"Suspense, romance, and a setting
so well-drawn that you'll feel like you're there—
Alderman delivers it all. An outstanding debut!"
—RITA Award–winning Author Marilyn Pappano

NOTHING TO HIDE

He walked back to the table and leaned across it,
both hands braced on the surface so that she had to
look up into his hard gaze. "You know where your
brother is. I want to talk to him."

She shoved her chair back and jumped up. "You're
wrong."

"I find that hard to believe."

"And even if I did _____ turning to
face him, he _____ ou. You're
not going to _____ Ken's life
during Dese_____ m now?
My guess is _____ 's killer, not
running."

"If you believ_ _ has nothing to hide, then convince
him to come in and talk to me, tell me what he knows."

She was shaking her head before he finished. "Gary
doesn't trust the authorities."

Chapman had come over to stand beside her at the
counter, too close for her peace of mind. And he was
doing it on purpose, trying to rattle her. "I can have
you arrested for obstructing justice, and if you know
something you're not telling me, I won't hesitate."

She sent a cool look his way. "You don't frighten me,
Mr. Chapman."

"Yeah, but I sure as hell bother you," he said softly,
leaning closer. Close enough that she could smell the
spicy fragrance of the soap he'd used in his shower.
"Now, why is that, I wonder?"

al eyes...do know," she continued. Then her arms crossed, "I wouldn't tell y... use me to get to him. Cory saved ... Mason Stone, so why would he kill h... that he's trying to find Kee...

A KILLING TIDE

P. J. ALDERMAN

LOVE SPELL NEW YORK CITY

For my grandmother.

LOVE SPELL®

December 2006

Published by

Dorchester Publishing Co., Inc.
200 Madison Avenue
New York, NY 10016

ISBN 0-505-52696-4

Printed in the United States of America.

Visit us on the web at www.dorchesterpub.com.

AUTHOR'S NOTE

Those familiar with the town of Astoria, Oregon, will note that I have taken literary license with a few of the building locations and the makeup of the East Mooring Basin. The new police station is in the correct location, but I chose to keep the old fire station in its original location.

I am indebted to the authors of several excellent books for my research about the Northwest Coast and its fishing communities. Quotes at the beginnings of the chapters come from *Myths and Legends of the Pacific Northwest* by Katharine Berry Jackson. *The World of the Oregon Fishboat* by Janet C. Gilmore provided me with wonderful details about fishing trawlers and maritime folklife. And for general information about Astoria, the Columbia River, and surrounding communities, I relied on the excellent writings of Timothy Egan, *A Good Rain*, and John Paul Barrett, *Sea Stories: Of Dolphins and Dead Soldiers*.

I am additionally grateful to all the people who have made this book possible. A special thanks goes to Lisa VanAuken for believing in me, and to Pam, Pat, Jo, Norma, and Royce, who took the time to read and provide me with excellent feedback.

If this book is accurate, it is because of the tireless efforts of these people. Any errors are mine alone.

A KILLING TIDE

> Where many die,
> I will make much water and little land.
> —*Myths and legends of the Pacific Northwest*

PROLOGUE

Astoria, Oregon, late winter, evening

Century-old clapboard buildings sat huddled together on the narrow triangle of land between Marine Drive and the roiling, four-mile-wide Columbia River. Sixty-knot gusts of wind shattered loose window panes, sheets of rain flayed peeling siding. A rusty streetlight groaned, its pool of light dancing on the darkened sidewalk. With each powerful new surge of the storm, the faded green awning over the door of the Redemption Tavern ripped farther away from its metal supports.

The door exploded open, and a man staggered out. Propping himself against the brick alcove, he peered into the night, eyes slitted against the wet. A Pineapple Express, damn their luck, straight out of the South Pacific. Someone'd probably die on the river bar tonight, wash up in Dead Man's Cove. Someone they all knew.

Shivering, he slipped into his pockets hands reddened and throbbing from hundreds of tiny cuts. Goddamn ratfish. Their fins cut like razors. In the last week, he'd flung enough of 'em off the port bow to last a lifetime.

He closed his eyes. He was tired—more tired than he'd realized. Prob'ly shouldn't have had all that beer. Someone from inside the tavern yelled at him to close the door, but he paid no attention. All he had to do was make it six miserable blocks, then he'd be home with Julie and the kids. He'd take a hot shower, eat a home-cooked meal. Get some sleep.

They wouldn't come for him at the house. Too many witnesses.

His hands fisted, the right one closing around the small snow globe he'd forgotten he'd put in his pocket. Frowning, he pulled it out, holding it up to the dim glow of the lamp above the door. Inside the glass, a miniature white fishing trawler floated on a pretty blue sea, glittery bits of snow falling all around it. The skipper's sister had given it to him for Bobby.

"Since Bobby's too sick to go out with you right now," Kaz had explained, looking a little embarrassed by her gesture.

Despair welled up, blurring his vision. She had no idea, no clue about the kind of trouble he was in—the trouble they were all in. Pretty little baubles couldn't fix anything, and there weren't going to be any happy endings. His shoulders slumped. With the snow globe still clutched in his hand, he pushed himself onto the sidewalk.

Rain immediately iced his face and ran inside his collar, soaking the front of his wool shirt. A car passed him, splashing black, greasy water over his boots. He shook a fist at it, but it never even slowed, its taillights disappearing into the swirling darkness ahead.

His mouth twisted. What a fool he'd been! But he never thought they'd find out, not really. And he'd been desperate—he'd had no other choice.

At least the skipper should've understood. After all, Gary was his friend. The two of them went way back. A small laugh escaped, its bitter sound immediately swept away by the wind. In all the years he and Gary had been together, he'd never seen Gary so angry, so . . . disappointed. So grim.

What have I done?

Then in the eerie quiet between wind gusts, he heard it—a faint scrape on the concrete. He spun around, peering into the rain-drenched night.

The street was empty, the only movement the quaking shadows of wind-whipped vegetation. His hands shook, then clenched hard, almost crushing the snow globe.

No. They couldn't find him, not yet.

Increasing his pace, he leaned into the next gust of stinging wind, scurrying past the last row of buildings. He ducked around the corner of a coffeehouse, and then from under its creaking sign, crossed a patch of grass to stand in the deep shadow cast by the concrete bridge abutment.

Footsteps.

He stared into the darkness, straining to catch a movement. Nothing . . . he saw nothing. Silent and still, he watched for several long moments, fear chasing each breath. Then he shuddered.

Swaying on his feet, he tried to gather his strength. He was so damn tired. Tired of running. Tired of trying to make things right again.

His head fell back and he looked up, letting the rain batter his face. Hundreds of feet above him, the steel deck of the massive bridge loomed, its tiny lights winking against the turbulent black sky. Steady streams of water poured off the structure, flooding the grass and soaking his boots.

Suddenly sensing movement behind him, he started to turn. Something heavy crashed down on his head, driving him to his knees. Pain exploded, radiating down his spine. Dazed, he shook his head and tried to look up.

Hands grabbed his coat, slamming him against the wall. Rough concrete gouged his cheek, and breath, hot and smelling of beer, huffed against his temple. "Where's the money?"

The voice was low and gravelly, and he immediately recognized it. Feared it . . . had expected it.

Can't tell.

His shoulder rammed against the concrete, and his collarbone snapped with a hot, grating pop. Nausea rose, thick and burning.

"*Where's the money?*"

He choked and sucked in air. "I'll pay you back . . . just give me a chance." The hands tightened like a vise, and he clawed at his throat. "Wait. *I'm begging you.*"

The pressure on his collarbone increased, and he screamed.

Dear God. They'll go after Gary, my family. "You'll never find it," he whispered.

White agony flooded through him, his entire body going rigid. He struggled, but his efforts were too feeble, too late. "I made sure," he got out, but his words were swallowed by the howling wind.

The hands loosened, and he fell, face down.

The grass smelled kinda sweet. Was that the ocean roaring? Didn't make sense. . . . He was by the river, wasn't he? He chuckled, but the sound only echoed inside his head. Funny. All those dreams he'd had over the years, the ones in which he drowned out on the river. He'd always figured he'd die crossing the river bar, but never like this. It shouldn't have been like this.

The storm was easing, its calm settling over him. Night closed in.

Julie will understand.

The fingers of his right hand loosened, and the snow globe dropped into the mud. He never even felt the last blow.

The maiden slept, but not soundly.
When the sun was high, she awoke.
All around her were skeletons and skulls.

CHAPTER ONE

She'd almost cut it too close.

Kaz Jorgensen opened the cedar plank door of the Redemption and stepped into the dimly lit interior of the waterfront bar. A gust of wind caught the door, slamming it against the alcove, and she had to use all of her strength to drag it shut.

Hanging her dripping sou'wester on a peg in the entry, she rolled the tension out of her shoulders. She'd been lucky today, very lucky. By the time she'd crossed the river bar, the seas had been running at seventeen feet. Waves two stories high had battered the trawler, making it groan and shudder beneath her feet, just like on that night fifteen years ago. The sense of déjà vu that had been plaguing her all day whispered once more across her nerve endings. She'd been lucky that night, too, but she'd been the only one.

Rubbing icy hands on her jeans, she glanced around the smoky, cavernous room, taking a quick

7

headcount. Everyone was there, thank God. Even her twin brother Gary and his friend Chuck, who were standing at their favorite place at the bar. Gary caught her gaze, glanced deliberately at his watch, and frowned. Shrugging, she held up both hands, then began to thread her way through the crowded tables.

She was halfway across the room, making her usual cracks and jokes to the fishermen she passed, when she noticed the stranger sitting in one of the booths along the back of the bar. Now wasn't that odd. Tourists didn't usually come this far into Uniontown. The Redemption was a working-class tavern in a working-class neighborhood, a little too rough for most with its worn, scarred tables and harsh, mingled odors of fish, grease, and creosote.

Then again, this guy didn't really look like a tourist—more like a lobsterman from the East Coast. Not that they got many of those out here. She glanced around, thinking he might be the source of the edgy mood she was picking up on, but everyone else seemed to be ignoring him. Oh, well. She shrugged. She'd find out all about him soon enough. In the years she'd been gone, the efficiency of the local grapevine hadn't diminished.

"You're late," Lucy McGuire said as she approached.

"Hi to you, too." Kaz dropped into the captain's chair across from her oldest and best friend, propping her wet sneakers on the extra chair. Catching the bartender's eye, she mimicked a drinking motion. Steve's brow arched, and he nodded.

"That's the second time this week," Lucy pointed out, taking a bite out of her Reuben sandwich. Her detective's shield glinted from the waistband of her pressed jeans, and her Beretta semiautomatic barely made a bulge beneath her charcoal wool blazer. An intricately designed antique silver clip tamed curly black hair at the base of her slender neck. Only Lucy could make a fashion statement out of the detective's informal dress code.

"I would've been here an hour ago if some *idiot* hadn't run through my lines," Kaz said by way of explanation. The tavern's only waitress appeared at Kaz's elbow with her usual—a pint of microbrew and a tablet of ibuprofen. Kaz shot Sandra a grateful smile, then continued. "Lost a half dozen pots, dammit. Remind me to hunt down the culprit after I've achieved the requisite level of pain-free frivolity."

"Frivolity? That's a word only an MBA would use, right? You learn that from one of those fancy clients of yours down in California?" Lucy shook her head. "Good thing I rescued you from that place. So how many crabs did you catch?"

Astoria born and raised, Lucy knew enough about fishing to know you didn't judge the size of your catch by the number. Kaz smiled, relaxing for the first time all day. "You don't count them, Luce. You weigh them."

Lucy just looked at her.

"Okay, the catch was light—a few dozen."

Lucy choked on a sip of beer, waving a hand in the air. "Wow."

"Hey, all that sun last year during El Niño changed the migration patterns."

"Big ones or little ones?"

"Oh, shut up." Kaz slumped more comfortably in her chair. "I'll have you know the business is starting to break even." Which was the excuse she'd given for returning home a month ago on a short leave of absence, even if it wasn't the *real* reason. Only she and

Lucy knew why she'd really come back, and coming home hadn't been without its risks.

She'd taken a huge gamble, leaving her junior partner in charge of their San Francisco consulting firm, Strategic Solutions. One simply didn't walk away from Fortune 500 clients, not without payback. They expected the boss to be there every day, and she was bound to lose a few of them. Right about now, she thought wryly, her competitors were probably rubbing their hands with glee.

But she'd made the right decision. Lucy's call early that morning a month ago had had Kaz's heart lodged in her throat. "Something's going on with Gary," she'd told Kaz. "He's acting weird, secretive." He needed Kaz's help, Lucy had insisted, and they both knew he wasn't going to ask for it.

Hearing the uncharacteristic worry in her friend's voice, Kaz hadn't even hesitated. She'd packed her laptop, told her partner she'd handle whatever she had to from Astoria, and booked the first flight to Portland. She'd made excuses to Gary about how she could use the break from her high-stress job, about how she figured she could use the downtime to help him get the family fishing business on its feet again. About how getting back out on the water would be good for her.

He hadn't bought her last argument any more than she had. She'd known coming home would cause old memories to resurface, to keep her awake late into the night. But she'd deal with them—she didn't have a choice. And though she hadn't been able to ferret out yet what was bothering Gary, she was working on it. In the meantime, she was helping out by putting some extra cash in the bank.

"Yeah, but you're breaking even because you're world class at pinching pennies," Lucy was saying. "Your brother, on the other hand, is world class at catching fish, something you don't seem to have the hang of yet."

"Hey. I've only been back a few weeks."

Lucy snorted, but Kaz ignored her, fiddling with the handle of her beer mug. "If Gary's going to make money, he needs a second crewman and double the pots. I ran some projections—"

Lucy crossed her eyes.

"Okay, fine, I'm shutting up now." Kaz picked up her beer. "To safe passages."

"Safe passages," Lucy repeated, clinking glasses and drinking. "So tell me you didn't just come into port— that you aren't that crazy."

"I'm not that crazy," Kaz replied obediently, swallowing the ibuprofen with another large sip of beer.

Lucy tossed down her sandwich. "Dammit, Kaz—"

"I'm handling it." She held out a hand, which she was pleased to see was only trembling a little. "See?"

"Yeah, right." Lucy shook her head.

Kaz knew all too well the risks she was taking, and that Lucy had a point. But the risks were short term and, in her opinion, worth the potential payback for Gary. In the last week alone, she'd been able to lay dozens of new lines and close to forty new crab pots—all while Gary and his crewman Ken continued to drag-fish. That kind of production would pay off big for Gary once she was gone.

"So who's the new guy?" she asked, cocking her head toward the back of the tavern and heading off the rest of what was becoming Lucy's nightly lecture on safety.

11

He was sitting by himself, eating a hamburger while he read *The Daily Astorian*. Obviously, no one had told him not to order the grilled food. Few locals except Lucy, who had a cop's cast iron stomach, were that foolish. For the first time, Kaz noticed the black German shepherd asleep at the guy's feet. Stretched out on the floor, the dog looked about the size of a full-grown deer.

Lucy glared at her a moment longer, letting her know that she didn't consider her lecture DOA, then relented. "New fire chief, Michael Chapman. He made the rounds to introduce himself a couple of days ago—comes from back East. When Richardson decided to retire, this guy applied for the job. Hizzoner, the mayor, took one look at his resume and snapped him up."

Kaz raised an eyebrow. "What'd he do in his prior life, save the Empire State Building?"

"Close enough." Lucy abandoned the rest of her sandwich and leaned forward, lowering her voice. "He's some kind of a big-time, washed-up arson investigator. The way I hear it, he and that dog of his brought down one of Boston's worst arsonists in decades, some guy who'd set dozens of fires and killed several people." Her expression turned grim. "I *hate* arsonists. They're sick little creeps."

Intrigued, Kaz sneaked a second glance. The guy definitely looked tough enough to bring down a serial arsonist. He had a rangy yet muscular build, with shoulders wide enough to make any woman's heart skip a few beats. His cable-knit sweater, faded and frayed jeans, and scarred leather boots marked him as a working man, which should've made him blend into his surroundings. Instead, the clothes merely served to intensify his aura of toughness. Dark, wavy, slightly shaggy hair fell across his high forehead, and his complexion was olive toned, a pleasant contrast to her fishing buddies, most of whom were fair-haired, ruddy-skinned Scandinavians.

Definitely good gazing material. Rough-edged, like he'd lived hard. "So why do people think he's washed up?" Kaz asked, her curiosity getting the better of her.

"The torch burned down Chapman's apartment, killing his fiancée." Lucy straightened and tossed her crumpled napkin on top of the remains of her sandwich. "Rumor is that Chapman wigged."

"Sounds like he had good reason," Kaz said, immediately feeling empathy for him. She knew all too well what that kind of loss did to a person. Then he looked up, his gaze locking on hers without warning.

He had light-colored eyes, maybe blue—she couldn't tell from this distance. But she had a sneaking hunch they'd chill her right down to the bone. His jaw was rock-hard, that much she *could* tell. And even though he was clear across the room, the intensity of his gaze was jolting.

She returned his look without blinking, a shiver dancing across her skin. She'd met guys like him in the corporate world—predators under the misimpression that their Armani suits added a veneer of sophistication, disguising what lay underneath. This guy needed her sympathy like she needed more well-intentioned grief counseling.

He nodded, the slightest incline of his head in her direction, then turned back to his meal.

"Kind of cute for a burnout, huh?" Lucy's voice cut into her thoughts.

Resisting the urge to shift in her chair, Kaz made a

noncommittal noise and drank more beer. "Maybe he wanted to downshift, live with a little less stress," she murmured, not believing it for one minute.

Lucy harrumphed. "If that's true, he'll go stark raving mad after one winter out here. Guys like him come out here to kick back, to live the supposedly idyllic, small-town life. After the first hundred inches of rain and thousand dollars of counseling to help them cope with all the peace and quiet, they de-web their feet and head back home."

Kaz snickered, her tension easing a little. Living on the north coast of Oregon *did* require a certain kind of fortitude. She'd always secretly thought that explained why one of the Native American tribes in the area had supposedly been cannibals. "Still, if he's got the kind of experience you say he does, maybe Astoria is lucky to have him," she pointed out.

Raised voices penetrated their conversation, and they both turned just in time to see Gary shove Chuck hard against the bar. The room fell silent.

Kaz jumped to her feet. She shook her head at Lucy, who was also rising. "I'm on it."

As she quickly crossed the room, a familiar sense of resignation settled over her. Lucy had been right about whatever she'd been picking up on. More often than not since Kaz had been home, her role seemed to be that of mediator in some confrontation involving Gary. She wished she knew what was bothering him. But so far, every time she'd tried to reach out to him, she'd gotten nowhere.

"I need your help, damn you." As she approached, Gary's large hands fisted in Chuck's shirt.

She ducked under Gary's arm and placed a hand on his chest. "Hey, Gary." Pasting a smile on her face, she glanced over her shoulder at Chuck. "What's going on, guys? You're starting to draw attention."

Beneath her hand, Gary's muscles were rigid with suppressed violence. Their genetic propensity for height had blessed him even more than Kaz—he towered a good six inches over her five foot ten. And whereas she tended toward a willowy frame, a stint as an Army Ranger and grueling years of drag fishing had given Gary a solid, powerful build. If he decided to turn this into a brawl, she wouldn't have a prayer of stopping him. "Yo, guys? You're turning me into a candidate for high blood pressure, here. What d'you say we—"

"Stay out of it, Sis," Gary muttered, not looking her way.

She risked a quick glance at Chuck, whose expression was calm. But then, Chuck was a freaking stealth machine—he always looked calm. Scarily calm. "Bad move, what you're thinking, man," he said, his voice barely a murmur.

A frisson of unease slithered through her. "What's this all about?"

Chuck spared her a look. "Not your business."

"You're making it my business," Kaz shot back softly, "as well as everyone else's." She angled her head toward the room. People's gazes were lowered, but they hung on every word.

"Problem?" The deep, resonant baritone came from behind and to her right. Kaz swung around, her shoulder connecting with Gary's chest and forcing the two men apart.

The new fire chief stood very close, feet planted, arms hanging loosely at his sides. He was taller than she'd realized, and if the crow's feet around his eyes were any indication, older than she would've originally guessed—maybe around forty. *Formidable* was the first word that leapt into her mind. If any more tough men showed up, she'd asphyxiate from the ambient testosterone.

She rose to her full height. "I'm handling it."

Chapman's hard gaze flicked over her; then he turned back to the men. "You two might want to continue this outside."

"Who the hell are you?" Gary demanded.

Kaz winced. Gary had an almost preternatural gift for irritating the authorities.

"Just a guy who wants to finish his dinner in peace," Chapman said, crossing his arms. The soft wool of his sweater glided smoothly over hard muscle. He widened his stance. "And I'd prefer that the lady not get hurt."

Kaz frowned. "I won't—"

"Oh yeah?" Gary overrode her. "And who asked you?"

Chapman shrugged and nodded toward his booth. "Zeke—over there—tends to get real stressed out." The dog let out a snore. "I do what I can for him."

Gary's face turned beet-red. "You're a regular comic."

Steve chose that moment to walk up on the other side of the bar. "Take it outside, Jorgensen. I don't want another fight in my bar."

Gary rounded on him, his expression lethal. "You've got no room to complain, *no room*. Hell, for all I know—"

Steve's normally pleasant expression hardened, his eyes going flat. "I *said*, leave. Now."

Kaz reached out and gripped his arm. "Gary. Please."

He glared at her for a moment, then jerked away. "Hell, I'm out of here." He tossed some money on the bar. When she reached out again, he glanced down at her, his expression momentarily softening. "Leave me be, Kaz." Then he shot a hard look at Chuck—a look, she realized, that was tinged with fear. "I've said what I needed to. You think about it." He snagged his coat off the back of the bar stool and shouldered his way between them.

Chuck slanted a chiding look at her while he paid his bill. "Stick to the sidelines on this one, kiddo." Then he followed Gary out the door.

She stood in the spot they'd vacated, staring after them, then huffed out a breath. Ignoring Steve, she turned back to Chapman, pasting another smile on her face. "You know, I really could've handled that."

He studied her without comment. She'd been right—his eyes were light blue, so light they were almost silver. And his gaze wasn't so much unfriendly as simply too . . . world-weary. She caught a whiff of his aftershave and gave brief thought to the odor of fish bait emanating from her clothes.

"Most women would hesitate before getting between two rough-looking men spoiling for a fight," he said finally.

With effort, she reined in her impatience. "One of those *rough-looking* men, as you put it, was my brother."

"Ah."

She leaned one hip against the back of a bar stool and crossed her arms. "What's that supposed to mean?"

He only shrugged, then held out a hand. "Michael Chapman."

"Yes, I know." His grip was firm, warm, and slightly rough. He held her hand a moment longer than was called for, and she pulled away, taking an involuntary step backward.

One corner of his mouth lifted at the movement. "Small town—word travels fast, I imagine." He waited.

"Oh, sorry." She introduced herself.

"Kaz." He cocked his head. "Unusual name."

"It's short for Kasmira, a family name—my grandmother's," she explained, then gestured vaguely toward the center of the room. "Well. I should be getting back—"

"I'm not keen on women getting shoved around in bar fights."

She ground her teeth. "Gary and Chuck can disagree on something as minor as whether Chicago has a chance to win this year's pennant race, but they're *friends.* Really, it wouldn't have gotten out of hand."

"Obviously you didn't think so, or you wouldn't have raced over to break it up."

He hadn't wasted any time pegging her faulty logic. Her voice chilled. "This is a small town, Mr. Chapman. You'll find folks around here won't appreciate you butting into their business."

A flicker of something, possibly humor, came and went in his eyes so quickly she might have imagined it. "Folks rarely appreciate my butting in, as you put it, no matter where they live," he replied, his tone dry as dust. "Ma'am."

Ma'am? She watched him walk back to his booth, annoyed with herself for letting him push her buttons. Protective males made her crazy, and Astoria had an entire flock of them. There had to be something in the water—this guy had been indoctrinated in less than a week. That is, unless he'd rolled into town already wired that way.

"Well?" Lucy asked as Kaz sat back down.

"Not a clue."

"What did Chapman want?"

Kaz jerked her shoulders upwards, still unsettled by her reaction to him. She was good at handling aggressive men—it'd been part of her job description for the last ten years. But Chapman had gotten the drop on her in less than thirty seconds—none of her usual defenses had kicked in.

Lucy was scanning the room, her "cop" expression on. *"What?"* Kaz asked.

Lucy hesitated, then shook her head. "You'd better have that talk with Gary, and soon. I don't want Sykes back on his case," she said, referring to the chief of police and her direct superior. "And I *really* don't want to be the one to haul your brother in on another assault charge on the chief's orders."

Kaz frowned. "Come on. That's stretching it, don't you think?"

"Two fights in one night? I don't think so. And you *know* this gives Sykes the excuse he needs to yank Gary off his parole."

"Whoa. Earth to Luce. Two fights? Steve mentioned the same thing. What're you two talking about?"

The light dawned. "Right—you weren't here yet. Gary and Ken got into it earlier." Lucy frowned. "Now that I think about it, it was the same kind of thing—a serious row that looked like something I might have to break up. Then Ken split, all suddenlike, and Gary seemed to cool down. Well, until a few minutes ago."

Kaz rubbed at an aching muscle in the back of her neck, the uneasiness she'd been feeling off and on since she'd entered the tavern returning in full force. Ken was usually already home with Julie and the kids by the time she made port, so she didn't see him all that much. Particularly now that his son was so sick. But he and Gary had always been tight, ever since they'd served together in Desert Storm. They had a lot of shared history—both from the war and from being out on the water together. Their relationship had had its rough patches, but their arguments had always been short-lived. Gary had always stuck by Ken, no matter what. In fact, both she and Lucy suspected that it had been Gary's loyalty to Ken that had landed him in jail six months back. Which made the fight Lucy was talking about incomprehensible. Kaz sighed. Just like the rest of Gary's behavior lately.

Lucy was waiting for an explanation, and Kaz dearly wished she had one. "Gary's been having nightmares—at least, I think he has. I can hear him pacing in the living room at night."

"About what?"

Kaz shook her head. "Maybe the war? I don't know. He's hard to read under the best of circumstances. But still, bar-fighting has never been his style."

Lucy's expression was grim. "Yeah, well, could've fooled me. And Sykes was here earlier—he saw what went down with Ken."

That wasn't good news. Sykes had a reputation for being dedicated to his job—folks in town were thrilled with his performance since they'd voted him into office. He'd worked hard to lower Astoria's crime rate, and he'd succeeded. If he thought Gary was a danger to the community, he wouldn't hesitate to throw him back in a cell.

Kaz went over what Gary had said to Chuck and Steve in those moments at the bar. Or not said, to be more accurate. The entire conversation had been way too cryptic for her peace of mind. She gnawed on her lip. "Look, you know those guys'll argue about batting averages, for Christ's sake . . ." Her voice trailed away as she took in Lucy's expression. "Okay, okay. If it'll make you happier, I'll go hunt Gary up and ask him some pointed questions."

Lucy immediately looked relieved, far more than Kaz would have thought was warranted. Which made her even twitchier. What wasn't Lucy telling her? "Of course," she said, trying to inject a lighter note, "I'll have to take a rain check on the pool game."

"Dammit—" Lucy sighed. "Sure, okay, I should get back to the station anyway."

Kaz glanced around the room, schooling her expression so that she didn't show the worry that was gnawing at her gut. None of the fishermen would make eye contact with her. And now that she thought about it, they'd been unusually silent out on the water earlier that afternoon. The typical radio chatter had been missing—along with the camaraderie. "Hmmm?" She realized Lucy had been talking to her.

"I *said*, you just don't want to get trounced again at eight-ball and owe me double or nothing on last night's bet."

"Like hell."

Michael Chapman leaned back in his booth and watched the Jorgensen woman leave. He'd noticed her the minute she'd come in—what man in the place hadn't? All that thick, waist-length, blond hair, that slim, athletic body, and those soft, chocolate brown eyes. All that attitude. He had to wonder what secrets she was hiding behind that attitude.

The way she moved reminded him a little of Jessica,

who'd had a similar, long-limbed walk, with the same hints of pride, independence, and feminine grace. He shook his head. Going down that old road would bring him nothing but heartache—and insomnia that only a large shot of scotch would cure. And he'd promised himself the move west would mean an end to those late-night drinks.

He hadn't paid much attention to women the last couple of years—a sad fact his friends in the Boston Fire Department had pointed out repeatedly—but the Jorgensen woman had caught his attention and held it. And after talking to her, he could sympathize with the reactions he'd seen on the faces of the other men when she'd arrived. A few had watched her with wistful expressions, a few with irritation. But the rest had looked relieved and maybe even exasperated— probably fishing buddies who'd been worried about her. He'd bet she drove them crazy on a good day, taking chances they shook their heads over and privately labeled foolish.

She'd certainly caused him a jolt or two when she'd waded into the middle of a brewing bar fight—one that looked as if it might get real ugly, real fast. Hell, that's what you expected from bar fights in places like this.

Sure, most of the people were typical of any waterfront tavern—hard-working, decent people. He'd been looking for just that kind of tavern when he'd come through the door, and he hadn't been disappointed. A place where he could relax, get a handle on the locals. Not that he hadn't expected the cool reception. Watermen were a fiercely independent bunch, used to being alone for days at a time. Ashore, they kept to their own kind, suspicious of newcomers. They might eventually cut him some slack because of the summers he'd spent crabbing on the Maryland shore, but he'd have to prove himself first.

The atmosphere in this place, though, was tense. And a few of these guys were definitely nasty characters—much more dangerous, he'd bet, than the rest of the bar's patrons. The type found in seaports around the world—drifters, criminals on the run from the law. He'd already been sizing them up and monitoring the brewing fight when the blonde had jumped in. She was damn lucky, even if one of them *was* her brother—she easily could've gotten roughed up.

He grimaced, reaching down to rub Zeke's stomach. The dog moaned appreciatively in his sleep. Christ. He'd learned his lesson, hadn't he? He had no business wondering what secrets the woman was hiding. And he could've sworn he'd beaten the Good Samaritan impulse out of himself, once and for all. In the past, he'd paid for that impulse, too many times to count.

He'd moved out west to find some measure of peace in his life, not to take on someone else's troubles. All he had planned for the next few days was to move his belongings, which had finally shown up several days late, into the Victorian fixer-upper he'd purchased for Zeke and himself on the east side of town. That and to renew his acquaintance with a few carpentry tools.

Shoving aside his half-eaten burger, he pulled out his wallet, adding an extra five for the tired waitress with the tense shoulders. As he did, he glanced around the bar one more time. He noted the closed expressions, the furtive glances, the air of desperation that permeated the room. Felt the undercurrents. And, in spite of himself, he was intrigued.

Those guys hadn't been fighting about anything as minor as Kaz Jorgensen had wanted him to believe. This town had secrets.

Too many secrets.

Chapter Two

Kaz arrived at the family's early 1900s bungalow above town to find the house dark, the driveway empty. After a moment's thought, she reversed out of the driveway and headed back in the direction she'd come. When Gary needed space, he sometimes slept on the *Anna Marie*.

She drove down the steep hills above the historic downtown district and then east on Marine Drive past shadowed, abandoned warehouses, remnants of a more prosperous era. Even though the rain had let up, the clouds were moving low and fast, and she had to hold the wheel firmly against the gusting wind. Gary was nuts to sleep on the boat. Even moored, it'd be pitching hard.

But then, Gary *had* been acting nuts lately. Okay, there, she'd admitted it. And God! She immediately wanted to take it back, because she might as well admit that Gary hadn't been improving in recent years—that she'd been deluding herself.

When Lucy had called her a month ago, Kaz assumed that she'd spend her two-week vacation the way she always did—working on the typical boat repairs—and as a side benefit, return to California sporting some improved muscle tone. She figured she'd take a few extra weeks, feel out Gary about what was bothering him. But she'd arrived home to a family business on the verge of bankruptcy, to boats in shocking disrepair, and to a stranger in the guise of her brother.

If anything since she'd been back, Gary had become even more reclusive, more prickly. Admittedly, with her out on the *Kasmira B* while he and Ken were bottom-fishing on the *Anna Marie,* she hadn't had that many opportunities to sit him down for a real talk. But he hadn't made the effort to hang around, either. Had that been deliberate on his part? Was he actually avoiding her for some reason? She shook her head.

Gary had a tendency to hole up like a wounded animal when he was hurting—he'd taken "time-outs," as he called them, more than once since he'd returned from Desert Storm. He wouldn't avoid her, and he wouldn't pick fights in bars. He'd withdraw—head for the hills where he could be by himself.

The fight six months back had been an aberration, she was certain. But if Jim Sykes used the fights tonight to revoke Gary's parole, Kaz *would* be concerned about Gary's state of mind. He'd never be able to handle a jail cell, not after what he'd been through in the war.

Spying his truck on the wharf of the East Mooring Basin, she heaved a sigh of relief and turned in, parallel parking behind it. The truck was locked up tight, so she headed toward the docks. Using the palm of her hand, she slapped the chain-link gate at the top of the steel ramp that led down to the docks. The gate refused to open.

She stared at it, perplexed. Someone had chained it from the inside. What idiot would do that?

Just then, she heard an odd, percussive, whooshing sound, and the wheelhouse of the *Anna Marie* exploded into flames.

Lucy drove to the new police headquarters located on the east side of Astoria, worrying the whole way. She was having second, third—hell, even twentieth—thoughts about having encouraged Kaz to come home. She'd hoped Kaz would have a calming effect on Gary, or maybe be able to ferret out what was going on with him. Instead, she might have placed Kaz in danger.

The truth was, Kaz tended to be oblivious about what was going on around her—probably because she spent way too much time hunched over those spreadsheets she loved.

Holding the wheel firm against a gust of wind, Lucy grimaced. Astoria had changed since they'd all been in high school together. The town had experienced an influx of rich vacationers who had bought up many of the old Victorian homes, using them as weekend getaways. The newcomers brought with them too much disposable income, as well as a thirst for parties where the flow of controlled substances went unchecked. In reaction, "We Ain't Quaint" bumper stickers had quietly shown up on many of the locals' trucks, and not-so-quiet clashes between the old and the new had become more commonplace.

From the looks of it, Gary had landed right in the thick of those culture wars. Lately, his behavior was giving Lucy some really bad moments late at night. And though she'd be the first to admit he'd been giving her bad moments ever since high school, this was different. Whatever he'd gotten himself into, she realized— too late—she didn't want him involving Kaz. Which was why she dearly wished she'd minded her own business and never placed that call.

It didn't help that Kaz carried around a boatload of guilt because of what had happened the night of the shipwreck fifteen years ago. She felt she owed Gary, that she was responsible for him. Which was understandable to a degree—Gary was the only family she had left. And when Sykes had railroaded him on that assault charge six months back, Kaz's level of guilt only seemed to rise. "Maybe if I'd been here, things wouldn't have gotten so out of hand," she'd told Lucy.

It was one thing for Kaz to try to talk to Gary, to see if she could help him sort through the personal problems that had plagued him since Desert Storm. But it was quite another if she got herself caught up in whatever else was going on. Gary was a big boy, and he could take care of himself. In fact, it was about damn time he handled his problems on his own. He needed to be shaken out of the rut he'd been in ever since the war—needed to acknowledge that the aftereffects of being a POW *hadn't* made him unfit company, for the fishermen *or* for the right woman. Lucy snorted and pulled into the left-turn lane, hitting her blinker. Yeah, right. He'd admit *that* the day pigs flew over the Columbia.

What mattered right now was that he needed to tell her—or some other cop, if he wasn't comfortable confiding in her—what the hell he was involved in, before he got in over his head. And he needed to keep Kaz out of it.

Lucy pulled into the brightly lit parking lot, suppressing a pang of homesickness for their old headquarters in the heart of Astoria's historic downtown district. Progress, she reminded herself, was good. Smiling hello to Joanne, she used her key card to open the secure door to the squad room.

"Everything quiet?"

"Yep," Joanne replied, with no hesitation in the rapid clicking of her computer keys. A single mom with five young boys, Joanne had said many times that her job as dispatcher was merely relief duty.

The place was empty except for Lucy's partner, Ivar, who sat at his desk, studiously working his way through a stack of files. A mug of green-colored liquid gently steamed at his elbow, and soft classical music played on a boom box confiscated from the evidence room.

Lucy dropped into the desk chair facing his. "I hope that vile-smelling stuff is for poisoning some perp, or else I'll have to request a transfer to the state police."

"Green oolong tea," he replied without looking up. "Full of antioxidants. You should try some."

"Over my dead body."

He nodded while he made a note in the margin of the page. "A real possibility, since you insist on eating red meat." He leaned back, stretching his legs out so far that his feet crowded hers, and eyed her with his typical air of calm.

Ivar was tall, thin, pensive, and when he bothered to speak at all, laconic. In the five years Lucy had been teamed up with him, she'd never once seen him lose his cool. Which actually made him the perfect partner, because she lost hers as often as possible. In fact, she considered a well-honed rant a work of art.

"Chief wants to talk," he said.

"Any idea what he wants?"

"Nope."

"Any chance I can delay this and go home for a good soak in the tub?"

Ivar shook his head in warning, and she glanced around to find Jim Sykes approaching her desk. He'd changed out of the tux he'd had on earlier for some kind of political fund-raiser. His "day" suit was baggy and rumpled, and he looked as if he'd been living in it for too long.

Sykes was an okay boss, mostly staying out of their way and letting them do their jobs but providing support when they needed it. She might not agree with how he'd handled Gary's prosecution, but he and Gary had a shared history that went way back—all of it rocky. Gary had always been particularly obtuse about the advantages he'd had over Sykes when they were growing up, about how hard Sykes had worked to overcome his disadvantaged childhood. It was only natural that Sykes resented him.

And to be fair, Gary had set himself up for a fall when he'd landed that punch, no matter how justified it had been. With Sykes standing no more than ten feet away that night, Gary might as well have handed him an engraved invitation to arrest him. The hotheaded idiot.

Sykes settled his large frame heavily against the edge of her desk. "I'm hearing rumors about the fishermen," he said without preamble. "That whole community is tense—they're hiding something."

Lucy sneaked a quick glance at Ivar, who was

frowning. So she wasn't the only one surprised by Sykes's statement. She'd heard hints of something big going down, but she hadn't heard about any connection to the fishermen. And she had yet to see any hard evidence. So far, the only people talking were a couple of small-time junkies who were trying to bargain their way into their next fix. Everyone knew those guys would say anything to minimize their time on the inside.

What surprised her was that the rumors had made it up to Sykes's level. The chief had worked hard in the last several years to cut the crime rate in Astoria, and the townsfolk were happy with the job he'd done. But few felt comfortable confiding in him.

She'd been out there pounding the streets, and as far as she could tell, no one was talking. Evidently Sykes's connections extended beyond the political.

His next words surprised her even more. "I'm making you the primary on the investigation. See what you can dig up."

She hesitated. She was the rooky detective on the force, so surely this assignment should go to Clint Jackson or one of the other, more experienced detectives. Then again, Sykes tended to support the careers of his officers, pass around the assignments so that everyone had a fair shake at promotion. Maybe he was giving her a chance to prove herself. Still, this didn't feel like a solid investigation to her—at least, not yet. "I don't know if that's warranted, Chief. Why don't I do some unofficial poking around and—"

"What I'm hearing indicates otherwise," Sykes interrupted. "You may not want to believe that your friends might be involved in anything illegal, McGuire, but my sources say they are."

"They're decent folks, just trying to make a living," she said quietly.

"Yeah, and until the government makes good on its buyout promise, that living is damn poor. I need you to use your contacts within the community to find out what they're up to. We don't want this thing exploding in our faces."

She glanced at Ivar again, to see his reaction. He was still frowning. So maybe that was what this was all about—the fact that her contacts with the fishermen were better than Sykes's. Of course, if he could provide her with a career opportunity at the same time, she knew he would. She could already see, though, that he wasn't doing her any favors. The words *conflict of interest* loomed large in front of her eyes.

Before she could frame a suitable response, Joanne poked her head into the room. "Chief—"

"Not now, Joanne," Sykes said over his shoulder, then stood. "Something's going down, I can feel it. Take Ivar with you, question the fishermen. Get results."

"Chief!"

"Dammit, Joanne! What?"

Michael Chapman was driving east on Irving Avenue, only a block from his new home, when the two-way radio crackled to life. He eased his foot off the accelerator and listened intently.

Swearing, he cranked the steering wheel hard, pulling a U-turn in the middle of the street and throwing Zeke across the back seat. He stomped on the gas, searching for a through street that would take him down to the waterfront.

* * *

For one stunned moment, Kaz simply stared. Then she threw herself at the gate, jerking it back and forth. *"Gary!"*

The flames leapt higher.

Backing up, she vaulted, hitting the top half of the gate with enough momentum to drag herself over. She ran down the ramp.

"Gary!" She glanced around for someone, anyone. The docks were deserted. *"Fire! Help!"*

The entire deck of the trawler was burning now, flames roaring off the bow and around the winch, aft of the wheelhouse. She strained to catch a glimpse of her brother, but all she could see silhouetted against the orange glow were the boat's mast and boom. A gust of wind shifted the flames toward her, and she fell back from the searing heat, crouching and flinging an arm up to protect her eyes. "Gary!"

The wind switched again, propelling the flames toward their other trawler, the *Kasmira B.* Kaz took advantage, leaping onto the *Anna Marie's* deck. Flipping open the nearest seat cover, she reached for the fire extinguisher.

It was gone.

The flames whipped toward her again, and she dove behind the wall of the wheelhouse.

She pulled herself into a crouch, coughing and trying to look through the open door to see if the passage to the engine room and galley was clear. Twice she had to pull back from the heat.

The boat's aged timbers crackled. The wall beside her, when she touched it, singed her fingers. She pounded on it with her fist. "Gary!"

No answer.

Edging around the corner, she assessed the stairs. Flames were burning down one side of the risers, but they were still partially clear. Pulling the hood of her coat over her head, she dove into the darkness below.

She landed hard on her hands and right shoulder on the engine room floor, rolling onto her back away from the flames that were burning next to the equipment. Inside, the roar was muted, but the heat was stifling. The timbers overhead hissed in the relative silence. Varnish from the ceiling plopped onto her coat, and thick, black smoke hung in the air. She pushed herself up.

Sweat poured off her, and a strong metallic flavor coated the inside of her mouth, making her gag. Her face and hands were unbearably hot—her skin felt like it was melting. She couldn't see more than a few inches in front of her.

She turned onto her stomach and took a cautious breath, but the air at floor level wasn't much better. The bitter, chemical odor of hot carpet assaulted her. Rising onto her knees, she crawled through the galley door. More flames, though smaller, ran in a line across the floor and were hungrily eating at the galley wall. With one hand stretched out in front of her, she crawled toward the fo'c'sle where the berths were. "Gary!"

The timbers overhead hissed and groaned in the silence.

Kaz stood, felt along the berths. She tripped over something, landing hard on her hands and knees, then got back up. The smoke was even thicker back here.

Dizzy. She shook her head. She had to keep going.

There. Her hand touched a boot, then clung to a jeans-clad leg. She sobbed and shook him, but he didn't move. Yanking hard on his jacket, she managed to roll him. He fell heavily onto the floor, wedged on his side against the storage locker.

The heat was getting worse. She couldn't budge him, and she seemed to be moving in slow motion.

No. Can't black out.

Gripping the heels of his boots, she threw her weight backward. He slid a few inches toward the stairs. She sank onto her knees beside him, her ears roaring.

Hands grabbed her from behind and yanked her to her feet. He floated out of the haze above her, an apparition in a black oxygen mask, black coat with yellow stripes, and boots. When he pulled off his face mask, she saw that it was Chapman.

"We've got to get out of here!" he yelled.

"No."

She heard a roar and looked up. Blue flames streamed across the ceiling from the engine room, reaching for her. Chapman dropped beside her, dragging her down, and covered her face with his arms. "Hang tight, they'll hose it down." He brought his face close to hers, pushing his mask over her mouth, and she gulped the oxygen greedily. Water rained down, scalding her scalp. She heard someone whimper and realized that it must be her.

Water began to fill the cabin—she was lying in several inches of it. *Gary's facedown in this.* She shoved at Chapman, hard.

He grunted and shifted sideways, and then rolled her with him, pulling her out of the stream of the hose. She pointed toward Gary. "My brother," she managed, but her voice broke.

"The deck . . . cave-in! Move it!" He pulled her to her feet and dragged her toward the stairs.

Kaz fought him, but he wrapped an arm around her middle and moved backwards, hauling her with him. She rammed her elbow into his solar plexus, and he slumped forward, his grip loosening.

Staggering toward the berths, she fell over Gary's body. She heard Chapman swear, but then he finally seemed to realize what she was doing. He ran a hand along both berths next to her, then knelt and hauled Gary up over his shoulder. Taking hold of her arm, he threw her toward the stairs. "Dammit, *move.*"

He propelled her up the stairs and through the door, then off the boat and onto the dock, not letting go of her until they were several yards away. She dropped to her knees, coughing and retching. Firemen raced past them, dragging hoses and shouting to each other.

Chapman laid her brother down several feet away, ripped off one of his gloves, and felt for a pulse. Then pulled back an eyelid.

She crawled toward them—toward Gary. *Please, God. Let him be alive.* Behind them, she heard a crash as the deck splintered and collapsed. Sparks flew over them on the night wind, and from the adjacent dock, the sea lions barked excitedly. She barely glanced back, just kept going.

Before she could reach Gary, Chapman pushed up his mask and threw out an arm to block her. She shoved it aside.

He turned then and gripped her shoulders, hard. His face was grim. "I'm sorry. He didn't make it."

"No!" she sobbed, pushing at him with both hands. His chest was rock solid and didn't budge. "I have to see him—" She froze, staring over his shoulder.

The man lying on the dock wasn't her brother. It was Ken Lundquist, their crewman.

CHAPTER THREE

Fifteen minutes later, Kaz sat on the back steps of an aid car, breathing oxygen from a mask attached to a portable tank. Her throat was raw, her skin hot and prickly. Flashing lights from emergency vehicles illuminated the area in rhythmic sweeps, hurting her eyes. Occasional gusts of wind caused the boats' riggings to clank like gunshots, adding a syncopated unreality to the entire scene.

To keep the growing crowd at bay, Chapman had roped off the wharf with yellow crime scene tape strung between sawhorses and the wooden railings. Fire hoses snaked across each other and down the steel grate ramp leading to the *Anna Marie*.

Kaz used a hand to wipe her eyes and felt grit smear across her cheek. In spite of the heat from the fire, she couldn't stop shivering.

God. Ken was dead. But how? In the three generations her family had been on the water, they'd never had a fire on one of their boats. The importance of fire safety had been drilled into Kaz and Gary at an early age—they never took chances. *Never*.

And yet, she was staring at the horrific evidence that proved someone had. Maybe electrical wiring had gone bad—somehow sparking near the fuel. The *Anna Marie* was used for drag fishing, so she hadn't been on the trawler much lately. Still, it wasn't like Gary to let a really critical repair go. She shook her head. Even if he had, as part owner, she was no less responsible. A man had died on one of their boats—a loving husband and father of two young children. Tears welled in her eyes, threatening to fall.

Why had Ken been on board? Usually, he had a beer or two at the Redemption and then went home early to Julie and the kids. Particularly now, because Bobby was sick with leukemia and going through chemo treatments. Ken *never* spent time on the trawler when it was in port. None of this made sense.

Maybe Gary could shed some light on what had happened. She'd already checked the *Kasmira B*, their other trawler, but there was no sign of him. Not that it was unusual for him to take off for a day or two, but his timing couldn't have been worse. Wiping her eyes, Kaz stood and scanned the crowd, then repeated the process, more slowly. Nothing. She begged a cell phone off the EMT and dialed their home number. No answer.

Numb, she turned back to the fire scene. Ken's body lay on the dock, the head and upper torso protected from the rain by a firefighter's coat. Lucy and Ivar stood over the body, along with the coroner. Kaz shuddered and closed her eyes. *Suck it up*. She had to pull it together, concentrate on what she needed to do *right now* to get through the night. And her first responsibility was to assist the authorities in whatever way she could to determine how this could've happened.

Another loud crash sounded, and she opened her eyes just in time to see the *Anna Marie*'s spool of fishnet and winch disappear into the holding tank in an explosion of flames.

After ordering the nozzle man to redirect his hose to the bow of the trawler, Michael turned and studied the Jorgensen woman. Her naturally pale complexion was washed of all color, and she looked shocky. He wasn't surprised, given what she'd just been through. Why in hell had she boarded a burning boat? Civilians always thought they could handle a fire, but they couldn't, dammit. In any fire, there were enough toxic chemicals to take out even the strongest person in a matter of minutes. His jaw clenched. He wouldn't forget any time soon the icy cold that had settled deep in his chest when he'd seen her dive into those flames.

He didn't like what he was seeing with this fire. It was burning way too hot, and in too many locations. That would have screamed "suspicious" to him, even if he hadn't hauled a body out of the hold. According to one of the firefighters, Kaz and her brother co-owned the boat. And the brother was on parole for assault—the near-brawl Michael had witnessed in the tavern evidently hadn't been out of character. He'd also seen Gary Jorgensen going at it with the guy who was now lying on the dock, dead. And Kaz—who had proved she was willing to do anything for her brother—was the first person on the scene of a suspicious fire.

So in all likelihood, what Michael had was a straightforward case of arson to cover up another crime—murder. He'd nail down the source of ignition, file his report, and let the police take it from there. Nothing complicated, no reason to get stressed out. No reason to feel the need to be the primary investigator on a case only two days after he'd hit town. No Goddamn earthly reason.

So why was his gut screaming for extra-strength antacids?

He frowned as Kaz handed the oxygen mask back to the EMT and stood on legs that were clearly still shaky. She was even paler than she'd been a few minutes ago, but she had a look of renewed determination on her face that spelled trouble. When she started walking toward the dock, he stepped into her path, placing a hand on her arm. "Sorry, but you can't go any closer."

She glanced up at him, her expression distracted. "She's taking on too much water. You'll sink her."

"I'm keeping an eye on the water level." Touching her was like touching a door with a raging inferno behind it. Disconcerted, he stepped back, removing his hand.

"I'll talk to the firemen myself."

"Can't let you do that." He pulled out a pencil and a small pad he kept with him for taking down notes. "Why don't we go over what happened here tonight."

"What?" She shook her head. "I have the right to protect my boat."

"She's a crime scene, for now. No one goes near her except authorized personnel."

"What're you talking about?"

"That fire was deliberately set." Her face blanched of all remaining color, and he shot an arm around her slender waist. "Whoa. Maybe you'd better sit—"

"That can't be," she whispered.

He watched her closely. Most people weren't that good at acting, but he'd seen all kinds. "I'm afraid it's a very real possibility."

After taking several deep breaths, she seemed to pull herself together, stepping away from him. Recognizing the pride and fierce self-control behind the move, he let her go.

"When will you know for sure?" she asked, her voice sounding more composed.

"After I go over the areas that burned, find the source of ignition."

She raised a slender hand to push her hair away from her face. When he saw the red, watery blisters that had formed along the outside edge of her palm, he reacted without thinking. His hand shot out, clasping hers, and he gently turned it so that he could examine the burn. "You need to have this taken care of," he said, his voice more gruff than he would've liked.

She glanced down and shrugged. "It doesn't hurt."

"It will once the adrenaline wears off. And I don't— you don't—want it to become infected and leave a scar." He forced himself to let go of her and pointed at the aid car. "Have the EMT put a dressing on it. And keep taking oxygen. Smoke inhalation is nothing to mess with."

He waited for her to head in that direction, but instead, she turned her back on him to stare at the fire, her shoulders hunched, her arms folded.

He shook his head. He was dealing with one stubborn woman. *And* a control freak, to boot. He needed to get some distance—she was a suspect. At the very least, she could be her brother's accomplice.

She kept glancing at the crewman's body then quickly away, as if she couldn't get over seeing him lying there. Was she horrified, or fascinated? Arsonists got off on watching their own fires—he'd seen it all too often. Then he noted the fine trembling of her shoulders—the same tremors he'd felt when he'd had his arm around her. The lady was holding it together by a very fine thread. She wasn't acting like an arsonist, or a murderer, or even someone's accomplice.

His instinctual urge was to protect her from what she'd have to face over the next few days. And that was a problem, a big one. *Time to pull it together, pal. Take a step way back.*

It was one hell of a coincidence that she'd been first on the scene—he couldn't ignore that. And the bottom line was that he had an investigation to run. He simply couldn't—*wouldn't*—allow himself to feel empathy for someone who was probably right up to her eyeballs in whatever had gone down on that boat.

Down at the dock, Lucy knelt beside Ken Lundquist's body, taking pictures while Ivar made notes and drew sketches. Jim Sykes stood a few feet away, observing. Her eyes burned, more from the effort to hold back tears than from the smoke in the air. Ken had been a good man. One of theirs.

They didn't get many murders in Astoria—this was only her second since she'd been on the force. The first one had happened last year, when some tourist had beaten his wife unconscious inside their motor home, then gotten liquored up and set the whole mess on fire, himself included. That scene had been gruesome, but this was far worse.

As she moved back to let Greg Ewald, the medical examiner, do his job, she sneaked a glance at Kaz. She looked like she was hanging in there, but it was hard to tell from this far away. She'd have to interview Kaz later, another chore that she wasn't looking forward to.

"This makes it pretty hard to ignore those rumors I've heard," Sykes said, breaking into her thoughts.

"Sir?"

"About the fishing community," he said impatiently.

Lucy held her tongue. She wasn't ready to start pointing any fingers or jump to any conclusions—not yet—but the chief had been on the warpath ever since he'd arrived. With the exception of the occasional loony tourist, crimes like murder and arson didn't happen in his town, and from all appearances, he was taking it personally.

Ewald straightened, having completed the in situ examination. He said something quietly into his tape recorder and then pulled off his surgical gloves, motioning for the EMTs to bag the body. "Going to be tough to get an exact time of death," he told her. "The fire retarded the rate of temperature loss in the corpse. I took a kidney temp, but—" He shrugged.

"Any preliminary determination on the cause of death?" Lucy asked, earning herself a glare. Ewald hated giving prelims, but dammit, she needed something to work with.

"Most likely blunt force trauma to the back of the head." Ewald's tone was truculent. "He's got grass stains and mud on his shoes and jeans—you catch that?"

"Yeah. The grass stains could've happened at any time, but it also might mean that the body was moved."

"They look fresh to me."

"Let's not get too exotic with the theories," Sykes interrupted. "Jorgensen probably followed Ken here after their argument in the Redemption and killed him. It's his boat, and he's our most likely suspect. Procedure says we need to concentrate on finding out whether he did it."

Light rain fell steadily now, and the fire was almost out. Kaz was shivering so hard and holding herself so tightly that she knew she'd have sore muscles by morning.

Chapman stood down on the dock, silhouetted against the orange glow of the dying fire. The flames reflected off his face shield, looking for one crazy moment like the comforting flames in a fireplace, seen through a window. Then he flipped his shield to speak into a portable radio, and the image dissolved.

The fireboat, the *Harry Steinbach*, which had been hosing down the other boats, turned a fog stream from its deck guns onto the *Anna Marie*. Chapman stopped a patrolman carrying a camera and pointed at the crowd. Then he headed back toward her, talking into the radio unit. ". . . don't hit inside the wheelhouse. I don't want the evidence washed away if we can avoid it." His deep voice had a calm, soothing quality to it.

But Kaz couldn't count on Michael Chapman to be either soothing or helpful. He thought the fire had been set on purpose, something she had trouble believing. And she'd be willing to bet, based on what he'd already intimated, that he thought she might be involved.

Of course, *that* idea was patently absurd—Lucy could vouch for her, or for any of the fishermen, for that matter. But Chapman was a newcomer—he didn't know any of them. What was it she'd told Lucy earlier in the tavern? That they were lucky to have him? Those words might be coming back to haunt them.

She'd been dead-on in her earlier assessment of his strength and determination, though—the man all but radiated a force field of authority. The volunteer fire-fighters, most of whom barely even knew him, were jumping at his orders. She knew those guys—they weren't prone to take orders from anybody, much less a newcomer. But he did seem to know what he was doing—the men had worked quickly and efficiently to put out the fire and protect the other boats.

She let out a sigh. The fact was, she should be grate-ful that Michael Chapman was here, no matter what she thought of him. This mess would get straightened out over time, she had no doubt of that. And if he hadn't shown up when he had, she'd be lying down on the dock next to Ken. Tonight made the second time in her life that she'd narrowly escaped death. But this time, she couldn't claim any of the credit for her survival—she owed her life to Chapman's quick think-ing. She didn't like being beholden to him. Not one bit.

She hunched her shoulders, trying not to look at the smoldering wreck of the *Anna Marie*. During junior high and high school, she and Gary had logged count-less hours together on the *Anna Marie*, upgrading and repairing her, as well as fishing off her. Kaz knew every piece of wood on that boat—had sanded it, painted it, caulked it. And she'd spent damn near every one of her summer vacations in the last ten years keeping the trawler seaworthy. The *Anna Marie* was . . . a friend, a family member. Tears welled again, and she blinked them away. Sentimental about a damn boat, when a member of their community was dead and she had much bigger problems on her hands.

She scrubbed her cheeks and distracted herself by watching Chapman—a strategy she was wryly aware had its pitfalls, given the lethal combination of his good looks and piercing intelligence. She was somehow drawn to him, and that scared her, because he wouldn't be on her side in all of this.

He was slowly scanning the crowd of onlookers and the jumble of fire, police, and aid vehicles, those knowledgeable eyes of his cataloging and filing away everything he was seeing. What was he looking for? Or whom?

She followed his lead, working her way through the crowd, then froze. Chuck was standing off to the left, his calm gaze trained on her. He sent her a quick, silent message she couldn't decipher, accompanied by the slightest of nods, then stepped back, immediately swallowed by the surging crowd. She strained for another glimpse of him, but she saw nothing. If Chuck was around, then so was Gary. He had to know she was there, and yet he wasn't coming forward. Before she could sort through the significance of that, Chapman walked over to her.

"Is that your truck over there?" he asked.

She looked in the direction he was pointing and shook her head. "It's my brother's. He frequently leaves it parked here." She was careful not to glance at the place where Chuck had been standing.

"So your brother was here tonight."

She hesitated, then shook her head again, the movement feeling as jerky and uncoordinated as one of those little dogs on the dashboard of a car. "I don't know where he is."

Chapman's pale gaze lingered on her for another moment, his expression giving away nothing. Then he turned and motioned to Clint Jackson, the cop who was keeping the crowd back. "One of you guys will want to impound that truck."

"Hey," Kaz said. "Wait a minute!"

"Standard procedure," he replied over his shoulder. "Your brother is a possible person of interest."

She stared at him as what he'd said sank in. "You think *Gary* would do this?" She waved her arm toward the docks. "The *Anna Marie* was built by my grandfather, named after our mother. Do you really think that her son, a third-generation waterman, would be the kind of person who could do this?"

"Anyone is capable of murder under the right circumstances. Setting a fire to cover it up is the easy part."

"Murder." She pressed a hand to her roiling stomach. "You think Ken was killed."

"Yes."

"And you believe Gary killed him," she said dully.

He turned back to her, his expression hard. "Your brother was seen arguing with the deceased earlier this evening in the tavern."

"No." Kaz shook her head. "You've got it all wrong."

"And I'm told your brother has a record of assault."

"If you knew the circumstances—"

"The circumstances are of no interest to me. Furthermore, in an arson investigation, it's standard to check out the owners of the property."

"Look." She strove for calm. "I'm sure you're used to things working differently in the city. But around here we take into account what we know about someone before we go around accusing him of something he isn't even remotely capable of!" Her hands were fisted at her sides, and she forced them to relax.

Chapman's expression was implacable. "Your brother seemed plenty capable of violence in the tavern."

God. He had it all worked out. Except he was wrong, he had to be. "What makes you so sure the fire was deliberately set?"

"I smelled gasoline when I first came on board. That, and the pattern of the fire—"

"We don't keep gasoline on board the *Anna Marie*—she runs on diesel. It's crazy to keep gasoline on board any boat. A fire at sea is every waterman's worst nightmare."

He started to speak, his expression showing the first real hints of impatience, then stopped and sighed. "You don't have to educate me about being at sea, Ms. Jorgensen. And the fact that someone used gasoline to start the fire when there was none on board makes it look even more deliberate."

He was right. My God. Someone had planned this. She stared at the now smoldering trawler. What in the world had Ken been involved in? And why had he come back to the boat so late at night?

"You were the first person on the scene? You saw no one else, no one running away from the boat?"

"No," she replied with a calm she wasn't feeling. "The marina is usually deserted this time of night."

"So why were you here?"

She hesitated. She'd have to be very, very careful with her answers. At least for now, until she could find Gary, talk to him, and straighten out this mess. With the odds stacking up so heavily against him, she couldn't take the chance that she'd provide information that could worsen his situation. "I wanted to talk to Gary," she said finally.

"Why here?"

"I didn't find him at home, and Gary sometimes sleeps aboard the *Anna Marie.* But before I could get to the boat, the fire exploded."

He glanced up from the notes he was taking. "Did the explosion knock you down, or was it more of a whooshing sound?"

"The latter," she said after thinking about it. "I realized that Gary might be on board, so I yelled for help and then ran to the boat."

"You called the fire in?"

"No. I didn't have my cell phone with me, and I didn't want to take the time to go back to the car to get it."

"*Someone* called it in. Who, if no one else was here?"

She stiffened. Did he think he would catch her in a lie? "I don't know," she said coolly. "Perhaps someone who has a view of the mooring basin."

He studied her, his expression turning speculative. "When I got here, the gate was chained shut, and I had to use bolt cutters. The other gates along the wharf aren't locked. Did you do that?"

"Of course not!" Then she remembered. "Someone had chained it from the inside. I didn't have time to deal with it. . . . I climbed over."

"So you thought it was your brother down below."

She gave a little shrug, refusing to reveal the terror she'd felt in those first few moments. "The wheelhouse door was open, and when we're in port, we keep it locked. We have expensive equipment on board— radios, a depth finder, radar—"

"Who has keys?" he interrupted.

"Just Gary. And me, of course."

"All right, what happened next?"

He was relentless, and he wasn't going to give up or go away until she gave him the answers he wanted. She repressed a sigh and told him about trying to use the fire extinguisher, about finding it gone. "We never move it, except twice a year to check that it still works."

"Probably tossed overboard." He made a note. "I'll have a diver check."

She pulled her coat tight around her, feeling the cold all the way to her core. It had begun to rain harder, adding to her discomfort, and the wind was picking up again, chopping the rain into drenching sheets.

What he said sounded plausible. Someone had deliberately set the fire and made it hard to put out, wanting to destroy the *Anna Marie*. None of the fishermen she knew would burn a boat. It would be considered a sacrilege, unless they were desperate to cover up something. *Like a body.*

She wrapped her arms tighter, inhaling the acrid odor of the smoke that clung to her clothes and hair. A new thought occurred to her. It had to be common knowledge that Ken was rarely on the boat when it was in port. So had Gary been the real target and Ken just an innocent bystander? Whirling, she started walking toward her SUV.

"Wait up," Chapman said, catching her arm. His hand was startlingly warm, his grip firm. "We're not done here. And you'll need to go to the hospital for tests."

"I'm feeling fine."

He moved his hand to her shoulder, forcibly turning

her toward the ambulances. "I'll have one of my men take you."

She dug in her heels, staring pointedly down at his hand. "You most certainly will not."

A look of exasperation flashed across his face, but he dropped his hand. "You really should go to the hospital, Ms. Jorgensen. You could collapse any time in the next couple of days from whatever you breathed when you were down in the hold."

He sounded concerned—almost. But she had other priorities—priorities that didn't include spending the night at the hospital being subjected to a lot of unnecessary tests.

"And I'll need your clothes."

She gaped at him. *"What?"*

"You were first on the scene, remember? And you *are* part-owner in the family fishing business, are you not?"

"If you're suggesting—"

"—that I'll need to test your clothes for accelerant. Standard procedure."

She really was beginning to hate that phrase. She started to answer, but broke off as Lucy, Ivar, and Jim Sykes walked up the ramp. Ivar came over to stand beside her. He didn't say a word—just used one of his big hands to rub gently between her shoulder blades. His compassion was almost the last straw.

Lucy walked up on Kaz's other side and slipped her arms around her, hugging her. "Are you okay?" she asked, sounding shaky herself.

"Yeah, mostly." Kaz tried to smile and failed, then nodded to Jim Sykes, who was shaking hands with Chapman.

"So," Sykes said, turning to her. "Looks like you've

got quite a foul-up on your hands. One of your boats out of commission, your crewman dead, and your brother possibly the prime suspect."

Chapman frowned slightly at Sykes, which struck Kaz as odd since he seemed to be thinking along the same lines. "You know Gary wouldn't do this, Jim," she replied as calmly as she could manage.

"Are you planning to issue a BOLO on him?" Chapman asked Sykes.

Kaz looked from one to the other, not comprehending.

"We need to talk to Gary," Ivar explained to her in his soft rumble. "Find out what he knows."

"Possibly armed and dangerous," Sykes confirmed.

"Hey," she yelped. "No way—"

Lucy shifted beside her. "Chief, I don't think—"

Sykes held up a hand. "Jorgensen has violated his parole, and he should be approached with extreme caution. It's in this community's best interests, as well as his, to bring him in off the street as soon as possible."

"That's way out of line," Kaz snapped.

Ivar gripped her shoulder gently. "With all due respect, sir—"

"You've known Gary all your life, Jim," she interrupted. "And you know damn well he'd never hurt Ken."

"Yeah, but I also know that his military training alone, with or without a firearm, makes him a deadly force." Sykes's tone softened. "You know as well as I do that your brother has been a walking time bomb ever since the war, Kaz. You need to stay out of this, and let us handle it."

"Why should I?" she shot back. "What I'm hearing so far doesn't give me any confidence that you will look for the person who really did this."

"Kaz," Lucy cut in. "Trust us to do our job. We just need to talk to Gary."

Kaz shut up. It was clear that she wasn't going to convince them of Gary's innocence, that she had to find him before anyone else did. If they tried to arrest him, she couldn't predict what he would do. And there had to be another explanation for all this—Gary simply wasn't capable of arson or murder.

Chapman had been standing back, observing all of them, his expression intent. For some reason, he didn't look any happier than she was. Then again, she was probably deluding herself. When it came to Chapman, she'd been deluding herself a lot in the last few hours.

His next comment confirmed as much. "So, Ms. Jorgensen. Your clothes. You can either go to the hospital with an official escort or give them to me here." His smile chilled her to the bone. "Your choice."

He watched all day and all night.
They thought he was only a skulking coyote.

CHAPTER FOUR

At dawn the next morning, Michael stood with Zeke on the north jetty of the mooring basin, waiting for the state lab technicians to finish their work on the *Anna Marie.* Pale sunlight pierced charcoal clouds, illuminating the rippled spines of exposed sand bars on the Columbia. Gulls screeched as they fought over the morning's catch, and on the docks, sea lions barked, their frenzied discussions broken only occasionally by the watery chug of a diesel motor as another fishing trawler headed out for the day.

Michael warmed his hands on his coffee cup while he gazed across the vast stretch of the Columbia. Although he'd been in town less than a week, each new day brought moments of beauty so stunning they took his breath away. The river's surface was misleadingly tranquil—here and there, a small eddy the only indication of the turbulence that lay hidden beneath. Softly framed by forested, evergreen hills, illuminated by the choreography of sunlight and clouds, the river fooled most visitors. Only those who lived by its shores understood that such daily theatrics came at a heavy price. Michael doubted he'd ever get used to the Columbia, even if he lived here for the rest of his life.

Initially, Astoria had reminded him of his summers on the Maryland shore. Driving into town that first day, he'd noticed what everyone notices at first—the steep hillsides with weathered clapboard houses clinging to them, the mooring basins with their neat lines of docked fishing trawlers, the sharp smells of the waterfront. Those sights and sounds and smells had brought back memories of a happier time in his life, a time when he'd felt a bone-deep satisfaction from helping his brothers bring in the day's catch.

But after less than a week of talking to Astorians, his impression of the town had quickly changed. On the Maryland shore, danger came from the storms that blew in from sea. One at least had warning. Here, danger was hidden in the submerged, shifting sandbars that could shipwreck your boat in a heartbeat, and in the treacherous current of an unforgiving river that drained an area the size of France into a narrow canyon. Michael had come away from his summers out on the Atlantic Ocean with a respect for the open water. But the Columbia . . . the Columbia made him uneasy.

He took a sip of coffee, its steam partially obscuring his view of a crab boat moving downriver. A slight breeze off the docks carried the scent of wet, charred wood from the *Anna Marie*. Zeke looked up at him, his expression eager as he whined softly.

"Yeah, I know, boy," he murmured. "You can smell it all the way up here, can't you?"

After an exhausting night of battling high winds and rain, Michael had gone home to shower and change clothes only an hour ago. Thanks to a small pump donated by the nearby boat works, the *Anna Marie* sat much higher in the water and was no longer in danger of being swamped. And the weather had calmed for the moment, but according to the radio, more storms were on the way. Which meant he had to hustle, because he wanted every damn bit of evidence off that boat.

He turned and stared back toward town, barely noting the jumble of homes and businesses that clung to the steep hillsides. The irony of his situation hadn't escaped him. He'd come over three thousand miles in hopes of living a more normal life, only to land right back in the thick of an arson-murder investigation. One that was dredging up memories he'd worked hard to bury. One that had all his instincts on red alert.

He couldn't help wondering about the timing of the fire so soon after his arrival. Had whoever was behind this been aware of his reputation and decided to target him? It wouldn't be the first time. He'd spent more than a decade tracking down firebugs who loved to play their cat-and-mouse games with him. Sick bastards who got off by matching their wits against his.

Then again, maybe it was simply a case of taking advantage of the new guy. Or, maybe he was just being paranoid. He shrugged. Not that it mattered—he'd catch the perp. And he had more immediate problems to solve than whether someone was messing with his head. Like local cops, who seemed more than willing to jump to conclusions before the evidence was processed. Like working out jurisdiction on the case, always a touchy subject. He shifted on his feet, vaguely unsettled. Like Kaz Jorgensen.

He might not have known her for more than a few hours, but he'd already figured out that she had no intention of leaving the investigation to the authorities. And he couldn't rule out the possibility that she was more directly involved than he wanted to believe.

The woman was a damn pit bull. After inhaling enough toxic smoke to put most people in the hospital for days, she'd agreed to rest and take oxygen for all of maybe five minutes before she'd begun making his life difficult. In more ways than one.

He didn't want to admit, even to himself, that he found her brand of loyalty and smarts appealing. Or that touching her shot more adrenaline through his system than a four-alarm fire. It was just chemistry, that's all.

He couldn't believe he was letting himself get distracted by a pair of soulful brown eyes and a sexy body. He knew the consequences of that kind of risky behavior. Five years ago, if he'd been less distracted, and if he'd been paying attention instead of planning his wedding, he would've known Phillips was targeting him and Jessica. He would've known Phillips was staking out their apartment, following Jessica whenever she went out. Waiting for the perfect moment, when she was alone.

Michael closed his eyes, forcing away the dull ache of those old memories. He'd paid the price, he'd learned his lesson. He knew better now.

Unlike Jessica, Kaz wasn't classically pretty. Hell, she wasn't really even his type. Her face was too narrow, her chin too pointed. But all that wild hair made him want to reach out and grab up handfuls of the stuff. And she had a surprisingly lush mouth—one that hinted she might not be nearly as controlled and self-contained as she wanted everyone to believe. What had really caught his attention, though, was that when it counted, she didn't back down. And in his experience, that kind of courage was very rare.

When he'd seen her dive down the stairs of the trawler, his heart had damn near stopped. She had guts, he'd give her that—she'd braved a ten-foot wall of flames to save what turned out to be a corpse. It made him wonder what she did for kicks—probably skydiving or bungee-jumping. Then again, maybe she was just whacked. One of the firemen had let slip that she consulted to Fortune 500 companies. It figured. When a person learned to swim with sharks at an early age, it tended to become a lifelong habit.

He should know.

He shook his head. Why was he even thinking about her? When it came right down to it, it didn't matter whether she was brave or sexy or just plain crazy. He had a job to do, and these days he *always* played by the rules. Rules that said one didn't get involved with anyone associated with an investigation. Rules that were there to remind him how self-destructive it was to think about her as anyone other than the sister of an arson suspect. Rules that, when he'd broken them in the past, had gotten someone he'd loved killed.

If there were even a remote possibility the arsonist was messing with his head, he couldn't take the chance of anyone associated with him getting hurt. And that meant keeping his hands off Kaz Jorgensen.

She was a Person of Interest *only* with respect to the investigation.

Zeke whined again, and Michael drank the last of his coffee, grimacing at its bitter taste even while he was relieved to have the distraction. He'd had better coffee in Boston, for Christ's sake. This was the Pacific Northwest, renowned for its damn coffee. So why was it he couldn't find a decent cup in this town?

The techs from the state crime lab were packing up and preparing to leave. He looked down at Zeke. "Okay, boy. You ready to rock and roll?"

Zeke barked and jumped in a circle around him, nipping at the hem of his sweater.

Michael pulled a pad of paper out of his pocket. "So here's the deal, pal," he said as they walked across the wharf and down the ramp to the dock. "You've got to be careful not to fall through the deck in a couple of places. We need to check out the wheelhouse, and getting there's going to be a little dicey."

"Mawroooo, rooo," the dog responded in his unique combination of moaning and dog talk. His expression was baleful.

"I'm not insulting you—it's just that you're not always so nimble of paw, you know?" The sea lions that had been lazing on the dock slipped into the water, and Michael had to grab Zeke's collar to keep him from going in after them. "Not a good idea, big guy. They'll have you for breakfast. Didn't you see the warning signs up on the wharf?"

He nodded good morning to the lead technician. "You guys do a thorough sweep of the wheelhouse and the flying bridge?"

"Yeah." The kid yawned. "We might've found a hair

off the guy, if we're lucky. One with the follicle attached. With all the soot, there's no way to tell the color until we get it back to the lab. Of course, it could belong to the owners. Or is one of the owners the torch?"

"Always a possibility."

The tech grunted. "Figures. We also dusted the lock for fingerprints, like you asked. Nada. But there's a hunk of melted metal that could be what's left of the ignition source."

"Good. I'll have more for you once I dig out the fo'c'sle and galley. What's your timeline on the hair?"

"We should have a preliminary opinion on the match to the vic by later this afternoon. DNA, you know the routine—like sometime in the next century, unless you've got clout." He grinned at Chapman. "Since you're new in town, I figure I've got plenty of time."

Michael tossed the dregs of his coffee into the water and crumpled the paper cup in his fist. "Put a priority on it. If you need someone with *clout* to call you, I can arrange it. I want this guy yesterday."

The kid held up both hands. "Hey, man, I was just kidding."

"And if you've got any DNA saliva collection kits, I need them."

Mumbling something about no sense of humor, the tech fished around inside his voluminous carryall and produced the tubes. "You know to keep these refrigerated, right? And I'll need chain of evidence forms. I don't want to be sitting in court six months from now explaining who had access to the evidence and could've contaminated it."

Michael slipped them into the inside pocket of his

jacket. "I'll handle any problems that come up in that area."

"It's your funeral, man."

He waited until the crime van had backed off the wharf, and then held back the tarp at the edge of the deck. "Here you go, Zeke. Jump!"

The dog looked at the decking, then at the dark, brackish water visible between the edge of the dock and the trawler's burned-through railing. He sat down on the dock, looked up at Michael, and yawned.

"Christ, dog. Down-shifting has turned you into a wimp."

"Raaaaa, raaaa."

Michael picked him up and transferred him to the boat, earning an enthusiastic licking for his efforts. Familiar with the routine, Zeke sat and waited patiently for his next command.

Once Michael had completed a scaled drawing of the fire scene, he pulled on surgical gloves. He and Zeke picked their way around the gaping hole of charred timbers over the hold and forward to the wheelhouse. Inside, the equipment was badly melted, the wheel charred black and partially disintegrated, the room scorched. Where the fire had burned hottest, the paint on the ceiling was blistered. But the walls were still intact, which meant that the fire had burned here only briefly before spreading quickly to other sections of the boat.

Even after being up all night, which impaired his sense of smell, Michael still had no doubt as to what odor he was picking up. "Okay, pal, are you getting what I'm getting?" He gave Zeke the command to go to work.

The shepherd crisscrossed the room, sniffing eagerly, then focused on a spot at the base of the wheel. He lifted one paw in a positive signal. Michael knelt beside him, studying the floor. Pulling out a pair of tweezers, he picked up a bit of cloth and held it to his nose. Gasoline. Placing the cloth inside a small, clean can, he tapped the lid shut, then continued his perusal. A short distance away, as the technician had indicated, lay a melted clump of metal, the remains of a piece of wire, and another smaller, scorched lump— possibly some kind of cheap timer. Michael pulled a large baggie out of his jacket and carefully put the whole mess inside. Then he sat back on his heels and surveyed the area.

He'd lay odds he was looking at what was left of a small space heater, its electrical cord, and a simple timer. The guy had probably stuffed the heater with gasoline-soaked rags. When the timer had turned the heater on, firing up the electrical elements . . . kaboom.

"Well, I'll be damned," Michael murmured. "Our torch seems to have known what he was doing, huh, Zeke? Now, isn't *that* a bad sign."

Marking the location of the ignition source on his diagram, he stood up, his eyes tracking the burn flow pattern down the stairs to the engine room and out the door to the foredeck. He stared at the decking, the hairs on his neck rising. He'd seen flow patterns hundreds of times, but this one. . . . The pencil he was holding snapped in two, and he swore at himself. *Don't go there.* There were similarities to his apartment fire, so what? So some burn patterns had become, for him, emotional triggers, like Rorschach inkblots. He'd cope, dammit. He had to.

He rubbed the back of his neck with a shaky hand and made himself focus once more. The perp had killed the crewman—maybe a fight had erupted, gotten out of hand, and he'd hit the vic too hard, accidentally killing him. That was Jorgensen's MO—evidently, he'd thrown a punch six months ago that had broken a guy's jaw.

Michael frowned and glanced around. Most people use whatever is handy to start a fire, maybe old rags and gasoline. Not a space heater. Had the Jorgensens actually kept a space heater on board? He supposed it was possible—it had to get damned uncomfortable out on the water during the winter. But in his experience, most crab boats had an oil heater down below for the crew. You simply didn't waste precious battery power on a current-hogging space heater.

As for the gasoline, Kaz Jorgensen had said they didn't keep any on board. Which made starting the fire not so easy. To use diesel, Gary would've had to siphon the tanks. And according to Kaz—*no, that's Ms. Jorgensen to you,* he reminded himself—they typically brought the boats in on empty, which meant siphoning would've been a bitch and a half. Besides, he and Zeke were smelling gas, not diesel.

Michael straightened and studied the layout of the mooring basin. The problem was, it would have been a hell of a lot easier to get rid of the body by dumping it in the river from the jetty. Nice, swift current, and a convenient storm as cover-up. The body would've gotten snagged under a dock somewhere downstream, which meant that it could've been days before it was discovered. Or it would've gone ashore, possibly as far downriver as Warrenton. Either way, dumping it in the water was less risky than leaving it on board the *Anna Marie*.

And why, if Jorgensen were the torch, had the guy

been willing to burn his boat? Had he needed the money? Or was he just tired of struggling to keep the family business alive, had decided to cash out, and Lundquist had been in the way? Michael made a note to check into the Jorgensens' finances. Kaz might have plenty of money, but that didn't mean her brother did.

It was fully light now, and he noticed that more fishermen were arriving. The crabbers would want to use the window between storms to lift and rebait their pots. Someone—he couldn't remember who at the moment—had said that the fishermen crossed the bar just before the tide turned, on the slack tide. That way if they got into trouble, at least the tide would carry them out to sea before their boat was reduced to toothpicks on the rocks or run aground on the sandbars. Michael grimaced. Hell of a way to make a living.

Several fishermen cast curious glances his way, but no one approached him. Those guys knew what was going on, he'd bet on it. Would they protect one of their own? Hell, yes. He'd have to interview them later, but he had no illusions as to their level of cooperation. He shrugged, sparing them one last glance. He'd deal with them when the time came.

"Okay, Zeke, what about streamers?" He pointed to a burn mark that flowed away from the wheelhouse door and around to the deck. "If I'd been in this guy's place, I would've run gasoline from here to the deck, where I'd pour a shitload of it, then I'd continue around the corner and down the stairs into the engine room. What d'you think? Have I got it right?"

"Mawroooo."

"If I'd known you had conversations with that dog of yours, I might not have hired the two of you."

Michael glanced over his shoulder. Wallace Forbes, Astoria's mayor and his new boss, was standing on the dock. "Don't try to come on board, sir."

"Wouldn't even think of it. Just stopped by to see how things were coming along."

Forbes was typical of politicians everywhere, dressed casually to put his constituents at ease, persistently cheerful, and always careful about what he gave away in a conversation. He wasn't a bad sort, necessarily, just the product of the electoral environment. Michael had never had much use for politicians, but he'd learned to live with them.

"Zeke is helping me confirm that this fire was deliberately set."

"From what I hear about that nose of yours, you already knew that," Forbes observed.

"Never hurts to have a second opinion."

"Now *those* are words to live by." Forbes pulled a cigarette out of a monogrammed silver case, tapped it a few times, and lit it. "So tell me you know *who* did it, as well."

Michael hesitated. "Fires have a way of burning up a lot of the evidence, and the weather last night was particularly foul. But with any luck, I'll find something useful."

The mayor nodded and looked out across the docks. He waved to the crew of a departing trawler. "Is there any possibility that it wasn't Jorgensen?"

"He had motive, as well as opportunity," Michael said, uneasy with giving the wrong impression. "But there are a few unanswered questions."

Forbes's gaze turned shrewd. "Like what?"

"I'd rather not say until I complete my investigation." Michael didn't think the mayor would want to hear that the method of ignition didn't match the crime.

The mayor watched him for a long moment through eyes half-shut against cigarette smoke and then chuckled. "Word has it you used to drive your superiors nuts."

Michael didn't respond. Forbes hadn't stopped by on a casual morning stroll along the waterfront, not at the crack of dawn. And he wasn't here to give Michael grief about his reputation as a maverick, which he had to have known about well before he'd hired him. Michael's buddies in the Boston Fire Department had told him Forbes had checked him out. Thoroughly. He hadn't just conducted a routine, cursory check—he'd made it a point to talk to anyone who would volunteer information about Michael. And while Michael resented it, he respected the mayor's thoroughness.

Forbes sighed. "You know, I've known the Jorgensens for most of my life. Knew their parents, too. Anna and Tim died in a freak storm—let's see—that would be fifteen years ago now. The twins would've been eighteen at the time. It was hard on them, real hard. Gary enlisted, ended up a Ranger in the army— in one of those elite units that does things the rest of us would rather not know about." Forbes shook his head. "Now Kaz, though, she went south and got herself one fine college education. Made a go of that consulting business of hers. People round here don't let on, but they're awfully proud of both of them."

He paused while he flicked some cigarette ash into the water. "Kaz was with her parents that night, you know. She barely made it to Sand Island, a nasty pile of shifting sediment just this side of the bar. She couldn't save her parents, and that's eaten at her. She hasn't been back, other than for her annual visits, in years. That is, not until about three weeks ago, when she showed up and started working the crab pots."

Michael remained silent, wondering where all of this was leading. The way he saw it, the fact that the locals thought highly of the Jorgensens didn't mean diddly-squat. The mayor might think that Gary'd had a couple of bad breaks, but that didn't mean the guy hadn't finally snapped. And the fact that Kaz had come back to town for an extended stay right before the fire wasn't exactly a point in her favor.

Forbes was smiling fondly, his expression distant. "She's a pistol, though, isn't she?"

"Yes, sir," Michael's reply was a little too heartfelt, but he didn't think Forbes had noticed.

"The irony is, until that shipwreck, folks around here thought Kaz was the most gifted female skipper to ever work the North Coast. She had this eerie sixth sense about the river bar. The fishermen used to just follow her across, knowing that if they did what she did, they'd make it home to their wives." Forbes watched the boats pulling away from the docks for a long moment, then sighed. "Fishermen are a superstitious lot—she'll have to prove herself all over again."

He turned back to Michael. "Heard you went in after her last night before you had backup in place. Thought you knew better than that, Michael."

Small towns. Michael wondered who had talked. He flipped his notebook shut and slipped it into his pocket. "I assessed the situation, made the decision to go in."

"I'd hate to think that business in Boston is still affecting your judgment."

Michael's voice went cool. "You knew what my reputation was. It's a little late to be having second thoughts."

Forbes nodded slowly. "True enough." He reached over to pat Zeke's head. The dog endured it with one slightly curled lip. "You know, people move out here for a number of reasons. Some of them just can't handle being in the city anymore—the peace and quiet is easier on their nerves. Some simply don't fit in anywhere else, and the folks out here are more forgiving of that than your average urban dweller." He paused. "I'm willing to bet you came out here for similar reasons."

Michael stared back, his expression impassive. He'd be damned if he would take the bait. "Was there anything else you wanted, sir?"

Forbes chuckled. "I also heard you were a real hard case." When Michael didn't reply, he shrugged and continued. "There've been a few run-ins between Gary and Jim Sykes in the past. Jim didn't grow up with the same advantages as the Jorgensens. His home life—excuse my French—sucked. Drunk mother, abusive father. More times than not, the only good meal Jim got was at school. But he's worked hard, risen above all that to become one damn fine chief of police." Forbes paused to draw on his cigarette. "A couple years back, Jim broke up a theft ring here in town that'd been driving us all nuts. Men were afraid to go to work and leave their wives, for fear the women would come home from the grocery store and walk in on a robbery in progress. Jim changed all that, and folks around here are grateful.

"I guess what I'm trying to say, Michael, is that if you do right by us on this case, the townsfolk aren't going to forget it. They'll be on your side from here on out. We stick by our own, no matter what."

"Yes, sir." Forbes was letting him know they'd over-look his checkered past, he realized, his mouth twisting. Just like they had with Sykes.

"Well." Forbes brushed his hand across the edge of the *Anna Marie*'s scorched railing, then rubbed the soot between his fingers. "I'm sure you're busy, so I'll be on my way."

"Thanks for dropping by, sir."

"Somehow, I doubt you were all that happy to see me, son," Forbes observed, his tone wry. He turned to go, then stopped and looked back. "Michael."

"Yes, sir."

"I don't think I have to tell you how much I appreciate having your expertise on this. I know you'll do everything you can to solve the crime fairly and impartially, and to bring the right person to justice."

Michael nodded. He hadn't missed the tension among the cops last night, with two of them flanking Kaz and sending a not-so-subtle message to the police chief that they wouldn't tolerate any subjectivity on his part. And Michael had also been neatly warned—no outsider would be allowed to run roughshod over one of their own.

But unless he was mistaken about the intent of this little visit, the mayor was willing to use him—the newcomer—to ensure that those friendships and loyalties weren't a hindrance to the investigation. He could've told Forbes not to worry. No one ever got in the way of his investigation—at least, not for long.

"Well, then," Forbes said, nodding. "I'll leave you to it."

Michael knelt and rubbed Zeke's chest while he watched the mayor walk away. He had a confusing fire scene, a beloved town daughter who was up to her neck in intrigue, and a boss who didn't trust the motives of his own police force. "Well, well, well," he murmured. "This town is looking less quaint all the time, huh, boy?"

"Raaaoow."

Blue Jay said,
"I am not dead . . . are you dead?"

CHAPTER FIVE

A mountain of water crashed against the window of the wheelhouse, pouring over the flying bridge and engulfing the wildly pitching deck. From inside the dream, Kaz watched helplessly as her father disappeared over the side into the darkness below. She heard as if from a distance her mother's scream as she crawled toward where he had been, an arm outstretched. Kaz opened her mouth to yell a warning, but no sound came out. It was too late. Another wave battered them, and her mother was gone.

Kaz wrenched the wheel hard to port, fighting to bring the trawler about, to get back to where her parents had gone overboard. But the trawler refused to change course. The window beside her exploded, razor-like shards raining down on her. The wheel spun out of control, slamming her against the wall. Dazed, she slid down until she was lying on the floor.

The trawler's bow reared up to the sky, then crashed

down in its final death throes. She inched toward the radio mike that swung wildly just out of her reach, but she was no match for the power of the storm. The trawler pitched again, this time to starboard, and she was thrown out the door and over the rail into a freefall.

Icy water slapped her down, pulling her into its black depths. Fighting her way back to the surface, she saw her mother floating facedown a few feet away. She reached out, only to be dragged farther away by the next wave.

Behind her, wood cracked, then splintered. The boom collapsed, and the trawler slipped beneath the surface. She turned back to where her mother had been, but the sea was empty. Kaz continued to search, fighting the massive waves until her limbs were numb. Exhausted, she grabbed a piece of decking that floated past, clinging to it.

"Take my hand," a voice said over the fury of the wind. She turned and saw Michael Chapman in his fireman's coat, rowing toward her in a small skiff, reaching out to her. "I can save you."

She sobbed and reached toward him, but as their fingers touched, his face dissolved into that of a ghoul, a relic hunter who plied the local waters, looking for skulls of fishermen. She screamed, shrinking away from his outstretched hand and sinking beneath the icy surface. Pulled relentlessly down, her lungs filled with water that stole her breath, her will to live. . . .

Kaz lunged up, clawing her way out of the nightmare and gasping for air. She scrambled into a crouch against the headboard of her bed, the harsh rasp of her rapid breathing disturbing the early morning quiet. Shuddering, she stared at the familiar furniture and knickknacks of her childhood bedroom, barely registering them.

It was just the dream. She repeated the phrase over and over inside her head, like a mantra. She lifted a shaky hand to shove damp hair back from her face and made herself look again at each of the sturdy pieces of walnut furniture her grandfather had built for her, to take in the pale morning light filtering through the sheer lace curtains of her south-facing window.

The nightmare had been occurring more often since she'd come home, and it didn't take a rocket scientist to figure out what had triggered it this time. Years of hearing the local legends about ghouls hunting for the skulls of drowned sailors, followed by the shipwreck when she was a teenager, and now last night's disaster—she would've been surprised if she *hadn't* had the dream.

Usually, the ghoul turned out to be whoever was hassling her at the moment. And Chapman certainly fit *that* bill.

She sagged into a sitting position, pulling the tangled bedcovers close to ward off the chill in the air. *Okaaay.* She let out a small, unsteady laugh, followed by an embarrassing hiccup. If she weren't careful, she'd get a visit from the little men wearing white coats. Yes, she'd just spent the better part of the last twelve hours with Chapman watching every move she made—grilling her, trying to make her slip up. And yeah, her life was stressful right now. Make that extremely stressful. Still, it might be a good strategy to avoid chatting up the local therapists over a beer— especially those with Freudian training.

She pushed back the covers and climbed stiffly from bed. Out of habit, she walked over to the window to gauge the weather. The skies were gloomy, the clouds gray and threatening to drop their moisture. But the wind was light, and for now, the rain was holding off. In the distance, she could actually see patches of weak sunlight over Young's Bay. She hugged herself, trying to sense the old connection with Gary—the one they'd always had growing up. Was he out there somewhere, standing at someone else's window, gauging the weather just like she was? Was he all right? Or was he running from a killer?

She wouldn't let herself even think about the other possibility—that somehow, he was involved. Not Gary. Not the quiet, gentle kid she'd grown up with. Not even the hardened, disillusioned man—the stranger—he'd become. She refused to believe it.

After Chapman had dropped her off around 3 A.M. and confiscated her clothes, she'd called every friend of Gary's she could think of, waking them up, which hadn't made her popular. No one knew where he was. Or, at least, no one was *admitting* they knew where he was. She'd checked his bedroom, but he hadn't slept in his bed. And his camping gear and army revolver were gone. That missing revolver was what had her the most worried. Gary *never* carried his gun.

Finally, the combined exhaustion of hard days on the water, being up all night, and being worried half to death had taken their toll. She'd pulled on one of Gary's Seahawks jerseys, hugging it around her as she'd dropped off into a fitful doze—only to awaken less than an hour later, feeling as if she were drowning.

She shook herself out of her reverie. She should be out looking for Gary—not dreaming about a past that she couldn't change. Or about a burned-out arson investigator, for that matter.

Michael Chapman thought Gary had run, a strong indication that he was guilty. But she knew that Gary had reasons to run other than guilt.

For twenty agonizing days at the end of Desert Storm, she and the rest of the world had watched and waited for the Iraqis to release Gary and four other POWs. He'd finally come home, quiet and withdrawn. His experiences had changed him from an amiable young man into a withdrawn stranger who had trouble sleeping through the night, who no longer talked about anything but the size of the catch. He'd never talked to anyone about that time in captivity—about what he'd endured. One thing Kaz knew for sure—if he were no longer able to handle closed-in spaces, no one could blame him.

She'd been so certain that spending time on the open water again would be his saving grace. That, and having Ken crewing for him. Ken knew what he'd been through. But now Gary might somehow be mixed up in whatever had happened to Ken—in murder and arson.

Chapman intended to prove that Gary had set the fire—she knew that as surely as she knew the tides. And Jim Sykes—well, Jim would do whatever it took to keep his town clean. If that meant throwing Gary in jail, he wouldn't hesitate.

Lucy had told her all about how people in Astoria thought Jim Sykes walked on water ever since he'd busted up a burglary ring. Kaz shook her head. Lucy had also confided that privately, Sykes's overzealousness on the job made her a tad uneasy. "He's taking 'by the book' to a whole new level," she'd said.

Since Gary was the most obvious suspect, she had no illusions that Sykes would waste time investigating anyone else. She was the only person, with the possible exception of Lucy, who was in a dicey position, who wouldn't readily accept that Gary was guilty. So the responsibility lay with her to prove them all wrong, Chapman *and* the police. Lucy had been right all along—something *had* been going terribly wrong with Gary. Maybe if Kaz had come home sooner, maybe if she had used more of her vacation time in recent years to hang out here in Astoria . . . *maybe*. She shook her head. Looking back wouldn't get her anywhere.

She needed a plan, one that would bring answers, and fast. Planning was her forte—she'd built an entire career around her talents in that arena. It was time to put those talents to good use outside the corporate boardroom.

She sighed, turning away from the window and heading for the bathroom. Getting the smell of smoke out of her hair and off her skin would be a first step toward feeling up to facing the day. The quick shower she'd taken last night before falling into bed hadn't even made a dent. So first, a long, hot shower. Then caffeine. She *definitely* needed lots of caffeine.

A half hour later, Kaz stood in her cheery turn-of-the-century kitchen, watching the coffee drip with excruciating slowness into a glass carafe and listening to the soothing sounds of the old house waking up around her—the ancient furnace in the basement kicking on, the whoosh of air through the cast-iron heating grates, the creaking of the structure as it warmed up.

She'd missed the old house. It represented home to her in a way that her condo in Stinson Beach never would. Her great-grandfather had built the Mission-style cottage for his young bride in the early 1900s, handling all the finish carpentry himself. The house wasn't luxurious by anyone's standards, but its high ceilings, built-in glass-fronted cabinetry and bookcases, and mahogany crown moldings made her condo feel cold and sterile by comparison.

Each of the rooms of the Astoria house held decades of memories, conjured up pictures in her mind of times when the family had still been together. They were good memories, memories to cherish. In the last decade, she'd led a full and productive life down in San Francisco, but in some ways, it had been a barren life. She'd been too busy, too focused on building her consulting business, and she'd let her relationships with family and friends suffer. Maybe she could be happier here than she'd been down south . . . no, that was crazy. She had a career, and a business she'd built from scratch. It was insane to think moving home would fill that empty place deep down inside her. Wasn't it?

When she heard pounding on the back door, jolting her out of her troubled thoughts, she jumped a foot.

Michael Chapman stood on the other side of the glass, his gaze watchful, his expression cautious. Zeke stood on his hind legs beside Chapman, both paws on the window ledge, looking in. The dog grinned, his tongue lolling out the side of his mouth. Chapman wasn't nearly so cheerful, but neither did he look all that ghoulish.

Rubbing suddenly damp hands against her jeans, she walked over and flipped the lock, opening the door. Zeke pushed against her leg, wagging his tail, and she leaned down to let him sniff her hand. "Don't you two have a home of your own to go to?" she asked Chapman. It was the first time she'd said something out loud since she'd awakened, and the words came out raspy. Obviously, the abuse her throat had gotten the night before hadn't helped her vocal cords.

"I went home after I left you for a change of clothes." Chapman handed her the morning paper that she had yet to retrieve off the lawn and sniffed the air appreciatively. "You going to share some of that coffee?"

His broad, Bostonian accent was stronger this morning than it had been last night, and he looked as tired as she felt—he probably hadn't gotten any sleep at all. Although she didn't need the diversion of having him underfoot, she simply didn't have it in her to refuse him the coffee. As far as she was concerned, coffee was one of the major food groups and should be featured prominently in international human rights laws. She pointed to a chair and then opened a cupboard door to retrieve a second mug.

He sat down at her oak pedestal table, slouching comfortably, his long, jeans-clad legs stretched out in front of him. His hair was damp and casually disheveled—he'd evidently showered on that trip home. But he hadn't taken the time to shave. A day's growth of beard darkened his strong jaw line, making his light-colored eyes even more startling in contrast.

Zeke collapsed at his feet with a moan, resting his chin on his paws. They both looked disgustingly relaxed and comfortable with their surroundings—a couple of confident males. Chapman's gaze was sharp, though, as was his dog's. The laid-back attitudes were a pose, meant to encourage her to relax her guard. She frowned and turned away to deal with the coffee.

Carrying the steaming mugs over to the table, she came to the point. "So why are you here?"

"I brought your clothes back. They're clean of accelerant."

"You didn't have them long enough to send them to a lab," she pointed out, taking a chair across from him and sipping from her mug.

"Zeke sniffed them. His nose is as good as any gas chromatograph, and he didn't find anything. I didn't see any reason to send them to the lab."

"So I'm no longer a suspect?"

One corner of Chapman's mouth lifted, drawing her gaze there. He had a very nice mouth, one that encouraged fantasies. And okay, she might need to revisit the whole Freudian dream-scenario issue. Then she realized the direction her thoughts were taking, and froze. *My God.* She wasn't actually *attracted* to the man, was she? How suicidal was *that?*

If he noticed her momentary distraction, he didn't comment on it, saying only, "It means I don't think you set the fire while you were wearing those clothes."

Typical of him to not give an inch. She barely managed to refrain from rolling her eyes.

He pulled a large manila envelope out of his jacket. "I'd like you to look at some pictures of the crowd from last night and tell me who you recognize— whether you see anything out of the ordinary, like a boat moored in the wrong location, a car that isn't usually there—that sort of thing."

She sat up a little straighter, even more on guard. "Why don't you show them to the harbormaster?"

"I'm headed there next. But this is your community— you've known the fishermen for a couple of decades, at least."

"I only spend a couple of weeks here each year—I haven't lived here for the last ten years."

He waved a hand, overriding her objection. "You might notice something or someone that the harbormaster wouldn't." Pulling the photos from the envelope, he spread them across the table. "Arsonists are pretty messed up in the head. Whoever did this might've hung around to watch."

So this was what he'd had Clint Jackson doing last night during the fire. Although still wary, Kaz was curious in spite of herself. She propped both elbows on the table and leaned forward.

Each photo had been taken to show a section of the crowd, and Chapman had arranged them on the table, from left to right, as she would've seen the crowd from where she'd been standing on the wharf. Sipping her coffee, she started studying them.

Michael leaned back, taking advantage of the opportunity to observe her. Up close, she looked exhausted, wrung out. Her hair hung in long, golden ropes down her back, still damp from her shower, and her face, stripped clean of any makeup, was still unnaturally pale. She wore a royal blue football jersey that was three sizes too large for her, jeans worn thin enough at the pressure points to have his imagination working overtime, and fluffy red wool socks. She looked sexy as hell. He gave himself a slight shake. *Don't go there. Focus on the job.* Yeah, right.

He couldn't help noticing the shadows under her eyes, or the hollows beneath her cheekbones. Anxiety had stamped deep creases on either side of her mouth. She'd finally bandaged the burn on her hand—the stark whiteness of the gauze stood out in contrast to the angry, reddened skin. Her hand had to be sore, and it bothered him more than it should that she might be hurting.

If she believed her brother was innocent, she must be under tremendous strain. But the hell of it was, she wasn't acting anxious—she was acting a little too much like an uncooperative witness. Or like someone who had something to hide.

She studied one photo at a time, moving methodically from left to right, her concentration absolute. Corporate barracudas concentrated like that—high-stakes players who couldn't afford to blink. Was that what she was? He shook his head slightly. His gut was screaming no, but he wasn't all that sure he could rely on his gut right about now.

She might not have lived in town in recent years, but she had to know most of the people in the pictures. Odds were she'd grown up with them, gone to school with them. The question was whether she'd be up front with him about whom she recognized, or whether she'd lie.

The knuckles on the hand that held her coffee mug whitened. She was staring at the photo on her far left.

"See something?"

She started, almost as if she'd forgotten he was there. It was a hell of a note—he couldn't keep his eyes off her, and she didn't even remember he was in the room. Any other time, he would've been amused at himself. But the fact that he was letting himself become attracted had him as twitchy as a cat in a room full of rocking chairs.

"These guys are all fishermen," she said abruptly, pointing to another of the photos and reeling off several names that he managed to jot down on the back of the envelope. "You'll recognize some of them from the tavern last night."

"And none of them were at the mooring basin when you arrived."

"No, I told you, it was deserted."

He propped a boot on top of one of the claw-foot legs of the table and studied her. She was holding back on him, dammit. "But you recognized someone else just now," he pushed. When she didn't respond, he rubbed a hand over his chin. He knew he had no right, at this point, to expect her to trust or confide in him, but it rankled, just the same. "Ms. Jorgensen—"

"I thought I might've recognized someone, but I was mistaken."

"Withholding information in a criminal investigation is a prosecutable offense."

Her jaw was set. "There's no one in these photos that I consider capable of arson or murder."

He leaned forward, picked up the photo she'd been staring at, and tossed it directly in front of her. "Leave the judgments up to the authorities—tell me who you saw."

Her soft brown eyes flashed at him. "I saw no one."

He waited her out, using the silence to try to unnerve her. The phone rang shrilly, startling both of them. She got up to answer it, but whoever it was must've hung up.

Michael picked up the photos and carefully stacked them. "I understand that you want to protect your brother," he said, giving her time to reconsider, "but it's unnecessary. If he didn't do it, I'll find out who did."

"Maybe, maybe not."

He started to snap at her, then sighed. "Look, if you're worried that I don't conduct thorough investigations, then let me set your mind at ease. I don't jump to false conclusions—I let the evidence tell the truth."

"I have only your word on that," she pointed out, sitting back down. "And frankly, I'm worried about your hidden agendas."

"I don't have any hidden agendas," he said, letting his voice reveal his irritation. "Although from what I've seen so far, you and everyone else in this town does." He leaned forward, lowering his voice. "I'd say that you're engaging in a bit of psychological transference, wouldn't you?"

Kaz stiffened. Even as her temper spiked, a part of her—the part that had spent ten years in corporate political battles—was impressed. He knew when to bide his time and when to go for the jugular—his interrogation skills were excellent. It wouldn't be wise to continue to underestimate him. Gary's life might depend on her ability to handle this man.

She refused to take the bait. "You could've had Lucy return the clothes—the harbormaster could've answered any other questions you have. You just wanted another shot at me, didn't you?"

A myriad of emotions flashed across his face, gone almost before she had a chance to label them—frustration, impatience, perhaps a little grudging admiration. His self-control was good—excellent—but a muscle ticked in his jaw, giving him away. Good. Maybe he'd investigate more thoroughly, checking out all the possibilities, instead of taking the easy way out. She hoped she could count on him not to take that easy path, but it was human nature to choose the most obvious solution. And over the years, she'd gained plenty of respect for the fallibility of human nature.

"We're on the same side, you know," he said finally. "We both want to catch whoever did this."

"That remains to be seen."

He didn't reply, his expression turning thoughtful instead. "Talk to me about the financial aspects of the fishing business."

Frowning, she got up to refill their mugs. And to stall. "What do you want to know? It's a tough business—it always has been."

"Are the marine stocks depleted out here the same way they are on the East Coast?"

"Yes." What was he getting at? "But the government just announced a buyout plan that, along with a reduction in fishing licenses, allows some fishermen to exit gracefully."

"Is your business profitable?"

She shrugged. "I'm working on it." Then she clued in and her mug clattered on the table. "If you're trying to imply that Gary or I would set fire to the boat to collect the insurance, you're way off base. Our boats represent a way of life to us—neither of us would ever burn our legacy. Besides, the insurance wouldn't cover the total cost of replacement."

"Maybe. Then again, maybe your brother had an immediate need for cash."

"Gary's needs are simple; he lives on very little," she retorted. "And he could've opted to be bought out, which would've given him plenty of cash. He didn't, he chose to stay in. Those who do can look forward to double the catches they've had in recent years."

"As long as the government doesn't change its quotas," Chapman pointed out. "And the government never moves that fast—Gary might've needed cash faster than he could get it from them."

"He could always ask me for a loan if he needed it."

"I know." Chapman was implying that he had already checked out her finances. She hated knowing that someone was poking around in their lives. "But would he?"

She shifted uneasily. Okay, so add perception to Chapman's arsenal of interrogation skills. When she'd suggested to Gary a week ago that she fund the worst of the repairs on the boats, he'd pitched a fit. "You'd be throwing good money after bad," he'd told her. It was as if he hadn't wanted her involved. At the time, she'd been hurt. Now, she wondered if he'd been trying to protect her.

When she didn't answer, Chapman got up to put his coffee mug in the sink. Then he walked back to the table and leaned across it, both hands braced on the surface so that she had to look up into his hard gaze. "You know where your brother is. I want to talk to him."

She shoved her chair back and jumped up. Keeping her back to him, she made a production out of assembling the ingredients for a protein shake. "You're wrong."

"I find that hard to believe."

"And even if I did know," she continued, turning to face him, her arms crossed, "I wouldn't tell you. You're not going to use me to get to him. Gary saved Ken's life during Desert Storm, so why would he kill him now? And Gary doesn't deal well with figures of authority. My guess is that he's trying to find Ken's killer, not running from the authorities."

"If you believe he has nothing to hide, then convince him to come in and talk to me, tell me what he knows."

She was shaking her head before he finished. "Gary doesn't trust any of you."

Chapman had come over to stand beside her at the counter, too close for her peace of mind. And he was doing it on purpose, trying to rattle her. "I can have you arrested for obstructing justice, and if you know something you're not telling me, I won't hesitate."

She sent a cool look his way while she measured out protein powder and put it into the blender. "You don't frighten me, Mr. Chapman."

"Yeah, but I sure as hell bother you," he said softly, leaning closer. Close enough that she could smell the spicy fragrance of the soap he'd used in his shower. "Now, why is that, I wonder?"

"Don't flatter yourself." She added yogurt to the blender, mixing the two ingredients together, then tossed in a couple of handfuls of frozen fruit. She leveled a steady look at him, tapped the lid on, and flipped the switch. The blender started making a hell of a racket.

After a second, Chapman reached out, hit the Off switch and, slanting an amused glance her way, fished out the spoon she'd left in.

She closed her eyes for a moment, feeling the heat creep into her cheeks. Then she busied herself pouring the shake into two glasses, holding one of them out to him. With any luck, his portion had some metal shavings in it.

He rinsed the spoon off in the sink, using the towel lying on the counter between them to dry his hands. Taking the glass from her, he set it on the counter, then removed a long tube containing a cotton swab from his jacket pocket.

She backed up a step. "What's that?"

"The lab techs found a possible DNA sample on the boat this morning. I'll need yours to rule you and your brother out."

She thought rapidly. Anyone would tell her that she was crazy to comply without consulting a lawyer, but she doubted she could find one on such short notice. The only lawyer she knew in town was the one her parents had used as executor of their will, and he'd retired years ago. Not that he would know anything about criminal law anyway.

She could call Phil, the lawyer she'd been dating for the last couple of years in San Francisco, but that would take a day or two—Phil wasn't known for returning calls he considered a low priority. And ever since she'd told him she wasn't ready to commit to marriage, she'd definitely been a low priority.

"I can get a court order compelling you to give me a sample, or we can get this over with right now," Chapman said, apparently reading her thoughts.

She hesitated a moment longer, then shrugged, too tired to continue fighting him.

He moved closer and held up the swab. "Open up." She complied, and he ran the swab expertly along the inside of her cheek.

His hand paused, the swab resting lightly on her lower lip, and she looked up, right into his heated gaze.

She could hear his heightened breathing, could almost feel the beat of his heart. His shoulders blocked out the light coming from the window behind him, creating a zone of intimacy around them. The heat of his body reached out to envelope her, and she wanted to lean into that heat, to surround herself with it, if only for a moment.

His gaze dropped to her mouth, and her breath hitched. *Bad sign.*

They both took a cautious half-step back.

His expression curiously grim, he put the swab inside the tube, sealing it and replacing it in the pocket inside his jacket.

She slowly released the breath she'd been holding and picked up her glass, taking a sip of it. Her hands were shaking. "When can I get access to the *Anna Marie*?" she asked, trying for a normal tone of voice. "I need to get her dry-docked."

"Soon. I'm almost done processing her for evidence." He drank a couple of sips out of his glass, probably out of politeness, then set it down on the counter. Walking over to the table, he picked up the envelope of photos. "You might want to think about the fact that someone who has killed once usually doesn't have a problem killing again."

She cocked her head. "Does that mean you think someone other than Gary did this?"

"Anything is possible, until the evidence proves otherwise," he replied. "One of those possibilities is that you could be in danger. Why don't you let me tag along, help you find your brother?"

She just snorted. "That was smooth, but I'm not quite that gullible. Or that rattled."

He shook his head. "Then I'll be on my way. Thanks for the coffee and . . . everything," he said, smiling a little. "Where do you buy your coffee, by the way?"

"My partner mails it to me from California."

"Figures." He gave Zeke a hand command and turned to leave, then stopped. "Do you keep a space heater on board the *Anna Marie*?"

She barely kept herself from reacting. "No, why?"

He shrugged. "Just thought I'd ask—it's not important."

After the two of them left, Kaz stood for a moment in the silence of her suddenly empty kitchen, waiting for her system to level out. Okay, she needed to reassess. She'd been ambushed by the strength of her response to him, but it was only a little unwelcome chemistry, that's all. Very unwelcome. She could handle it. Handling men on a personal level had never been her strong suit, as Phil was always quick to point out. But she'd deal with Chapman. She sighed and rubbed her forehead. And maybe, just maybe, if she repeated that to herself enough times, she'd start to believe it.

She had no illusions that she'd seen the last of Chapman—he'd probably made it only as far as her curb and would hound her every move. Or simply sic his dog on her.

He'd been more accurate than he knew. She *did* have a good idea of where Gary had probably gone to ground. Well, at least, the general area. And she knew whom to ask—if he had a phone, she already would've called him.

After he'd ducked out of her view the night before, Chuck must've stood at the back edge of the crowd, watching. She'd recognized him in the photo and was still a little surprised he'd allowed himself to be seen. Someone had had a hand on his arm—a hand that wore a ring she'd know anywhere. The gold, embossed signet of Astoria High School, Class of '88. Gary had been there, watching from a distance.

How long did she have before Chapman showed the photos to Lucy, who'd have no trouble identifying that blurred image? Or before he asked Lucy about the space heater, which she knew that Gary regularly stored in his truck and used in the wheelhouse on long drag-fishing trips? An hour, maybe two?

Picking up Chapman's glass, Kaz downed the other half of the protein shake. She could use the boost, and right now, a few metal shavings were the least of her worries.

CHAPTER SIX

After stopping for gas, Kaz drove west on Marine Drive, then veered off along the north shore of Young's Bay. The tide was out, exposing deeply carved, milk-chocolate-colored ridges of mud at the bay's edge. Tufts of bright green grass and burnt-orange reeds topped each ridge, and where the water had drained away, silvery lines etched the shiny surface of the mud. The lines deepened into gullies that eventually dumped into the section of the bay where calm water could still be found, patiently reflecting the grays of the sky above. As Kaz drove, she spotted at least a dozen great blue herons wading in the shallows. Eagles, plentiful in the winter months, fished from the ends of old logs and rotted piers jutting out of the water.

She kept an eye on her rearview mirror, hoping to spot any cars that might be following her. A mile back, she could've sworn she'd glimpsed Clint Jackson in a patrol car. All Gary needed, at this point, was for her to lead the cops right to him. There was no one behind her now, though. And she might've imagined Jackson, but Chapman was another matter entirely. Maybe he wasn't following her, but she doubted it. And she could kick herself for not noticing what make and model of car he drove.

Crossing the Wallooskee River, she drove through dairy farm country until the highway started winding its way through the foothills toward its ultimate destination, the old logging town of Mist. After another ten minutes, she came to the Elk Preserve.

People who wanted a lot of privacy and very few visitors had homes near the preserve, well hidden in the forest. The foothills of the Coast Range had been logged at least twice in the last century, and some of the more recently clear-cut areas resembled pastures full of nothing but dead stumps—stump farms, the locals called them. The older cuts, which had happened before logging companies had been obliged to replant, had grown stands of mixed, native forest as nature had intended.

Chuck Branson had eighty acres of older forest, up a now-defunct logging road on the southeast edge of the preserve. He'd moved there after Desert Storm, buying the land out of the money he'd earned fishing summers in Alaska. For the first two years, he'd lived in an army tent while he, Gary, and Ken had built his cabin from the trees on his land. The sign at the entrance to his property read, *If I don't know you, you shouldn't be here.*

He meant it.

His gate was locked with the kind of padlock that would take C-4 explosive to breach, so Kaz parked her SUV in front of it and climbed over.

The woods glistened in the morning light, and a tiny winter wren warbled shrilly from a nearby bush. Up ahead, a doe and her yearling browsed. As Kaz passed by, they watched curiously but didn't bolt into the brush.

Sounds traveled oddly in the woods, muffled on level ground, then amplified up ravines through the trees and underbrush. From his front porch, Chuck could hear a twig snap a thousand feet away. He wasn't fond of surprises—it hadn't been serendipity that had led him to build his cabin at the top of the ravine. And he had, Kaz was certain, been tracking her since she'd crossed onto his property.

Although she hadn't heard him, the hairs on the back of her neck had been standing up for several seconds when Chuck suddenly materialized beside her, halting her before she was even halfway to his cabin.

His Chicago Cubs sweatshirt had seen better days but matched his worn, baggy army fatigues and battered combat boots. In his left hand, he balanced the gleaming stock of a shotgun so that its barrel leaned against his shoulder. Chuck had always had chiseled, blunt features, and he rarely made the effort to soften them by smiling. His pale brown hair, shaved close to his skull, heightened the sense of danger that he exuded.

"War games?" she asked lightly, nodding at his weapon.

"Patrolling the perimeter."

"Why? Worried that someone will find out Gary's here?"

He took his time answering, pulling out a hand-rolled cigarette and lighting it. "That's none of your business," he said gently.

"He's my brother."

Chuck shrugged. "He doesn't want your help."

"Tough." She lifted her chin, ignoring the hurt his comment caused. "He's got it anyway."

Chuck didn't respond, waiting with an eerie kind of stillness he'd perfected in the military.

"I saw you at the fire last night," she said, hoping to get an explanation of the message he'd been trying to send.

He drew on his cigarette, then removed a bit of tobacco from the tip of his tongue with two blunt fingertips. "You could've been hurt, going onto the boat like that."

She folded her arms. "I'm still in one piece, aren't I? The same can't be said for Ken."

"He was a good man, but he made mistakes."

A chill passed through her. "Are you saying that Ken was killed because he was in some kind of trouble?" But Chuck merely shook his head. She hugged herself, trying to shake off her unease. "Where did you go after you left the tavern last night? I wanted to talk to you."

He looked amused. "Checking on my alibi, Kaz?"

"What were you and Gary arguing about?" she clarified, her teeth clenched.

"We already told you to butt out." He took another drag on the cigarette, then shrugged, looking off into the distance. "Had a date with the lovely barmaid Sandra."

Kaz hadn't noticed Sandra in Chapman's photos, and she certainly hadn't heard that Sandra and Chuck were an item. Chuck didn't form attachments easily— Gary and Ken being the only exceptions that she was aware of—which made his explanation improbable at best. So the real question was, why was he making a point of providing himself with an alibi?

"Lucy said that Gary argued with Ken before I got to the tavern. Do you know anything about that?"

"It was nothing."

"Not according to Lucy. She says Gary was pretty angry." Kaz waited, but he didn't comment further, and her frustration notched up. "Chuck, I have to talk to Gary."

"He'll contact you when he needs to."

"So you *do* know where he is."

"Didn't say that."

Her patience abruptly ran out. "Quit being such a damn spook," she snapped.

He smiled slightly, a hint of affection showing in his hazel eyes. "But I'm so good at it."

Well, he was right about that. Her breath was expelled on a half laugh, and then she sobered. "Look. I know you're loyal to Gary—that you feel you owe him. But you might not be doing him a favor this time. If I'm going to help him, I need to find out what he knows."

"You know better than to think Gary had anything to do with Ken's death."

"I don't," she said quickly. "But the cops are on a mission to pin this on him." She hoped this bit of information would sway Chuck—he wasn't any fonder of the authorities than Gary was.

But he only shrugged, saying, "Then Gary would be right to lay low."

"Is that what he's doing—laying low?"

"Not necessarily."

She controlled the urge to scream. "The cops won't give up, you know that. This is too big—Sykes can make a name for himself by bringing down Ken's murderer. Show that he's dedicated to keeping the community safe."

Chuck fieldstripped his cigarette, rubbing the bits of tobacco between his thumb and index finger, his expression contemplative. "Gary doesn't need or want your help," he said finally. "He wants you to stay out of it. You could be in danger."

Angry, she made a chopping motion with one hand. "That's not important right now."

"Yes, it is." Chuck suddenly focused his intense gaze on her, and she had to work hard not to show her uneasiness. Sometimes he seemed to look right into her soul, as if he knew things about her even she didn't know.

She'd never understood Chuck, not even back in high school. He was a ghost, a shadow on the perimeter of her life, waiting and watching. For what, she'd never understood. And whenever she got close to discovering it, he retreated, disappearing behind an implacable facade. "So you've talked to Gary," she tried one more time.

"I talk to Gary all the time, you know that."

"Since the fire last night," she clarified impatiently.

"I didn't mean to imply that."

She threw up her hands. "Fine. At least tell me that he's all right, that he's not in danger."

"He's fine. Gary can take care of himself."

His comments gave her some measure of relief. Taking a shot in the dark, she asked, "Do you know how many days of supplies he had with him? What area he headed into?"

Chuck gazed at her, his expression giving away nothing. "If he wants to get seriously lost up there, you won't find him. *I* couldn't find him."

That much was true. Gary had training in wilderness survival and evasion. And he knew the foothills of the Coast Range intimately—they were *his* mountains.

She started pacing the small clearing they were standing in. From the bare branches of a nearby alder tree, a Steller's jay scolded her, its rich blue plumage standing out against the evergreen backdrop of the fir trees beyond. "The new fire chief thinks Gary killed Ken and then set the fire to hide the crime."

"That's ridiculous, and you know it." Chuck shifted the butt of the shotgun to the soft cushion of leaves at his feet. "Gary renounced violence after the war. He wouldn't hurt anyone, not even a cockroach. He was protecting Ken six months ago when he punched out Svensen."

"You know that, and I know that, but Gary's the prime suspect. I've *got* to talk to him, find out what he knows, and figure out a way to prove he didn't do it." She wrung her hands, and then rubbed them on her jeans, feeling like she was jumping out of her skin. Maybe she'd better back off on the caffeine.

"There are a lot of cockroaches in this town."

She stopped pacing. "What?"

Chuck rubbed the barrel of his shotgun with an index finger, his expression hard, his eyes unfocused. "They need to be wiped out before things can get better."

She'd always tried hard, since Chuck was Gary's friend, not to ask herself what he was capable of. He'd been a Ranger, like Gary and Ken, and the three of them had been tight ever since the war. But the rumor was that Chuck had also contracted out to the CIA as a sniper in Iraq. And when he made one of his cryptic comments like just now, it was hard not to remember—and not to use her fertile imagination to embellish on—those rumors. "What are you talking about?"

"Nothing. Go home, that's all. Lock your doors, don't get involved. Gary won't appreciate it if you do."

She shivered uncontrollably. What was going on in Astoria? Had her home town changed that much in her absence? So much that she couldn't even trust childhood friends?

She inhaled the crisp, clean mountain air, drawing it deep into her lungs, but it did nothing to allay her anxiety. "At least tell Gary to get in touch with me."

Chuck looked noncommittal.

"Please."

He hesitated, then nodded. "We'll see." He grasped her arm in an almost courtly manner and turned her downhill, toward the gate. "I'll walk you back." He waited politely while she decided whether to acquiesce—an illusion, since he was leaving her no choice. Then he escorted her off his property, melting into the woods once she was safely on the other side of the gate.

Kaz climbed into the SUV and jammed the keys in the ignition. Then she leaned back, staring blindly at the dense green wall of vegetation in front of her. Nothing, she realized, was as it seemed. It was as if everything she'd thought was real was simply part of a well-constructed facade, created by friends to protect her from a harsh reality they'd decided she couldn't handle.

She had to laugh at the irony. No one had ever tried to protect her in the corporate world. They'd tried to bulldoze her, outmaneuver her, or when all else failed, ruin her reputation. They hadn't succeeded—she'd used what she'd learned to get where she was today. And yet her childhood friends, whom she'd thought knew her better than anyone in California, seemed determined to shelter her.

Michael Chapman, though, stood out as the exception. He seemed intent on throwing the truth in her face, almost as if he were throwing down a gauntlet. He clearly wanted her to accept his challenge, but what was the nature of it? Was it a quest for the truth? Was he *that* dedicated to seeing justice was served? Or was she imagining it? Was she so frustrated by the half-truths and evasive answers she was getting from her friends that she was eager to trust a total stranger instead?

She shook her head, starting the SUV. Sitting around speculating wouldn't get her anywhere.

She backed up, then on a sudden hunch, turned uphill past Chuck's place toward one of the area's more primitive campgrounds. Towering, old-growth firs with trunks far larger than she could put her arms around shaded the small area, their canopies shutting out any light that would have allowed undergrowth to flourish. The forest floor was littered with pine needles and old, fallen rotting logs, cleared here and there to provide level spaces in which campers could pitch their tents.

Parking on the side of the road, Kaz glanced around to verify that the campground was empty, then got out of the SUV. After orienting herself, she stepped a few yards into the woods on the north edge of the property, to where an ancient Douglas fir tree had fallen and was now functioning as a nurse log to newer trees and ferns.

She knelt in the decaying woodland debris behind the log and studied the space beneath it. As she'd suspected, there were faint signs of recent digging. Removing some small branches and twigs that had been used to camouflage the entry, she used her hands to scoop soft dirt and rotted bits of bark out of the way. There was a small cave, not much more than an indentation in the ground, which would easily be mistaken by most campers as some animal's den. Except that it wasn't—it was one of the many hidden locations Gary used to store supplies up in the hills, in case he needed to disappear into the back country for a few days. He'd made a habit of maintaining his "stashes," as he called them, ever since Desert Storm. She'd always thought his behavior excessively paranoid, but now she was simply glad he'd planned ahead.

Feeling with one hand along the cool dirt walls all the way to the back, she prayed that a fox or a raccoon hadn't decided to take up residence. The cavity was empty—of both animals and supplies.

She sat back on her heels, dusting off her hands. Gary really was on the run, as she'd feared. Why? Chuck obviously believed in his innocence, as did she. So why would he run? To avoid being jailed on the parole violation? She didn't think so. More likely, he'd stand his ground with Sykes, daring him to take action. No, something more was at stake. Either he was running because he was guilty, or because he was regrouping before going after the killer himself. Both possibilities scared the shit out of her.

She stood and studied the surrounding woods. They were silent, too silent. The birds had stopped singing, and no small critters rustled in the brush, foraging for food. The back of her neck tingled in warning.

Was someone watching her? It couldn't be Gary. If it were, the animals wouldn't have taken cover—they knew he wouldn't harm them. Animals had a sixth sense that way.

Breathing shallowly, she stood where she was, casually scanning the vegetation around her, straining for a whiff of scent, for anything that would identify the intruder. But after a few long moments, the birds came out of hiding, and Kaz's sense of someone watching her faded away. She let out the breath she'd been holding. Maybe the intruder had been of the four-legged variety. Or maybe she'd been overreacting.

She glanced around one more time, still harboring the faint hope that Gary might be nearby. But she knew any effort to find him would be fruitless. Chuck was right—Gary was too good to leave behind any trail, even if she knew which direction he was headed. Frustrated, she returned to the SUV.

Once she was on the highway, she reviewed what had happened the night before. To be guilty of killing Ken and setting the fire, Gary would've had to head directly to the marina after leaving the tavern. After all, she hadn't been more than forty-five minutes behind him. And Ken had to have been on the boat already—there wasn't enough elapsed time for them to meet elsewhere, go to the boat, and argue—all before Ken was killed and she'd witnessed the first explosion of fire.

So why had Ken been on the boat? What had he been up to? It all came back to that. She had to find out where he'd been and what he'd been involved in. It was her only hope of figuring out why Gary had run, or of proving his innocence.

As she passed the Elk Preserve, a nondescript, dark green sedan passed her going in the other direction, and she glanced over to see Michael Chapman driving. Seconds later, shots rang out, and her window exploded.

CHAPTER SEVEN

Kaz raised both hands instinctively, causing the SUV to veer sharply toward the ditch. Yanking the wheel back, she barely missed the deep, water-filled marsh that bordered the road. The SUV careened around a sharp curve, then skidded onto the shoulder as she hit the brakes. Cutting the engine, she sat there in the sudden silence and shook.

Tires screeched behind her. She heard a door slam, then running footsteps. Fumbling with the door handle, she jumped out as Chapman reached her.

He gripped her shoulders hard with both hands. *"Are you all right?"*

"Yes." She dragged in air, trying not to hyperventilate.

"Did the bastard hit you?" He moved his hands over her, checking for injuries.

"No."

"Where? Where are you hurt?"

She batted at his hands. "I'm *fine*—he missed me."

Chapman lurched back, letting her go as if he'd been scalded, then turned away. A muscle worked in his jaw. Kaz watched him try to regain control, surprised by his reaction. It made sense that he might be concerned, but he was acting panicked, almost frantic.

After a moment or two, he said in a calmer voice, "Which direction did the shots come from?"

"Inside the preserve, I think."

"Get back inside the car." He gave Zeke the command, "Guard," and then headed in that direction.

Michael jogged back toward the preserve, his heart pounding so hard his chest hurt. When he'd heard the shot, then seen her car swerve . . . God help him, he'd thought she had been killed. In less than the time it had taken to react, he'd been right back there on that night, five years ago, driving up to the raging inferno that had been his apartment, slammed by the knowledge that Jessica was gone, that he was too late to save her. His gut-wrenching fear now was the same as it had been then—and so was his cold rage. Not Kaz—not again.

He forced himself to slow to a walk, to gulp in deep breaths. He could feel the terror fighting for supremacy over the adrenaline, scrambling his concentration, shattering his nerves. *You're no good to her this way.* Now wasn't the time to lose it. Later, when he was alone, he'd let himself think about how all those feelings he'd been so sure he'd buried had come rushing right back at the first sound of those shots, ambushing him.

Opening the gate of the preserve, he stepped inside, then paused. All he could hear were the birds chirping and the wind rustling the dead stalks of grass. He closed his eyes, listening for the faint sounds of someone's retreat—the slight crackle of dried grass, the snap of a small twig. But there was nothing. The shooter was long gone. The tension in his shoulders eased, and he started his search.

About fifty yards down the road, just inside the fence line, he found what he was looking for—a small, circular area of matted grass. The son of a bitch had knelt there, hidden in the tall reeds, and simply waited for her to drive by. He must've followed her out to Branson's, then circled around in front of her.

Dropping down on one knee, Michael studied the ground carefully. The shooter had been careful—no spent shell casings, no cigarette butts or candy wrappers. No evidence. Michael could envision him as he'd knelt there, totally silent, very patient, and very cool. At the right moment, he'd simply aimed and taken his shot. Michael's hands clenched. And come damn close to killing her. Whoever it was, the shooter was a professional.

Michael stood and looked at the surrounding grass. He could just make out, from a bent reed here and there, the bastard's path through the meadow toward the back of the preserve. No doubt he'd parked on a local road on the far side of the preserve, so that he could leave undetected. Michael wanted to follow his trail, to see if he could find any evidence that could be used at a later date, but he'd already left Kaz alone for too long. He'd come back later, and he'd find something, even if it was only a partial footprint.

No one was that good.

By the time Michael returned, Kaz was already chastising herself for not insisting that she accompany him.

The look on his face, when he saw her still standing there, was one of pure rage. "Don't you ever listen? I said, *get in the car.*"

"Why? Whoever it was, they're long gone." Her point was reasonable but only served to make him more angry. What was going on with him? "Look, it was probably some idiot hunter. The preserve has problems with poachers—"

She huffed irritably as he shoved her aside and leaned inside her car. After a few seconds, he took a pocket knife out and used its blade to pry something out of the ceiling. A bullet.

He examined it closely, then pulled out a plastic baggy and dropped it in. "I'd guess fifty-caliber." He held the bullet up for her to see. "Know any hunters who go around shooting elk with a sniper rifle? I don't."

Her knees turned to rubber, and she slumped against the side of the SUV. Someone had shot at her on purpose. She tried to laugh but the sound came out shaky. "Well, at least he was a lousy shot, so that leaves out the people I know."

Chapman's expression turned thoughtful. "Not necessarily. Maybe he wasn't trying to hit you, even though he came damn close. Maybe it was a warning."

She became aware of the chill in the air and hugged herself. "But why? I don't have anything to do with this. And if he thinks this will permanently scare me off . . ." Her voice trailed away as Chapman snorted.

"Anyone who knows you wouldn't be likely to make that mistake. Not that I wouldn't be happy if you came to your senses—"

She glared at him. "Wrong comment to make."

He ran an agitated hand through his hair, making it look even more disheveled than usual. "This is *exactly* what I've been talking about. Civilians always get hurt when they get in the way."

"In whose way?" she shot back.

He took a step toward her, his expression full of fury, and she backed up. "If I wanted you out of my way," he said, his voice arctic cold, "I'd have you arrested, not shot. What kind of person do you think I am?"

What Lucy had told her in the tavern about his being burned out flitted through her mind. Could he be that unstable? He certainly had been acting strangely in the last few minutes. But those were the kind of thoughts people were having about Gary, and then using them to jump to unsubstantiated conclusions. She refused to do the same. Though she already regretted her comment, backing down wasn't the answer, either. The only people who wouldn't get mowed down by Michael Chapman were the ones who stood up to him. "So what *are* you doing out here? Following me? Don't you have something more important to do, like gathering evidence off the *Anna Marie* so that I can get her dry-docked?"

"No thanks to you, I was able to deduce that Chuck Branson is one of your brother's best friends and is, in fact, the second man you were talking to in the tavern. So, *as part of the ongoing investigation,* I thought I'd see if he knows where your brother is." Chapman's voice turned sardonic. "I gather I'm not entirely off base, seeing as how you're within a mile of his place."

She shrugged. "Chuck won't tell you anything. Not if he wouldn't tell me."

"Would Gary pull a stunt like this?"

"Of course not!" If Chapman could even ask that question, what did he think Gary capable of?

"It makes sense. He has the training, and he knew he wouldn't hit you, so he fires a warning shot, hoping to get you to go away."

She shook her head. Gary would never shoot at her, even if he knew he wouldn't hit her. "You're so far off base—"

"He has a history of run-ins with the police, and a record of assault. Just how well do you really know your brother?"

She refused to acknowledge how close to home his questions were. He'd hit on her greatest fear—that she didn't really know her brother as well as she thought she did. That he might've turned into a complete stranger, someone capable of doing exactly what Chapman was suggesting. Placing her hands on her hips, she said, "The man Gary punched out that night wouldn't even press charges—Sykes was the one who prosecuted. And Gary and Sykes have some past history. But why bother explaining? You've already got Gary tried and found guilty."

Chapman made a dismissive motion with his hand. "What about Chuck?"

She thought about it for a moment. "I don't know," she admitted. "Chuck's . . . well, weird. I think he's got some CIA stuff in his background."

"He's sure as hell got something spooky going on— his records are sealed."

"Gary, Ken, and Chuck were all in the army together. There's no way Gary or Chuck had anything to do with Ken's death—they were all too tight."

"They could've had a falling out. You haven't been

around much lately, so how would you know?" When she didn't answer, he continued. "You came out here hoping to talk to your brother, didn't you?"

She tensed. The interrogator was definitely back; the concerned man, gone. "Chuck and I talked about last night." That much, at least, was the truth.

"Does he know where your brother is?"

She shrugged. "If he does, he isn't saying."

"If Gary asked, Chuck would help him. Maybe take a pot shot at you, to warn you off."

Chuck could easily have circled back around after he'd left her. She'd given him plenty of time, since she'd gone to the campground. He would have heard her drive in that direction. When he'd been with her, he'd been carrying a shotgun, but that didn't mean he didn't have quick access to other weapons. In fact, it was a virtual certainty that he'd been heavily armed— he always was.

"And that could've been what they were arguing about in the tavern last night, am I right? That Gary wanted Chuck's help," Chapman said when she didn't answer.

She had to admit that it made some sense.

"And that's why you drove out here, isn't it? To see if Gary was hiding out here."

"Yes, all right?" she snapped, feeling goaded. "But Chuck refused to tell me anything, other than that he'd had a date with Sandra after he left the tavern. So I guess we can cross him off our list of possible suspects."

"He wasn't on mine, until this happened." Chapman rocked back on his heels, his hands shoved in the pockets of his jeans, a stance that emphasized his lean hips and wide shoulders. He studied her thoughtfully for a moment. "Who's Sandra?"

She realized he'd have no way of keeping the locals straight at this point. "The waitress at the Redemption."

"I'll check her out."

She raised an eyebrow. "Why bother, unless you think someone other than Gary could be the murderer?" He gave a noncommittal shrug. "And if someone is shooting at me, that means I can't be on your list of suspects anymore, right?"

"Maybe not, but you're sure as hell on my list of uncooperative witnesses."

She stared at him, refusing to back down. "You know, sooner or later, you'll have to consider that whoever killed Ken might not be Gary—that Ken could've met someone else on the *Anna Marie* for some reason we don't yet understand."

"I'm keeping an open mind."

God, the man was stubborn! She yanked open the door of her SUV and got inside, brushing bits of glass off the seat. She'd have to drop the car off at the dealer's. With the kind of winds they got on the coast, taping plastic over the broken window would last about five minutes. Which meant dealing with another insurance claim. She sighed and hung her head for a moment. The adrenaline was beginning to wear off, leaving her punch-drunk with fatigue.

Almost as if on cue, it started sprinkling again. More weather was moving in, and the sky to the southwest was dark and threatening.

Pushing the door shut behind her, Chapman leaned both arms on the edge of the window. He was very close, which wasn't helping her already erratic pulse rate. The man appeared to get a kick out of invading her personal space, a habit that should have annoyed

her, if her libido were behaving. "I'll follow you to the
police station so that you can report this."

Which would raise questions she didn't want to answer, at least, not yet. "It's a waste of time to bother the
cops with this."

"The police should have an incident report on file,
in case anything else happens to you, so that they can
establish a pattern."

She didn't like the sound of that, but she shook her
head. "I prefer to keep this to myself."

He watched her for a long, silent moment with those
silvery blue eyes, then nodded once, the movement
abrupt. "I get it. You don't want to put your friend Lucy
in an awkward spot about what you were doing out
here." He laughed, but there was no humor in it. "You
people really do stick together, don't you? But then
again, it's okay to get in the newcomer's way, isn't it?"

"Okay, yes, you're partially right." She wished he
weren't quite so astute. "Lucy's been my friend for all
of my life. Her hands are tied right now, and she
doesn't need Jim Sykes breathing down her neck
about a conflict of interest. I'm sorry, but I do take that
into account. Those issues don't exist with you."

"Not yet, they don't," he said, very softly.

She stilled. "Pardon?"

He shook his head. "Forget it. Why don't Zeke and I
follow you to the mechanic's and give you a ride
home? That is, if you don't give me the slip between
here and there."

Narrowing her eyes, she reached down and started
the engine, putting the SUV into gear. "Don't bother.
The dealership is less than a mile from my house—I
can hoof it."

"I'll give you a lift," he repeated firmly. "If you're at home and without transportation, I figure that limits the amount of damage you can do to my investigation for the next few hours."

She was amused. "You forget that I've lived here most of my life. I won't be without a car for any more time than it takes to make a call or two."

Gunning the engine, she pulled onto the highway, gravel and dirt spurting from beneath her tires. When she glanced in the rearview mirror, he was still standing there, his hands in his pockets and his dog at his side, watching her drive away.

CHAPTER EIGHT

Lucy hung up the phone and eyed the Kleenex box on her desk, which Ivar judiciously moved out of reach before she could hurl it at the far wall of the squad room.

"Tell Papa," he said.

"I could've used the stress relief," she complained. Ivar just waited her out. "Okay, fine. We've got no exact time of death." She picked up a pencil and tapped it rapidly on her desk blotter. "The heat from the fire makes it impossible to pinpoint by body temperature any more accurately than a range of about two hours."

Ivar flipped through his notes. "Ken left the bar around eight last night. Kaz found him on the boat a little over one hour later."

"So that's our time frame for the murder," Lucy agreed, then held up a hand. "But wait, it gets better. Ken had bits of concrete embedded in one cheek, and mud and grass on the heels of his boots."

"Hmmm."

"Not a lot of boats are made of concrete," she hinted.

"Body was moved."

"Gold star time." Lucy flopped back in her chair, causing it to squeak in protest. "Shit. We don't have a murder scene."

Ivar's long, narrow face took on a brooding look, which meant he was headed into his silent mode. She *hated* his silent mode. For long stretches of time, she couldn't even get monosyllabic responses out of him. Unrewarding in the extreme. Not to mention that she was convinced it wasn't healthy for any human being to be *that* quiet.

She paused to drink warm soda out of the can that had been sitting on her desk for . . . she couldn't really remember how long. Hopefully, the caffeine didn't disappear along with the carbonation. Jim Sykes chose that moment to walk in the back door carrying a latte, which he took into his office. She wasted a couple of seconds, fantasizing about forcibly removing that cup from his possession, then considered the ramifications to her career.

Sighing, she said, "Okay, I've got a theory." She framed a picture in the air with her hands. "Here's how it happened: The killer did him on the boat, then dragged him off the boat, hunted around for some concrete to scrape his cheek with, then dragged him back on the boat." Ivar snorted, and a new thought occurred to her. "Why kill him and then move him to the boat when there's a perfectly good, raging river to dump him in? This whole thing—"

"—doesn't make sense." She swiveled around in her chair. She'd last seen Chapman around 2 A.M., right before she'd headed off to the hospital for the preliminary autopsy. Now there were deep grooves of exhaustion bracketing his mouth—he'd probably guarded the boat himself for the remainder of the night. A sign of dedication, or obsession?

"The killer knew what he was doing when he started the fire," Chapman said as he settled tiredly into the chair beside her desk, propping one boot on his knee. He gave them a quick rundown on the ignition method. "Who in this town would have that kind of knowledge?"

"Half the men in this town have military or Coast Guard background," Lucy mused. "There aren't a lot of options growing up here—signing up for a stint is pretty common. Get three squares, play with lots of neat toys, and then get your schooling paid for after. I considered it myself." Ivar rolled his eyes, and she kicked his foot.

"Jorgensen would know a thing or two about fire," Ivar said. "So would Chuck Branson. Both are ex-Rangers, and Rangers are trained in diversionary tactics."

Lucy shifted uneasily in her chair. She'd been having a hard time—throughout the long night and all morning—wrapping her brain around Gary as a possible suspect. She didn't like the position she was in, or the strong feeling eating away at her gut that her loyalties were impossibly divided. And knowing Gary, he'd be amused by her moral dilemma. The jerk. "I could say the same about anyone with a stint in the military police or the Coast Guard," she pointed out. "They both have to be able to spot and investigate arson." She looked at Chapman. "What about your own backyard? Arsonists, many times, are volunteer firefighters, right?"

"I'm checking that out, but none of them have an obvious motive. Do you know the cause of death?"

"Not officially. Unofficially, someone bashed his skull in from behind." She drank the last of her soda while she brought him up to date on the forensics. "From the angle of the blow and spray patterns of the blood, it could've happened while he was still upright, if the perp is tall enough, or after Ken was unconscious and lying on the ground."

"Interesting."

"Yeah. Why kill him elsewhere, then move the body onto the *Anna Marie* when there's a perfectly good river with the Current from Hell a few steps away?"

"I'd wondered the same thing." Chapman drummed blunt-tipped fingers on her desk. "On the one hand, we don't know that he was killed close to the river, so we can't assume that it would've been convenient to dump him there. Still, going to the trouble to put him on the boat doesn't compute."

"Need to take soil samples and concrete scrapings," Ivar said.

Lucy cocked her head. "Ken usually walked home from the Redemption," she said, thinking out loud. "So we start at the tavern and work in a radius out from there."

"What about insurance money as a motive?" Chapman asked. "Maybe Jorgensen burned the boat for profit."

"Nuh-uh." Lucy had no doubts on that score. "Gary loved that boat—he'd never burn it. Besides, he left the tavern at least a half hour after Ken did, so if Ken were killed and then moved to the boat, Gary didn't have the time to do the crime."

"Unless the murder occurred close to the mooring basin," Ivar pointed out.

"So you're suggesting what?" Chapman asked Lucy. "That there's a possibility that someone might be framing Jorgensen?"

Lucy sighed. "I don't know *what* I'm suggesting, because I can't think of a reason for anyone to frame Gary, either."

"As theories go, it's farfetched." Chapman leaned forward. "You know these people, grew up with them. What would get Jorgensen to the point that he'd be desperate enough to kill?"

"Up until six months ago, I would've laughed you out of the room when you asked me that question. Yeah, I know, Gary's got that assault conviction. But there's a story behind that." Lucy pursed her lips. "Gary's been acting weird lately. And, yeah, I've been wondering why. But I still can't believe he'd kill someone."

"He's got the training."

She shook her head. "Since he came home from the war, he's renounced violence. The bar fight was an exception. Hell, for all I know, he's converted to Buddhism—he spends way too much time meditating and communing with nature." She shrugged. "I suppose it works for some folks."

"He didn't strike me as the passive type when he was getting ready to bash Ken's face in last night in the Redemption."

Chapman was right, and it bothered the hell out of her. "The point is," she said stubbornly, "I'd stake my reputation on the fact that Gary wouldn't kill anyone."

"What reputation?" Ivar rumbled.

"Shut up," she suggested, kicking him again, then gave the problem some more thought. "We'd be better off finding the real murder scene and linking the forensics to the body. If we're lucky, we might be able to use Luminol on the concrete and pick up blood spatter."

"Evidence collection from the boat is almost complete," Chapman said. "But if Lundquist really were killed elsewhere, we may not find much more. The galley and fo'c'sle were pretty much trashed by the fire."

"I can pull together a list of anyone who might have the knowledge to start a fire that way, and if they have any connection to Ken, check their alibis."

"Good. You ever going to impound Jorgensen's truck?"

"It's still at the wharf?" Lucy muttered several choice four-letter words under her breath. "Brenner!" she shouted. A uniformed officer stuck his head into the squad room. "Try to pick up Gary's truck sometime this century, will you?" She turned back to Chapman. "Anything else?"

"Only that our perp is no slouch in the brains department. He made damn sure the area on the boat where Lundquist would've been found burned from both above and below. He left the hatch open to ventilate the fire, and soaked the decking with gasoline, which ensured that the entire deck in that area would collapse."

Lucy snapped her fingers. "Damn, I forgot. Get this—according to Ewald, there was evidence of severe bruising on Ken's body, already partially healed." Both men stared at her. "He'd suffered at least one beating in recent days. And I can't come up with even a farfetched explanation as to why Gary would've been beating on Ken—that's even more bizarre than Gary killing him."

"What about the normal amount of knocks he would've taken out fishing?" Chapman asked. "The waters around here aren't exactly smooth sailing."

Lucy shook her head. "Too much bruising, and in all the wrong places. Whoever administered the beating knew what he was doing. He inflicted the most damage where it wouldn't be seen—around Ken's kidneys, and on his back and ribs."

"And where it would also cause the most pain—the kind of beating that sends a message," Chapman's expression was thoughtful. "So we've got a carefully planned arson and a victim who was in some kind of trouble with people who don't play nice. Did you talk to the wife?"

"Yeah, nada, but she's acting scared. We've subpoenaed his bank records, and we're looking into any calls he made from his home or his cell phone. Maybe we'll get lucky."

"What about the bartender? Could he have overheard something?"

"We interviewed him this morning, but didn't get much out of him. Steve makes a point of turning a deaf ear—that's how he stays in business in a community like ours."

"A lot of unanswered questions," Ivar mused. "Too many illogical events to assume the easiest solution. Need to gather all the evidence in one place, then study it carefully."

"I agree," Chapman said.

Lucy rolled her eyes. "I tell you what—you two pick through the little bits of stuff in the collection bags and cans. I'll take a drive and see what I can find by the tavern. I need some fresh air."

But Chapman clearly wasn't through with her. "Kaz

is damn smart, and Gary can't be a slouch if he was a Ranger, right?" He ticked off the points on his fingers. "Jorgensen had motive—the argument in the tavern. Means—access to the boat and the knowledge to start the fire. And opportunity—his truck was found at the wharf."

Lucy decided she wasn't all that happy with Chapman's one-track mind. "When's the lab work coming back from the boat?"

"Some later today, the rest in a couple of days." He pulled a manila envelope out of his jacket and tossed it onto her desk. "Photos of the crowd from last night. I'd appreciate it if you'd take a look at them."

"Fine." She broke off as her phone rang. "Yeah." She listened a minute, and then said, "Yeah. Give me fifteen." She hung up and gave him a hard look. "Just so you know, Kaz had nothing to do with this."

"You may be right, but if her brother did it, at the rate she's going, she'll go down with him."

"Meaning?"

"She's withholding information from me. Obstruction of justice."

Ivar nodded. "Sounds like her."

"Hey," Lucy said.

Ivar shrugged. "She'd do anything for Gary, you know that."

"That doesn't mean she'd break the law unless she had a damn good reason."

Ivar remained silent, then raised both hands when Lucy glared at him.

"Just so I'm not working totally in the dark here," Chapman said, his tone sarcastic, "do you two want to volunteer anything about your relationships with the

primary suspects on this case?" He looked at Lucy.
"You and Kaz were together last night at the tavern."

"We're all friends," Ivar assured him before Lucy
could explode.

"And that's all?"

"We all want the same thing—to find the real perp.
Murders don't happen in our town—and Ken was a
friend. We'll get whoever did this to him," Lucy said.

A look passed between the two men that Lucy
couldn't decipher, and after a moment, Chapman
nodded as if satisfied and stood up. "I've got a lot of
work to do before dark," he said, and turned to go.
"And I figure I've got maybe twenty-four hours before
your friend is on my case about dry-docking her boat."
He stopped, one corner of his mouth lifting. "Then
again, I don't really have even that long, do I? Once
you leave here and provide Kaz with a car, she'll be
mobile again."

Lucy flushed.

"Call your friend off, before she gets herself hurt," he
suggested.

"She won't listen to me on this one." His brows
arched, and she sighed. "Kaz feels responsible for
Gary, feels an obligation to help him."

"The shipwreck fifteen years ago," he guessed.

She gave him a quizzical look, and he explained
about the conversation he'd had with the mayor. "Kaz
figures she should've been able to save her parents
that night, and she's felt guilty ever since," she said.

"Could she have?"

Lucy shook her head. "But you can't tell her that.
There were gale force winds that night, and storm
surge well over thirty feet. Most of the waves were at

119

least fifty feet, crest to trough. For you landlubbers, that's a five-story building. The miracle is that *she* survived. But the way she sees it, Gary's had a harder time than she has, partially because of losing their parents."

"And you don't have any influence over her."

"On a lot of things, sure, but not this."

"Then let's arrest her as a material witness."

Lucy hooted. "That'd last about as long as one phone call to her lawyer ex-boyfriend in California. He'd have her out on bail within a couple of hours."

Chapman looked frustrated, and Lucy had to wonder why. Surely he'd run up against much worse in the course of his career.

"See to it that you keep her out of my way, or I *will* have her arrested." He nodded at both of them and walked away.

"Well, well," Ivar said.

"What?" Lucy asked.

"Chapman and Kaz. Bad timing, though."

"*What?* No, no, no." Lucy was appalled. "What makes you think that? Oh, wait—you mean that mano-a-mano moment the two of you had?"

"Chapman asked if I was in a relationship with Kaz," Ivar explained. "Clears the way for him."

Lucy wondered if her partner had been ingesting too many herbs. "He didn't even sound like he liked her."

Ivar looked amused. "And your point is?"

"Oh, right, crazy me." She mock-slapped her forehead. "Why would I possibly think a guy has to *like* the woman he goes to bed with?"

"He likes her—he's just not happy with her at the moment because she's interfering with his investigation. What's more interesting is that I'm not sure he was even aware that he was establishing territory." He caught Lucy's look of disbelief and shrugged. "Male intuition."

"Yeah, and I'm the damn Easter Bunny. If you get any more woo-woo on me . . ." Her voice trailed off while she gnawed on the idea. "You've heard the rumors about him, right? That he was placed on administrative leave by the Boston Fire Department after the fire that killed his fiancée? That there was some question as to whether he could've saved the arsonist in the fire six months later?"

"Yup. You telling me you're upset about a serial arsonist who got himself killed?"

"Of course not."

"So?"

"So Kaz already has enough problems on her plate."

"Especially if she's being her typical, driven, nosy self," Ivar said, his tone wry. "I noticed you didn't tell Chapman about the rumors."

Lucy shrugged. "Just because the chief claims he's got incriminating information on the fishermen doesn't make it true. And we don't know whether it's connected to the fire. I didn't see any point in sending Chapman off in that direction."

"Get real. No one controls where that guy goes but him."

CHAPTER NINE

It was only early afternoon, but the weak winter light was already showing signs of fading. Kaz trudged up the hill to her house from the car dealership. It would take two days to order the window and have it installed. With Gary's truck impounded by the cops, she hoped Lucy came through fast.

A patrol car was parked across the street from the bungalow, and she changed course, veering in its direction. Clint Jackson. So he probably *had* been following her.

"He's not here, Clint," she said when the cop lowered his window. "Go home."

"Now, Kaz, you know I can't do that. My orders are to keep the house under surveillance."

"Why? If Gary sees your car, he'll be gone before you even have a clue he's around."

"Maybe, maybe not." Jackson rested an arm on the edge of the window. "Your brother's not God—we'll get him sooner or later." He smiled at her, but it wasn't a friendly smile. "Collaring your brother could be damn good promotion-making material. I'm in line for detective this year. You'd be wise to stay out of my way."

Kaz smiled back pleasantly. "If memory serves, I used to babysit you, didn't I?"

"Stuff it, Kaz."

"You want me to bring you some tea and cookies while you waste the taxpayers' dollars?"

"Go to hell."

She stomped back across the street. Okay, so not all the cops on the force were like Lucy and Ivar. Some were Neanderthals. And if the Neanderthals caught up with Gary before Lucy and Ivar did. . . . Her stomach knotted. She couldn't let herself think about that.

As she entered the house through the kitchen door, the phone rang. She jogged into the living room to answer it, only to have whoever was on the other end hang up on her. Just what she didn't need right now—some oblivious idiot calling the wrong number, over and over. Her tolerance for idiocy was at an all-time low, starting with her own.

Being attracted to Michael Chapman was the ultimate in stupidity, and reckless, besides. She couldn't understand her over-the-top reaction to him, or her apparent inability to function intelligently around him. All she had to do was take one look at that rugged physique and curly dark hair, and all her brains flowed out onto the floor and rolled around like just so many marbles.

She yanked open the refrigerator door and stood there, staring inside. Gary was her only remaining family. His future and happiness were at stake, maybe even his life. And here she was, getting sucker-punched by good looks and a pair of pale blue eyes shadowed by hints of a tragic past—something for which, of course, she'd have way too much empathy. She expelled a breath. *Get a grip.* She couldn't afford to be distracted, no matter how powerful that distraction proved to be.

She gave up on the meager contents of the fridge, grabbed a handful of saltines, and walked back out the kitchen door. Waving cheerfully at Jackson, who flipped her off, she cut across the neighbor's side yard to walk the six blocks downhill to Julie and Ken's house. It was past time that she paid her respects and asked Julie what she could do to help out.

The Lundquists' home was in Uniontown, an older, working-class section of Astoria filled with small, Victorian-style homes crowded onto a steep hillside directly above Marine Drive, the main highway through town. The bridge towered high over the river and the abandoned, rotting warehouses at the water's edge, allowing the huge freighters en route to Portland to pass underneath. To bring the cars back down to street-level, the bridge deck spiraled down over Marine Drive, ending at a stoplight on the river side of the highway. The result was that the bridge's railings almost touched the homes that perched on the hill, making them appear to crouch over the bridge. Homes in Uniontown might be more modest than their Victorian cousins farther uphill, but they still commanded a stunning view of the river and the bluffs on the Washington State side.

Julie and Ken's house looked slightly neglected, and the yard was not as neat as it had been a couple of months ago. The shades were drawn. Kaz couldn't hear any sounds from inside but rang the doorbell anyway. While she waited, she listened to the sounds from the waterfront and the traffic on the bridge. After a moment, the door opened.

Julie stood in the doorway, wearing a simple black blouse and black cotton slacks. Her pale brown hair was scrubbed back from her thin face into a ponytail, her hazel eyes red-rimmed from crying. "Kaz," she said, her voice dull.

"I'm sorry," Kaz said, spreading her hands. "I don't even know what to say."

Julie stared at her for a moment and then gestured for her to enter. Kaz stepped over the threshold and then halted, her eyes widening. The house was a mess—books and papers strewn about the living room, cushions from the couch ripped open and lying on the floor, lamps toppled and broken. What used to be a pile of paperwork—probably hospital bills—now lay in a haphazard line of loose pages flung across the carpet.

"What in the world?"

"Someone broke in while I was at the funeral home." Julie swiped at a tear, then added bitterly, "What kind of person robs people while they're arranging for a memorial service?"

"You called the police?"

"No."

Kaz looked around the room, her gut screaming at her. The destruction had a methodical feel to it—someone had been searching for something. "You have to call the police, Julie. I can help—stay here with you, if you want. But you have to report this."

"No!" Julie said, her voice sharper. She seemed to collect herself, drawing a breath. "No," she repeated more calmly. "No more cops. They were here all morning, asking questions I couldn't answer."

Her eyes slid away from Kaz's. She was lying. Why? "Then let me help you clean up."

Julie ducked her head. "I don't need your help." She bent down to retrieve a broken toy and a stack of children's books. When she straightened, her expression was wary. "So why are you here? If it's to ease your conscience about what Gary did, then—"

"No, that's not it at all," Kaz said quickly, startled. She knelt to pick up a stack of bills, trying to be helpful, but Julie quickly snatched them from her hands.

"Then what brings you here?"

Kaz hesitated. "Julie, had Ken been acting any differently lately? You know, angry, maybe? Or desperate?"

Julie laughed without humor and waved a hand at the dilapidated furniture and threadbare carpets. "Look around. Who wouldn't be feeling desperate?"

"I meant, well, more desperate than just the day-to-day stuff."

"The day-to-day stuff is a pile of bills we can't pay, Bobby's chemo treatments, a furnace that decides when and how long it will work . . ." Julie's voice trailed away, and she stared down at the shards of a broken glass lamp shade at her feet. She knelt and picked them up, tossing them into a wastebasket that sat in the middle of the room.

"How is Bobby?" Kaz asked. Julie had been driving him to Portland for treatments for a number of months. Kaz couldn't imagine what it was like to watch a small child struggle with the side effects of chemo. To live daily with the fear that you might outlive your son.

"Bobby's fine."

"Gary mentioned that Bobby was having a tough time with side effects."

"That's over or, at least, better."

Kaz took in Julie's closed look, her rigid posture. "Can I help out with the medical bills? Or perhaps babysit when you have to go to Portland?"

"No, look—" Julie stopped and ran a nervous hand over her thin ponytail. "I appreciate it, really I do. But my mom is paying for Bobby's treatments, and I don't want your help, Kaz."

"But—"

"Having you around is a reminder, okay? Of what your family has taken away . . ." She turned to Kaz, resolute. "Perhaps you should leave."

"Julie, Gary didn't do this, I know he didn't." Kaz reached out a hand, but the younger woman stepped back.

"I know you'd like to believe that, but Gary hasn't been okay for a long time now. Ken stuck with him out of loyalty, and because no one else would crew for him."

"That's not true," Kaz said, shocked. "I know Gary can be difficult at times—" She took in Julie's mulish expression and changed tactics. "I'll prove that Gary didn't do this."

"You should let the police handle it."

"Did Ken indicate what he and Gary had been arguing about?"

"*No*," Julie said. "Look, Kaz, there's nothing I can do to help you. Ken never said a word to me, other than to mention here and there when Gary had been a jerk on the water that day."

"At least tell me whether Ken came home last night."

"No." Julie's face crumpled. "The last time I saw him was early Saturday morning, before they left port. I never saw him again, until I went down to the morgue to identify him."

"I'm sorry," Kaz said again, feeling helpless. She turned to go.

"Kaz." Julie's sharpened voice stopped her. Rage blazed out of the young woman's eyes. "If Gary *didn't* kill Ken, then I want to know who did. You find out who the hell did this to my children."

"I will, I promise."

Lucy bounced a tennis ball against the far wall of the squad room while she waited for Ivar to summarize his stack of notes into what she figured was the Master Note he wanted to have with him when they went out to investigate possible murder sites. She'd already rolled her eyes, paced, and tried her best to annoy him in inventive ways, but he wasn't budging. If he spent even five more seconds writing in that neat little script of his, she was going to club him to death with the butt of her service revolver. "You about done?"

"You've already asked me that three times." His head never lifted from his task. "Why don't you go drop off your car for Kaz?"

"I already have, which you would've noticed if you weren't so driven to organize your life to death."

Jim Sykes emerged from his office. She snagged the ball midair and dropped it into her drawer. This afternoon, the chief was wearing a tailored, dark blue wool suit, tasteful tie, and spiffy, tasseled loafers. "Where the hell does he get the money for those kinds of clothes?" she muttered out loud, envious that his clothes budget was clearly more substantial than hers.

Ivar glanced up. "Inheritance. His aunt died about a month back."

"Huh."

Seeing them, Sykes rerouted from the coffeepot over to their desks. "McGuire. Status?"

"Yessir." She brought him up to date. "Brenner should have the truck heading for the impound right about now. If there's anything in it, we'll find it."

"What about Jorgensen? Any sign of him?"

She shook her head. "Clint is staking out the house, but so far, no go. We talked to Gary's fishing buddies early this morning, but no one's seen him."

"Talk to his friend Branson and see if you can pick up any clues. If Jorgensen's headed into the hills, we're better off bringing in the dogs before the scent gets diluted by all this rain."

Lucy made sure she didn't show the alarm that skittered along her nerves. "I don't think we're at the point where we need tracking dogs, sir."

"Murders are typically solved in the first forty-eight hours, McGuire, if they're going to be solved at all. And we're already—" he glanced at his watch, which looked as expensive as the rest of his outfit, "—almost twenty hours into the investigation. I don't want anyone dawdling."

"I've still got a number of people I can talk to, who could get a message to Gary so that he can turn himself in, if it comes to that."

"Good." Sykes shoved both hands into his pockets and stared at her. "The Jorgensens are good friends of yours. You got a problem with that? 'Cause if you do, I need to know right now so I can reassign you."

Lucy hesitated. She *did* have a problem with it, but she also wasn't willing to let anyone else on the detective squad be charge of the investigation, not if she could avoid it. No matter how difficult it was for her, it was far worse for Kaz and Gary. And it was her fault that Kaz was involved at all.

The truth was, Lucy couldn't handle having Gary's fate rest in anyone else's hands. Not that she was the world's greatest detective, but she'd never be able to keep her nose out of the investigation, so she might as well make sure it was run fairly, even if that meant she had to be the one to slap the cuffs on Gary. "No, sir. No problem."

"Good." Sykes nodded and turned to go, then stopped. "So why are you two still here? Don't you have a murder scene to locate?"

Lucy managed to contain her glee as Ivar hurriedly gathered up the rest of his notes. When the chief wasn't focusing on being a social climber or setting up a press conference, he was very good at his job. Sometimes in surprisingly useful ways.

CHAPTER TEN

Deep in thought, Kaz walked back up the hill to pick up the car that Lucy should've left for her by now. Julie's attitude had been puzzling—one minute unfriendly, the next nervous and almost afraid. And though Kaz hadn't expected a particularly warm reception, she hadn't thought Julie would assume Gary was guilty. Julie knew how tight he and Ken were. If she were convinced Gary had murdered her husband, did the rest of the town believe that as well? It was a depressing thought.

Not for one minute did Kaz believe that the Lundquists had been the target of a random burglary. And based on the way Julie had been acting, she didn't believe it either. Someone was looking for something, something that perhaps Ken had put on the *Anna Marie* and had gone back to retrieve. Had the murderer followed him there and killed him? And if Julie thought Gary was guilty, why hadn't she been willing to call the police and report the burglary? She'd had the perfect opportunity to add to Gary's woes.

Kaz shook her head as she reached the edge of her yard. So someone thought that Ken had something worth burglarizing the Lundquists' house for, maybe even killing for. And, possibly, Julie knew what it was. Given Gary's argument with Ken in the tavern, it was a safe bet that Gary also knew what it was. But, Jesus, what could it be? The only thing Gary and Ken ever handled that was of any value was a few fish.

She was no further along in figuring out what was going on. In fact, she was more confused than ever. Some super sleuth she was turning out to be. Clearly, she should stick to dealing with Fortune 500 executives. Even with all their political agendas and power plays, they were turning out to be downright straightforward in comparison to her hometown friends. Another depressing thought.

She glanced at her watch. The river was starting into flood tide, so the fishermen would be coming into port soon. She was counting on them to help her— they had to know what was going on, what Ken had been mixed up in. Those guys kept track of their own.

Lucy's street car was a shiny black Jeep Cherokee, complete with roll bars, which she rarely pulled out of her garage. The city provided her with a patrol car when she was on duty, and weather permitting, she biked to the police station to stay in shape. Kaz retrieved the keys from underneath the floor mat, climbed in, and cranked the key. The engine growled to life, attesting to the excessive amount of horsepower under the hood. The clutch had a different feel than the one in Kaz's SUV, and she burned it more than Lucy would've liked as she backed out of the driveway.

*   *   *

Ten minutes later, Kaz pulled onto the wharf at the mooring basin. Many of the boat slips were still empty, but there was a line of trawlers coming upriver. Her timing was good.

Someone had removed the crime scene tape from the parking area so that it now only surrounded the *Anna Marie*. And the cops were there with a tow truck, working on Gary's pickup. She parked the Jeep, then walked over to give Brenner her key to the pickup so that they wouldn't have to jimmy the locks. If she couldn't manage to help Gary in any other way, she could at least keep his repair bills to a minimum.

As she headed back toward the docks, she spied Chapman and Zeke on board the burned trawler. Gathering more evidence, no doubt. He kept poking around in her and Gary's lives, asking questions. Doing his best to invade her personal space. Okay, so the trawler wasn't really her space. But even if she hadn't been working on the *Anna Marie* lately, she still considered the trawler part of the family. And she resented the hell out of the intrusions. It was all she could do to keep herself from marching right over there and demanding that he let her on board.

Several of the fishermen who'd already made port noticed her approach, and they didn't look happy to see her. She grimaced. Funny how her status had gone from "buddy" to "outsider" in less than a day. Then again, she reminded herself, nothing was as it seemed. Maybe they'd never considered her their buddy.

Karl Svensen was standing on the bow of his trawler as one of his crewmen brought the boat in close to dock. "Karl," she said when he drew close enough to hear her. "I need to talk to you for a moment."

"Well, Kaz, that doesn't mean I want to talk to you." He shoved aside a stack of crab pots. "I'm busy."

Karl was the fisherman who had refused to press charges six months ago, even though Gary had broken his jaw. Kaz had never been able to ferret out what the argument had been over. The usual rumors had circulated—one had it that they'd fought over a woman; another, over fishing territory. But Kaz had never bought into those rumors, especially since Ken had also been there that night. She'd bet money that Gary had been protecting Ken, which was what Lucy and Chuck also believed.

She turned so that whoever was close could hear what she was saying. "Someone here must know what Gary and Ken were arguing about at the tavern last night."

"We don't tell tales out of school," Svensen retorted. "This doesn't concern you, Kaz."

"The hell it doesn't." She was sick of hearing that. "It's my brother that the cops want to pin this on." She looked each one of them in the eye, and they dropped their gazes, embarrassed. But no one was forthcoming. "You're his friends. Do you really want him to take the rap for this?"

"Gary hasn't been an easy person to get along with in recent years, Kaz." She turned toward Bjorn Ewald, the captain of one of the larger trawlers and the medical examiner's brother.

Bjorn was a mountain of a man, well over six feet, with red hair and a bushy beard. And he had a huge family to match—eight children at last count. When Gary needed extra crew, Bjorn sometimes lent out one of his teenage sons. Kaz had always liked Bjorn.

"Maybe not," she acknowledged his comment. "But

that doesn't make Gary a murderer." She turned back to Svensen. "Who was standing next to Gary and Ken last night? You, Karl? They were standing near where you always sit."

Svensen uncoiled the bow line and jumped onto the dock to tie off. "Who told you that?"

"No one—I took a wild guess. So you were there?"

He shrugged. "I didn't want to tell you, because I knew that if you found out about the argument, it'd upset you."

"Knowing what I'm dealing with is better than not knowing anything at all. What were they arguing about?"

"All I heard was that Gary was real upset with something Ken had done. Ken told him that he hadn't had any choice. And Gary got even madder, told him that if he didn't fix it, he'd be sorry." Karl's eyes kept darting toward the other fishermen.

Was he lying? "Did you talk to Ken?" she asked.

"No."

"Witnesses in the bar say that you weren't exactly uninvolved," she said, taking a shot in the dark.

He climbed back on board his trawler and started stowing gear. His expression was no longer even marginally friendly. "Even if I know more than I've told you, I'm not saying anything else."

"Where were you last night around eight-thirty? You weren't in the bar—I would've seen you."

"Butt out, Kaz."

"I can't do that," she said evenly. "My brother is about to take the fall for something he didn't do."

Karl's smile was cold. "Are you sure about that? I'd rather face down forty-foot waves than your brother, given the mood he's been in. And like I said, I heard him threaten Ken."

Her anger bubbled to the surface. "Are you willing to swear to that in court? Because that's what it will come down to."

He shrugged. "No skin off my nose. You Jorgensens have never done any favors for me."

"I'm not looking for favors, Karl. I'm looking for the truth."

"Yeah, well, I've already told you everything I'm going to, so why don't you take a hike so I can get straightened away and go home?"

"Fine. If you remember anything else, would you please give me a call?"

"I won't."

She stood there a moment longer, rubbing her forehead to ease the headache that was starting to pound, then turned to leave. Bjorn came out of his trawler's engine room, rubbing grease off his hands with a rag. "Don't pay any attention to Karl," he said, his voice low so that it wouldn't carry. "He's grumpy because his catch has been so light lately."

Kaz searched his face, but all she saw was concern for her. Bjorn hated to see people at odds. "Are you sure that's all it is?"

His expression turned wary. "I don't know anything, if that's what you're asking."

"Don't know, or won't say?"

"Kaz . . ."

She made an angry gesture with her hand. "Never mind. When push comes to shove, you guys don't seem very willing to help one of your own."

"That's not true, and you know it."

"Do I? I'm asking a lot of questions, but no one's giving me any answers."

"You were gone a long time."

"I'm still part of this community, dammit."

"Give it time—the guys will come around. You've already made a difference on the insurance and other stuff you've helped the guys with, and they know it. But people are slow to trust around here in recent years."

Kaz stared out across the river, her hands on her hips. "Yeah, well, time's up. Gary needs help now, and you guys aren't exactly riding to his rescue."

"Has it occurred to you that the best thing you can do is to stay out of it?"

"I don't believe that."

Bjorn fiddled with the netting on a crab pot, then seemed to come to a decision. "The rumors are true," he said in a low voice.

Kaz felt a chill ripple down her spine. "What are you talking about?"

"Some of these guys are involved. You've got to stay out of it, Kaz. You could be in real danger. Let the cops handle it."

"Who's involved?"

"No way. Even if I knew for sure, I wouldn't tell you. I won't be the cause of you ending up badly hurt, or worse, dead. Ken was *killed,* Kaz. And these guys think he was murdered to send a message."

"Is Gary involved?" she asked, her voice harsh with urgency. "Do you know what Ken was into?"

Bjorn shook his head. "Look, I've already said more than I should have. I'll check your crab pots for you, if you want. That's all I can do, for now."

She stared at him, frustrated, then her shoulders slumped. "I'm scheduled to go out tomorrow, but thanks for the offer."

* * *

When Chapman saw her approaching the *Anna Marie,* he came over to the dockside railing. Silhouetted against the late afternoon light with his face in the shadows, he looked every inch the tough investigator—hard, maybe even a little dangerous. This was a man who kept going until he got the answers he wanted, no matter how long it took or who got in his way. Normally, she appreciated—even respected—that kind of tenacity. Normally.

Something stirred within her, and she ruthlessly squelched it. No sane woman would ever get involved with a man like Chapman. He was carrying around a load of baggage, just like she was. That alone made him someone she should be wary of. And if he decided to, he could put Gary away for life. "I need to come on board to start assessing the damage, make a plan for repairs," she said, taking the offensive.

He shook his head. "Not an option. The boat is still a crime scene."

She stared across the river, trying to control her runaway emotions. So far, the day had little to recommend it. And she was having a hard time, all of a sudden, holding it together. Maybe she was still suffering from the effects of smoke inhalation. That might be why she was exhausted and felt . . . fragile. God! She hated feeling like this.

"I've spent the last ten years creating solutions to problems and implementing them." She tried to control the tremor in her voice. "It's what I'm good at. Waiting, on the other hand, is something I don't do well."

"Imagine my surprise."

She gave him a sharp look, her tolerance for sarcasm at an all-time low. "The business can't afford to have one of the trawlers out of commission for any length of time," she said through gritted teeth. "I need to get on the *Anna Marie*. Now. And I don't think you have the authority to keep me off her for very much longer."

Chapman eyed her for a moment, and she hoped he couldn't see how tight she was strung. It was a faint hope—the man saw everything. He seemed to come to a decision. "I could use a helper for gathering evidence. That would get you on board—but not give you totally free rein. How's that sound?"

"Do you even need to ask?"

He held up a hand to stop her from jumping on board. "You'll do *what* I say, *when* I say it, and you'll do it the way I tell you to. Agreed?"

"Deal."

An hour later, they were standing on soggy, blackened carpet in the galley of the *Anna Marie,* working as quickly as they could to beat the approaching darkness. Zeke was watching from the burned upper edge of the deck with what Kaz could have sworn was an expression of self-pity. He wanted to be involved.

"What are we looking for?" she asked Chapman, poking through bits of charred timbers and ashes.

She needed a distraction, so that she didn't break down and cry. She'd never considered herself the sentimental type, but seeing the destruction on the *Anna Marie* up close was hard. Huge sections of the deck had burned through and collapsed into the compartments below. Netting from the spool sat puddled in a melted mass of goo on the floor of the hold. And the beautiful woodwork that she'd hand-sanded and painted in the family colors, now resembled charred sticks.

The wheelhouse was still standing, but the floor of the flying bridge above was buckled and unstable. All the equipment—radar, shortwave radios, sonar—was gone. And that was just the inventory of what had to be repaired and replaced. Who was going to restore the essence of the *Anna Marie?* She'd been a companion on thousands of trips, part of so many of the good memories Kaz and Gary shared.

Chapman straightened and held out a shiny object. "This, for one thing." She struggled to control her emotions and remember what they'd been talking about. "It's the padlock from the door between the engine room and the galley, correct?"

She leaned closer, then nodded. It was in remarkably good condition—she would have thought it would've melted in the high temperatures.

"It was probably protected by the falling wood to some extent, and the fire would have burned with less heat down here than up top where the accelerant was," he said, reading her mind.

She leaned over his hand to examine the padlock more closely in the waning light.

"What?"

"See these scratches?" She pointed to the marred surface around the keyhole. "Those weren't there before." The significance of those scratches hit her. "Wait. That means whoever opened it didn't have a key. So it couldn't have been Gary."

Michael nodded slowly. "Possibly. Unfortunately, it doesn't exonerate him."

"What do you mean, it doesn't? It's clear proof!"

"Ken could've done this—he didn't have a key. Correct?"

"But what possible reason did Ken have to get into

the hold of the boat late at night? And for that matter, what reason could he have that he didn't want Gary to know about? All he had to do was ask to use his keys."

"Not if they'd been fighting. And these scratches could've been put here any time in the last several weeks—maybe on a day when Gary forgot his keys. But it certainly opens up the possibility that someone was after something."

Just like at the Lundquist home. She started to tell him her suspicions about the burglary, then held back. She was afraid he would think Gary had done it. And he was right—this didn't, unfortunately, let Gary off the hook. In fact, it could be used against him, if it could be proven that Ken had a legitimate reason to fear Gary. Her shoulders sagged.

Chapman bagged the padlock and put it in a brief-case he'd brought to the boat. His tone sympathetic, he said, "I'll have it checked for fingerprints. Maybe we'll get lucky." He studied the area where the berths were. Most of the decking had fallen onto that area. "Which berth was Ken in?"

Kaz thought back, reliving those first moments as she'd tried to find Gary, choking and blinded by the thick smoke. She shuddered. "I landed about here," she said, pointing. "Then I crawled . . ." She turned, her finger following the path she'd taken last night. ". . . it must have been the starboard berth. I pulled him out of the bunk and he fell against that storage locker."

Chapman paused, then nodded. "That matches my memory of where I picked him up." He picked his way around the winch, which had landed in the center of the galley when it had fallen through the deck, and started removing burned timbers from the berth.

Kaz moved over to help him, but he waved her

back. "Stay back—I'll hand wood out to you, and I need you to stack it neatly in one pile. Then I'll get the lab guys back out here to go over everything."

She huffed a little but did as he directed. They worked for several minutes in surprisingly companionable silence, with Zeke whining every once in a while, becoming more and more impatient with his inactivity.

After Michael had cleared the worst of the timbers, he knelt down and surveyed the area without touching it. "We're in luck," he said quietly. "A lot of the berth is still here—just scorched. And I could be wrong, but I'm not seeing any obvious bloodstains."

Kaz craned her neck to look over his shoulder. Why did he think bloodstains were so important?

"Most mortal head wounds bleed a lot," he said, answering her unspoken question. "There was a lot of blood on Ken's clothing. If there are no correspondingly large bloodstains on the berth, then it confirms our theory that Ken was killed elsewhere and moved onto the boat. And that's premeditated arson."

Kaz stared at him, her throat closing. "No matter what else Gary could've done, he's incapable of planning to burn the *Anna Marie*," she managed. Chapman looked at her, his expression both grim and . . . pitying. She turned away, walked over to the stairs, and sat down among the soggy debris. "I know you don't believe me, but deep down, Gary has a gentle soul. What he had to do in the army tore him apart inside. He didn't do any of this—I *know* it."

Chapman opened his mouth to speak, but his cell phone chirped. He reached into his pocket, pulled it out, and flipped it open. "Chapman . . . yeah, I'm down at the boat right now . . . interesting. I'll come by in a bit—I want to see for myself." He disconnected and turned to Kaz. "Let's get moving. I've got to drop by the police impound lot, and we're done here until I can get the lab guys back."

She wanted to ask him about the call, but from the expression on his face, she knew she had a snowball's chance in hell of getting him to tell her. "When can I dry-dock the *Anna Marie*?" she asked instead.

"Not yet."

CHAPTER ELEVEN

The sun was gone by the time Kaz pulled into her driveway, and twilight lurked on the edges of the clouds. The wind had picked up, splattering occasional raindrops against the windshield. Below her in the downtown district, the outlines of old brick buildings stood silhouetted against the fading light. Out on the river, running lights glittered on the fishing trawlers, spotlights at the tops of their masts illuminating the churning waters of their wakes as they chugged upstream. Two large freighters were anchored for the night off the waterfront, their towering hulks dwarfing the other vessels.

A car door slammed, and she glanced in the rearview mirror. Lucy had driven up and parked behind her. Kaz climbed out of the Jeep and followed her into the kitchen.

Lucy hunted through the refrigerator, pulling two bottles of beer out and handing one plus a pizza box to Kaz. "I figured you'd forget to eat. Where're the paper towels?"

Kaz pointed to the far counter and then sat down, placing the pizza box in the middle of the table. She propped her elbows on the table, scrubbed her face with both hands, and worked hard on getting her brain to function. "I need to keep the Jeep for a couple of days. Don't ask why."

"Why?"

"If I tell you, you'll yell."

"I've just spent two hours scraping concrete and digging in the mud. Make my day—I could use someone to yell at right about now."

Kaz sniffed. "I'm no punching bag."

"Yeah, but as my friend, it's your duty to be there for me." Lucy handed her a slice of pizza on a paper towel. "Rumor has it that your SUV is at the dealer's, missing a window. Since you're still among the living—though not necessarily sounding like it—I won't ask if you were in danger."

"That would be good."

"Kaz . . ." Lucy shook her head and took a large bite of peppers, onions, and anchovies. Her eyes closed, the expression on her face bordering on bliss. "There is a Higher Being. Don't you want to know *why* I was digging in the mud?"

Kaz stared at her slice of pizza, trying to work up an appetite. "Is it okay to tell me?"

"Of course not—I'll have to kill you right after dinner." Lucy gave her a quick rundown, then snorted. "My big find of the day was a snow globe."

Kaz shot out a hand, grasping Lucy's arm before she could take another bite. "Describe it."

Lucy rolled her eyes. "Geez, Jorgensen. It was a little glass ball—you know, with the little bits of snow inside?"

"A white fishing trawler on a blue sea?"

"Whoa." Lucy quickly sobered. "Tell me right this minute how you knew that."

Kaz let go of her arm, the relief flowing through her almost making her giddy. "I gave it to Ken last week, for Bobby."

"Yesss." Lucy pumped her fist in the air and reached for her cell phone. "Ivar? Yeah, listen. Pull the concrete and mud samples from under the bridge and make them top priority, okay? And meet me there in a half hour." She hung up. "You know what this means, right?"

Kaz nodded. "If Ken were killed by the bridge, Gary couldn't have done it—he didn't have enough time. The murder scene is at the other end of town from the *Anna Marie.*"

"Exactly." Lucy gnawed on her lower lip. "So we see if we can link the mud and concrete from the bridge to the samples from the autopsy. If they're a match, it's a step in the right direction. But we'll need more than that to convince Sykes." She took another bite of pizza. "How're you holding up?"

Kaz put her slice down, reality sinking back in. And with that, the gnawing sense of desperation that she'd been feeling all day long. "Gary's holed up somewhere, Luce, and I can't figure out why. If he didn't do this, then someone may have been trying to kill *him,* not Ken. And so far, I'm doing a damn poor job of helping him."

"My guess is that if he needs help, he knows where to find it. Gary's got people all over who'll help him and keep quiet about it."

"Julie Lundquist told me that no one but Ken was

willing to crew for him anymore, and the guys at the marina indicated pretty much the same."

"That's pure bunk. And Gary's got buddies from the military in several of the neighboring towns. The fishermen may not be real happy with him right now, but I think that's related to what's going on."

Kaz's panic subsided a little. Lucy was right—Gary knew several vets who lived up in the hills, which meant he had access to supplies for as long as he needed to hide out. Long enough for Kaz to ferret out who could've done this. She should've realized that herself, which was one more sign she wasn't firing on all cylinders. If she could get some sleep and then keep digging for answers—

"I don't like that look on your face." Lucy frowned at her. "You need to take a step back and let me handle this."

Kaz kept silent.

"I mean it," Lucy insisted. "I need to conduct the investigation by the book—it's Gary's best hope of coming out of this cleared of any wrongdoing." She pointed a finger smudged with tomato sauce at Kaz. "And you need to quit letting guilt about what happened fifteen years ago color your judgment."

Kaz shook her head. "Gary hasn't had the breaks I've had. And I haven't been here for him."

Lucy snorted. "He got himself into this, he can get himself back out. I was wrong to ever make that phone call to you."

"You know he won't last even one night in jail."

"He should've thought of that before now. Hell, he should've thought about that six months ago when he punched out Svensen for dissing Ken."

A new thought occurred to Kaz. "Do you think the two incidents are related?"

Lucy looked thoughtful, then shook her head. "Nah, how could they be? Too much elapsed time." Her expression became grim. "I saw the photos from the fire."

Kaz's stomach clenched. "Did you say anything to Michael Chapman?"

"I've managed to avoid him for the last couple of hours."

Abandoning any pretense of eating, Kaz kicked back from the table, staring out the window at the garden that Gary had maintained for her all these years, which now looked bedraggled in the late winter rains. "Chapman's all but convinced Gary did it—he's just looking for evidence to convict, at this point."

"Yeah." Lucy sighed. "That was my impression, too. He thinks you're withholding evidence from him. Are you?"

Kaz hesitated, then shrugged. "Nothing important."

"If you know *anything,* you should tell us." When she didn't respond, Lucy glared at her. "I don't believe this—you're willing to let Chapman get away with railroading Gary? You won't let me help?"

"Chapman outranks you—"

"Like that's ever stopped me before. That guy gets in my way, I'll mow him down."

Kaz chuckled and held the cold beer bottle against her forehead, trying to ease her headache. "This is where I'm supposed to be grateful you're armed and have poor impulse control, right?"

"Hey, that's why I joined the force. I figure if I lose it and shoot someone, they probably had it coming."

"Just as long as the person you shoot isn't my brother."

Lucy sobered. "You know I wouldn't do that. I could never hurt Gary."

Kaz studied her friend's face, seeing the truth there. She'd always wondered, in the back of her mind, whether Lucy had a thing for her brother. But if she did, she'd kept it well hidden over the years. Which wasn't exactly in character.

Lucy wiped her hands with a paper towel and picked up her beer. "We executed a search warrant at the Lundquists' today. God! That was hard."

Kaz frowned. "What were you looking for?"

"Anything related to the crime—it was a general warrant. The place was a mess. I thought Julie usually kept it pretty neat and clean."

"She does. Someone tossed it."

"What?"

Kaz shifted in her chair, realizing what she'd given away. "I went up there earlier, to pay my respects—"

"And to pry information out of the poor woman."

"—right. And she told me she'd been burgled. Wouldn't let me call you or help clean up. What are the chances of a burglary—"

"Happening the day after Ken was killed?" Lucy shook her head. "Slim to none."

"Yeah, that's what I thought. I wonder what they were after."

Lucy picked up another piece of pizza and contemplated it. "Do you think Gary did it?"

"I hope not." Kaz considered, then shook her head. "I don't think so, but I can't prove it."

"So," Lucy mused, chewing slowly. "What would Ken

have that someone would want? Something small enough they'd tear apart the house looking for it? Shit. This case gets weirder by the hour."

Kaz stood up and got them another beer. Beer seemed to be all her stomach was accepting without staging a rebellion.

"What's your take on Chapman so far?" Lucy dug into her third slice of pizza, having no such problems.

Kaz hesitated. "Why are you asking me?"

"*Hell.* Ivar is right—you two have a thing going."

"We do not! Chapman's too stubborn, too overbearing, too . . . too—"

"Sexy?" Lucy leaned forward, dropping her pizza. "Please tell me you are not interested in this guy."

"It's just chemistry. No big deal."

"I'm serious. We don't know jack about him, except that he lost it on some arson investigation back East. Well, okay, and that he's related to the Boston Police Commissioner."

"Whoa." Kaz looked at her, shocked. "You told me he was an arson investigator. You didn't say anything about his being associated with the police."

"He isn't. But the latest info that's floating around on him is that the police commissioner was his guardian during his formative years. His parents were killed in a car crash, or something, and the commissioner was a family friend who stepped in to keep him and his brothers out of foster homes."

"Where do you *hear* this stuff?"

Lucy shrugged. "Ivar told me, and he heard it from somebody on the force, who probably heard it from someone in the mayor's office . . . you know how this shit gets around."

"So Gary and I are up against an experienced arson

investigator who just happens to have deep ties to law enforcement." Kaz shook her head, closing her eyes as depression settled over her like a wet bank of fog. "Shoot me now."

"The point being," Lucy said firmly, "that it wouldn't be smart to get involved with Chapman right now, or even—speaking from a purely one-night-stand-no-attachments point of view—jump his bones." She twisted the cap off her beer and lobbed it into the trash. "Not that he doesn't have very nice bones. And not that you'd ever be practical enough to consider sex as a recreational sport instead of the first step toward Happily Ever After."

"Phil would argue that my failure to commit was the reason we broke up," Kaz pointed out, experiencing the twinge of guilt and sadness that surfaced whenever she thought about him. "I'd say that makes me commitment-phobic, not the other way around."

"Yeah? Well, Phil's a twit. A good lawyer, maybe, but definitely a twit."

A laugh sputtered out of Kaz. "Come on. He's a nice guy."

Lucy just snorted. "Chapman's definitely *not* a twit, but until we have a chance to see how this guy really handles himself . . ." She gave Kaz a stern look.

"Okay," Kaz admitted. "So I looked a little more closely at Michael Chapman than usual, but that's all. I'm not dead, but I'm also not crazy."

"Since when?" Lucy shot back, then harrumphed. "So tell me what you really think of him."

Kaz pursed her lips. "He doesn't know the people involved," she said after a moment, "so it's easy for him to think that Gary's the obvious suspect. Whether or not he'll keep digging if there are unanswered questions . . ." She waggled her hand to indicate that she thought he might go either way. "For some reason, my gut is telling me that he's honorable, that he'll work to find out the truth. But you know how good my instincts are when it comes to men."

"The track record from hell."

"Hey."

"Well, it's not like any of those 'suits' you dated down south—including Phil—had any redeeming qualities, other than their ability to pay for tickets to the symphony."

"A minute ago you were accusing me of being too serious about relationships. Now you're suggesting that I'm mercenary?"

"Of course not. You were working under serious limitations, being in the corporate world. Not to mention that since the shipwreck, you haven't let *anyone* get close to you."

Kaz stared at her, shocked for the second time that evening. "Oh, come on." Was Lucy right? She *had* been more comfortable on her own in recent years . . . God. She hoped she wasn't turning into some kind of eccentric. She liked the idea of being married, and someday, she wanted to have children. She'd been busy building her career, that was all. She frowned. *Had* she pushed Phil away? He certainly thought so— he'd accused her of it the last time they'd talked.

"And, of course, you've been deluded for the last ten years as to what constitutes quality of life," Lucy added, breaking into her thoughts.

"Nice to know you have such a high opinion of me and my chosen lifestyle," Kaz said, her tone dry.

"*Prior* chosen lifestyle. I don't see you packing your

bags and heading back any time soon. Am I right, or what?"

At the moment, Kaz couldn't even think about a permanent move back to Astoria. It was a decision she had no idea how to make, or even when she would be able to make it. Her partner was doing a good job so far of handling the issues that had cropped up, but sooner or later, she'd have to go back. Even if she'd noticed since coming home that it felt right, somehow, to be here, she couldn't take the time to sort it all out. And for now, what was happening in California or even in her personal life had no relevance for her when balanced against Gary's problems.

Oblivious to Kaz's inner turmoil, Lucy rolled right on, her expression turning more businesslike. "I'll keep an eye on Chapman. But stay away from him, and let me handle him."

"That won't be easy. He thinks he can get to Gary by following me around."

"Gee, I'd say the man isn't dumb. You *do* know where Gary is, right?"

Kaz hesitated. "Possibly."

"If I were Gary," Lucy mused, "I'd head for the high country around Saddleback Mountain. He's camped in that area for years, and he knows how to lose himself up there. And up near the peak, it's damn near vertical, which would discourage all but seasoned climbers from following him." When Kaz didn't say anything, Lucy nodded and stood up, closing the pizza box and carrying it over to the door. "Try not to get shot at again while you're in my Jeep. It isn't paid off yet."

"Thanks for the pizza and conversation," Kaz said,

meaning it. Lucy had always been there for her, during some of the worst moments in her life.

"Yeah, I can tell you were wild about the pizza. Let's just get through this, so we can pick up our nightly pool game again. I'm starting to go into withdrawal."

Later that evening when Kaz's phone rang for the umpteenth time that day, she'd already taken a long bath and finished her third beer, which had gone straight to her head. Miles Davis was playing "Kind of Blue" in the background, and she was stringing her seventh crab pot while she tried to formulate her strategy for the next day. She was beyond exhausted, but still jumping out of her skin.

The phone rang again.

"Dammit!" She considered not answering—it would probably be another hang-up. But whoever it was, they weren't giving up—the phone continued to ring shrilly. Sighing, she dropped the spool of steel mesh wire inside the crab pot's iron frame, got up, and started hunting for the portable in the mess of newspapers and printouts on the coffee table. On the eighth ring, she unearthed the unit and punched the little green button.

"Yes, hello."

There was no sound on the other end, except for someone breathing. After a long moment, she heard a click, and then a dial tone.

CHAPTER TWELVE

At Astoria's main fire station downtown, Michael tossed his pencil on top of his notes and sketches relating to the investigation. He reached down to pet Zeke, who snored peacefully from his favorite place under the desk.

The station was quiet in the evening. Since the Astoria Fire Department was made up largely of volunteers, the firehouses weren't manned around the clock. Instead, on-call firefighters kept their gear with them.

Michael liked it that way. It gave him undisturbed time to think through the complexities of an investigation. To get inside the arsonist's head, to feel what the guy had felt when he'd lit the match or set the timer. Michael frowned. For some reason he hadn't yet put his finger on, that connection was eluding him on this case.

He read through his notes once more. So far, the forensic evidence was inconclusive or just plain nonexistent. The lab techs were in the process of comparing the human hair they'd found to the victim's, but the unofficial word was that it wasn't a match. The hair was blond, a possible match to either Kaz or Gary. But Astoria had a huge Nordic population, so that was hardly conclusive. The DNA tests weren't yet complete, so he wouldn't know for certain for another day or so.

Michael had spent the dinner hour interviewing the fishermen as they came into port, and he'd come away with one overriding impression—that they were afraid. What could possibly have these fishermen, who each day braved some of the world's most dangerous waters, so spooked? And talking to Lundquist's widow and the bartender at the Redemption had been even less illuminating.

Michael had a whole town full of people who weren't talking. Even if he cut them some slack for being wary of outsiders, their reaction was still extreme. This town had a secret, one that caused people to clam up tight. He'd seen real fear in the eyes of the fishermen and the bartender. Something, or someone, was putting a lot of pressure on them.

What really stuck in his craw was that the detective in charge of the case, McGuire, was acting like she had a good idea of what was going on, but even *she* was holding out on him. And the other one, the tall, thin quiet one, seemed to be content to take most of his direction from McGuire. So much for cooperation between the departments. Who was McGuire protecting? The Jorgensens, the fishermen, or all of the above?

He picked up his sketch of the fire and stared at it one more time. Pools of gasoline had been dumped on both the fore and aft decks, resulting in the caved-in sections over the hold and the fo'c'sle. The crewman's body had been lying directly under the largest pool of gasoline, virtually guaranteeing that the deck would cave and burn the body. There was no doubt in Michael's mind that the arsonist had intended to leave very little forensic evidence behind.

Michael smiled grimly. The torch had miscalculated there—he hadn't foreseen Kaz's determination. If she'd shown up a few minutes later, they'd be matching dental records, or DNA from bone marrow, to ID Lundquist. She was also damn lucky to be alive, and the thought of what could have happened if Michael had arrived only a few minutes later was still giving him waking nightmares.

The torch had also poured streamers down the stairs and through the engine room to the galley, breaching two locked doors. Lundquist's wife had verified that no one except Kaz and her brother had keys to those doors. Both locks showed signs of having been tampered with recently, which might be a point in Gary Jorgensen's favor.

Tipping the scales in the other direction, however, were the records on Jorgensen's military training, which had finally arrived a few hours ago via e-mail. Although most of the material had been deleted for security purposes, the type of training he'd received had been clearly documented. Jorgensen could have set that fire in his sleep, with very little forethought or planning. And if he'd had quick access to a space heater, then Michael could no longer argue that the method of ignition required advanced planning. Jorgensen could have simply killed in a rage and then covered it up.

At this point, Michael had more damn inconsistencies and unknowns than he had evidence. Like the fact that Lundquist's body had been moved after he'd been killed, possibly from a location that wouldn't have given Jorgensen the time to do the crime. Like those two scratched locks. And it was those inconsistencies that were definitely giving Michael heartburn.

Then again, maybe his heartburn was because of Kaz. The more time he spent around her, the more he was starting to care about her. Okay, certainly the way she looked invited him to indulge in a few fantasies. But the way her mind worked—*that* was the real appeal, and that *was* scary. She was smart, savvy, and . . . not boring, he realized. She'd never be comfortable, but he was discovering that comfortable wasn't all it was cracked up to be. Kaz was . . . fascinating. Challenging. *Hell.* The woman was part of the investigation. End of story.

She knew more than she was letting on—she'd seen something in one of the photos. And if McGuire had seen what Kaz had, she wasn't letting on. He'd gone over and over the Polaroids, but he couldn't figure out what—or who—had caught Kaz's attention. Dammit, he didn't trust her. And what had him truly worried was that he wasn't sure his libido cared.

He sighed, leaning back in his chair. What was it about moving to a new town that made a person think about new possibilities? Possibilities that he'd never let himself consider in recent years? Ever since Jessica's death, he'd avoided long-term relationships. Anyone close to him could become a target, and that was reason enough, to his way of thinking, to steer clear of commitment. If his actions on this investigation ended up putting Kaz at risk, he'd never be able to live with himself.

He knew his buddies back East thought he'd crossed the line that night five years ago when he'd tracked down his fiancée's killer. He'd never be able to prove that he'd acted honorably. Going in alone had been a mistake, because there had been no witness to corroborate his version of what had really gone down inside that burning building. The guy had had a death wish—he'd had no intention of going back to jail. Michael would have to live with the rumors for the rest of his life. He shook his head. *Move on, pal. The past is just that—past. There's nothing you can do to change it.*

What *had* changed was that sometime between leaving Boston and arriving in Astoria, his attitude about the future had shifted. The minute he'd laid eyes on Kaz, he'd started thinking in terms of a more committed relationship with someone. But other guys got to have the house with the wife, the two-point-two kids, the dog, and the white picket fence—not him. Hey, he had the dog, didn't he? That was enough. It had to be.

He blew out a breath. This case was frying his brain—he needed a distraction. Picking up his cell phone, he speed-dialed and waited for the pick-up on the other end. "Hey, Mac. Still playing politics?"

His long-time friend and police captain in Boston snorted. "Every chance I get. You know how I love kissing ass. Especially your surrogate papa's."

David Waltham, Boston's police commissioner, hadn't been happy when Michael had informed him of his plans to move to Astoria. After trying unsuccessfully to change Michael's mind, he'd started targeting Mac, his theory evidently being that Mac could convince Michael to come back home. Unfortunately, he could use the carrot-and-stick approach with Mac—he was Mac's boss.

"So when *are* you moving back, pal? We've got a pool going on how long you're gonna last out there in the boonies, and I need some insider information here—I could use the cash."

Michael smiled. The guys hadn't changed—they'd

bet on when the first raindrop hit the sidewalk outside, if nothing else came to mind. "You're going to lose this one, Mac. I'm not coming back."

"Oh, man, don't tell me that. I'll have to quit my job or else get myself fired."

"You want me to tell him to lay off?"

"Hell, no. I'm getting a kick out of it. For once, the commissioner isn't getting his way, and it's about damn time."

Michael couldn't argue with that. He'd be forever grateful that David had stepped into the void left by his parents' deaths, but that didn't mean the years he'd lived in David's house had been easy ones. Waltham was smart and powerful, and he had one of the most forceful personalities Michael had ever come up against. It wouldn't hurt David to lose a few battles now and again. "I need a favor, Mac."

He heard his friend sit up in his chair, probably taking his feet off the jumble of papers that always littered his desk. Michael envisioned the serious, all-business look that had come over his friend's face. When Mac took notice, no one could beat his laserlike concentration. "Shoot."

"Someone might be messing with me out here. I need you to check around quietly, see if you can find out who's been checking into my background."

Mac let out a low whistle. "What the hell's going on, buddy?"

"Just a little arson and murder, timed a little too conveniently." He waited while Mac swore, then continued. "It could be nothing—I'm just being cautious."

Mac harrumphed. "Like your instincts on this crap are ever wrong." There was a moment of silence. "You all right?"

"Yeah."

"Maybe the commish is right—maybe you should come home."

Michael could hear the worry in Mac's voice. He'd spent more than one night convincing Michael that he had to come back from the edge, that he had to stop his self-destructive ways. In fact, if it hadn't been for Mac shaking some sense into him, Michael wasn't at all sure he'd still be around to harass firebugs.

"Quit worrying," he reassured Mac. "The bottle of scotch is safely locked away. I'm up against someone who's clever, that's all. Get me that info, and I'll be fine."

"If you say so." Mac sounded dubious. "Hey. Maybe I should take a trip out there, check the place out."

"And here I was thinking the commissioner was the one acting overprotective."

Mac sighed. "Okay, okay. I get the hint. What else can I check into? You got a name you want me to run through the computers?"

"Not yet. But send me some coffee beans."

"You're kidding. . . . aren't you?"

"Two pounds of my special blend, from the shop in Faneuil Hall."

"Shit, Chapman. Is that place rusting your brain cells?"

"Just send me the damn coffee."

"All right, all right. How 'bout I overnight them?"

"I'm not made of money. Send it priority mail—I can wait that long." Just. Michael already planned to dip into Kaz's stash whenever he could until his own arrived. But he didn't mention that to Mac—he didn't want his friend getting curious. The next thing he'd hear was that they were betting back in Boston on how soon he'd be getting laid.

He talked to Mac for a few more minutes, catching up on some of the gossip back home, then ended the call with a promise to check back in a day or two, after Mac had had time to do some nosing around.

He leaned back in his chair, stretching and thinking about how badly he needed the break he'd counted on but wasn't getting because of this case. When it was over, he promised himself, he'd use some power tools. Knock out a wall or three. Then he'd be back to normal. That is, if he could figure out what normal was, these days.

He heard a car door slam outside. The chief of police, Jim Sykes, loomed on the other side of the glass door. He waved, and the police chief opened the door, walking into Michael's office. "Working late only a few days into the job, eh?"

"No choice in the matter." Michael gestured to an empty chair beside his desk. "Have a seat." Zeke lifted his head and moaned low in his throat, and Michael gave him a soft command. The dog subsided but didn't go back to sleep.

While Sykes settled in, Michael examined his reaction to the man. The way he'd felt last night hadn't been a fluke—he didn't like the guy, but he couldn't put his finger on why. On the surface, Sykes seemed okay. A little overzealous, maybe, but dedicated to his job. And Michael understood overzealous—he'd seen a lot of colleagues in Boston act the same way. Politics could either work for or against you, and many of his buddies felt that if you were smart, you actively made it work for you. Michael had never personally subscribed to that philosophy, instead going his own way, not really caring what anyone thought.

The police chief drew out a slim cigar. He raised his

eyebrows, and Michael kept his expression even while he unearthed a used coffee cup to serve as an ashtray. He had a real hatred of smoke in any of its forms. Most arson investigators didn't feel that way—they actually liked the smell of smoke. And many of them were three-pack-a-day addicts, feeling a genuine affection for anything that burned.

"Came by to welcome you to the community," Sykes said after lighting up. "It's great to have someone with your background in town."

"Thanks." Despite his tailored suit and expensive haircut, Sykes had the look of a man who drank too much. The flesh around his eyes was puffy and his cheeks were webbed with numerous small red blood vessels. Then again, a lot of cops drank. And Michael shouldn't be casting stones, given that he was working on kicking that late-night scotch-on-the-rocks himself.

Sykes settled more comfortably in his chair, then chuckled. "I have to admit, I had an agenda for stopping by tonight. I'm hoping to convince you to join the Big Brothers here in Astoria. The program has a special place in my heart, and I make a point of asking all my officers to spend some time with disadvantaged kids in the community, to let them see that we're more than just a uniform, that we're human beings, too."

His request took Michael a little by surprise, though now that he thought about it, it made sense. Sykes would be particularly sensitive to the problems of children who grew up without good role models at home.

"I don't know." Michael hesitated. "I was an only child—I'm not sure I know how to be a Big Brother."

"Not a problem. I want these kids to start a dialogue with us now, before they get started down the wrong path."

"I'd be of more help after I've been here awhile, once I have a better feel for the community."

"Once you get your feet wet, you'll do fine," Sykes assured him. "Both as a role model and as a fire chief. Think about it—that's all I'm asking. You can give me your answer later."

Michael nodded.

"People around here take some time to warm up to newcomers. We've had a lot of folks move out here and then leave within a year or two. So we tend to hold back some in the beginning." He drew on his cigar, then tapped some ash into the cup. "Give it a while—you'll find folks a lot more willing to talk to you."

"I doubt this investigation can wait that long," Michael said wryly.

"Which is the other reason why I stopped by—to suggest you take it easy on this one—let the police be the primaries. We've got a lot of history with Jorgensen. He's been on my radar for a long time."

Was it Michael's imagination, or did Sykes want him out of the way? And if so, why? Simple territorial jealousy? Career aspirations? Given what the mayor had told Michael, the career angle made sense. The police chief was probably an elected official, and right now, Sykes had the citizens on his side for lowering the crime rate. He wouldn't want a messy murder/arson screwing up his reputation for upholding law and order, especially not in an election year.

"Jorgensen has a police record," Michael said conversationally. He'd pulled it earlier that afternoon—Gary had a lot of arrests, but the only conviction was for the one assault, and it hadn't carried any jail time. Kaz might've been right about that arrest—there was something that didn't smell kosher about it. And when

Michael had asked the bartender at the Redemption about it, he'd clammed up. Fast.

Sykes shrugged. "There were a couple of fights on the waterfront, run-ins with my guys on several occasions, and, of course, the assault charge." Sykes puffed on his cigar. "My opinion? Jorgensen's a tinder keg waiting to blow."

"Still, it's quite a leap from a bar fight to murder and arson. Are you convinced he did it?"

"We found a tire iron with blood on it and a pile of gasoline-soaked rags under a stack of crab pots in the back of his pickup truck. I've got what I need to charge him with first degree murder and first degree arson, and I'll be drawing up the warrant as soon as the lab reports come back."

Michael was silent while he digested this new information. "Do you think that's wise?" he asked finally. "The investigation isn't complete, in terms of the fire or the crime scene."

"We've got enough to move forward." Sykes released an acrid cloud of blue-tinted smoke, and then leaned forward. "Jorgensen's been a danger to this community for years, and I want him off the streets. If I hadn't pulled him off that fisherman six months ago, he'd have killed him."

Zeke whined. Sykes raised an eyebrow.

"He doesn't like smoke." Michael placed a hand on Zeke's neck to soothe him. "You had any success locating Jorgensen?"

"Not yet, but we will. He can't hide forever in a community this small. And he'll get in touch with Kaz eventually—he won't be able to help himself. Those two are like peas in a pod."

"I'm new to the community, admittedly, but it was

my impression that folks around here like the Jorgensen twins. Wouldn't you be better off, in terms of community relations, waiting until all the evidence is in before arresting him?"

Sykes shrugged it off. "Kaz and Gary got a lot of sympathy when their parents drowned, but that doesn't make them saints. In my opinion, this town has been going too easy on them for a long time. Kaz's always been a little too loose with her favors, you know what I mean? She had quite the reputation in high school."

Michael managed to not react—to stay seated—as the rage boiled up. He'd always disliked men who talked about women as if they were lower-class citizens. But this was the first time he'd had to restrain himself from smashing in a guy's face. "I don't imagine that has much bearing on the case," was all he said, but someone who knew him well would have been alarmed by the change in his tone.

"Maybe, maybe not. I've always figured that someone with loose morals is capable of anything. There's no doubt in my mind that she'd help that brother of hers get away with this—if we give her the chance."

Unfortunately, Sykes had a point, even if his reasoning sucked. Michael started to tell the police chief about the inconsistencies that were cropping up, but for some reason, he stopped himself. He also didn't mention the shooting, or that he was worried about Kaz's safety. He realized that he didn't want Sykes anywhere near Kaz, even if he was the chief of police, and even if he had the reputation of being the town's savior. He'd take his concerns to McGuire and her partner. "One of my guys mentioned that you and Gary Jorgensen have some personal history."

Sykes's eyes went flat. "You wouldn't, by any chance,

be suggesting that I'm letting personal feelings get in the way of doing my job?"

"Might be." Some distant part of Michael's brain was surprised that he was pushing the man, but he couldn't seem to stop himself.

The tension in the room was thicker than the fog that was rolling in off the water. Zeke growled, and Michael tightened his grip on the shepherd's collar.

Sykes's cell phone rang, breaking the silence. Without taking his eyes off Michael, he reached two thick fingers into his pocket and pulled the phone out. "Yeah." He listened for a minute. "I'll be right there," he said, then pocketed the instrument. "You want to be real careful before suggesting things you don't know much about," he said, his voice soft.

Michael didn't respond. If Sykes were merely a chauvinistic jerk, just another small-town cop acting aggressively for the sake of his career, then Michael was making an enemy he could ill afford. But the remark about Kaz had set him off, and he found it hard to regret his actions. Even though he knew it indicated he was taking the case too personally himself.

Sykes leaned over, deliberately dropping his cigar into Michael's coffee. "You're new in town, Chapman, so I'll cut you some slack. This time. But don't ask me something like that ever again."

"Is that a threat?" Michael asked softly.

"Might be." Sykes's smile was feral. He stood, looking down at Michael. "I'll make sure Detective McGuire provides you with a copy of the paperwork on the warrant. In the meantime, I expect to see your report on my desk in the morning."

Michael rose. "I don't turn over results of any investigation I'm working on until I'm finished. And I take my orders from Mayor Forbes, not you." He walked toward the door of his office. "McGuire will get a copy of my paperwork when it's ready, and not before."

Sykes followed, stopping at the door. He was sweating more than when he'd come in, enough to ruin that pretty silk shirt he was wearing. "Jurisdiction over this case rests with the police department, Chapman. I know what goes on around here—I've lived here all my life. If someone sneezes inside their house out on Young's Bay, I hear about it. And I take murder in my town real personally. You'd be wise to consider that before you go mouthing off."

Michael smiled pleasantly. "I'll be sure and give that some careful thought."

After the police chief left, Michael pulled out a plastic baggy and carefully dropped the half-smoked cigar into it. He'd send it to the lab to have Sykes's saliva checked against the DNA found on the boat, just in case Sykes had been traipsing all over Michael's fire scene. Besides, it'd give him no small amount of satisfaction when it became known that he'd had Sykes checked out.

Michael stood there, rubbing the back of his neck while his gut screamed at him. On his way home, he'd drive by the Jorgensen house, just to make sure everything looked okay. He wouldn't stop, and he sure as hell wouldn't let himself touch Kaz. Touching would be bad, given the state he was in. But he wouldn't be able to sleep, he knew, if he didn't at least drive by.

He needed to know she was all right. That was all.

An hour later, Kaz awoke with a jolt, her heart pounding. Before she was even fully alert, she was reaching for the baseball bat she'd put next to her bed. What

had awakened her? Her hand on the bat, she lay still and listened.

There. A rustle, a floor board creaking—the one in the living room that they'd never been able to fix.

Someone was in the house.

She slipped out of bed and pulled on her sweats, trying to make as little noise as possible. Then she picked up the bat and crept into the hallway. The moon had come out, its bright light streaming in the window high over the stairs.

She crept forward, avoiding the floor boards that creaked. At the top of the stairs, she stopped to listen again. The sounds were louder now—intermittent thumps, then the slight squeak of a piece of furniture as it was shoved across the hardwood floor. Whoever it was, they were opening drawers, pulling books off the built-in shelves . . . the shelves that her grandfather had built. The shelves that she and Gary had sanded and varnished last week—one of the few projects they'd worked on together, in harmony, since she'd come back. The bastard had better not be putting any scratches on those shelves.

She gripped the bat tightly and started down the stairs. He'd be able to see her in the moonlight, but who cared? He'd come into their house, was going through their belongings.

Halfway down the stairs, she paused on the triangular landing where the stairway took a ninety-degree turn. The front door was standing wide open. On top of everything else, the jerk was running up her heating bill.

"Hey!" she yelled and leaped, clearing the last several steps and landing on the area rug in the entry.

CHAPTER THIRTEEN

The intruder exploded out of the living room, running for the front door. Kaz swung the bat at his midsection, but her aim was off. The bat glanced off his shoulder and hit the wall. Plaster rained down onto the floor.

He rounded on her. A black ski mask covered his face, and he was huge—outweighing her by as much as seventy-five pounds. Big enough to do some real damage. Adrenaline flooded through her.

She swung the bat again, but he stepped inside the arc and used both hands to shove her, hard. She went flying backwards.

The stair railing broke her fall, but the weight of the bat overbalanced her. She crashed down hard on the risers, her hands releasing and then shielding her face as it fell on her. Hot shards of pain lanced through the vertebrae in her back and her head.

Scrambling to her feet, she retrieved the bat, but he

was gone—out the door and off the front porch in a single leap. By the time she ran down the porch steps, he'd vanished.

She came to a halt on the front sidewalk, swearing and gulping in the cool night air. Then she made a quick trip around the outside of the house, her bare feet turning numb from contact with the cold, damp ground.

He was gone.

Back on the front sidewalk, she searched up and down the street, hopping from one foot to the other. That was when she saw him.

He was slouched against the pole of a burned-out streetlight on the opposite side of the street, smoking a cigarette. She stalked over to him, her bat tightly clenched in both hands in front of her. But as she got nearer, she realized that it wasn't the intruder.

"Careful with that thing," Chuck said when she reached him. If he thought her state of undress was odd, he didn't comment.

Glancing beyond him, she searched the alley between two of her neighbors' houses. Empty. She lowered the bat. Her hair hung in a disheveled mess around her face, and she shoved it back with her free hand. "Why didn't you stop him?"

"Who?"

"The man who came running out my front door. Black clothes, ski mask?"

Chuck's gaze sharpened, his expression becoming less remote. "What are you talking about?"

"Someone was in the house."

"Just now?"

"I woke up, he was in the house, and I chased him out." She glared at him. "I can't believe you didn't see anything. What good is all that Super Spy training if you don't even notice a bad guy right under your nose?"

"I just got here." He grasped her elbow and half-dragged her back across the street to her own front yard. She had to jog to keep up. "Stay here while I check things out."

"I've already done that . . ." Her voice trailed off as he disappeared around the corner of the house.

He was back in less time than it took for her to complete a few yoga deep-breathing exercises. "No one there."

"I could've told you that." A suspicion formed in her mind. "What are you doing here?"

"Figured I'd keep an eye out, in case there was any trouble."

"Good job. Why would you think there'd be trouble?"

"There's trouble just about everywhere these days. Read the paper."

She narrowed her eyes. "I could do without any of your cryptic remarks right now."

He glanced down at the bat and raised one eyebrow. "Going after him with that was stupid—he could've had a gun."

"Gee, I didn't have a gun handy—Gary has it with him."

Chuck didn't even blink. "Can you call Lucy, get her over here to stay with you?"

"I'm doing just fine by myself." Kaz folded her arms. "And you still haven't answered my question about what you were doing here. For all I know, you're the person I chased." Although, she admitted silently, he would've had to pull off the world's fastest change of clothes.

Chuck shook his head.

"Your timing is awfully coincidental."

"Leave it alone."

"Where's Gary?"

At the sound of an approaching car, he whipped his head around. "Cavalry," he said, and melted into the night.

Kaz muttered several choice words and then turned toward the vehicle that pulled up at her curb. Michael Chapman. Her heart rate sped back up. Great. Like she needed more excitement in her life right now.

Chapman got out of his car, walked around to the passenger side, and unbuckled the seat belt around Zeke. They both strolled over to where she stood, their pace unhurried. Chapman's sharp gaze took in the baseball bat, the sweats she'd pulled on with Gary's Seahawks jersey, her bare feet. She could only imagine what type of impression she made. "Interesting getup for a late-night stroll."

"I had an intruder, and I took care of him." Her tone was short. "What are you doing here this late at night?"

"Checking up on you, which appears to have been a good idea." He frowned. "You used a baseball bat? That was stupid."

Kaz's temper ramped up a notch. "Contrary to what people seem to think about us Jorgensens, we don't go around with guns strapped to our bodies or hidden under our pillows. And I haven't spent a lot of time in my life contemplating how I'll handle midnight intruders. This *used* to be a safe town."

He closed the distance between them and grasped her chin, turning her face so that he could see it better. Something cold flashed in his eyes. "Is that your only injury?"

Kaz edged away, unnerved by the effect of his touch. She raised a hand to her head. As if on cue, a lump at her temple started throbbing. "I fell on the stairs when he pushed me. I'll have a few bruises, but nothing serious."

He rocked back on his heels and put his hands in his pockets, almost as if he didn't trust himself not to touch her again. "What was he after?"

"How the hell should I know?" She stomped up the front porch steps and through the open door. He and Zeke followed her into the living room. "Probably has to do with the weird phone calls I got today." She started stuffing books back onto the shelves, and he moved to help her. "Hang-ups."

"Christ." Michael dumped a pile of paperback thrillers on the shelf and turned to face her, his face grim. "You know they were checking to see if the house was empty."

"Well, it wasn't." She went into the kitchen and filled the teakettle with water, then located some herbal tea bags. He followed her in, and she could feel his pale eyes on her, probably assessing how hysterical she might be. Okay, maybe she was acting a little over the top, but it had been an extremely stressful twenty-four hours. And her house was becoming a regular superhighway, what with both the Friendlies and Unfriendlies who thought they could come and go without so much as a "by your leave."

Zeke sat down beside her and leaned heavily against the back of her left knee, almost buckling it. While she waited for the water in the teakettle to boil, she rubbed the top of his head. The dog moaned and gurgled with pleasure. "This dog thinks he's a person."

"Shepherds have the intelligence of a five-year-old

child. He's perfectly capable of reading your moods, reacting much the same as any other human being would. He just has trouble communicating in a language that we humans understand."

"So if he had vocal cords, he'd be telling me that everything's all right, now that he's here," Kaz said, her voice wry.

"Something like that." Chapman took a tea towel off the cupboard door in front of the sink, and then retrieved a handful of ice from the freezer, which he wrapped inside the towel. He held it out to her. "It'll help the swelling."

She took it, touched by his concern, and held the ice up to her head, wincing at the cold.

"So far, you've been lucky." He folded his arms and leaned against the edge of the counter. When she started to protest, he quelled it with a hard look. "No, dammit. Let me finish. This morning you were shot at, now you've been attacked in your own home."

"He wouldn't have attacked me if I hadn't attacked him first," she mumbled, earning herself another glare.

"*Next* time, the guy might not be so polite. Now, are you going to tell me what the hell is going on?"

"I don't know." The look on his face was skeptical. "I *don't.*"

The kitchen was silent except for the sound of Zeke's tail thumping on the floor. She reached down and rubbed his head some more.

"Why would someone break into this house?"

She chewed her lip. There had to be a connection between the Lundquists' place being tossed and her intruder. Which meant that someone thought either Ken or Gary had something they wanted. It also indicated that Gary might be more involved in this mess than she wanted to believe. The risk of telling Chapman her suspicions was that he would leap to the wrong conclusion about Gary. But she was running out of options—she had to tell him.

She filled Chapman in about the break-in earlier that day at the Lundquists' and about Julie's secretiveness. "I think there might be a connection."

His expression was both angry and incredulous. "You *think*?"

"Okay, there's a connection. But I refuse to believe that Gary's behind the break-ins. For one thing, he has no reason to break in here and toss his own home."

Chapman nodded. "All right. I'll grant you that. But what about a partner, a person he might've had a falling out with? Most burglars are hoping to score one of three things: drugs, guns, or cash. Are you sure Gary isn't involved in some kind of drug smuggling?"

She gave him an incredulous look. "*Yes.* After seeing what drugs did to men in the military, Gary won't touch anything stronger than aspirin. And he isn't motivated by money—he'd never risk ending up in jail just to score some cash."

"What about the other fishermen?" Chapman asked. "Doesn't Astoria have a problem with heroin smuggling?"

Kaz tried to remember what Lucy might've said to her about drug trafficking. "The cops have known for years that heroin is coming through here, going upriver to Portland. But there's never been even one rumor of anyone I know being involved with drugs, and no one in the fleet has ever been arrested."

The teakettle whistled, and she turned to deal with it, but Chapman waved her off. "Sykes dropped by my office a little while ago." He brought the kettle, a ceramic teapot, and two cups over to the table. "They're getting ready to swear out a warrant against Gary."

A cold numbness spread through Kaz, and she reached for the back of a chair, dropping into it. "My God."

"They found what they think is the murder weapon in Gary's truck."

"But that makes no sense! Gary's not dumb enough to leave that kind of evidence lying around."

"He could've been in a hurry—or could've been scared off when you arrived."

She shook her head. "He wouldn't have run from me—he would've tried to protect me from whatever was happening." While Chapman poured tea into her cup, a piece of the puzzle fell into place. "Someone's trying to frame him."

"Possibly."

"It's obvious—" she broke off. "What did you say?"

"I said, you may be right."

Kaz stared at him. "Earlier this afternoon, you were hell-bent to convict my brother."

He slanted her a chiding look. "I was leaving open all possibilities," he corrected. "But now too many things aren't adding up."

"Like what?"

"I'm not at liberty to discuss that. Let's just say that a few of the findings might be inconsistent with someone killing in a fit of rage, then panicking and setting a fire to cover it up. I'm having the rags from the truck tested to see if the accelerant matches what I found on the boat." He set the teapot down. "But you're right—finding the murder weapon in the truck is too damn easy."

His words brought her a huge measure of relief. To

have someone agree with her, to not have everyone think she was crazy or blinded by her loyalty to her brother . . . Michael Chapman still wasn't her ally, but he *was* proving to be open-minded.

But why was Gary hiding out, if he were innocent? Surely Chuck could provide an alibi for him. She sagged in the chair. It was all, suddenly, overwhelming.

She tried to raise the mug to her lips, but her hands were shaking too badly. The hot liquid spilled, soaking through the bandage that covered her burn. She sucked in a sharp breath, her eyes watering from the pain.

Chapman leaned across the table and placed his hands on hers, helping her hold the mug steady while she took a sip. The warmth, both from his hands and from the tea, was a blessed relief. "Thanks," she said, her breath hitching alarmingly.

"It's the adrenaline," he said quietly. One corner of his mouth lifted. "You'll be fine in a couple of hours— back to your old, feisty self. Until then, you'll feel like you got flattened by an eighteen-wheeler."

She tried to smile back at him, but failed. Their gazes held for a long, silent moment; then he cleared his throat. Releasing her hands, he got up and rummaged through drawers until he found the first aid kit. Sitting back down, he took her hand in his and proceeded to remove the soaked bandage.

Kaz let him, almost paralyzed by his gentleness. His touch was difficult to reconcile with the tough image he typically projected, and it added a new layer of complexity to his personality. If she'd been paying attention, she would've been able to predict that gentleness, based on how he treated Zeke. But she'd blocked out those kinds of observations, trying to convince herself that he was the enemy.

He's not acting like the enemy now, the voice inside her head whispered. And she was having a hard time not imagining how nice it would be to have those hands touching other parts of her body.

While she was trying to rein in her unruly thoughts, he examined the burn. "It's healing well, but I don't think hot herbal tea is beneficial." His voice was wry as he dug through the jumble of packages in the kit to find some ointment. After spreading it with a light touch, he opened a package of gauze bandages and taped one over the blisters.

She hadn't said anything the whole time he'd worked, hadn't been able to while he had her hand in his. "Um, thanks," she muttered, pulling back and concentrating on her tea.

"No problem," he said, sounding amused. He watched her for a moment, his expression thoughtful. "I want you to take me with you when you go out on the water."

"*What?*" She jumped up to rinse out her cup. Just what she needed—twelve hours in close proximity to the most disturbing man she'd met in recent years, a man she was starting to feel a real connection with. And wasn't *that* a terrifying thought? The day she agreed to what he was suggesting was the day she ought to have herself committed to some nice, quiet sanitorium. "No way."

She had rules, ones that she hadn't broken since the shipwreck. Never again was she going to be responsible for taking someone over that river bar. She couldn't take the chance, not after that night all those years ago. It had taken her years to recover, to find a way to live with the fact that she hadn't been able to save her parents. She couldn't go through that again.

"I know what I'm doing, and I won't be in your way," he said, his voice calm. "I need to get a feel for what goes on out there, listen to the conversations on the radio."

He'd followed her over to the sink, and suddenly, he was standing way too close. Her already stressed system headed toward overload. "I hadn't decided yet whether I was going out," she said, stalling.

"You need to lift your pots, don't you?"

As usual, he was right, and he knew it. She had to get the newly strung crab pots into the water and empty and rebait the others. And it seemed that he'd come to the same conclusion she had—that they might overhear something in the fishermen's chatter that would give them some clues. Of course, the fishermen might also reveal Gary's hiding place, and with a warrant outstanding for Gary's arrest, Chapman would have no choice but to tell the police anything he overheard.

"I don't take crew out with me, ever."

He frowned at her. "Why not?"

She shrugged. "Just a rule I have. It's dangerous. And newcomers don't have a clue what they're getting into."

"I trust you." His eyes gleamed with the irony of his statement. They both knew she was still suspicious of his motives.

She grabbed a washcloth from the sink and started scrubbing a drop of tea that had gotten spilled on the counter. "Well, you shouldn't. Trust me, that is."

He was silent for a moment. "Funny. I didn't take you for a coward."

Her head whipped up. "*What?*"

"You don't want to be responsible for me out there,

so you're running scared. I'm betting you've been scared for the last fifteen years. Ever heard of getting back up on the horse after you've fallen?"

"How *dare* you—"

"Hell, yes, I dare." He leaned forward, his face only inches from hers. "You want this investigation solved, don't you? Your brother cleared?" When she didn't respond, he continued, relentless. "You'll dive into the hold of a burning boat, but you won't take me across the damn river bar. I've got news for you—no one's responsible for me but me. I'm asking you to take me out there, so *I'm* the one taking the risk. You're just driving the damn boat—you're not God."

He was right, and when he put it that way, she felt foolish. But he didn't know the conditions out there, so he didn't really know what he was asking. She started to shake her head.

He moved even closer, placing a hand on the edge of the counter on either side of her, boxing her in. "Here's the deal. You're not going anywhere without an escort, not after what's happened today. I won't have you in danger. So if you want to get those crab pots in the water, I'm going out with you. Either that, or I arrest you as a material witness, right here, right now."

She stiffened. "That's blackmail," she snapped.

"Yeah. So deal with it."

She wanted to punch him, and that shocked her. She wasn't a violent person. No one had ever gotten under her skin to the point that she wanted to hit him. In some dim recess of her mind, she knew she was out of control, overreacting. But she *hated* being backed into a corner, *hated* having decisions forced on her.

She stared at him, silent but defiant.

"I'll work for free," he said softly.

"Damn straight you'll work for free," she said faintly, realizing belatedly that she'd been coerced—or charmed, she wasn't sure which—into agreeing to his plan. She frowned. "The business can't afford to pay anyone right now, unless I send you home with a few crabs for dinner."

He smiled, satisfied with his small victory. "When do you plan to go back out?"

"I must be crazy," she grumbled. "Rule number one—don't take someone you don't trust out on the water with you."

"You trust me. You just don't want to admit it."

"You know, I really hate it when someone tells me how I feel."

He reached out and ran a finger over the bruise that was beginning to form on her temple. His touch was featherlight, but it shot through her, heating her to her core. She started to ease away, but he shifted even closer. She could feel the warmth radiating from his hard body, and she had the insane urge to cuddle against him, to soak up all that heat. She leaned away, lifting her chin.

He looked amused at her reaction. "I'll bunk down on the couch in the living room for the night." His voice had thickened, taking on a seductive quality.

It took her fogged brain a moment to process what he'd said. "You want to stay *here?* I don't think so."

"On the couch," he stressed, still smiling slightly, but with a hint of cockiness now. "Unless you prefer otherwise?"

"No!" She swallowed audibly, twice. Where was her much-vaunted poise when she really needed it? He still had her boxed in, and he was so close that neither one of them had to speak louder than a low murmur.

She cast about for an excuse. "I'll be fine. I doubt the intruder will come back tonight."

He hesitated, clearly not convinced, then reluctantly nodded. "All right. But I leave Zeke here."

"Fine," she said quickly.

His gaze dropped to her mouth, and her pulse headed for the stratosphere. He was going to kiss her. She couldn't decide whether the idea turned her on or terrified her.

He leaned down until his lips were only a whisper away, then stopped, his incredible, silvery eyes locking with hers. They questioned her silently. He had the kind of eyes she could have stared into for days.

She used the temporary reprieve to suck in some much-needed air. Laying a hand on his chest, she pushed slightly, testing his resistance. He didn't budge. "*Not* a good idea." Her voice sounded weak even to her own ears.

"Probably not," he murmured, "but I don't seem to be able to help myself." Sliding his warm hands under the heavy fall of her hair, he cupped the sensitive area at the base of her skull, holding her head still while he brushed his mouth across hers, barely making contact. His lips were warm, firm, and tasted of the herbal tea they had just drunk.

She shivered. His kiss was as light as his touch had been a moment ago, and just as devastating. An invitation rather than a demand, it was more of a turn-on than he could possibly know.

Her knees threatened to buckle, and she grabbed the edge of the counter to brace herself. "Wait," she said, hearing the edge of desperation in her voice.

He trailed his lips along her jaw line to her ear, nipping the lobe and then using his tongue to sooth the small hurt. "I'll stop if you want me to," he whispered, his breath warm on her neck.

Fisting her hand in the material of his sweater, she shuddered. She *didn't* want him to stop—she didn't want to pull away from the seductive promise of what might be developing between them.

Reading her reaction, his eyes darkened. Placing both hands at her waist, he lifted her onto the counter, then parted her knees and stepped between them. Capturing her lips, he kissed her, hard.

The man knew how to kiss. She moaned deep in her throat and parted her lips, inviting him inside. He didn't hesitate, tasting her deeply, his tongue capturing hers and luring her into a duel that hinted of what it would be like if they were to take this to the next level. She wanted to glue herself to every inch of him. And she wanted that incendiary kiss to go on and on.

Think about Gary. What you want isn't what's important here.

She managed to drag both hands down to his hard chest and push, her body already protesting as she did. "I want you to stop," she managed, her voice unsteady, her breath hitching with regret.

He froze for a long moment, breathing hard and staring at her. Then he sighed and leaned his forehead against hers.

"It's just chemistry," she said, trying to convince herself.

"More like a nuclear explosion," he muttered. He straightened, easing away from her slowly, grimacing at what the movement cost him. Reaching out, he rubbed her lower lip with his thumb, almost destroying what was left of her resolve. His expression was curiously sad. "But you're right—bad timing all around."

He told Zeke to stay and walked over to the kitchen door, then turned back to her. "What's between us isn't going away. When this is over—"

"I'll probably be going back to California," she said quickly, though the thought made her slightly ill.

"We'll talk," he said firmly. "And my name is Michael. It's time you started using it, don't you think?"

Once he was gone, she slid down the front of the cupboards until she was sitting on the floor, her knees bunched up. Zeke leaned over and licked her face, then grinned at her, his tongue lolling. Bemused, she raised a shaky hand to pat the top of his head. "I could be in a little trouble, here, Zeke."

"Rawrooo."

She dropped her forehead to her knees and rubbed Zeke's chest. Then on a sigh, she dragged herself to her feet. That kiss had been the knockout punch for a long, miserable day. She'd deal with the ramifications tomorrow, when she could be more rational about how irrational it was to start a relationship with a man she barely knew. One who could turn her bones to water with only a look. One who felt like he might be the man she'd been waiting for all these years. And wasn't *that* just a scary thought?

But right now, all she could think about was falling into bed.

Sleep. She desperately needed some sleep.

But it was not to be. At 4:15 A.M., Kaz was awakened from a restless doze by Zeke, who exploded into a frenzy of barking and leapt at the darkened silhouette of a man standing in the doorway of her bedroom.

CHAPTER FOURTEEN

The man reached in, grabbed the door handle, and slammed the bedroom door shut only a split second before Zeke hit the door, scratching and growling.

"Dammit, Kaz! Call off the dog." The voice on the other side of the door was muffled, but she would have recognized it anywhere.

"Gary!" She threw back the covers and scrambled out of bed. Grabbing Zeke's collar, she flung open the door. "I've been worried sick," she said, hugging him.

He held her close for a long moment, then gently set her aside. Crossing to her window, he drew shut the curtains, then prowled the small space beside her bed like a big, restless cat. Zeke watched him warily, growling low in his throat.

Even in the shadows, Gary's face was haggard, his cheeks hollow. His forehead and jaw were streaked with dark grease paint, adding to the starkness of his features. And he looked gaunt, as if he hadn't been eating.

She pressed her lips together, swallowing a sound of distress. "It's too dangerous for you to be in town. Why are you here? Where've you been staying?"

"I won't tell you that." He rounded on her, pointing a finger. "You stay out of this, Kaz."

She folded her arms. "What's going on, Gary?"

"Nothing you can do anything about."

"Is that why you've been avoiding me the last couple of weeks? Because of this?"

"Yes." He came over to where she stood, placed his hands on her shoulders. "I want you to go back to California. Tomorrow. Just pack your bags and go."

She shook her head.

His large hands squeezed her shoulders. "Please, Sis." Then he pulled her close again, and sighed. "I couldn't bear to lose you."

She laid a hand against his cheek. "Tell me what's going on," she said softly. "I can help you. What are they looking for?"

He jerked his head up, stark fear washing over his features. "What d'you mean?"

"Someone's been calling here, then hanging up. I had a visitor, around midnight, who was searching through the bookcases in the living room. And the Lundquists' house was tossed earlier today."

"Sonofabitch!" He turned away from her, slamming his fist against the wall. Zeke snarled, and she knelt to soothe him. "You've got to go stay with Lucy, where you'll be safe." He paced some more, then stopped, running his hands through his hair. "Dammit, I didn't want you involved. These guys play for keeps, Sis. God, look what they did to Ken."

"Who *are* these guys?"

"No way."

"Tell me you aren't trying to handle this alone." The thought terrified her. "That's it, isn't it? You're staying here in town, not up in the back country where you'd be safer, trying to find out who's behind this. If the cops find you—"

"I've got some people helping me."

"Chuck," she guessed.

Gary shrugged and resumed his pacing. She couldn't remember ever seeing him strung this tight. If Chuck were helping him, that gave her some comfort that he wasn't alone. And maybe some of the fishermen were on his side—people like Bjorn. It made sense. Without their help, he'd be spotted immediately. Still, he and Chuck had no business being vigilantes, if that's what they were doing.

She sat down on the edge of the bed. "Go to Lucy and Ivar, tell them what you know. It's the only way."

He shook his head. "Not an option." He stared down at Zeke, then held out a hand for the shepherd to sniff. "Why do you have that new guy's dog here?"

"Michael left him for my protection after the break-in this evening." She bit her lip. "Someone's trying to frame you, Gary."

He laughed grimly, the sound harsh in the relative quiet of her room. "You think I don't know that?"

"The cops found the murder weapon in the back of your truck. They've issued a warrant for your arrest."

"Yeah, Chuck told me." Before she could ask how Chuck had found out, Gary shook his head. "Chuck has his sources—I don't ask."

"Clint Jackson is staking out the house—he's been here off and on since this morning."

Gary snorted. "I saw him. He was sitting in his car, half asleep when I came in the front door. He never even saw me." Gary looked momentarily amused. "You don't have to worry about him catching me."

"But there are others out there looking, according to Lucy."

"I just came by to pick up a few things." He knelt, taking her hands in his. "Stay out of this, Sis. For me."

"Not an option," she said, mimicking him.

"You have to trust me on this. If I'm worrying about you, then I can't concentrate on stopping these guys. This Chapman, can he protect you?"

"I can protect myself."

"Not from these guys—don't even think that. If you get in their way, they won't hesitate to kill you." He gripped her arms and shook her gently. "Dammit, you're all I've got left."

"Then you know how *I* feel."

"At least go out on the water, act like everything is normal. You'll be pretty safe out there—the guys won't let anything happen to you. And don't go anywhere on your own. Promise me that much, at least."

"What about you?"

"Forget about me—I'm not important." When she opened her mouth to protest, he shook his head and stood, forcing her to look up at him. "You listen to me, Kaz. This time, your stubbornness could get you killed."

"And you don't need to be a hero," she said quietly.

He snorted and let go of her. "No chance of that at this point." His smile was sad, his expression becoming more distant. "But they aren't going to get away with this, not in my town."

He walked over to the window, easing the curtain aside, then swore softly. "Looks like Jackson has actually decided to take a walk around the house. Pity you can't sic the dog on him." Gary pulled a .45 Ruger out of his jacket, chambered a round and flipped the safety on, then handed it to her. "Keep this with you, even when you sleep."

She took the gun reluctantly. She knew how to use it—Gary had insisted on teaching her years ago—but she'd never been comfortable handling it. "Tell me how to get in touch with you."

He shook his head. "If you need anything, find Chuck." He walked to the door and opened it, then looked back at her, worry evident on his face. "Good-bye, Kaz."

Tears burned behind her eyes, and she panicked. "Gary—"

"Take care. Do what I'm telling you."

And then he was gone.

Kaz dropped down onto the bed, staring at the empty doorway. She picked up the pillow, shoving the pistol underneath. For several long moments, she stared at the moonlit glow of the white pillowcase.

Then she grabbed the pillow and hurled it across the room.

Two hours later, Lucy was sitting in her living room in her rattiest sweats, mainlining coffee, eating cold pizza, and watching a rerun of a World Cup Soccer match while she cleaned her gun. Normally, she slept until the very last minute each morning, then headed into the police station and had her caffeine hit there. But this case was driving her nuts, so she'd gotten up early, figuring that watching the game and sniffing gun oil would help her relax enough to think things through.

In her opinion, soccer was a great sport. Its players exhibited the perfect blend of grace and athleticism, with the right amount of competitiveness thrown in. She snorted. Unlike football players, whom she'd always been convinced got away with culturally sanctioned assault and battery. Most linebackers and defensive tackles were lucky they'd landed a place on a team somewhere—otherwise, they'd be doing ten to fifteen in the state pen.

The United States soccer team scored a goal, and she let out a whoop. Then she removed the firing pin from the Glock, inspecting it closely for wear. The only use the gun had ever seen was on the firing range, but still, a careful cop kept her equipment in top condition.

Sykes had gotten the warrant issued for Gary's arrest in record time, dropping it on her desk the night before. He'd also assigned two more teams of cops to search for Gary, putting Clint Jackson in charge. And that worried the hell out of her, because Clint wasn't, to put it mildly, her first choice for the job. Of course, her opinion might be colored by the fact that Clint was a redneck, chauvinist asshole who got off by objectifying women. The guy made her see red every time he swaggered into the squad room. She didn't mind being treated like she was one of the guys—that was actually what she preferred. But Clint had let it be known more than once that he thought any skills she had were best used in the bedroom.

Still, no matter what her personal feelings were about him, she was convinced she was right to be worried. She wasn't the only one on the force who thought Clint could be a little too rough on prisoners, not to mention a little too trigger-happy. If Gary decided to put up a fight . . . she shook her head. The dumb shit needed to turn himself in. Why the *hell* hadn't he made contact with her and told her what was going on? Surely he trusted her. He had to know she'd do whatever she could to ensure that he was treated fairly.

Maybe he trusted her, but didn't have the confidence in her ability to help him. She pondered that while she ran a small brush through the barrel of her gun, scouring it of any gunpowder residue, then shook her head, muttering under her breath. No. She was just being insecure, which was a bad habit of hers. Gary knew she was good at her job, and Gary knew she was loyal to her friends. She'd never given him any reason to think she'd let him down.

She sensed rather than heard a movement in the doorway and looked up. Then jumped a foot. "Shit!"

Gary was leaning against the doorjamb and watching her with an amused expression on his face, as if she had conjured him out of thin air. "Jesus, McGuire. You clean your gun at six-thirty in the morning?"

"You scared the hell out of me!" she shouted at him. "Don't do that—I could've shot you."

"Your gun is in itty bitty pieces."

"I can have it back together in under seven seconds."

"Yeah, and I can render you unconscious in under two."

She already should've pulled her backup gun, and she cursed the lack of caffeine in her system that was making her brain function like molasses. "You here to turn yourself in?"

Gary grunted and moved out of the doorway. Keeping a wary eye on her picture window, he leaned over and picked up her coffee mug, draining it. When the taste registered, he grimaced. "Christ. What the hell is this?"

She snatched the mug away from him and headed for the kitchen to refill it. "I reheated yesterday's."

"You're hopeless in the cooking department, you know that?" he said, following her. He leaned against the counter, muscular arms crossed, looking tall and lethal in his camouflaged army fatigues and grease paint. "Convince Kaz to lay off. I don't want her mixed up in this."

"You convince her."

"I tried—she isn't buying it."

So he'd been to the house and talked to Kaz. Lucy handed him the coffee mug, then palmed the .38 she'd retrieved from the kitchen drawer, pointing it at him. "I've got to arrest you, Gary. I can help you, but I have to take you in."

He shook his head. "Point that somewhere else, will you? I don't want you losing that infamous temper of yours and shooting me."

"Hands behind your head, fingers interlocked. You have the right to remain silent. Anything you do say can and will—"

Carrying his coffee, he walked over to the refrigerator, looking inside. "Got anything to eat besides pizza? I'm a vegetarian these days."

"You can't just ignore me!"

He shut the door, sighing. "You're not going to shoot me, Luce, and I'm not going to turn myself in. So put that thing down, before I feel the need to take it away from you."

"I'd like to see you try," she snarled.

He grinned and winked. "And I'd like nothing better than to try, darlin'. But I've got places to go, people to see."

Pure, hot, sexual awareness arrowed through her,

heating her. She swore, de-cocked the gun, and laid it on the kitchen table. Dropping into a chair, she rubbed her face. No way was she going to let him see how much he'd gotten to her with one remark and a sexy smile. "Okay, what d'you want to talk about?"

"Kaz. Convince her to go back to California." Gary's brows drew together. "Hell, you're the one who called her and told her to come back. So fix it."

"You know about that?" Lucy felt the guilt slide through her.

"Yeah. What a dumb-ass move."

She bristled at his remark, but she refrained, just barely, from snapping at him. He had a point. Kaz was acting recklessly, and displaying a tenacious stubbornness that was half the reason Lucy had had a sleepless night. And it *was* her fault that Kaz was involved. "Like she's listening to me any more than she is to you."

He sat down in the chair opposite her, and she noticed for the first time how exhausted and anxious he looked. Her stomach started to churn as she considered what could make a badass, ex–Army Ranger like Gary so paranoid. "Can't you arrest her or something?" he asked.

"Phil would have her out in an hour, you know that."

"Then put her in protective custody."

"Gee, all our officers are busy out looking for you."

He grunted. "I noticed. Okay, so move in with her."

"Gary . . ." She shook her head, then folded her arms. "I've heard rumors for a couple of weeks now about the fishermen. Care to tell me if they're true?"

"No."

"Want to confide in me about what you're doing?"

"No."

She gritted her teeth. "Where were you the night before last while the *Anna Marie* was burning down to the waterline?"

"Camping."

"Try again," she shot back. "I saw you in the photos Chapman took of the crowd."

He glared at her. "I went to the mooring basin to spend the night on the trawler, but I hooked up with Chuck instead. Satisfied?"

"Not by a long shot." He wasn't telling her everything, and the knowledge that he didn't trust her to help him hurt so much she was having trouble breathing. She forced herself to pin him with her hardest interrogation stare. "Did you go onto the *Anna Marie*?"

"No." He leaned forward, close enough to pump up her pulse rate. His eyes shone with a feverish intensity. "You know I didn't kill Ken. Quit playing cop for just one damn minute and listen to me. Kaz is in real danger. Did she tell you someone broke into her house last night?"

Lucy swore.

He smiled grimly. "Yeah, I didn't figure she'd raced to the phone to call you."

"Do you know what they wanted?"

"Yeah."

She glared at him. "You going to share with me?"

"No." He stood and walked to the back door. "Figure out a way to keep her safe—that's all I'm asking."

"You can't just waltz out the door! I'm an officer of the law and there's a warrant out for your arrest."

"You never saw me—I wasn't here." He paused in the open doorway. His expression was hard, but his eyes were haunted. She shivered as cool air wafted over her. "Watch your back, Luce."

Two seconds later, he was gone, and she was left sitting alone in her kitchen, listening to the quiet ticking of the clock on the wall.

Well, hell. She'd just let a wanted felon walk out her back door. She'd throw something, but there was nothing within reach that she could afford to break.

CHAPTER FIFTEEN

When Kaz awoke around nine, her first sleep-fogged thought was that she felt like a mummy, wrapped from shoulders to toes. Then she remembered that Zeke was stretched out along one side of her, on top of the covers.

After Gary had left, she'd given in and let the dog sleep on the bed. She had a sneaking suspicion that Zeke was afraid of the dark. He'd been so rattled by their late-night visitor that the only way she could get him to quit pacing, his claws click-click-clicking on the hardwood floor, was to invite him into her bed.

Zeke's forepaw lay across her stomach, holding her down, and his head lay on her shoulder, tucked into the crook of her neck. He was sound asleep, his hind legs twitching as he chased imaginary prey. She lifted his paw and tried to roll him over. He groaned, snuffling against her neck and licking her ear, then went back to sleep.

It was the same ear that Michael Chapman had licked the night before.

Muttering to herself about the male gender, she lifted the edge of the covers and eased sideways out from under Zeke, half-falling onto the floor beside the bed. She dragged herself to her feet and went into the bathroom.

After brushing her teeth and throwing cold water on her face, she glanced in the mirror. Big mistake. Two nights of little sleep had left her looking wan with purple smudges under her eyes. Worry about Gary had added hollows to her cheeks. She was starting to resemble a scarecrow.

Taking a quick shower, she turned it to bracing cold at the end, forcing herself to stand under the icy stream until she was awake. Then she tamed her wet hair into a French braid and applied light makeup. After rummaging around in her dresser, she pulled on a clean pair of jeans, a turtleneck, and a heavy cotton sweater.

As she dressed, she assessed the weather. The wind was picking up in velocity, splattering rain drops against the panes of her bedroom window. Another storm was moving in, and it looked like it might have some punch to it. She'd check the marine forecast, but she was certain there'd be gale force winds and at least fifteen feet of storm surge, even close in to shore. No one would be going out crabbing today.

Sighing, she grabbed the pair of running shoes she had drying on the heat register and headed downstairs. Rounding the corner into the kitchen, she came to a halt.

There was a cup of freshly brewed coffee sitting on the edge of the counter, doctored the way she liked it with a small amount of cream. It held down a handwritten note. She picked up the coffee and the note, noticing that Zeke was gone. Before she could read it, the phone rang.

She reached for the handset, then hesitated, unsure if she could cope with another hang-up. The phone rang again. She couldn't ignore it—it could be anyone, even Gary. Just this once, she wished her brother were into technology and had installed Caller ID. She sighed and picked up the portable unit.

"So glad you thought to call me about the break-in." Lucy's voice had a distinctly sarcastic edge to it.

Kaz relaxed. "What could you have done? Send the lab guys over to dust for fingerprints?"

"For starters, yeah."

"He was wearing gloves."

She heard Lucy groan. "Don't tell me how you know that—I don't want to hear."

"I noticed when I swung the baseball bat at him."

"Jesus Christ." There was a pause while Lucy drank something. "Does the word *caution* mean anything to you? The guy could've had a gun."

"That's already been pointed out to me, more times than I wanted to hear," Kaz said mildly. "Did you call for a reason?"

"So where the hell was the surveillance team? Jackson or Brenner should've been right outside."

Kaz shrugged. "You tell me. When I chased the guy out the front door, there was no one out there." She didn't add that Jackson had been there later, when Gary had shown up for a visit.

Lucy sighed loudly. "All right. I'll send over a team to check for fingerprints, just in case. And I'll also find out where Jackson was—he should've been there.

Can you *please* stay out of trouble for the remainder of the day?"

Kaz didn't bother to answer. She could hear Lucy shutting a door and walking somewhere outside, her steps crunching on gravel. She was probably leaving for the station. A new thought occurred to Kaz. "Hey. How did you know that someone had broken in here?"

"Your jerk of a brother." Lucy disconnected, leaving Kaz standing in the middle of her kitchen holding a dead phone. She realized her mouth had fallen open, and she snapped it shut. So she wasn't the only one Gary had visited last night. Interesting. And since Gary wasn't behind bars this morning, that meant Lucy hadn't arrested him. Even more interesting.

It appeared that the men in their lives were giving both of them trouble. Speaking of which—she stared at the note she still held in her hand, focusing on the bold, black scrawl. Michael's handwriting was as forceful as the rest of his personality.

"I assume the weather's too lousy to go out," he'd written in large, slanted letters. "And I didn't figure you'd want me to join you in the shower—at least, not yet." She smiled a little at his audacity, feeling a trickle of heat as an image of the two of them together under all that steam snuck into her mind. Then she frowned as she read the rest of the message. "*STAY PUT.* Zeke and I have work to do. We'll be back this evening. *GET SOME REST.*" That was it—he hadn't bothered to sign it.

She crumpled the note in one fist and tossed it into the trash. The man had more than his share of arrogance. Unfortunately, it didn't make him any less attractive.

* * *

By late morning, Kaz was pacing her living room like a caged animal. Each wind gust rattled the loose pane in the south window that they'd never gotten around to glazing, and even though she'd closed the damper on the fireplace, puffs of ash floated onto the floor. Rain now came down in drenching sheets, and she could feel the barometric pressure dropping like a stone. Coastal storms had always made her itchy, and this one was no exception.

She'd already downloaded her e-mail and taken care of any outstanding issues from the San Francisco office and her clients. That had taken less than an hour—her partner had things well under control. It seemed to be working out fine to telecommute, at least, for a large part of the workload. Which had her thinking about the possibility of a more permanent, commuting-type setup, and of letting her partner handle more of the day-to-day responsibilities. Still, it would've been nice if there'd been enough work this morning to keep her from going stir-crazy.

"Stay put," she muttered, stacking a pile of books in the bookshelf, then adjusting them so that they lay on their sides, then moving them to a different shelf altogether. Like she could just sit around, doing nothing. Another hour of this and she'd need tranquilizers.

She couldn't see the mooring basin from this end of town, but she hoped none of the fishermen had gone out before the storm hit. Worry for them had been nagging at her since she'd awakened. Most likely, they were camped out in the Workman's Café on the waterfront, waiting to see if the weather let up. Or on their boats, killing the time by knocking off some of the items on their ever-present lists of needed repairs.

But her concern for the fishermen was nothing next to the hysteria that threatened to bubble up whenever she thought about Gary. He was out there, somewhere close by, trying to catch people who were capable of murder. *And* trying to evade the cops who all, with the exception of Lucy and Ivar, wanted his head served up on a platter.

What did it all mean? A nervous widow, fishermen who were too scared to talk, and something that people wanted. Was it drug-related, as Michael seemed to think? *Were* some of the fishermen running drugs? Could that have been what Bjorn had been alluding to when he'd said that some of them were involved?

But if so, how had Ken gotten mixed up in it? It didn't make sense—he was a family man, not a drug runner. She couldn't imagine him taking those kinds of chances, not with his wife and kids. Then again, Bobby had been horribly sick, and Ken would do anything for him. But Kaz knew beyond a doubt that Gary wouldn't touch drugs, not for any reason.

She stopped fiddling with the books and blew out a breath. To hell with it. The least she could do was check up on the fishermen. And maybe one of them would let something slip, provide some small bit of information she could use to figure out what to do next.

Snagging her sou'wester off the hook by the back door, she headed out into the storm.

Halfway to the mooring basin, she changed her mind and pulled a U-turn, heading back toward Uniontown. At this time of the day, the Redemption was mostly deserted. She figured Steve would have time to talk to her and could perhaps shed some light on what had happened two nights ago. Pulling into the parking lot, she set the Jeep's brake and hopped out, jogging across the gravel to the door.

She paused inside the entry, shaking off the rain and letting her eyes adjust to the dimness of the room.

Steve was behind the bar, totaling up last night's receipts. "Hey, Kaz." He smiled, his expression friendly.

Like most of her contemporaries in town, Steve had gone through school with her. Although they hadn't run with the same crowd, she remembered Steve as being one of the good guys. She'd heard some rumors that he'd gone a little crazy after his divorce a few years back, but the divorce had been particularly acrimonious, so he'd probably had good reason.

If Steve looked the other way sometimes when it came to what went on in his tavern, it was understandable. A bartender heard a lot, knew a lot. And if he made a habit of revealing what he knew to anyone who would listen, he'd be out of business in a hurry. Astoria had a healthy rumor mill, but in an odd way, most of the locals disapproved of anyone who talked out of turn. There were unspoken rules about who you should talk to, and about how much you could reveal. Right now, Kaz was counting on those rules, because as the sister of someone who was involved, she was on the list of people Steve could talk to, if he chose. She also wanted to find out why Gary had felt that Steve had no cause to criticize him that evening.

"I need to know what Gary and Ken were arguing about two nights ago," she said without preamble.

Steve shook his head, his expression turning wary. "It was pretty busy, Kaz. And you know I make a habit of tuning out."

"You were standing right here the whole time—you could hardly miss what they said."

He didn't reply, busying himself with rinsing out glasses.

Her heart sank. He wasn't going to help her, any more than the fishermen were. She slipped onto one of the barstools and leaned her elbows on the bar. "They've charged Gary with arson and murder. Steve, if you know something . . ."

He sighed. "I'll tell you exactly what I told Lucy and Ivar, and that new fire chief guy. I didn't hear anything important."

So Michael had already questioned Steve and hadn't mentioned it to her. He was conducting an investigation, she reminded herself. He wasn't obligated to keep her informed. But still, it bothered her that he wasn't being entirely straight with her. "Okay. What did Gary and Ken say that night that *isn't* important?"

Steve shrugged, then glanced around the mostly empty room before answering. "They were arguing about something to do with the crab pots."

She stared. "That doesn't make any sense. They drag-fish—I'm doing the crabbing."

Shooting her an exasperated look, he said, "I don't try to reason through what I overhear, Kaz. All I know is that Gary told Ken to shape up or else."

"Or else, what? Was he threatening to fire him?"

"Not as far as I could tell. It sounded more like a disagreement about how they were handling something."

"Was Ken upset? Or nervous?"

Steve paused and thought about it. "It's kind of hard to tell, with him being so laid back most of the time. But yeah, he did seem to be kind of edgy."

"Who was standing next to them at the bar?"

His face closed up. "I already answered these questions for the authorities. You're wasting your time, to say nothing of sticking your nose in where it doesn't belong."

"Who was standing there, Steve?"

"Karl Svensen, okay? Now either order something from the kitchen, or get the hell out of here and let me get back to what I was doing."

So she'd been right about Karl. "Was he part of the argument?" she asked.

"I didn't notice."

She was certain he had, but wasn't going to tell her. "Why was Gary so angry with you that night?"

"I wouldn't have a clue." Her disbelief must have shown, because he shrugged. "It was just some crackpot remark your brother made because he was pissed. I'm sure he resented my interference."

He was lying, but for the life of her, she couldn't figure out why. She stood up. "If you think of anything else, please call me, okay?"

He picked up the pile of receipts and put a rubber band around it, then met her gaze, his expression remote. "There's nothing else to say."

"Well, thanks anyway."

He shook his head. "Don't thank me, Kaz. Just mind your own business."

"Why does everyone keep saying that to me?" she wondered out loud.

"Because there are things going on around here that you don't need to know about."

She stared at him, experiencing the same sense of unreality as she'd had the day before when she'd talked to Chuck. Steve looked worried, maybe even afraid. But whatever it was that was bothering him, she had no way of knowing—he'd said all he was going to. She blew out a breath. "I'm beginning to think

205

I have no clue what is going on in my own home town."

"You don't."

"I live and work here, too, dammit," she said, sick of the obfuscations.

"Not for the last ten years."

Two blocks away in Uniontown Park, Lucy and Ivar stood in the driving rain in their police-issue slickers, hunched over the body of a small-time local drug dealer. Someone had stabbed him multiple times in the chest, then dumped him in the back of one of the abandoned warehouses on the water's edge. Lucy pulled her collar up, swearing under her breath at the foul weather. Hell of a way to start off the work day. First Gary, now this.

Rigor had set in, so the guy had probably been killed sometime the night before. "Two murders in as many days," she said aloud. "And we're supposed to believe they aren't related? I don't think so." She looked at Ivar. "Just what the hell is going on in our town?"

His expression pensive, Ivar watched Greg Ewald work the body. "Don't like the feel of this."

"Now there's an understatement."

"You think Gary could've had a hand in this? Or Chuck?"

Lucy pressed her lips together. That was *exactly* what she was worried about—that Gary and Chuck were on some kind of vigilante mission. Gary hadn't come right out and said anything that would lead her to believe that. But she knew, somehow, that that was what he was up to. And where he went, Chuck went. Still, she couldn't believe Gary would commit murder, even to rid the town of a drug dealer. And it didn't make sense—unless what had happened to Ken was somehow tied into the drug scene. It wasn't as if Gary had lost it and was going around town killing off any scumbag who happened to cross his path.

She realized Ivar was looking at her oddly— probably because he'd never seen her silent for that long. "Nah. If Chuck had done it, he would've walked up behind the guy and slit his throat. This isn't Gary's style, either." Ivar gave her an odd look, but she shrugged.

She turned as Clint Jackson approached, dragging with him a thin, nervous man. "Well, well. Look who we've got, Ivar. Briggs, ole buddy. Just why am I not surprised that you're hanging around?"

The drug addict shifted nervously in his soiled, torn sneakers, his dilated eyes darting around, landing anywhere but on the body. He seemed oblivious to the fact that he was soaked to the skin and shivering. "I didn't do nothing, I swear."

"Of course you didn't," Lucy soothed. She noted the spittle in the corner of his mouth, the unhealthy pallor, the physical twitches. He hadn't gotten his usual fix, and he was going into withdrawal. Interesting. "So maybe I can help you out a little, Sammy, in return for a little information. Did you see what went down here?"

"I ain't talkin'. It wouldn't be healthy."

Lucy snorted. "Since when do you care about anything but your next fix?"

Sammy threw up two filthy hands, his eyes wild. "Hey, this one's too hot. I tell you what's goin' down, and no one's gonna sell to me ever again."

Even more interesting. She leaned closer, unfortunately close enough that she could smell how long it had been since he'd had a bath. The rain wasn't even making a dent in the state of his personal hygiene, and if that odor transferred to her sweater, she'd make it her personal goal to put him away for a long, long time. "So maybe we'll get a little something out of the evidence lockup, Sammy, to keep you going while we have our little chat."

The addict's eyes lit up. "Really? You can do that?"

"Sure," Lucy said easily. She ignored Ivar's frown.

But Sammy caught it, and his expression turned angry. "You're lying to me." He spat at her feet. "Cops. You think you're above the law, that you can do anything, get away with anything."

She shot a glare at Ivar for giving her away, then patted Sammy down, removing a small baggie of grass from his inside pocket. "Look what we have here."

"Hey! That's personal use only."

"Yeah, but Sammy, you've already got two convictions on record. This little ole bit of weed is going to send you up the river for the rest of your life."

"What! No way, man. You can't do that. I'll get me a lawyer."

"It's called three strikes, Sammy. Maybe you've heard of it?"

"You *bitch!*"

Lucy turned and nodded to Jackson. "Put him in lockup for now. I'll deal with him later."

As Jackson dragged him away, he yelled, "I ain't telling you nothin', you hear?"

After he was out of hearing distance, she turned to Ivar. "That went well."

Ivar shrugged. "Probably won't tell you anything for

a couple more hours. Needs to start really hurting first."

"He saw what went down, what d'you want to bet?" Lucy frowned. "But he looked more scared about talking to us than he was about being sent up for life."

"Yeah. Wonder why."

Troubled, she turned back to Ewald. "So, preliminary cause of death?"

The medical examiner stood and stripped off his latex gloves. "Unofficially, someone stabbed the life out of him. And enjoyed it."

She shivered, then covered up her reaction before Ivar noticed it. "Well, hell."

Kaz had always loved the mooring basin, having spent most of her childhood in or around it. In some ways, the maze of docks with their neatly moored fishing boats felt more like home than the bungalow in town did. But what she'd missed most of all, when she was down in California, were the smells—the unique, pungent blend of stagnant water, fish, and diesel, contrasted by the clean, crisp smell of the wind as it blew off the ocean. Cities had their own intriguing aromas—the corner deli, the bakery down the block. If she moved away from San Francisco, she would always miss them. But up here, the air carried the scents of her past, providing her with a strong reminder of who she was.

She sat in the Jeep on the wharf, staring at the tableaux below her while rain drummed on the canvas roof. Bjorn was on his boat, repairing a net under a hastily rigged tarp that probably wasn't keeping much of the rain out. The rest of the marina looked deserted—not many people wanted to work in a storm. She told herself to quit woolgathering and hopped out of the Jeep, locking it.

As she walked down the dock, Bjorn motioned to her to join him under the tarp. She climbed on board and sat down on the stern bench, shoving aside a block and tackle. "I appreciate that you told me what you did yesterday, Bjorn."

He shook his head. "I never said anything."

"I had a visitor last night."

His head came up sharply. "You okay?"

"Yeah. He wasn't after me; he was searching for something." She watched Bjorn's face immediately close up. "And I'm betting you know what he wanted."

"If I did, I'd tell the cops."

"Would you?"

He shrugged. "Maybe, maybe not, okay? I've got a family to think about."

He was right, and she felt like pond scum for pressing him. "I'm sorry. I'll go." When she stood, he looked relieved. She couldn't stop herself from asking one more question. "Gary paid me a visit, too. He thinks I'm safer out on the water than in town. Is that what you think?"

Bjorn hesitated, then nodded. "Maybe. Gary okay?"

"He's strung pretty tight. I'm worried about him."

Bjorn glanced around the marina before speaking. "No matter what Karl said yesterday, Gary's got friends around here."

"That's good to hear," she admitted. "But there's a warrant out for his arrest, and unless you guys start telling me or the cops what you know, he's still in danger."

"And if we *do* talk, we'll end up like Ken."

She hesitated. "Bjorn, is this about drugs?"

He shook his head. "No more."

She gave up and turned to leave. "If this lets up, I'll be going out tomorrow, taking Michael Chapman with me." She tried to dispel the tension in the air. "The guy'll probably puke all over my running shoes when he sees the river bar."

As she'd hoped, Bjorn chuckled. Then his expression turned serious. "Most of us don't trust Chapman, Kaz. And the fact that you're letting him on the *Kasmira B* won't help matters for you."

"I'll have to take that chance." She jumped back onto the dock. "Safe passage tomorrow."

"You too, Kaz. You too."

She was ten yards away when she heard him call her name. She turned.

"Better not come down here again, Kaz, unless it's to take the boat out."

She nodded to indicate she'd heard his warning, then continued up the ramp. Standing next to the Jeep, she let the rain wash over her, so tired she had to hold herself upright with a hand against the hood.

Clint Jackson was parked a block away, watching her. He was probably hoping she'd lead him to Gary. She almost laughed out loud. Fat chance of that.

Ignoring him, she opened the door of the Jeep and climbed in, then put her arms on the wheel and rested her forehead against them. Karl Svensen was standing on the deck of Bjorn's boat, his face set, his gestures angry as he talked. He must've been on his boat, watching while she talked to Bjorn. She closed her eyes, unable to care at the moment.

She had no idea what, if anything, she'd uncovered that could help Gary, and no clue where to go next. Never in all her life had she felt so alone. It was as if people were going out of their way to make her feel like an outsider. She straightened. Well, it wouldn't work. After allowing herself this little two-minute pity party, she'd figure out what to do next. She'd be damned if she'd let Gary down.

The passenger-side door abruptly opened and Michael Chapman slide inside. "Amateur sleuthing not going as well as you'd like?"

She turned her head. Raindrops glistened on his dark hair and black Gore-Tex jacket. His eyes gleamed, and his expression was sardonic, but he still managed to look sexy as hell. She closed her eyes, bracing herself against the jolt of heat she experienced whenever he was near. "What are you, some kind of bad penny?"

"I was driving by when I saw you walk up from the dock. I see you didn't take my advice about staying home." His tone turned gentle. "You know, civilians always get hammered when they get in the way."

Was that a glimmer of sympathy she saw in his eyes? Or pity? She stiffened her spine and sent him the coolest look she could manage. "Are you bothering me for a reason?"

He regarded her with a slight smile, as if he were well aware of the double meaning behind her words. The interior of the jeep was suddenly too warm, the cramped space far too intimate. She edged around in her seat, propping her shoulders in the corner, so that she could face him. The last thing she needed was a repeat of last night's idiocy, especially since she now knew that he wasn't being entirely forthcoming with her about the investigation.

"Why don't you think about us working together on this?" he suggested, surprising her. "I could use your insight into the community."

She raised an eyebrow. "And you'll keep me informed as to the progress *you're* making, right?"

"As much as possible, I will."

She shook her head. "If I can't expect Lucy to do that for me, why would I expect you to?"

"Maybe because, at some point, you have to trust someone," he pointed out. "Otherwise, you're on your own. I could be wrong, but I don't see any evidence that your friends are rallying around you, eager to help."

"That's unfair," she protested. "Lucy and Ivar have jobs to do."

"And the fishermen? I don't see them acting too supportive."

"They have their own worries. Besides, it's possible—" She stopped, realizing what she'd been about to say.

"—that they're helping by hiding your brother," he finished for her.

She didn't respond.

He shook his head, reached out, ran a thumb gently down her cheek. "I don't want you to get hurt," he said softly.

Her eyes locked with his, and she saw the truth there. He cared about her, cared about her safety. She started to lean toward him, then straightened when she realized what she was doing. She drew a steadying breath. "I'm okay," she assured him. "The phone calls have stopped, and I seem to have an official escort." She gestured at the police cruiser.

Michael glanced in Jackson's direction and frowned. For some reason she couldn't fathom, he didn't seem to be reassured. He shook his head, rubbing his thumb across her lower lip in a brief caress, as was becoming his habit. "Think about letting me help. Please." He pulled back and opened the door to get out. "I'll drop off Zeke this evening, and you can give me your answer then."

She watched him walk down the ramp to talk to the fishermen, her lip tingling where he'd touched it, and she shivered. Maybe he was right about the investigation. And maybe, just maybe she really wanted to believe him, to lean on him, if only for a few minutes. But she couldn't take the chance of trusting him.

For Gary's sake, she had to handle things by herself. Which would be easier if she got some sleep. After three visitors in one night, following on the heels of the fire the night before, she was running on empty. She needed a little refueling, maybe a short nap. It wasn't like her to feel sorry for herself. Maybe inhaling all that smoke on the boat had temporarily zapped her drive.

She'd go home, soak in a hot bath. Let her mind wander for a half hour. Maybe something would occur to her, some idea of what to do next.

Then again, maybe she should just go soak her head.

CHAPTER SIXTEEN

When Kaz came downstairs at dawn the next morning, Michael was standing in her kitchen, watching coffee drip, and tending an omelet. He'd dropped by late the night before, staying long enough to leave Zeke and bump up her blood pressure, even though he hadn't come within ten feet of her. He was the last person she'd seen before falling asleep, and now he was the first person she was seeing after awakening. That didn't feel as awkward as it should have—it felt . . . good. Right.

This morning he wore snug-fitting jeans and another sweater that did illegal things to the width of his shoulders. He looked well-rested—an effect she had yet to achieve, what with her nightmares and her doggy-breath bed companion. She almost snarled.

He glanced at her as he expertly moved the two halves of the omelet onto plates. "Morning."

She grabbed a mug. "Don't you have a kitchen of your own?"

"Still packed."

"How'd you get in?"

"Zeke let me in." She narrowed her eyes at him, and he cocked his head toward the kitchen door. "It was unlocked." He pointed the spatula at her. "That was careless."

"But I locked it," she said, startled. "I checked all the doors and windows before I went to bed. Zeke got restless around midnight and started pacing. But after a few minutes, he settled down. I'm sure no one was in the house or he would've gone crazy."

"Maybe he scared someone off before they got inside. Who has keys to this place?"

"Lucy and Gary, that's it." She prayed that he wouldn't ask the next obvious question—whether Gary had been there. She didn't know if he'd come back, and she didn't want to lie to Michael any more than she was forced to. Every time she did, she felt like she was betraying him. Which was a problem, a big problem. Because in order to protect Gary, she might not have any other choice.

"You keep a spare key hidden outside?" Michael asked.

"No."

"Would Lucy come in and not tell you?"

She shook her head.

"What about what's-his-name—Chuck?"

An interesting question. Had Chuck come back last night to keep watch? She shivered, and then realized Michael was waiting for her to respond. "Maybe, I don't know. He's been hanging around."

Michael's expression turned grim. "You didn't tell me that."

She shrugged. "When I confronted him, he said he was looking out for me."

Michael seemed dissatisfied with her answer, but he didn't press her. He brought the plates over to the table, sat down, and nodded at hers. "Eat."

She sampled the omelet and was pleasantly surprised. Okay, so he could cook. She didn't have much luck with omelets, but this one was cooked to perfection, lightly browned on the outside and filled with a fragrant mixture of grilled vegetables and some kind of creamy, tangy cheese. She dug in.

He sipped his coffee, seemingly content to watch her. "Where's Zeke?"

"In my bed," she answered between mouthfuls of food. She shot him a dark look. "Your dog has as much nerve as you do."

He looked amused.

"Hey," she said, pointing her fork at him. "I didn't ask you or your dog to invade my life like this. And I didn't ask you to fix me breakfast, or to—to—"

"Show you what you might've been missing all these years?" His smile bordered on cocky. At her snort, he shrugged. "Have you forgotten? I'm going out with you this morning."

She *had* forgotten. Just what she needed—hours of nerve-racking work in close quarters with a man who had her on pins and needles every time he came within twenty feet of her.

"What about Zeke? You can't bring him with you."

"The guys at the station agreed to babysit him. As soon as we drop him off, we're good to go."

Great. It was going to be a long day.

* * *

Thirty minutes later, they had the crab pots loaded on board the *Kasmira B*, the diesel engines warmed up, and the routine check completed. Kaz put the trawler in reverse and backed away from the dock, while Michael cast off the lines and pulled in the rubber bumpers that protected the trawler from banging against the dock when she was moored. Kaz steered toward the fuel pumps and pulled alongside.

While the computerized pump was verifying her credit card, a new thought occurred to her. If she were looking for the perfect place to hide something, she knew right where she'd put it. And Gary and she thought uncannily alike—at least, they always had in the past.

She handed the fuel nozzle to Michael and leapt onto the dock. "I'll be back in five. Once the tanks are topped off, go below and change. Use Gary's long johns, the cotton and wool socks, the float coat, and the fur-lined gloves."

Climbing the ramp up to the wharf, she jogged along the east side of it back toward land. Off to her left was the warehouse that contained all the cold storage units used by the fishermen. She and Gary kept their own unit, storing frozen halibut and tuna until they could negotiate a favorable price.

She fished the key out of her front jeans pocket, unlocked the padlock on the steel door, then cranked the handle. After checking to make sure the soles of her shoes were dry so that she wouldn't stick to the icy floor, she stepped inside. The cooler was essentially a large freezer with steel walls and a concrete floor, and it was kept precisely at zero degrees Fahrenheit, the optimum temperature for storing frozen fish. Overhead, the compressor hummed loudly, doing its job. On her right, a stack of large tuna lay in a slatted, wooden tray, cleaned and ready for market.

She closed her eyes. *Please, God, let me be wrong.* Because if she wasn't, then she would have to admit that Gary was deeply involved in what was going on.

Despite the unnatural chill inside the cooler, she rubbed sweaty palms against her jeans, then forced herself to walk over to the frozen fish. Flipping the top one over, she used both hands to pry the frozen flesh of its belly apart. Inside, she found what she'd been hoping she wouldn't—what someone was so frantically looking for. Carefully wrapped packets of hundred-dollar bills. Lots of packets.

With shaking hands, she threw that fish aside, then checked the others, several dozen tuna in all. They were all stuffed with packets of money.

She repacked the last tuna and backed away, one hand pressed over her mouth. *Oh God oh God oh God.* She was staring at what had to be several hundred thousand dollars. Gary had known about the money the night before last—had he had it all along and not told her? Was he really tracking down the killer, or was he in on it?

"Everything all right?"

She whirled around.

Michael was standing in the doorway, watching her.

She swallowed, nodded, and walked toward him. "I thought Gary might've left some extra pots in here, that's all. Let's go. We're going to miss the tide."

He leaned against the doorway, hands in his pockets, and studied her with that pale, knowledgeable gaze of his, his expression as cool as the dawn air. She held her breath.

Then he shrugged, smiling without humor. Had she imagined the flash of disappointment in his eyes? "Whatever you say, boss."

CHAPTER SEVENTEEN

She was lying.

Michael stood in the galley, warming his hands on the oil stove and staring out a portal on the starboard side of the boat. He was at eye-level with the surface of the Columbia, which was an odd perspective. The water, which looked smoother from a distance, bounced and lapped past the glass, in concert with the dipping and rocking of the boat. Now and again, a cormorant would float by, startled into flight by Michael's close proximity. In the distance, barely visible through the top half of the small window, he could see forested hills and sand-colored cliffs.

They'd passed through banks of fog, short but fierce rain squalls, and the occasional bit of sleet. But he wasn't focused on the weather they'd be battling to lift the pots. He was thinking about Kaz and what could have made her face drain of all color in that storage unit.

Just when was the woman going to start trusting him? He'd done everything he could, short of compromising the investigation, to show her that he was trustworthy.

Something had rattled her. But whatever it was, she wasn't talking. She'd shut herself inside the wheelhouse and hadn't said a word to him since they'd headed out.

He understood he was the newcomer, but dammit, he'd hoped that she was feeling at least some of what he was. They had something special—he *wasn't* imagining it. Something that could last long after all this was behind them.

He pulled himself up short. What the *hell* was he thinking? He'd kissed the woman *twice* and he was already thinking about long-term? Even more to the point, he couldn't believe he was thinking long-term about a woman who was lying to him. He had rules about the people he let get close to him. He didn't tolerate subterfuge, and Kaz was a walking hidden agenda.

Okay, to be honest, he had to ask himself whether, if he were in her position, he would confide in the investigator on the case. He shook his head. It was a tough call. She had to know that as fire chief, he had the authority to arrest her brother. So he probably needed to cut her some slack. But it stung that she didn't trust him.

The arson case felt hinky, the murder wasn't making sense, and the town fairly oozed with secrets, of something really ugly lying just beneath the surface. Add to that, he had a steadily growing, very bad feeling that she was in danger. What if she got hurt because he couldn't solve the case fast enough? What if she were killed?

To hell with it. Tossing the rest of his cooling coffee into the small galley sink, he filled a mug for her from the thermos and headed upstairs to the wheelhouse to confront her. She had her back to him, consulting the navigational charts that covered the walls. The radio chattered intermittently but was still mostly quiet—they were one of the first boats out.

She jumped a little when he reached around in front of her, the coffee mug in his hand. When she glanced his way, he noted that she was still pale, and that there were deep lines of strain bracketing her mouth.

"Thanks," she said, taking the coffee from him but not meeting his gaze.

He smiled grimly. He had to be six kinds of fool to take this woman on. "Time's up," he said. "Tell me what's got you so spooked."

She stiffened, then shrugged casually. "That's funny, that's exactly what I asked the fishermen yesterday," she said lightly. "Didn't do me any good, either."

"Yeah, but if you don't level with me, I'll toss your body overboard to feed the sharks."

"Nothing much in these waters except a few great whites. I'll take my chances."

He leaned a shoulder against the doorjamb. "I am not amused." When he reached out to touch her shoulder, it was rigid. "Trust me," he said, his voice low.

She turned and searched his face as if she were looking for some kind of reassurance. He waited. Then she lifted a hand in a what-the-hell gesture and let out a strained laugh. "I think I've got the what-everyone's-looking-for angle figured out."

As she described what she'd found, Michael felt cold dread settle deep inside him. "That's the kind of money that motivates people to commit murder."

"Yeah."

"Who has keys to the cold storage unit?"

"The guy who owns the warehouse, Gary, and me," she said, her reluctance to answer clear.

"Any chance the owner is dirty?"

She frowned. "It's possible, I suppose. But it doesn't make much sense, does it? Why use someone's locker and risk discovery?"

Michael nodded, waiting while she checked their bearings and adjusted the heading slightly. "You realize this means that your brother is in this right up to his neck."

She stared at the distant horizon, her lips pressed together. "Yes," she said finally. "Though we probably disagree as to his motive. I've been thinking about it, and I think that Gary found out whatever Ken was into and was trying to extricate him. And maybe that meant helping him hide the money."

The idea had some merit. Michael wondered again if Gary was being framed. But there would be no logic to whoever was looking for the money putting it in the locker to frame Gary. No. Gary had put it there—that fact was inescapable. "Unless you can prove that Gary wasn't the one who murdered Lundquist and set the fire, knowing what he's up to doesn't help you much."

"I *know* that," Kaz said, sounding frustrated.

The trawler was starting to rock more as they neared the breakers, and Michael planted his feet more firmly to better ride out the pitching. "What else haven't you told me?"

"Nothing important," she said, too quickly.

"Right," he said, letting sarcasm bleed through. He ran a hand through his hair, still angry.

"Look, let's listen to the radio while we lift the pots and take it from there, okay?" Her expression was pleading.

"When we get back to port," he told her, his patience at an end, "you're handing the money over to your pal Lucy. And you don't make a move without me—I just became your round-the-clock shadow." She started to protest, and he reached out with both hands, yanking her around to face him. "*No.* You don't get a choice on this one. I'm not letting another person I care about die on my watch. Got that?"

"Don't confuse me with your fiancée," she shot back. "I don't need your protection."

He froze. He'd given away more than he'd intended, and she'd tossed it right back in his face. "I don't care what you want," he said, his voice going cold, his hands gripping harder. "If I have to, I'll have Sykes confine you. I'm sure he'd be happy to oblige."

Her face grew even more pale. "You wouldn't."

"Unless you cooperate, you're about to see exactly what I *will* do."

Her lips trembled, her eyes filling. He felt like a slug, even while he was still furious with her. He wasn't in the habit of making women cry.

She jerked out of his grip, turning her back to him. "We're about ten minutes away from the bar. You should get below."

"I'm staying right here."

She turned back, and their gazes clashed. She was the first to look away. Was that remorse he was seeing on her face? Hell, he was probably just fooling himself.

"Then shut the door," she said. "I don't want to be standing in a foot of water while I navigate."

* * *

Fifteen minutes later, the coffee Michael had ingested was threatening to make the rest of his day miserable. Huge waves were coming at the trawler from all directions, and remaining on his feet was impossible unless he braced himself against the wall and hung onto the equipment console. In all his summers of crabbing back East, he'd never been this close to being seasick.

Kaz stood, feet braced with both hands on the wheel, for all outward appearances cool and calm in the face of what was sheer insanity. But her eyes moved continually—from landmarks, when they were visible, to the navigational maps, and then to her equipment.

He wasn't just impressed, he was in awe. His respect for her skills had increased tenfold in just the last five minutes. He knew the Columbia River bar was the most treacherous stretch of water in the Lower Forty-eight, but until he'd experienced it, he'd had no clue. Waves battered them relentlessly, crashing over the trawler in a crazy jigsaw pattern and tossing the boat about like a toy. A person had to be crazy as a loon to tackle this every day. No wonder she wasn't worried about the occasional intruder in her home—the guy would have to be armed with an Uzi to make her even break out in a sweat.

As they climbed a vertical mountain of water out of the next trough that had him pondering the wisdom of his lapsed Catholicism, he glanced to the stern. In between the massive walls of water, he caught sight of a line of trawlers, all following them. That line was a hell of a show of confidence. The other fishermen might not be willing to admit they wanted her out here, but the fact that they were following her lead through the Graveyard of the Pacific made its own statement.

"You do this every day," he said, breaking the tense silence that still remained between them.

"Most days, yeah." Her response was absentminded. "This is pretty calm today."

He nearly laughed out loud. The swells were over ten feet. And how long would it take the trawler to break apart if she made a mistake? No more than a few minutes, he was certain. He couldn't even think about what it must have been like for her that night fifteen years ago. He fought down the urge to demand that she turn around and take them back to port where she'd be safe—to demand that she never do this again. To tell her that he couldn't handle it if she went out and never came back. "You need counseling," was all he said.

She shot a quick smile at him. "Nah. I had counseling, right after the shipwreck. It didn't stick."

He shook his head.

She gestured at the horizon with one hand. "This is all part of a tradition—going back, for most of us, at least three generations. I may have left this life behind, and I may have had some bad experiences out here, but I'm discovering that it's still a part of who I am."

He couldn't deny what she was saying—his brothers back East felt the same way. They faced harsh conditions, but nothing like this. "Why not dock somewhere down the coast?"

"All the good mooring basins have river bars." She paused to listen to the radio for a minute, then continued. "Other than the fish processing in Coos Bay, the buyers are all right here in Astoria. The river bar is an inconvenience"—she rolled her eyes at the understatement—"but it's a fact of life."

"And death."

"Yeah." She pushed the trawler up and over the crest of another wave. "Gary has always said that you have to be lucky, each and every day you're out here. Because if you aren't, all the skill in the world won't make any difference."

She fell silent, her face unaccountably sad for a moment, then she seemed to shake off her thoughts. He wondered what she'd been thinking about—maybe her parents, or friends she'd lost out here. Maybe both.

Michael watched her navigate another monstrous swell, thinking about the kind of courage it took to face the waters that had taken away two family members. His family had been lucky—they hadn't lost anyone in more than fifty years. But he'd seen the effects of such tragedies on the other fishing families back East. He'd always been in awe of their acceptance of the hardships they put up with, year after year.

And although the woman standing before him was, in many ways, like his brothers' wives, she was also very different. She was brave, to the point of taking insane risks. Loyal to those she cared about. But what kind of person abandoned—even for a few months—a lucrative consulting practice in plush, comfortable surroundings, for the freezing, miserable dangers of the Columbia? The kind of person who valued her family over what money could buy, he realized.

He'd been blind, not really understanding how desperate she must be to clear her brother. And he'd been a fool to think he could ever have a casual relationship with her. It would be an insult to everything she held dear—for that matter, everything that he valued, as well. And yet, short-term was all he could let himself have—he'd decided that long ago. The honorable thing for him to do would be to walk away, to not let what was between them go any further than it already had. Not unless he was ready to change his mind about what he wanted.

Suddenly the waves lessened in intensity, and the rough water changed texture. They'd left the river bar behind and entered the Pacific. The set of Kaz's shoulders visibly relaxed, and she turned to him with a slight smile that was perhaps a peace offering. "We've got about forty-five minutes 'til we reach the pots. Let's use the time to get warm—it'll be our last chance for a while."

He wanted to touch her, to rub those proud shoulders and soothe the rest of the tension out of them, but he held back. Instead, he said, "I'll bring you some more coffee—I'm going to wait a bit."

"While you're down there, throw on hip boots and a sou'wester, along with rubber gloves. You don't want your hands icing up when we start lifting the pots."

They traveled south, hugging the coast, until they came to a string of buoys whose colors matched the stripes painted on the sides of the *Kasmira B*—black and green. Fishermen had their own colors to distinguish their string of crab pots from others laid in the same area.

The weather, Kaz noted, was getting nastier. The wind had picked up, and there was considerably more sleet and snow mixed in with the rain. She cut the engines down to a low rumble as they came alongside the first buoy. Then she stepped out on the deck, dressed in hip boots, pulling on her gloves.

Michael was already kneeling alongside the railing.

He glanced up at her. "I'll lift and rebait—you steer the trawler."

She shook her head, moving the hydraulic block that they would use to haul the pots out of the water into position. "It would be better if we had a second crewman, but you're stuck with me. It'll go faster if I help."

They worked in companionable silence for the first twenty minutes or so—she was surprised at just how companionable. Michael had slipped easily into the rhythm of the work—lifting the pot while she chopped the frozen bait with a cleaver, working with her to throw back the females and undersized males, then baiting and dropping the pot back into the water, only to repeat the process with the next one down the line. Every so often, she stopped to readjust their position along the lines, then came back out on deck to help.

The catch was looking good, thank God. The business needed the money—this was only their second "lift" of the season. If the catch stayed this steady, it might cover some of the money that had already gone out the door. She'd worried when the pots were mostly empty a few days ago, and she'd begun to wonder whether she'd have to move her pots out slightly deeper. They were at twelve fathoms now—a good depth in most years.

She glanced sideways at Michael. He was working steadily and not saying much, evidently content with the screech of the gulls, the lap of the water against the hull, and the sound of the wind. They were both icing up from the freezing spray and sleet, though, and would need to take a break soon.

He was good. Almost as good as Bjorn's son. And they were progressing many times faster than she could on her own. It was almost as if Michael could anticipate her next move. She tried not to dwell on it, tried not to think about how nice it would be to have him on board on a regular basis.

She'd never felt this kind of easy companionship with Phil, not in the three years they'd been together. She'd always had to struggle, to concentrate on making the relationship work. With Michael, everything felt natural. Maybe Lucy was right when she'd claimed Phil hadn't been the right guy. Maybe the right guy was standing beside her now. It was a scary thought, and one that she wasn't willing to explore in her current circumstances.

But it was becoming harder and harder to lie to Michael, even through omission. She hadn't told him about Gary's visit night before last, and that wasn't sitting well with her. She didn't really think he'd use the information to launch a manhunt for Gary—she hadn't thought that for a while now. The truth was, she didn't have it in her anymore to keep Michael in the dark. He'd been right when he'd told her that she'd have to trust someone. And her gut was telling her he was the one she should place her trust in. She came to a decision. Once they were back in port, she'd sit down and level with him.

She stopped chopping bait to listen to the chatter on the radio for a minute. The fishermen had been talking continuously for the last half hour, joking with each other, reporting fake locations meant to confuse the larger, commercial trawlers who might horn in on their catch, and generally keeping each other company. She recognized almost all of the voices— Svensen's, Bjorn's, those of Jacobsen's crew, and others. Svensen was nattering on about something having to do with too many dogfish in his net when she stopped and stared at the radio.

Michael straightened from throwing crabs over the side. "What?"

She listened for another few moments and then shook her head, perplexed. "Nothing, I guess. It's just that Svensen gave out a location that wouldn't fool very many people—it's too close in to shore. I thought he was smarter than that."

"Maybe not. How well do you know him?"

She shrugged. "We grew up together, but I'm not all that fond of his type."

"Type?"

"The kind of fisherman who only gets into the business for the money," she explained. "He fell into an inheritance, bought up several trawlers from folks who'd tried their hand at fishing and had failed, and put a lot of crews behind hauling big catches, fast. Make the money and get out—that's his attitude. Guys like him don't last through the lean years, because they fail to meet their expected profit margin and there's no love of the work to see them through. From what I hear, no one expected him to make it this long."

"What about the other guy you were talking to earlier?"

"Bjorn?" She grabbed another handful of frozen bait and brought the cleaver down hard. "He's okay, third generation, like us. He's got a large family—several of his teenage sons are already crewing for him. One of them helps Gary out from time to time."

"Kaz."

The change in the tone of his voice alerted her and she turned around. She saw the broken line he was holding up. "Sonofabitch." She stabbed the cleaver into a hunk of bait and dropped down to look over the side, then along the line of buoys as they stretched out into the distance. She stood and moved into the wheelhouse to run the trawler up to the next buoy. "Check it out."

Michael leaned over the side and snagged the buoy. He connected the line to the hydraulic block and hauled up the first pot. On the other end of the pot, the line had been cut, just like the one before.

Her lips trembled. "Let's check the others."

For the next hour, they ran the rest of the first half of her lines. Each buoy had one pot attached, then the line was cut. All in all, she estimated that they'd lost well over half the pots, maybe three-quarters. It was a devastating financial blow, not so much the pots but what had been in them. Unless Gary relented and let her invest some of her money in the business, it could go under.

Someone had done this, and made it look good enough so that no one would notice. That took time and determination. She returned to the wheelhouse and unhooked the handset for the radio. "This is the *Kasmira B*, over."

"*Kasmira B*, nice to hear from you." Bjorn's voice boomed across the airwaves.

"We've got a problem here. You guys see anyone around my lines the last couple of days?"

"State your situation."

"Lines cut, pots not retrievable." She waited. Michael came to lean against the door, pulling off his rubber gloves and rubbing the ice from his coat.

The radio remained silent.

She clicked to retransmit. "I repeat, lines cut, pots

not retrievable. I'd appreciate a report of who y'all have seen over here lately."

Silence.

Her gaze met Michael's. His expression was hard. She swore and tossed the handset onto the console.

"How bad is it?" he asked.

"Bad enough." She rubbed the back of her neck. "Let's take a break and then see what else we can salvage."

She headed down to the galley, and Michael followed. While she was pouring coffee, he came up behind her and put his hands on her shoulders. She tensed, not sure she could stand the sympathy without breaking down.

He overrode her resistance, pulling her back against him and wrapping his arms around her. "This will all be over soon, and these guys will come around." He placed his chin on top of her head. "Maybe they didn't want to talk because I was on board."

"Maybe." But she didn't think so. She sniffled once, appalled at how close she was to tears. For something of so little consequence compared to everything else she'd faced in the last week, the cut lines were, for some reason, the last straw. But she knew it wasn't the lost pots, not really. It was the silence on the radio that had gotten to her.

Michael tightened his arms for a moment, then let her loose. He moved around her, got sandwiches out of a Styrofoam cooler, unwrapped them, and handed one to her. "Eat."

She stared at the sandwich, which looked totally unappetizing. "Do you always push food as a panacea?"

"I can think of other remedies, but they're harder to implement when swathed in four layers of foulweather gear."

That got a small laugh out of her. "Valid point." She took the sandwich.

They ate in silence for a few minutes, warming themselves next to the oil stove. The ice on their clothing melted, making a soggy mess of the carpet.

"So what now?" Michael asked.

"We pull what we can, then head for port. I'll see if it's possible to get a diver out here, but with these currents, it's probably a lost cause. Someone knew what he was doing."

"Someone who knew your colors, and who knew what to do to inflict maximum damage. Someone in the fishing fleet."

"Yeah." She tossed down the rest of her sandwich, no longer able to swallow. She simply couldn't fathom it. Someone not only wanted to frame Gary, but to put them both permanently out of business. That took a lot of hate. Or a lot of desperation.

She'd faced hostile corporate boards, and over the years, she knew she'd made some enemies. They'd undercut her and take her next client maybe, or try to block the merger she was working on. Tit for tat. But that was nothing like this.

This felt personal.

It took them five hours to run the rest of the lines. She'd lost almost all of the pots. Tired and discouraged, she turned the *Kasmira B* in the direction of port. The ride back over the bar was a silent one, but Michael never left her side. She was grateful for that, more than she should have been. His silent support felt better than anything she'd experienced in days. And it felt right that he was there beside her, regardless of what Bjorn and the others thought.

They docked the *Kasmira B* well after dark, then went straight to the storage unit to retrieve the money and take it to Lucy.

It was gone.

Under the mist was a black cloud,
hiding the water.

CHAPTER EIGHTEEN

When Kaz and Michael walked out of the storage unit, several police were waiting for them. Lucy's expression was grim, Ivar's sympathetic. Kaz froze, horrible images running through her mind. They'd arrested Gary, he was hurt . . .

Sykes stepped forward and handed her a folded document. "General search warrant," he told her. "Covers your cold storage unit, your boats and vehicles, and your house. We're looking for evidence related to the arson and murder of Ken Lundquist."

Releasing the breath she'd been holding, Kaz took the document, unfolding it with shaking hands. As she read, disbelief and anger filled her. The impersonal legalese brought home the gravity of Gary's situation. And hers. "You already have an arrest warrant," she said, looking up from the paperwork. "Why are you doing this?" Clint Jackson, who was standing next to Sykes, smirked at her.

"We've arrested your brother in the past and couldn't make it stick," Sykes said. "This time, I'm personally making sure the DA has all the evidence he'll need to convict."

Kaz rounded on Michael. "Did you know about this?" He hadn't made any calls on his cell phone while they were out on the water, but he could have been aware of the plan all along and not told her. God. Would she never learn? She'd trusted him, been ready to confide in him.

He reached out a hand for the document, and she shoved it at him. After skimming through it, he shook his head. "I only knew about the arrest warrant."

She wanted to believe him. But he must have suspected this would happen. Why hadn't he warned her? For that matter, why hadn't Lucy? The betrayal stung, and her eyes welled with tears.

Appalled, she turned her back on Michael, swiping her hands across her cheeks. She held out her key ring to Sykes. He took it, telling her to wait nearby. He and Clint walked into the storage building.

To put some distance between herself and the others, she walked over and sat down on the cold, wet concrete curb of the parking lot. The truth was, she couldn't say with any certainty what Michael—or Lucy and Ivar, for that matter—thought about Gary's guilt. Most of the time, they sounded like they believed he was being framed by someone, as she did. Could she really count on anyone to be as firmly in Gary's court as she was?

She couldn't shake the feeling that events were spinning out of control. If Sykes and Jackson had searched the unit even a few hours ago, they'd have found the money and been able to use it to build the case against Gary.

It made sense that Gary had moved the money—maybe after he'd seen her go into the storage unit that morning. Fear for him made her stomach cramp. If he'd moved the money while they were out, then he had to be hiding nearby, perhaps using one of the many abandoned warehouses that were strung out all along the waterfront. The crumbling old buildings were some distance from Astoria's business district—only fishermen would be close enough to see him coming and going, and they wouldn't say anything. At least, she didn't think they would. But still, he was taking insane risks, moving around in broad daylight.

Lucy came over and dropped down beside her, giving her a hug. "I tried to call you several times today—"

"We were out working the crab lines."

Lucy's expression turned wry. "So I heard, from just about everyone at the Redemption. No one was happy about your taking a newcomer out."

Kaz shrugged.

"The chief got Judge Banks on his cell phone," Lucy explained quietly. "Banks was out elk hunting and was reluctant to issue a warrant over the phone, but after Sykes told him about the blood on the tire iron matching Ken's, he didn't really have a choice."

Kaz relented a little. It was unrealistic to think that Lucy could have controlled what Sykes did. But how much should she tell Lucy? That was the question of the hour. Since the money was gone, what was the point in revealing what she'd seen? Then again, the money was tied in to all of this, somehow.

Glancing toward the storage unit to make sure that Sykes was still out of hearing range, she said, "We've got problems." She motioned the others over and brought Lucy and Ivar up to date.

"When there's that much money floating around, it's usually related to drugs," Ivar pointed out.

Lucy nodded in agreement. "Which gives us the possible connection to the murder of the drug dealer." She told Kaz and Michael about the body they'd found yesterday morning. "The second murder definitely doesn't look premeditated—more like someone who needed a fix turning violent." She got to her feet and started pacing. "We've got a local methadone treatment clinic that was burglarized late this afternoon, what looks like a supply disruption on the street bad enough to escalate to violence, and a huge amount of cash." She shot Kaz a disgusted look. "Floating around God knows where."

"What?" Kaz raised her hands. "How was I supposed to know it would disappear while I was out?" Lucy gave her a look that told her she'd already figured out that it hadn't disappeared on its own, but she didn't say anything.

"It's got to be money that would've been used to buy drugs," Ivar said. "Someone stole drug money, and the drugs it would've purchased never got to the street."

Michael spoke up. "So maybe the fishermen are running drugs. Taking money out to sea for a rendezvous, then bringing the drugs back."

"If so, it's a damn near perfect setup." Lucy blew out a breath. "The Coast Guard wouldn't stop those guys to conduct searches—their boats wouldn't be considered suspicious."

"Gary's not part of this," Kaz insisted, sounding like a broken record even to herself. "There's got to be another reason why he had all that money." She appealed to Lucy. "You *know* he wouldn't be involved, Luce."

"Actually, I agree," Lucy said. Ivar frowned at her, and she shrugged. "I think Gary's being framed, so sue me." But her expression remained troubled. "It's a damn good question, though, what he was doing with all that cash in the storage unit."

"Maybe he got it from Ken," Kaz suggested, thinking out loud. "Maybe that's why they were arguing that night in the tavern. If Ken thought someone was after him, he could've asked Gary to keep the money someplace safe.

"But if Ken were dealing drugs, why would he need anyone to safeguard the money?" Lucy shook her head. "That's cockeyed—he would've been exchanging the money for the drugs, not hiding it. And we've gone over his bank and phone records. Nada. He doesn't fit the profile."

"Profile?" Kaz looked from Lucy to Ivar.

"He has—had—a stable home life, there've been no dramatic changes in his lifestyle," Lucy explained. "Then again, Gary doesn't fit the profile either, based on our investigation into your financial records."

Kaz stared at her. "You've been looking at our *bank* records?"

"Yeah." Lucy shifted, sending her an apologetic look.

Kaz looked away. All of a sudden, she was sick to death of the whole mess. She wanted this investigation out of the way of her friendships with the people here in town she cared the most about.

A new thought occurred to her. "What if Ken weren't involved with drug running but stole the money for some reason?"

"That could work," Michael said, looking thoughtful. "He yields to temptation, then gets in trouble and goes to Gary."

"That would also explain the sudden supply disruption at the street level," Ivar mused.

"Didn't you tell me Ken had suffered more than one beating a few days prior to being killed?" Michael asked Lucy. "So he stole the money, the bad guys were onto him, and they beat him up as a warning a couple of times. When he didn't pony up, they got rid of him."

Kaz looked at both of them in shock. "Bjorn told me the fishermen thought Ken had been killed to send a message," she said, remembering.

"Yeah, I can buy that." Lucy chewed on her lip. "But that doesn't explain why they framed Gary."

"If Ken went to Gary for help and Gary created heat by asking too many questions . . ." Michael shrugged. "Framing Gary kills two birds with one stone."

"But why would Ken have been stupid enough to steal drug money?" Lucy asked. "I knew him pretty well—he never struck me as being either stupid or suicidal. Anyone with half a brain knows not to steal from drug dealers."

"According to what Gary told me, Ken had horrific medical bills for Bobby's leukemia," Kaz said. "Ken loved Bobby—he'd have done anything for him. And watching him go through chemo treatments . . ." She shuddered, unable to imagine what it must have been like to watch your own child suffer that way. "If the rendezvous with the drug supplier is happening at sea, maybe Ken thought he wouldn't get caught."

Lucy shook her head. "We checked out the medical bills. The mother-in-law is paying for them."

Julie had indicated the same to Kaz, but Kaz wasn't so sure. At the time, it had been her impression that Julie was lying. And Kaz had just gotten Ken and his family signed up for health insurance a week ago, which made the cancer a preexisting condition that wasn't covered. The bills had to have been enormous.

"Whatever the scenario," Ivar said, "Gary is in this up to his neck."

"He's trying to find out who's involved," Kaz insisted. She stopped speaking while Sykes and Jackson locked up the storage unit and walked past them toward the docks, then continued. "At least, that's what Gary told me."

Lucy groaned loudly. "And you didn't tell me this earlier?"

Kaz risked a glance at Michael. His expression was set and furious. Well, she knew how *that* felt—weren't they just the pair? And the hell of it was, she didn't want it to be that way between them. "Think about it," she said, pushing him out of her mind. "Someone else has to be involved, or I wouldn't be getting phone calls. Gary would have no reason to do that."

Lucy looked seriously unhappy. "Dammit, Kaz, you could be in real danger."

"I keep telling her that," Michael growled.

"We need more information," Lucy said. "I can start running checks on the finances of some of the fishermen—look for recent changes in lifestyle, that kind of thing. But we need hard evidence."

"A discussion with Gary right about now would be very useful, to find out what else he knows," Ivar mused.

Kaz stood up. "I'm heading home."

"No," Michael said firmly. "You'll wait right here until I get a change of clothes from my place; then we can go together."

"The cops have a surveillance team at my house, in case you've forgotten." Her voice was cool. "And Sykes and Jackson will be right behind me to search the house. I don't need you."

He strode over to her and knelt, taking both her hands in his. His grip was warm, his expression serious. "I didn't know about the search warrant, I swear," he said, keeping his voice low. "Don't do something foolish because you're upset with me."

Before she could react, Lucy grabbed Michael's arm. "Excuse us." She yanked him to his feet and walked him several feet away. "You're getting too close," Kaz heard her tell him in a low voice. "Back off."

Michael's expression turned hard. "Are you questioning my objectivity?"

"Maybe I am."

He took a step forward, and Kaz rose to intervene, then stopped at his next words. "I'm going to protect Kaz," he said, his voice tight with anger, "no matter what. If that blows my objectivity all to hell and back, then so be it. I don't really give a damn what you think." Then he turned to include Kaz. "Don't you two think it's about damn time you trusted me?"

"You're taking my *laptop?*" Kaz asked Sykes, shaking with fury. He and Jackson had arrived just after she'd gotten home. Michael was only a half hour behind, still angry that she'd refused to wait. Not that Sykes had given her any choice.

She and Sykes were standing in her living room while Jackson carried out boxes of files, printouts, and equipment—all of her records on the fishing business, as well as the records for her consulting business down in California. All of her bank statements, all of Gary's correspondence, all of her *personal* e-mails to

Phil, for God's sake. She reached for the phone. "I'm calling my attorney."

"You'll get it all back, don't worry," Sykes replied, gathering up the loose stacks of printouts that had been strewn across the coffee table. He tossed her keys back to her, his expression curiously angry.

He and Jackson had practically torn the house apart, becoming more angry as they worked and refusing to answer her when she demanded to know what they were looking for. And Clint had seemed to get an almost prurient satisfaction out of going through her personal belongings. If it were the last thing she did on this earth, she would prove they were wrong about Gary, wrong about her.

Clint paused at her front door as they were leaving. "We're going to nail Gary this time, Kaz. Count on it."

A few minutes later, she walked into the kitchen, yanking open the door to the freezer and staring at her choices for dinner without really seeing them. Maybe she was going about this all wrong. Who in the fishing community was capable of running drugs? Bjorn was one of the more successful fishermen in town. He hadn't taken the government's buyout offer, and he was still operating several boats. But she couldn't imagine that he would be tempted by anything illegal. And if he were in trouble, she would have seen some sign—maybe that he wanted to sell one of the boats. Of course, it was possible the reason he was doing so well was that he had a second, very lucrative source of income.

She shook her head, slamming the freezer door. This was getting her nowhere. Bjorn was the last person she should be suspecting. So far, he was the one who was the most supportive of her, though that wasn't really saying much. After all, what had he really told her? Certainly nothing that could be substantiated. Maybe that was his strategy—sound helpful while keeping her in the dark. Oh, for—she stomped over to the window and looked out at the dark, empty street. Were things so bad that she was wondering whether one of the nicest guys in the fleet—the father of eight children, for God's sake—was a cold-blooded murderer?

When it came right down to it, the only fisherman she could stand to accuse of drug smuggling was Karl Svensen. He *had* refused to press charges against Gary six months ago, but recently, he'd been neither helpful nor friendly. And according to Steve, he'd had some kind of run-in with Ken. She wasn't privy to Karl's finances, but they couldn't be all that great if his boats came back into port on the light side. Of course, that could be said about every fisherman in Astoria, including her.

She sighed. She was going in circles, and those circles were bringing her right back around to Ken. He was the only person who'd had obvious financial pressures. Chemo and hospital stays like Bobby's were expensive, and she'd never been under the impression that Ken's mother was all that wealthy.

On a hunch, she pulled the Portland phone book out of the kitchen junk drawer, looking up the number for the hospital where Bobby was being treated. The clock on the wall above the stove indicated that they were well into the dinner hour, but maybe hospitals kept their offices open later than other businesses.

She dialed the number. When the receptionist answered, Kaz asked for the business office and was informed that it was closed. So she asked to be transferred to the children's oncology ward.

While she waited, she rehearsed what she would say. She jumped when the head nurse answered on the second ring. "Um, yes, hi. This is Julie Lundquist, and I wanted to check on the status of our account. I think I may have paid one of the bills twice, by mistake—"

"I'm sorry," the nurse said, "but it's after hours, and the office is closed. If you could call again tomorrow morning—"

"Um, I knew that," Kaz said. "But it's kind of an emergency. See, I've overdrawn my account, and I know it's late, but I'm trying to reconcile my checkbook while Bobby gets a little sleep—he's having so much trouble sleeping right now—and I'll be getting overdraft notices that I can't afford—"

"Oh, poor thing," the nurse said, her voice instantly sympathetic. "It's so hard to watch children go through chemo."

"Yes," Kaz agreed quickly, feeling a giant twinge of guilt at her deception. "It would really help if you could pull up my records on the computer and take a peek at the last payment I sent you, you know, so I could verify the amount?"

"I'm not supposed to—"

"Please."

"Well, I don't see how it could really hurt . . ." The nurse seemed to come to a decision. "Hold on and I'll see what I can do." After tapping on the computer keys for a moment, she said, "Please verify the last four digits of your social security number for me."

Kaz froze, trying to remember Julie's number from when she'd filled out the insurance forms for the Lundquists last week. "8166." She held her breath.

"Okay, here we go. You haven't sent us anything for a long time. Your last check to us was dated four months ago."

"I see," Kaz said hesitantly, amazed that it had been so easy, and then said, "Um, I thought that I might've overpaid. Can you give me the outstanding balance?"

"Well, that's odd. You don't have a balance." The nurse tapped some more. "Oh, right! I remember now. We received that anonymous donation that wiped out your outstanding balance. Our bookkeeper told us about it. We were so excited that someone would do that for Bobby."

"Anonymous?" Kaz repeated, dumfounded. Then she realized the woman had to be talking about Ken's mother. "Oh, you must mean the payments from my mother-in-law."

"Nooo," the nurse said, sounding confused herself now. "The payment was anonymous, and there's a notation right here in the file that they called you to give you the good news about your unknown benefactor. Your mother-in-law hasn't paid anything in quite some time."

"That's right," Kaz said quickly. She started to end the call, then thought of one more question. "When was that payment made again?"

"Hon, you must really be out of it. They called you this afternoon."

Kaz recovered quickly enough to laugh nervously. "You know, I am. I've been losing so much sleep— well. Sorry to have taken up your time." She hung up before the woman decided to get suspicious, then stood in the middle of the kitchen, lost in thought.

So Ken had probably been using the drug money to pay for Bobby's treatments. It made sense. And Julie must have known about it and lied to cover it up. She'd *known* that the burglary wasn't real, that they'd been looking for the money. That explained her edginess when Kaz had been at the house, and her unwillingness to talk to the police. But there was no doubt in Kaz's mind who had made the payment earlier today.

Slowly setting the portable phone down on the counter, she acknowledged the full import of what she'd just discovered. The anonymous payment was *exactly* the type of gesture that Gary would make, especially in light of Ken's murder. Of all the information she'd unearthed to date, this was the most disturbing, because it meant that whoever had killed Ken would now be after Gary.

Kaz paced for another moment, trying to control her anxiety, and then pulled a frozen meal at random from the freezer. She popped it into the microwave. She had to get in touch with Chuck, right away. Gary's only hope of staying alive was to turn himself in. And that meant she needed to drive out to Chuck's that evening.

She opened the junk drawer to rummage for a pad and pencil. She'd leave a note for Michael. He'd be angry, but there wasn't any help for it. If Michael was with her, there was no way either Chuck or Gary—

Her only warning was a slight shifting of the air behind her. She started to turn, but he was on her too fast, a gloved hand encircling her neck. Before she could even think to struggle, his arm locked hard around her waist, and he jerked her backwards so that her feet were dangling in the air. Then he half-carried, half-dragged her, kicking and squirming, into the darkened living room.

Terror surged as he choked off her air. She clawed at the hand at her throat, unable to do more than scratch the leather of his glove. The hand tightened, and her vision turned gray.

She flung her other hand up and back, trying to claw his face, but all she got was a handful of some kind of soft wool material.

A ski mask.

He lifted her higher against his body. She tried to kick backwards, but he was holding her off balance and she couldn't get a good enough angle to inflict any real damage. Her ears started roaring.

No. Don't give in.

She threw her head backward as hard as she could, hitting him in the face. He howled, and his grip loosened. Gulping in air, she curled her body over his arm, forcing him to bend forward, then threw herself backward, causing him to lose his balance and fall to the floor.

They crashed into the coffee table, then fell sideways, landing in a heap on the area rug with him underneath. She rolled away, scrabbling to get the distance she needed to kick him—his knees, his groin, his ribs—anywhere she could hurt him. But he recovered faster than she'd anticipated. In one swift move, he was on her, slamming her against the hardwood floor with enough force to knock the air out of her lungs.

He was heavy, and strong. *But not fit.* Even as she struggled to drag air into her lungs, she dimly registered the softness on his chest and stomach.

She kneed him, but he dodged to the side, deflecting her aim. A lamp crashed to the floor beside her, shattering. She jerked her head sideways to avoid the exploding shards of glass.

Using both hands, he rammed her head hard against the floor. Pain exploded, stars swimming at the blackened edges of her vision.

Sliding both gloved hands around her throat, he squeezed, cutting off her air. She glared at him, defiant, but couldn't see anything except his eyes gleaming at her through the holes in the mask. But she could hear his harsh breathing, smell his sweat. *Sweat never lied.* He was scared. A surge of hope ran through her.

His hands loosened slightly, and she gulped in air to scream. Then they tightened again, choking off any sound she could have made. She bucked and squirmed, but he had most of his weight on her, and she couldn't move more than a few inches. Over the thumps they were making in their silent struggle, she heard the weird, disassociated pinging of the microwave as it finished cooking her dinner.

She continued to fight him, using her hands to punch and scratch him, anywhere she could reach. He never spoke, just eased the pressure on her larynx once in awhile so that she could draw in enough air to keep from passing out. Then he'd cut it off again, his teeth flashing at her in a grin. He was toying with her, and he was enjoying it. Her efforts were futile.

She subsided, exhausted and trembling.

And heard his soft, low, laugh.

"That's better," he whispered. "This was a demonstration of what will happen to you if you don't give us the money. You won't know when I'll come back, and you won't be able to stop me any more than you could this time. Nod your head if you understand."

She nodded reluctantly, straining to memorize details, anything that she could later use to identify him. He had to be someone she knew. Somehow, she was certain of that fact. A sob of frustration worked its way out of her throat.

"Good girl," he whispered. "You've got twenty-four hours to return the money. We'll be in touch."

He grabbed her hair and used it to pull her head up, then jerk it back down.

The last thing she remembered was the floor rushing up at her left eye, and then everything went black.

CHAPTER NINETEEN

"Kaz? Come on, sweetheart, wake up. Talk to me." The voice, deep and filled with urgency, came at her out of a smothering fog of pain. "That's right, hon. Open your eyes."

She tried to obey him but could only get one eye open. Someone was holding her hand, gently stroking her cheek. There was a light way above her, and its brightness hurt. Then she saw the shadow of someone leaning over her. Michael.

She moaned and gulped in air. Breathing hurt, she discovered.

"You're okay," he said softly. "You're safe."

She thought she could hear sirens, but the pounding inside her head overwhelmed all other sound. Beside her, a dog whined. Zeke. He licked her hand. Raising it, she touched her temple, which seemed to be the source of the pain. It felt funny—wet, and the wrong size, somehow.

"Easy," Michael said softly. "Don't touch that. Let's have the EMTs take a look, okay?"

"What—"

"When I drove up, the kitchen door was standing open. Zeke found you on the living room floor, out cold."

Memories came flooding back. The man in the ski mask, how he'd cut off her air, the awful feeling of helplessness. *The threat.*

Twenty-four hours. She had only twenty-four hours to find the money.

She struggled to rise, but Michael's gentle hands held her down. "Don't move, sweetheart.

"Help . . . sit up."

"Not until the EMTs check you over."

She could focus a little better now with her one eye. Michael's expression was fierce, at odds with the soft, crooning quality of his voice. He must be scared. "I'm okay." She struggled again to sit up.

He grumbled something and rose, scooping her up off the floor in one fluid motion. Walking over to one of the easy chairs, he settled her in his lap, keeping his arms tight around her. The abrupt movement made her dizzy, and she laid her head against his shoulder, closing her eyes.

For one moment, she'd lean on him. The terror still had its hold on her. She'd been so damned helpless. She shuddered. Her throat was sore, and she placed a hand on it.

Michael's gaze sharpened. He brushed her hand aside, saw the bruises, and his expression became even harder. He said nothing for a moment, and then, "Did you see who attacked you?"

Two EMTs arrived, cutting off her reply. One of them

knelt beside the chair and grinned at her. "Hey, Kaz. How ya feeling?"

"Like someone . . . flattened me."

He nodded and looked at Michael. "Sir, if you'll set her down and move out of our way—"

"Not a chance," Michael replied, his voice implacable. "Check her right where she is."

The EMT eyed him and decided not to argue. She continued to lean against Michael while the EMT checked her pupils, took her blood pressure, and asked her simple questions to determine if she was alert. He cleaned her face with an antiseptic wipe and placed a temporary bandage over the cut on her forehead.

"Pupils are okay," he said, packing up his instrument case. "But let's take a ride to the hospital, Kaz. You'll need a CAT scan and some stitches."

"No, I'm all right." She shrugged out of Michael's arms and got shakily to her feet, gripping the arm of the chair for support as a new wave of dizziness attacked her.

Michael stood and put an arm around her. "Dammit, you'll go to the hospital, even if I have to carry you there myself."

She started to argue, then subsided when she saw the mixture of fear and rage on his face.

Her teeth were chattering, even though the air in the kitchen was toasty warm. Not a good sign. And the cut on her forehead was beginning to throb. She sighed. "Help me out to the ambulance?"

Four hours later, Kaz lay on a bed in the hospital emergency ward, waiting. They'd stitched up the cut on her forehead, then strapped her to a table and run her through a giant tube to take pictures of her head. Someone was supposed to come by with a verdict as to whether she would live, but she wasn't sure she cared. She wanted to get out of there. Right now. She hated hospitals. The last time she'd been here, she'd been in the basement morgue to identify her parents' bodies.

Her whole body hurt, all the way down to the cellular level. Getting slammed into a hardwood floor a couple of times—then landed on by a two-hundred-pound gorilla—did that to a person. But she'd just have to take large quantities of aspirin. The sense of urgency and dread, which had settled somewhere in the vicinity of her solar plexus, was growing with every passing minute.

Twenty-four hours, the voice inside her whispered. That's all she and Gary had, if she believed her attacker. And call her crazy, but she didn't think he was the kind of guy who'd be flexible.

Michael and Lucy chose that moment to come through the curtains that surrounded her bed. They were arguing, as usual. Lucy's expression when she glanced Kaz's way was worried, her eyes full of regret.

"Where the *hell* was your surveillance team?" Michael asked. "She was a sitting duck."

"Jackson called them off. They received some kind of tip on Gary's whereabouts that they're following up on. I didn't find out until just a few minutes before I heard your call come in."

Kaz shivered, the bad feeling inside her getting worse. Were they closing in on Gary? He had the training—theoretically, he could elude them for days.

The emergency room nurse popped her head in.

"The doctor wants to keep you overnight for observation," she announced cheerfully. "We've got a room all set up."

"No," Kaz said, making her hoarse voice as firm as she could. "I'm leaving." She swung her legs over the side of the bed, then had to wait a moment for the dizziness to recede again.

The nurse rushed over and pushed her back onto the bed. "That requires the doctor's signature, and he's not available. Why don't you lie down—"

Kaz huffed out a breath and leaned sideways on one elbow, squinting at Lucy through her good eye. "Show her your gun," she said, sotto voce.

Lucy rolled her eyes.

Using an arm to keep the nurse at bay, Kaz slid until her feet touched the floor, then grabbed the edge of the bed in an effort to stand up. The nurse tut-tutted and waved her hands.

Michael cleared his throat. "There were no cracks in her extremely hard head, right?" The nurse nodded reluctantly. "Then I'll keep an eye on her for the night. Hunt up the doc and get him to sign the release papers." When the nurse opened her mouth to protest, he added, "Do you really think she'll stay put?"

"Where're my clothes?" Kaz demanded, glaring at her. The nurse threw up her hands and left. Kaz sank back down on the bed, the effort she'd made having exhausted her. She hated these feelings of weakness. She didn't have time for them.

While they waited for the nurse to return with her clothes, Lucy commandeered the only available chair, pulling it up to the edge of the bed and sitting down. "Talk," she ordered.

As best she could with a throat that was refusing to work, Kaz told them about the attack. "He was convinced that I knew where the money was."

Michael's eyes were on the bruises beginning to form on her neck. "Did he try to strangle you?" She could hear the rage churning just beneath the surface of that quiet tone.

"I don't think that was his intention. He was controlling me by cutting off my air supply."

Michael turned abruptly on his heel and walked over to the window, standing with his back to them.

Lucy watched him, a worried frown on her face, then turned back to Kaz. "Can you describe the guy?"

"Not really—he was wearing a ski mask."

"Height? Weight?"

"He was heavier than me—I'd say by at least seventy pounds. And he was tall enough to lift me off my feet, so he has to be over six feet."

"So six-two, maybe three, around one-ninety to two-ten. What else?"

"He was strong, but . . . he had a gut." She couldn't stop the shudder that went through her. "He used his weight to subdue me."

Michael turned to look at her, his expression stark.

"He had brown eyes, I think," she continued, forcing herself to think back to those moments when Ski Mask had had her pinned. "But it was dark, so that's just an impression. Thick wrists, pale skin . . . and dark hair, fairly thick, on the back of his wrists."

"What about smells? Aftershave? Was he a smoker?" Michael asked.

"Sweat," Kaz remembered, wrinkling her nose. "His clothes were . . . damp with it." She closed her eyes. She'd been helpless—completely helpless—for the first time in her life. Even on the trawler the night her parents had died, she hadn't felt that helpless. She'd rather face down another thirty-foot storm surge than cross paths with that guy again. Pressing her lips together, she blocked out her thoughts. "I think he was the same guy who was in my house two nights ago. This time, I did some damage, I think, to his nose."

"Of course you did." Lucy grinned. "Any rings on his hands?"

Kaz shook her head. "He had on leather gloves—black." She folded her hands in front of her in an effort to stop their trembling. "He said I had twenty-four hours to return the money."

Michael swore, walked back to the foot of the bed, and gripped the metal railing. "That's it. You're out of it, from here on." He turned his fierce gaze on Lucy. "I want her in protective custody—that's a formal request. I want someone with her every damn minute until we catch this guy. And I want her in a safe location."

"No," Kaz said, raising her hand when he would have roared at her. "Don't you see? We don't have any time left. Sykes thinks he's closing in on Gary. I have to get to him before they catch him. We have to find out what he knows."

"He can talk to Lucy. I want you out of it."

"He won't talk to anyone but me," Kaz insisted.

"Tough," Michael said, his voice rough. "I won't have you hurt, not again."

"That's not your call," Kaz said evenly. She watched the hurt and frustration come into his eyes, and she was sorry for it. But she knew—was more certain than ever—that she was the only one who might have a chance of getting Gary to talk. Yes, she hurt, and yes, she was scared. She wanted nothing more than to climb into bed, pull the covers over her head, and sleep forever—preferably in Michael's arms. But she didn't see an alternative—she had to talk to Gary.

"She's right," Lucy said, causing Michael to utter a succinct swear word. "If Gary's willing to talk to anyone, it would be either Chuck or Kaz." Lucy didn't look any happier about it than Michael. "I questioned the junkie we found at the scene of the second murder again, and he's not still talking. I even threw the three-strikes prison sentence at him as a threat, and he won't budge. After you two left the mooring basin, I also talked to several of the fishermen at the Redemption. *No one* is talking—they're scared out of their wits. I don't have any suspects, dammit, and Kaz is my only hope of finding some leads I can pursue." She turned back to Kaz. "I assume you're going to contact Chuck."

Kaz nodded.

Michael heaved a sigh and scrubbed a hand over his face. "What's your plan?"

"To drive out to his place and talk to him."

"Won't work," Ivar said, appearing at the edge of the curtains. His long face was somber. "We found Chuck about a half hour ago in your backyard. The EMTs are bringing him in right now, but they aren't optimistic. Whoever got the drop on him beat him almost to death."

CHAPTER TWENTY

Numb from the news about Chuck, Kaz shooed every-one out and pulled on her clothes, gritting her teeth against the pain and dizziness that kept threatening to swamp her. She walked slowly toward the waiting room where Michael was pacing, just as Chuck was be-ing wheeled down the hall on a gurney. She froze, tak-ing in his blood-soaked clothes. One side of his face was purple, and his lips were swollen and split in sev-eral places. Splints immobilized his left arm and leg.

When she whimpered, he opened his eyes. He lifted his free hand. "Sorry . . . didn't protect . . ."

She rushed over to him, holding his hand in both of hers. "It's all right—don't talk."

". . . let Gary . . . down . . . promised . . ."

"No," she said softly, tears blurring her eyes. "You *didn't*. He understands. You're going to be all right."

The emergency room doctor who had sewn her up

261

came around to move her out of the way. "That's all—we've got to get him into surgery. *Now.*"

But Chuck gripped her arm hard, his expression fierce under the pain. "Get . . . away from . . . here."

She leaned closer. "Where's Gary, Chuck? I have to talk to him."

"*No* . . ." He shook his head back and forth, agitated.

The doctor placed a firm hand on her shoulder and pulled her away. "I said, that's *all.*"

Chuck whispered something, then started mumbling.

"Wait," Kaz said urgently, then bent down, putting her ear next to his mouth. "Say it again, Chuck."

". . . boats . . ." he whispered, then lapsed into unconsciousness.

"Shut up. Just . . . shut up and let me take care of you for a little while." As Michael eased Kaz into the passenger side of his car, he tried to control the panic and rage that had been eating at his insides for the last four hours. He'd almost lost her, that was all he could think about. It had been so close.

From the back seat, Zeke licked the side of her face, whining, and she raised a hand to pet him. Michael leaned across her to fasten her seat belt. "For once, quit trying to handle everything yourself."

"We have to go to Bjorn's," she said.

"No, we don't. We're going back to your house, where there's a police presence, and you're going to let me put you to bed. Dammit, you need rest. You have a head injury, and I can tell you're hurting—" he stopped, his voice almost breaking, and shook his head.

She laid a hand over his on the seat belt fastener, and he turned his head to look at her. "Twenty-four hours," she repeated quietly. "That's all I've got." He was so close he could see every small scrape and abrasion the bastard had put on her.

Unable to respond without snapping at her, he straightened, slammed the car door, and walked around to the driver's side. He got in, fastening his seat belt with jerky movements. Then he leaned back, closing his eyes. If the guy had hit her a little harder . . . been a little rougher . . .

He couldn't shake the feeling that someone was playing him, trying to make him lose his cool and screw up. He had to calm down, think more clearly. It was his only hope of keeping her safe.

"Why Bjorn's?" he asked when he felt more in control.

"I think he might know where Gary is."

"If I take you there, *then* will you come home with me?"

"After we talk to Gary, I will spend the rest of the evening in bed," she said, obviously hedging.

Frustration surged through him. He wanted to rage at her, yell at her for having taken so many chances . . . for being who she was, he realized. The real reason he was angry was that he'd let her down, let *himself* down. He hadn't been there when she'd needed him. So the blame lay squarely with him. Again. And God help him, because in the space of only a few days, Kaz had become as important to him as life itself. He'd loved Jessica, but his feelings for Kaz were different somehow. Stronger, and more urgent. Almost as if he didn't have any say in it all— he had to be with her, or he'd spend the rest of his life regretting it.

But he couldn't think about that now—that was exactly what the killer wanted him to do. He wanted Michael to act irrationally and emotionally. To panic, so he lost his edge, so he'd miss something. Starting the car, he put it into gear. "How do I get to Bjorn's?"

She gave him the directions, and five minutes later, they were parked in front of Bjorn's house. Before he could come around to help, she climbed stiffly from the car on her own. That damned independence again. She seemed grateful, though, when he put his arm around her to help her up the walkway.

She moved slowly, almost shuffling her feet. She had to be hurting bad. Although they'd filled a prescription for pain medication at the hospital pharmacy, she had refused to take it, worried, she'd said, that it would keep her from thinking clearly. "Stubborn woman," he muttered under his breath. He'd let her get away with acting tough for another hour or two, but eventually she'd take the pills, even if he had to grind them up in her food.

Bjorn answered the door on the first ring of the doorbell—he'd probably seen them drive up. He took in her injuries and bruises, then turned to Michael. "What happened?"

"I was attacked," Kaz said. "Chuck's in the hospital—we don't know if he'll pull through."

Bjorn's face crumpled as he slumped against the doorjamb. "I can't do this anymore," he muttered to himself. Then he seemed to remember his manners and held open the door, showing them into a large living room cluttered with comfortable chairs and children's toys. "Sit."

Michael gently eased Kaz into the nearest chair but remained standing. He turned to Bjorn, resolute. "If you know something, now's the time to tell us."

"I think you know where Gary is, know who's hiding him," Kaz said.

Bjorn walked over to the huge old fireplace that dominated one side of the room and stared into the flames. After a moment, he shook his head.

"Gary's backup is in the hospital," Michael said, pressing. "He's been staying close by—Kaz saw him two nights ago. We need to get to him, find out what he knows."

"How do I know you won't arrest him?" Bjorn asked. "He isn't part of this, you know."

"You can trust Michael," Kaz said.

The words flowed over Michael like a soothing balm. It was the first time, despite all they'd been through, that she'd given him any concrete indication she believed in him.

Bjorn looked at Michael. "Gary doesn't want her involved."

"She's already at risk," Michael said. "Her attacker gave her one day; then he's coming back."

Bjorn looked from one to the other of them, then sighed and squared his shoulders. "He's been staying on the boats—mine, Jacobsen's—moving a couple of times a night, then hiding out in the abandoned warehouses on the days we're out on the water."

"Where is he right now? Which boat?" Michael asked.

"Jacobsen's 70-foot trawler, the *Alliance*."

"Thank you," Kaz said softly, getting up to walk over and give him a brief hug.

He gently hugged her back, his eyes sad. "I hope I've done the right thing. You'll be careful?" With the last question, he looked to Michael for confirmation.

Michael nodded. "I'll take care of her. She's not getting out of my sight until this is finished, not again." He'd handcuff her to her bed if he had to. Her days of risk-taking were over.

Bjorn saw his determination, heard the emotion in his voice, and frowned. "That thing back in Boston—you let that guy die in that fire?"

Michael raised an eyebrow, but shook his head. "No, but I'll never be able to prove it."

Bjorn studied him for a long moment, then nodded. "Just handle this honorably, that's all we ask."

"You have my word on it."

They drove straight to the mooring basin, but the *Alliance* was locked up tight, its portholes dark. When they spied two search teams a couple of blocks down, Kaz looked sick to her stomach.

They spent another forty-five minutes searching other trawlers in the vicinity, as well as the closest warehouses, but there was no sign of Gary. If he were around, he wouldn't let them find him, not with the cops so close. Giving in—only because she was probably hurting from so much activity, if the pinched, white look on her face was any indication—Kaz allowed Michael to drive her back to the house.

Zeke trailed them into the kitchen, hovering close to Kaz. Michael made her sit in one of the kitchen chairs while he rummaged around in her cupboards, finally coming up with a can of chicken noodle soup. Standing at the stove, he kept an eye on her while he stirred the soup. When she got up to help, he exploded. "For God's sake, let me do it!" Then he stopped, reeled in his emotions, and continued in a calmer voice. "Just let me help. I need that."

"It wasn't your fault," she said.

"I should've been here—I shouldn't have let you come back here alone. My gut was screaming at me, and I didn't listen to it." He set the saucepan aside and went over to her, kneeling down to put his arms gently around her. It felt reassuring to hold her, to know that she was alive and warm and safe. "I can't stand that you've been hurt, that you won't let me handle things for you."

She rested her head on his shoulder for a moment before looking up at him. "Don't you see?" she said quietly. "I'd like nothing better than to check out. But there's no time."

His arms tightened for a minute, and he pressed his lips gently to hers. It was a kiss meant to reassure and soothe both of them. He wanted more, but he forced himself to let go. "At least let me feed you."

She smiled wryly. "Your specialty."

"Yeah."

He served the soup and they ate in silence for a few minutes.

"I should've been paying more attention," she said in between spoonfuls. "He must've come in while I was on the phone to the hospital in Portland."

He looked at her curiously, then listened while she related what she'd discovered.

"So Ken was using the money to pay for Bobby's treatments—that would be the only reason he would take the chance of stealing drug money," she said. "And I think Gary may have made the anonymous payment." The expression on her face was one of frustration. "I *have* to get to Gary, but I can't figure out how."

The swelling in her cheek and eye looked like it was going down. He got up to add more ice to the cold pack. Then he refilled her soup bowl and placed it back in front of her.

"I want you to take a time-out for the night," he said quietly. "Get a good night's sleep—let your body heal a little." She started to shake her head, and he leaned across the table, taking both of her hands in his. "Just listen to me. I don't think there's anything you can do tonight. You have no way of knowing where Gary is or how to get hold of him. And you need the down time. Hell, *I* need the down time."

"I've got some places I can check—"

"Places you can get to in the dark?"

He watched the emotions flit across her face—worry, frustration. And finally, resignation. "Okay, for a few hours."

He squeezed her hands. "Thank you," he said simply.

Kaz hadn't been asleep long when the sound of Zeke's tail rhythmically thumping on the hardwood floor woke her up. As she opened her eyes and tried to move, she realized Michael was in bed with her, and that he was holding her close, both arms wrapped tightly around her. He must have come back upstairs after he'd tucked her into bed, to sleep beside her and protect her. She'd unconsciously curled into him in her sleep, her head resting on his shoulder, her arm on his chest.

She raised her head to peer into the darkness, hoping to identify what had awakened her. At her slight movement, Michael immediately stirred.

"What?" he rumbled.

"Someone's in the house, I think," she said softly.

"Damn straight." The voice came from the bottom of the bed.

They both bolted upright, Kaz moaning at the quick movement, and Michael reaching under his pillow for the gun. She stopped him with a hand on his arm. "It's all right, it's Gary."

"Hell of a way to keep my sister safe, Chapman." Gary walked around to Kaz's side of the bed, cursing as he almost tripped over Zeke. After making sure the curtains were closed, he switched on the lamp on the nightstand.

"Are you okay?" Kaz asked him, her eyes squinting in the sudden glare. He looked even worse than he had forty-eight hours ago. His clothes were filthy, and his eyes held the feral look of an animal who knew it was being hunted down.

"Seems like I should be the one asking that question. Bjorn told me what happened." He knelt by the side of the bed, taking her chin in his hand and turning the bruised side of her face toward the light. His lips tightened. "Dammit, Kaz, I told you to stay out of this. I told you you'd get hurt."

She shook her head. Michael had climbed out of bed and was pulling on a sweater. He'd been sleeping in his jeans, she noted, but had taken off his boots and sweater. "You aren't safe here," she said to Gary. "You know about Chuck?"

Gary nodded, his expression angry and frustrated. "The hospital has him listed as critical."

"You're well informed for someone on the run," Michael said, his voice mild.

Gary looked at Michael. "I haven't been on the run. I want you to get Kaz out of town. This mess is about to blow wide open."

Kaz made herbal tea and scrounged together a sandwich for Gary. When she entered the living room with the tray, Michael and Gary were already talking quietly.

"It's our speculation that the fishermen are running drugs," Michael was saying to him.

Gary accepted a mug from Kaz and nodded. "Ken figured it out before I did."

"Did he steal drug money to pay for Bobby's treatments?" she asked.

"Yeah, the fool. And he paid the consequences. I tried to talk him into giving the money back, although I wasn't sure it would save his sorry hide. But he'd already used some of it. After the second time they beat him up and threatened to go after his family, he gave the rest of the money to me to put in the locker." He shot an exasperated look at Kaz. "And then you go looking for it. Smart move, Sis."

"I figured if you had something they wanted, the locker was the place you'd hide it."

"Yeah, and that analytical mind of yours put you right in the line of fire." He shook his head, then picked up his sandwich. "Cutting the lines on the pots was a warning. They'll threaten your life, next."

"They already have," Michael said and told him about the ultimatum she'd been given. "Who else besides Bjorn in the fishing community knows about my background?"

Gary stopped wolfing down the sandwich to look at him curiously. "Pretty much everyone. Why?"

"Because I think someone's messing with my head on this. The use of fire to cover up the murder, at the same time I come to town—" He shrugged. "The fire could've been a convenient way to use my status as a newcomer to slow down the investigation. And it's not the first time someone I care about has been targeted."

He sent Kaz a look that warmed her all the way through. Then as what he'd said sank in, she frowned. She hadn't even considered that angle. Lucy hadn't told her the real source of the rumors about

Michael—just that the cops had been talking about him. But Bjorn had clearly known the details of Michael's background—he'd indicated as much when they'd talked to him earlier in the evening.

Gary's expression was speculative. "You could be right, but it doesn't help us, unless you can prove that someone checked you out."

Michael nodded. "I've got a call in to a buddy of mine back East. I should hear from him in the morning. Who told you about me?"

"Bjorn." Gary frowned. "But he could've heard it from any number of people."

Michael shrugged. "I'll find out, sooner or later. In the meantime, I won't have Kaz at risk because you want to play vigilante."

Gary's gaze turned hard. He set aside his empty plate. "If you think I like doing this—"

"Then turn yourself in, tell the cops everything you know."

"If I do that, I'm as good as dead."

"I can get you protective custody," Michael said.

"That won't stop them."

"Gary," Kaz interrupted, placing a hand on his knee. "At least tell us who's involved—give us something more to go on, so that we can help out."

"No, I want you out of it." Gary got up and started pacing. "I'm close. I only need one more day to put it all together."

"Is Karl Svensen involved?"

Gary whirled around, pointing his finger at her. "You stay away from Svensen and his crews. They don't have any loyalty to us, and they won't lift a finger to help you."

"So that's what the fight was about six months ago,

and why Svensen never pressed charges. Ken had found out what Karl was doing, and Karl threatened him. You stepped in to protect Ken."

"I didn't know what was going on, but yeah. Svensen took a swing at Ken, and I stopped him. At the time, it surprised the hell out of me when he refused to press charges." Gary growled in frustration. "Dammit, Kaz, haven't you heard anything I've said? If you go any further with this, they'll kill you without even flinching."

"Who else is in on it?" Michael demanded. "Either tell us what you know, or I call the cops now. Jackson is right outside."

Gary abruptly sighed and sat down. "I'll talk if you promise to take Kaz out of the equation."

"Done."

"Hey!" They both ignored her.

"They're using the Redemption as their meeting place," Gary told Michael. "The back room. And yes, before you ask," he said to Kaz, "Steve is in on it. I don't know what they have on him, something that happened around the time of his divorce. He's turning a blind eye to the meetings. He could finger every damn one of them if he wanted, but I can't get him to talk. I searched Svensen's boat, but I didn't find anything, other than some notations in the ship's log that could've been drop-off points."

He shook his head. "Bjorn's in the clear, but I think he knows what's going on. If he does, he's not saying, and I don't blame him. He's got his kids to think about. The supplier is someone offshore, probably a Triad offshoot. The buyer's right here in Astoria. Most of the drugs are going upriver, only a small amount is staying here in town."

"Who's the buyer?" Michael asked.

"No one you can do anything about. He's set up so well no one can touch him—at least, so far, but Jacobsen and I are planning to follow Karl and observe the handoff, then take the information to the right people. And that's all I'll tell you. Now will you please get Kaz the hell out of town? I can't finish this unless I know she's safe." He pinned Michael with a hard glare. "If you're sleeping with her, the least you can do is take care of her."

"You're jumping to the wrong—" Kaz started, but Michael cut her off.

"My intentions are honorable," he said evenly. "And I resent the implication that I would use her in any way."

"And *I* resent the fact that you think I would *let* him use me," Kaz said to Gary, angry with both of them and trying to ignore the warm feeling she was getting from Michael's declaration. "Neither of you can make decisions for me. I'll do whatever I think is necessary, and no one is responsible for my actions except me."

Gary didn't reply, but turned back to Michael. "You moved in awfully fast after I split. I'm not happy about that."

"Get used to it," Michael suggested. "I'm not willing to let her get hurt again."

Gary hesitated, then nodded. "Fair enough. But if you've taken advantage of her in any way—"

"Oh, for God's sake," Kaz exploded. "Will you two listen to each other? You sound like we're living in Regency England. I've been taking care of myself for a long time. If someone doesn't recognize that, and damn quickly, I'll throw you both out of the house."

"I'd like to see you try," Michael growled.

"There's a cop right outside," she retorted.

He shook his head at Gary, and they exchanged a see-what-I-have-to-put-up-with look, which made her even angrier.

Gary got up and handed Kaz his empty mug. "I'll let you two lovebirds sort this out—it's time I got out of here. Twenty-four hours, that's all I need." His expression turned wry. "At least try to keep her out of my way during that time."

"I'll keep her safe," Michael replied. "But I still think you should go to the cops on this."

"Not yet."

Michael closed the back door behind Gary and leaned against it, watching her with an expression she couldn't fathom while she cleaned up the dishes. Something about the look on his face was making her nervous. He watched every move she made, almost as if he were deciding what to do next.

She grabbed the dish towel and dried off the counter around the sink. *He was in bed with you,* the little voice in her head whispered. In truth, the thought had been percolating in the back of her mind since she'd awakened. Even while Gary had been there. *Not in the chair across the room—in your bed. Holding you like he'd never let go.*

He pushed away from the door, walking slowly toward her, his expression intent. She backed up, saying the first thing that came to mind. "I can't believe you two, thinking you can make a plan to 'take care of me' without even asking me what I want."

He shrugged, but kept coming toward her. "We know what's best in this situation—you don't."

"Bullshit." She backed up another step, her retreat abruptly stopped by the edge of the counter. Lifting her chin, she said, "I make the decisions concerning my life."

"Not this time." He came to a stop in front of her and looked down at her, his silvery eyes burning with a suppressed emotion she couldn't put a name to. "Quit using the issue of your independence to dodge the real issue here."

She swallowed. "What real issue?" she whispered.

"Whether or not we're going to make love tonight."

In an instant, she went cold, then hot. Now she knew what that look on his face was—it was the look of desire. He wanted her, and knowing that was enough to make her knees turn to water.

She could think of a thousand reasons why this wasn't a good idea. They had a killer closing in, maybe even waiting nearby for the perfect moment to strike. Chuck was in the hospital, in critical condition. And Gary was out there somewhere, laying a trap for the killer that could blow up in his face.

Michael took one more step, a step that brought him so close that everything else flew out of her mind. All she could think about was the strength and heat of his body, and how much she wanted to explore it. It was pure insanity, but she couldn't seem to make herself care.

Leaning over, he braced his hands on either side of her. His face was only inches from hers, his expression rigid from tension. "Are we?"

"Are we what?" she breathed.

"Going to make love. Tonight."

She reached up, curving her palms over the hard muscles of his shoulders, feeling the heat of his body through the soft wool of his sweater. She tried to force herself to think rationally one more time. "I—"

He captured her lips, cutting off any protest, however weak, she would have uttered. His kiss burned away her remaining resistance, its fire streaking through her, all the way down to her toes, curling them. Her hands dropped to his chest and fisted, her mouth softened and molded itself to his. She was incapable of doing anything but kissing him back.

Much too soon, he broke off the kiss, stepping back and leaving her wanting more, much more. They were both breathing hard.

"Kaz." He took her hands in his. "I want more than this one night."

It was crazy, what he was proposing. She lived in San Francisco and ran a consulting firm. He was a firefighter who'd seen unimaginable violence and human evil, who might have to arrest her brother. The problems they faced in a long-term relationship were overwhelming. And yet, this felt so right. She didn't make decisions lightly, but this one seemed so natural, so easy. She lifted her chin and looked him square in the eye. "All right."

He let out a slow breath, smiling a little for the first time. But she could still sense a hesitation in him. "Are you sure you're up for this?" he asked softly, running his hand lightly over her bruised face. Even now, he was thinking of her well-being, not willing to do anything that would hurt her.

She rose on her toes and linked her arms around his neck. "It'll hurt more if you *don't* make love to me."

CHAPTER TWENTY-ONE

Michael bent and picked her up, carrying her upstairs and down the darkened hallway to her bedroom. He laid her down gently in the center of the bed, taking care with her injuries. The small lamp on her bedside table was still on, casting a soft glow throughout the room. He made no move to turn it off.

Stepping away from the bed, she watched as he unbuttoned his shirt, revealing a broad, muscular chest sprinkled lightly with dark hair narrowing to a vee at his waist. Her fingers gripped the bed covers, itching to hold him, to run her hands over those hard planes and muscles, to soak up all that heat. She caught her breath as his hands moved to his jeans, unbuttoning them. He pushed the jeans and his briefs down in one move, stepping out of them, and then straightened.

He was magnificent—all muscle and sinew, all hard lines of masculine elegance. She couldn't breathe.

He smiled, then placed one knee on the edge of the

mattress and leaned over her, grasping the edges of her football jersey with both hands. "Your turn," he said, his voice a deep, sexy rumble. He tugged the jersey off over her head, leaving her naked except for her panties. Then he lay down, the bed dipping under his weight, and stretched out beside her.

He seemed content to look at her, to take his time driving her wild by doing nothing more than touching every part of her body with his incredible eyes. No one had ever done that, just looked at her as if she looked exactly the way he wanted her to, as if he wanted to experience the anticipation of what would come next. "You're so beautiful," he said quietly.

She trembled, and reached out to lay her palm against his chest.

He caught her hand in his, kissing her palm in a way that made her shiver. "No," he said softly. "Let me."

The shadows of the darkened room closed around them intimately, and he drew her closer, warming her with the entire length of his body. He reached up to smooth her hair, gently finger-combing the silky blond strands so that they flowed over her shoulder and down over her right breast. His fingers lingered there for a long moment, his touch unbearably light and teasing. Heat built inside her, and she arched involuntarily into his touch, but his hand moved on.

Down, over the slight swell of her lower stomach, down to the edge of her panties, never even hesitating as he slid them off, dropping them on the floor beside the bed. Then to the sensitized insides of her trembling thighs. His fingers trailed fire, all the way up to her core.

He cupped her. She moaned aloud, dampening his hand. His gaze flew to hers, the silver of his eyes darkening to a stormy gray.

"Michael—" she panted, fighting against the building pressure, surging against his hand to try to ease the ache. She was ready, so fast it almost frightened her.

"Shhhh." He soothed her, leaning down to kiss her softly, then with more insistence, taking her with his tongue, mimicking the movements of his hand as he stroked her, explored her.

Her hips bucked off the bed, the exquisite pleasure almost more than she could bear. When she thought she couldn't take any more, he slid two large fingers all the way into her, pressing upward.

The climax hit her hard, arching her body tautly, scaring her with its intensity. She tried to pull away, but he held her gently, immobilizing her with his body, continuing to stroke her. Waves roiled through her, great rushes of heat, starbursts of pleasure. He wrung every last spasm out of her, then brought her slowly, gently back down to earth. She collapsed against the tangled bedcovers, unable to think or even to breathe.

He leaned down and kissed her lower belly, then moved up to her breast. Taking it into his mouth, he tugged on it softly with his teeth, and she felt the need start to build all over again. She gasped and sobbed.

He laughed softly, his warm breath causing her nipple to pucker almost painfully. "Didn't I tell you I was going to show you what you'd been missing all these years?" He moved away for a moment to deal with protection, then slid over her, settling heavily between her thighs.

The delicious weight of him galvanized her and she reared up, hooking her hands around his neck and pulling his mouth down to hers. Their hearts beat crazily against each other, but in unison. "Don't make me wait any longer," she whispered, sighing against his mouth.

"I couldn't, even if I wanted to."

He fought the urge to rush, to possess. She tasted as he'd imagined she would, only better. She felt, as he settled over her, as he'd imagined, all soft and yielding, only better. He wanted her at a gut-wrenching level so deep down inside him that he was afraid to let himself go, afraid he'd just take and take, consuming her until there was nothing left.

Holding himself rigid, he slipped inside her, letting her adjust to him. He saw her eyes widen with shock, their soft brown glazing over with pleasure. She murmured against his lips, tightening her hold on him, cradling him.

He was big, bigger than she'd realized. For a moment, she wasn't sure she could take all of him, and she pulled back slightly, alarmed by the intensity of what she was feeling. He withdrew a little, then surged forward again, seating himself deep inside, touching the core of her, making her arch mindlessly.

After a long moment, he started moving. Pulling back, then pushing, long, slow, deep strokes that drove her wild. She'd never known a man to take such care, to give so generously. She watched in his fierce gaze, seeing his control slip away as he settled into a strong, powerful rhythm that rekindled a driving need deep inside her, taking over her very self, flinging her into a world she'd never known, never even had a glimpse of.

Her vision grayed, every cell in her body building toward an explosion even more powerful than the last one. Her pulse galloping and roaring in her ears, she dimly heard his hoarse calling of her name, then his long moan. She peaked and exploded, crying out as, arms wrapped around each other, they slid down through crashing waves of pleasure.

He settled heavily on top of her, his chest heaving. For several long moments, Kaz lay there, reveling in the feel of him covering every inch of her, listening to his heart as its beat eventually slowed in concert with hers.

She rubbed her face against his shoulder, inhaling the damp, musky, already familiar scent of him. Never before had she felt this . . . connection, either during or after sex. What she'd experienced in the past seemed, in comparison, like lukewarm companionship. This, though, this was . . . cataclysmic. She was bound to him now, in some way that she couldn't define. She'd surrendered a part of herself that she hadn't known existed, that had been lying dormant all these years, waiting for the right man to come along.

Lying there in the quiet of the night, she listened to the sound of Michael breathing, and she worried. About what they'd experienced, about how either of them could ever casually walk away from it, about how much she already was in love with him. And about the fact that sooner or later, she might be leaving town, going back to California. Then she thought about Gary and where he was right now, while she was lying in bed, guilty in her sated pleasure.

Michael stirred and turned on his side, taking her with him, wrapping his arms around her. Cocooning her from the outside world, if only for a few more hours. "Don't think about it," he said quietly. "We'll sort it all out."

CHAPTER TWENTY-TWO

Kaz awoke to the sound of Michael talking softly on the phone, his voice low. "Yeah, I understand. They'll keep him there for now? . . . Right. I'll let her know."

She threw back the covers and sat up—slowly. The throbbing in her head was down to a dull roar, probably because she'd been able to sleep for the first time in days. But the rest of her body was, if anything, stiffer and sorer. She tentatively stood up, wincing, and used one hand to hold onto the headboard. Funny how she hadn't felt any of this while Michael had been making love to her a second time last night. Slowly, gently, and with such exquisite care. Or again this morning, their whispered words and low moans gently disturbing the predawn quiet. She smiled at the memory.

"What are you doing out of bed?"

She turned to find him standing in the doorway, a coffee mug in one hand. His hair was damp, his face freshly shaven. Even with a scowl on his face, he was adorable. And all hers. At least, for now. "What time is it?" she asked, smiling at him.

"Early afternoon."

"What?" She gaped at him. "Why didn't you wake me up?"

"Because you needed the sleep," he replied evenly. "Don't expect me to do things that aren't good for you."

She grumbled at that as she walked unsteadily across the room. "What are you supposed to let me know?"

"It's not good news."

She stopped, searching his face. "Gary?"

He nodded. "They've taken him into custody."

She put out a hand, leaning heavily against the dresser. "Is he okay?" she whispered.

Michael hesitated. "According to Lucy, he resisted arrest. She says he's roughed up but refusing treatment. They're holding him at the station until he's arraigned later this afternoon."

Kaz pulled open a dresser drawer and starting yanking clothes out at random. "I want to see him."

"That may not be possible—"

Her head whipped around. "I *will* see him." She bumped the drawer shut with her hip and grabbed the pile of clothes on top of the dresser. "If I can get him to tell me who the Astoria connection is, then we can take over his investigation."

"We?" Michael folded his arms and smiled slightly at her.

"Yes," Kaz said, and waited.

"All right." He nodded. "As long as we work together on this."

She sighed with relief, falling a little more in love with him. "I'll take the world's fastest shower, if you'll hunt up the world's largest bottle of aspirin."

* * *

An hour later, Michael dropped Kaz off at the station, extracting a promise from her to call him at the fire station when she was ready to leave. The light was already starting to fade. She couldn't believe she'd slept away most of the day. There was almost no time left.

She opened the door and, catching Joanne's eye, pointed at the interior security door. Joanne released the lock and waved her on through.

Lucy and Ivar were both at their desks, going through the stacks of papers that Sykes had taken from her house yesterday. Ivar had her laptop open in front of him, and he was tapping on the keys, a frown of concentration on his face. As she approached, he looked up, his expression relieved.

"What's your password?"

Kaz shook her head. "If anyone else were asking, I'd tell them to go to hell." She walked around to his side of the desk and typed it in for him.

"Someone's been accessing the fishermen's bank accounts, posing as Brenner, giving out his badge number," Lucy told her, scrubbing a hand over her face. She looked like she'd been up all night, and she clearly wasn't happy about it. For the first time in as long as Kaz could remember, Lucy's clothes were wrinkled. Her hair was mussed, even escaping its barrette. "When I called the bank first thing this morning, the manager's comment was, 'But I gave all this information to your officer yesterday afternoon.'" She sighed. "Never mind that the guy didn't think to ask for a subpoena. I don't suppose that was you?"

"I didn't think of it, but I wish I had," Kaz said, earning a glare. She perched on the edge of the chair beside Lucy's desk, reaching out to pick up the muddy snow globe that was sitting there. Shaking it, she watched the snow drift down around the fishing trawler while she considered. "Could've been Gary, though."

"Yeah, that was my second thought."

Kaz set the snow globe back down and leaned forward. "Where is he? I want to see him."

Lucy hesitated, the expression on her face scaring Kaz. "What's wrong? Is he all right?" she asked.

Lucy nodded. "For now. The chief has him on suicide watch, though."

A small whimper escaped Kaz's throat. "For God's sake, why?"

"He's despondent, refusing to talk, and refusing to eat." Lucy leaned back in her chair, looking truly defeated for the first time since the investigation had begun. Her eyes held hints of desperation mixed with frustration, and more—an emotion that Kaz couldn't put a name to. "I can't get through to him, Kaz. He just keeps repeating that I need to convince you to leave town."

Kaz leaned forward. "Take me to him."

"He's only allowed to see his lawyer." Lucy bit her lip. "But he's refusing legal representation."

"Then let me talk to him. Tell Sykes that I'm standing in for Phil until I can get him to fly up here."

Lucy shook her head. "A family member can't stand in for a lawyer. Anything he told you would be admissible in court."

"Put me in a room with him and turn off the intercom," Kaz pleaded. "Five minutes, that's all I'm asking."

Lucy glanced at Ivar, who made a production out of ignoring them both. Then she checked the rest of the squad room before nodding. "All right—five minutes. But if Sykes shows up, you're out of there. This is irreg-

ular as hell—I could lose my job over a stunt like this."
She rose. "I'll have him brought out to one of the interrogation rooms."

"*Thank you.*"

"Don't thank me yet. And Kaz—be prepared. He put
up a hell of a fight. It took four of our guys to subdue
him, and they weren't too happy with him by the time
it was all over. Two of them are in the emergency room
right now, getting stitched up."

Kaz waited at Lucy's desk until she returned, then followed her into a room that was at the back of the building, halfway down the hall that led out to the parking
lot. When she entered, Gary was sitting in one of the
chairs, his hands and legs in shackles. Clint Jackson was
standing guard in the corner. Lucy motioned for him to
follow her, and after a moment's reluctance, he did.

Once they were alone, Kaz rushed over to Gary.
Very gently, she took his face in her hands and turned
it up to the light. His nose was bloody and slightly
crooked, his lips split and ballooned to twice their
normal size. Small cuts and areas darkening to bruises
covered his face.

Gently, she unbuttoned the three shirt buttons that
hadn't been ripped off and inspected his ribs. Black
and purple splotches covered them. A small sound of
distress escaped her lips. Who could have done this to
him? What right did they have to cause this much
damage?

He'd barely moved when she touched him, but his
eyes slowly focused on her. He licked his lips and
tried to speak, but she shushed him. Laying her head
on his shoulder, she tried not to cry. To see him this
way, in shackles, made her want to throw up. She swallowed hard and, schooling her expression, raised her

head. "So," she said, keeping her voice as light as she could. "I guess I should see the other guys, huh?"

One side of his mouth lifted slightly. "Kaz . . ." The word came out slurred, almost garbled. He closed his eyes and grimaced.

"Talk slowly and quietly." She glanced around at the closed door and the window, then moved so that anyone looking in wouldn't be able to read his lips. "They can see us but Lucy said she'd leave the intercom off for a few minutes to give us some privacy. Tell me everything you know, and Michael and I will take it from here."

He shook his head, then closed his eye as he dealt with the pain the movement seemed to cause him. "Get . . . out of . . . town."

She took his face gently in both her hands and looked directly into his eyes. "Listen to me, Gary. We can help. Find the evidence to clear you."

"I . . . don't matter . . ."

"Yes," she said fiercely, "you do. Don't you dare let them win, damn you. You *tell* me, and then you *stay alive* until I can get you out of here."

He stared at her for a long minute. "Trap door," he managed. "Svensen."

Kaz thought rapidly. "The trap door in Steve's office?" All the old waterfront bars had shanghai trap doors—doors in the floor that led to the water below the pier. In the old days, sailors had regularly been shanghaied, or kidnapped, and taken out to sea to serve as indentured crew on ships. "So Svensen goes to the tavern, picks up the money, then drops into a boat below the pier?"

Gary nodded, then sucked in a breath. "Svensen takes out . . . to be swapped for drugs." He tried to wet his lips with his tongue, and she rose to get him some water out of the cooler. She held it to his battered lips and trickled it into his mouth. He gave her a grateful look as he swallowed.

"Who is Karl's contact?"

Gary shook his head abruptly, then winced. "No . . . no way. . . . Too dangerous."

Kaz let that go while she paced and thought it through. So how did Karl get away with regularly meeting someone out on the water and not being seen by the other members of the fishing fleet? The last piece of the puzzle fell into place. It was the obvious solution, and she'd even heard Karl say it herself. She hadn't put it together until now. And, she realized, no one else would have either. It would have escaped everyone's notice. Only a fisherman would have caught on, and only over time.

"You said you found notations in Karl's ship's log. Did any of them match this?" She repeated what she'd heard Karl say over the radio when she and Michael had been out. Gary nodded.

She resumed her pacing. Okay. So she had the list of drop-off locations, and she also knew which one was for the next rendezvous. She had to find Svensen, follow him. If they could catch him in the act, they'd have enough leverage on him to get to whoever was in charge. Was today a day that they'd make a drop? It was Friday—a day most fishermen superstitiously avoided going out on the water. Which made it ideal—fewer people would be out there to observe what was going on. She'd bet Svensen was going out tonight.

She hugged Gary again, carefully, trying to will some of her strength into him. "I want you to rest, and to not worry. But most of all, I want you to stay alive until we get back, all right?" He didn't respond. "I'll get you out of here, by tomorrow at the latest."

"Sure."

Kaz frowned at him. Something wasn't right. She opened her mouth, but just then, she heard a commotion outside the door.

The door opened, and Sykes strode in, trailed by Lucy. He leaned over the table, his expression angry, one eye showing bruising underneath. "What the hell is going on in here?"

"Why the hell hasn't he been treated?" Kaz demanded right back, not answering his question. "He could have internal injuries."

"That's a damn good question. McGuire?"

Lucy stared at Sykes, speechless.

"Do you mean that you didn't know about this?" Kaz asked, confused.

"Of course not. I've been out of the office since we apprehended him, putting ice on this black eye," he said. "You shouldn't be in here, Kaz—it's damned irregular. There's no way I'm allowing this case to get screwed up, no way I'm giving you an opportunity to tell the judge that we compromised the process. Gary can see a lawyer, and that's it." He turned to pin Lucy with a hard look. "Was this your idea?"

Kaz deflected him, answering for her. "I was concerned about Gary's condition and demanded to see him. Clearly, he's in no shape to be making decisions for himself. I will be immediately calling a lawyer to represent him, and I'd like you to delay arraignment until he can get here."

Sykes shook his head. "We'll temporarily assign him a public defender. There's no way I'm letting the DA agree to bail, anyway, not after the fight he put up when he was arrested. So all he has to do at the hearing is plead 'Guilty' or 'Not Guilty.' "

Kaz didn't like it, but she knew she couldn't stop him. "Why do you have him on suicide watch?"

Sykes stared at her for a long moment. "This is the first I've heard of it—I'll check it out." He came around the end of the table and took hold of her elbow. "You're leaving, now."

Lucy, who was standing slightly behind Sykes, cocked her head toward the squad room, indicating that she wanted to talk.

Kaz glanced at Gary, who was watching the exchange with intense concentration. When he realized she was looking at him, though, he immediately dropped his gaze back to the floor. Something was horribly wrong, she could feel it. Gary was acting oddly, and Sykes was acting . . . almost considerate. Sykes hadn't been considerate toward a Jorgensen in twenty years. But then, she realized bitterly, he knew he'd won—he had his man. So what did he have to lose at this point by being nice?

"Go," Gary said, the word almost a whisper. He had slumped back in his chair, pain clouding his expression.

She jerked her elbow out of Sykes's grasp, walked back over to Gary, bending down. "What?"

Gary drew a long, shaky breath. "I'll be all right," he said, his voice stronger than it had been since she'd come in. "Just . . . go."

Sykes grasped her arm more firmly and pulled, motioning toward the door. She gave in and, with a last glance at Gary, allowed the police chief to escort her from the room.

She walked over to Lucy's desk and retrieved her

jacket. "I'm headed for the marina, then the Redemption. I'll call Michael on my cell phone and update him."

Lucy was already shaking her head before Kaz finished. "You know he wanted you to wait for him."

"There's no time, he can catch up with me." She glanced at her watch. Slack tide was in just under two and a half hours. She turned to leave, then stopped, looking over her shoulder. "Was there something you wanted to tell me?"

Lucy hesitated, then shook her head. "Not yet. There's something I need to check first. But Kaz—be careful."

At the fire station, Michael was stapling the last of his notes together and placing them in the arson investigation file when his cell phone rang. He dropped the file folder on the desk in front of him and reached for it. Recognizing the Caller ID, he smiled and picked up. "You ship me those coffee beans yet?"

"Sent them out yesterday. Tasha at the coffee shop sends her best. How the hell you keep them sniffing around when you don't put out, buddy, is a mystery to the entire staffs of the fire and police departments of the Greater Boston Area."

"Right." Michael's voice was wry. Mac didn't know that Michael had finally broken his long run of celibacy. And in the most fantastic way. He smiled a little, remembering last night. His married friends had been right when they'd told him that making love to the woman you'd fallen *in* love with was a totally different, completely shattering experience. He felt like he'd been turned inside out, that he'd crossed some invisible threshold and was now looking at the world with an entirely new perspective.

"Yo, buddy. You still there?" Mac's voice held a note of curiosity.

Michael forced his mind back to the present. "Any word on who's been checking me out?"

"The mayor of your cute little burg called a few of the higher-ups, including your surrogate papa, but that's no surprise. And someone from the police department evidently talked to Geoff Whitford who, as we all know, loves you just the way you are. The sonofabitch probably blabbed everything, out of spite."

Michael wouldn't be surprised. Mac was right—Whitford had resented him for more than a decade, because of an incident during Whitford's rookie years. Michael had been the one to write him up, and to point out to the brass that Whitford wasn't good management material. If he could make Michael's life difficult, he would leap at the chance. "You know who placed the call?"

"Couldn't ferret that out. So, when are you moving back?"

"Not in this lifetime."

"Says the person with the addiction to quality caffeine."

Michael's phone beeped, indicating another incoming call. "Gotta go. Say hello to Sharon for me."

"You're behind a little, pal. That's what living in the boonies gets you. This week, it's Susie."

Michael shook his head, smiling, and ended the call, picking up the next one. It was the state lab. "Tell me what you've got."

"I've got trouble with a capital T." The lab technician, for once, was dead serious. "You'd better get over here. Now."

CHAPTER TWENTY-THREE

After Kaz left, Lucy watched Sykes go down the hall to his office, enter, and close the door. She wandered over to the vending machine against the far wall and fed quarters into it, punching the button for a can of soda with more force than was necessary. *Okay, think.* Something wasn't adding up, and if she had more caffeine in her system, her fuzzed-out brain would be able to figure it out.

What she'd just overheard didn't compute. Clint Jackson had told her that Sykes had been the one to put Gary on suicide watch. But Sykes was acting as if this was news to him. So someone was lying. And when she put that together with Gary's refusal to talk to the cops all along, then the way he'd resisted arrest, she didn't like where all of it was taking her. Somewhere, there was a dirty cop. The obvious choice was Jackson.

Could he be the in-town buyer of the drug-smuggling ring? The fishermen couldn't be handling it on their own—they were just the runners. But a cop? She knew these guys. She had trouble believing that any of them would be in on drug deals.

Then again, who better than a cop? A cop would have the inside track on investigations and undercover narc work, and he or she could make sure that their runners and dealers were never arrested.

She remembered what her snitch had said the other morning at the warehouse. *You cops, you think you're above the law.* A shiver ran through her.

Jackson made sense—he'd been in the right places all along. He'd been assigned surveillance on Kaz's house, yet was suspiciously absent when she'd had break-ins. Hell, he'd even been in on conducting the search warrant. He'd been in the vicinity and easily could have attacked Kaz afterward. And he'd been present at Gary's arrest. How many of Gary's injuries were *really* the result of resisting arrest?

She slapped the wall beside the vending machine with her hand, then leaned against it, closing her eyes. If she were right, then Gary was in real danger. He knew too much to be left alive. And if anyone could get to him in the station house, a cop could. *And make it look like suicide.*

She gulped down soda. Although she didn't like it, she had no choice—she had to take her suspicions to Sykes. If she was wrong, well, then she'd look like a fool. So what else was new?

No question that the guys on the force wouldn't trust her from here on out. Cops stuck together—they didn't rat on each other. And it wouldn't be the first time she'd jumped to conclusions and then had to live down the consequences. But sit by and watch Gary possibly be murdered? *No.*

She turned and walked down the hall to Sykes's office. His door was still closed—she could see through the window that he was on a phone call. When he finished, she tapped on the door and opened it, entering. She closed the door behind her.

Eyebrows raised, Sykes motioned for her to sit. "What's on your mind, McGuire?"

"Sir, I'd like you to delay the arraignment."

He frowned at her, leaning back in his chair, his hands behind his head. "I've already been through this with Kaz. Jorgensen doesn't need his own lawyer to stand there for five minutes and enter a plea."

"That's not what I'm talking about." Lucy leaned forward in her chair. Her best strategy was to convince Sykes that the case wasn't yet solid enough. "I've uncovered some information indicates Gary might've been framed."

Sykes went abruptly still. "What makes you think that?"

"Well, for one thing, Gary's not stupid enough to leave the tire iron where we could find it. And," she continued before he could argue, "the time line doesn't work. I got the lab results back, and given the match of the concrete and mud samples with the bridge, Gary wouldn't have had time, after leaving the tavern, to meet up with Ken, kill him, then transfer him to the boat and set a time-delayed fire. Kaz was right on his heels—"

Sykes held up a hand to stop her. "Look, McGuire. I understand that you haven't worked that many homicides, so you wouldn't necessarily be aware that, in cases like these, not all the evidence lines up neatly. There's always some detail that doesn't seem to make sense. But that doesn't mean Jorgensen is innocent. The man ran, which is a strong indication that he's guilty as sin. And he resisted arrest."

"I think I can explain that," Lucy said urgently. "If I'm right about a theory I'm working on. One that I'd like your permission to follow up on."

Sykes took his time pulling out a cigar and lighting it. After a couple of puffs, he motioned for her to continue.

She drew a breath and plunged in. "You said, a few minutes ago, that you didn't know Gary had been placed on suicide watch."

Sykes stared at her through a cloud of smoke, his expression blank. "So?"

"So Clint told me before you got here that *you* were the one who had put Gary on suicide watch." Lucy waited for a reaction, but he said nothing. "Don't you see? If Clint is in on this, and Gary knew it, he'd be afraid to turn himself in."

"Whoa." Sykes sat forward abruptly. "McGuire, you need to be real careful before you go around accusing your fellow officers of something illegal."

"But what if Clint put Gary on suicide watch because it would make a good explanation if he winds up dead?"

Sykes didn't say anything for a long moment, and she resisted the urge to shift in her chair. Finally, he nodded thoughtfully. "Interesting theory. Do you have any proof?"

"Not yet, but I'm working on it. And Kaz could have plenty later this evening."

"Oh?" He pinned her with a hard look. "You letting a civilian get mixed up in this?"

"Do you think I could've stopped her? Her brother's in jail, accused of a crime he probably didn't commit—"

"We don't know that," Sykes said, his tone firm. "I'm still inclined to believe that he's guilty. But he may not have been working alone—almost certainly, he wasn't. Where is Kaz right now?"

Lucy hesitated. She'd opened the door—she could hardly refuse to answer. "The mooring basin."

He stubbed out his cigar in the ashtray and stood, indicating that their meeting was over. "I'll look into what you've said. I don't want one cop investigating another on my force. And I'm sure as hell not initiating an official investigation into one of my detectives until I have more proof. I plan to go through with the arraignment. If you pick up any other information, you need to tell me right away, is that clear?"

"Yes, sir." Lucy stood and turned to go.

"McGuire?"

At the door, she turned back. "Sir?"

"Good work."

At the Redemption, Kaz sat in the darkened corner of the same booth that Michael had occupied that first night, sipping a glass of beer and watching the other patrons in the bar. She'd tried Michael at the station, but there had been no answer. Then she'd left a message on his cell phone. So far, he hadn't shown up.

Svensen was there, along with Jacobsen and others. It was now two hours before the end of slack tide. If Svensen was going to make a move, he had to make it soon.

Steve hadn't been happy when he'd seen her arrive, but if he suspected why she was there, he'd given no indication.

Karl drank the last of his beer and paid his bill, then headed for the back hall. Anyone watching him would assume that he was simply going to the men's room, but his actions had a studied casualness about them.

After a minute, Kaz got up and followed him. The back hall was dimly lit, like the rest of the bar. Several doors, all closed, led off it, and at the very back, a door led outside, probably to the edge of the pier. Svensen was nowhere to be seen.

Kaz walked down the hallway to Steve's office door. She turned the knob quietly, opened the door a crack, and glanced inside. The room was empty. She stood there for a moment, perplexed. Then she heard a toilet flush in the men's room, and footsteps. She ducked into the office, closing the door behind her.

That had been close. Evidently, Karl really had come back here to relieve himself of all that beer. Then the footsteps turned and came back down the hallway.

The knob of the office door turned. She glanced around, frantic for a hiding place. She could crouch on the far side of the filing cabinet, but if he came in, he'd surely see her. At the last second before the door opened, she dove underneath the desk, curling herself up as best she could inside the cavity between the two rows of drawers and pulling the chair back into place.

The door opened, temporarily letting in the noise from the bar. The bar noise was abruptly shut off as Karl closed the door and latched it, locking it from the inside.

Kaz concentrated on breathing shallowly and quietly.

The light came on, and she watched boot-clad feet walk over to the file cabinet. He opened a drawer and she heard him slide file folders to the front, the plastic of their frames clacking as he shoved them together. He must have taken something out, because she heard it thud down on top of the cabinet. As quietly as possible, she shifted so that she could put her head down on the floor and look out from under the edge of the desk.

Karl stood with his back to her, unwrapping a package. She heard a rustling sound, possibly of heavy plastic being unwrapped, then he slammed the drawer shut, picked up the package, and turned around. Just before she ducked back into the desk, she saw that whatever he had was covered in black plastic. Her movement brought her butt up against the other wall of her hiding space. The wood of the desk creaked ever so faintly.

He stopped, turning back toward her hiding place. She stopped breathing.

After a long moment, the light went off, plunging the room into darkness. Then, silence. He wasn't leaving. Her air was running out, her heart pounding so loud she couldn't believe that he couldn't hear it.

Finally, he crouched in the far corner of the room, pulling back the carpet there. He reached for something in the flooring, flipped it up, and used it to pull open the trap door. The smell of the river, carried on a waft of cool air, flowed into the room, and she heard the waves lapping against the pilings below. There was a shuffling noise, then he dropped through the door, pulling it closed after him.

Kaz sucked great quantities of air into her deprived lungs. After a moment, she climbed out from under the desk. Gary's information had been dead on—Karl was probably on his way upriver to the mooring basin. She had only minutes to spare if she wanted to follow him.

Rounding the desk, she slid on silent feet to the door and cautiously opened it. The hallway was clear, so she slipped out, closing the door behind her. Smoothing her clothes and hair, she walked back into the bar. Steve gave her a sharp glance, then seemed to sigh. He nodded, his expression serious, his eyes worried. She smiled reassuringly at him.

Walking over to her table, she sat down and drank the last of her beer, setting the mug down unhurriedly, then placed some folded bills under the edge of the glass for Sandra. She stood and walked calmly out the door.

Once outside, she broke into a run.

CHAPTER TWENTY-FOUR

Fifteen minutes later, after losing a battle with herself, Lucy walked back toward the interrogation room to talk to Gary one more time in the hopes of getting him to cooperate. She needed to stay out of it, let Sykes handle it. But she couldn't—she just . . . *couldn't*. Where Gary was concerned, she might as well get used to it—she had no objectivity.

As she reached out to open the door, she glanced out the window at the end of the hallway. And what she saw froze her in her tracks.

Sykes was standing in the parking lot next to a police cruiser, talking to whoever was inside. He said something, threw his head back and laughed, then reached inside the window to clap the cop on the shoulder. Then the cruiser backed out of the parking spot, turning and giving Lucy a clear view of who was driving.

Clint Jackson.

She leaned against the interrogation room door, closing her eyes. Sykes hadn't believed her. She made a sound of self-disgust. And why would he? She was the rooky detective, the one who had no experience. The one with the rep for jumping to conclusions.

She stood in the hallway, an internal debate raging within her. Gary was in grave danger, she *wasn't* wrong about that. She had to buy him some time. But how? The thought of his dying . . . she shuddered. She knew what she had to do, the only thing she *could* do. A laugh tinged with hysteria escaped. So they'd thought she was impulsive before? Well, hell. They didn't know the half of it.

She glanced toward Ivar's desk. He was sitting where he'd been for the last two hours, still working on Kaz's computer. Should she tell him what she was up to? In less than a second she had her answer—a big-time NO. He was better off not knowing, not being a party to an illegal act. She didn't need to take his career down along with hers.

Squaring her shoulders, she opened the door to the interrogation room and told Brenner, who'd been standing guard, to leave. Gary looked down at the floor, refusing to acknowledge her presence, just as he had since they'd brought him in. Desperation overlaid the other emotions she was feeling. If she was right, she had only minutes to get through to him. Once he was arraigned and locked up for the night . . .

She pulled up a chair and sat down. "So," she said with a casualness that belied what she was feeling. "I'll bet you don't have any way of knowing, since you haven't spent a lot of time in our cool new police station, that the men's room is right by the back door."

Gary's head slowly came up. He stared at her with his good eye.

"The back door that leads directly to the parking lot, and beyond that, to those old warehouses," she added.

He shook his head. "What are you doing, Luce?"

She leaned forward and lowered her voice. "I don't think you'll be alive, come morning. Am I wrong?"

He just stared at her, his expression giving nothing away.

Anger at his indifference to his own safety bubbled up, edged with panic. "And I don't think you resisted arrest. They beat you, just like they beat Ken. Didn't they?"

No response.

She kept going doggedly, determined to get through to him. "You know, rumor has it that you have a weak bladder."

After a long moment, he nodded.

Relief flooded through her. "Then you'll need to go to the men's room after all that water Kaz just let you drink." She stood up and took hold of his elbow. "Let's go. *Now.* There's no time."

He shuffled along beside her docilely enough. To anyone glancing their way, it looked like it was supposed to look—that she was escorting the prisoner to the restroom. Once inside, she quickly checked the rest of the stalls, then took a key out of her pocket and unlocked his hand and leg cuffs. "Okay," she said, standing back and assuming a fighting stance. "Make it look good."

Gary shook his head. "Can't . . . hurt you."

She rolled her eyes. "It has to look like you overpowered me. That is, if I'm going to stand a chance of keeping my job when this is all over."

He shook his head again, and glanced at the closed door. "Find . . . another way. Can't do it."

She blew out an exasperated breath, dropped her hands to her hips, and angled her chin at him. "Just knock me out, dammit. I've taken worse on the mat at the gym. Do you want to live, or not?" She glared at him, then went for the taunt that might make him angry enough to do what was necessary. "Or is that it? Finally, you have to choose to save your own hide so that you can save Kaz's. Wouldn't want you acting out of self-interest, now would we?"

He growled and reached for her, placing his hands on her shoulders, cupping the curve of her neck. His thumbs caressed the sensitive skin behind her ears. She tried to control the shiver that went through her at his warm touch but wasn't quite fast enough.

One corner of his mouth slowly lifted. "So I . . . still . . . get . . . to you." His expression was affectionate. His hands tightened just slightly.

"Oh, just shut up—" The darkness came quickly, swamping her.

The last thing she remembered was being gently lowered to the floor and the whispered words, "Sorry, love."

"Like you thought, the accelerant was gasoline," the lab technician said.

Michael stood in the basement lab at the State Police facility in Warrenton, glancing through the paperwork the technician had handed him.

"And it matches what was found on the rags in the back of Jorgensen's car." The tech pulled the sheets out of his hand, held them side by side, then pointed at the two gas chromatograph readings. "That's not definitive, since most of the gas around here comes from the same refinery, but along with everything else . . ."

Michael glanced at his watch, worried about the passing time. He had to get back to the station to pick up Kaz soon. He wouldn't put it past her to get impatient and strike out on her own. The woman needed a keeper. And so far, the tech hadn't given him any reason for his demand that Michael drop everything and drive out there. "Why the hell—"

"And I've got a match on the DNA," the tech interrupted him. He rummaged around on his desk, then held up two DNA diagrams which, sure enough, looked identical. He was shifting from one foot to another and glancing nervously Michael's way.

Michael's heart sank. It had to be either Gary or Kaz. Which didn't prove that either one of them had committed the murder, but it left him with no way to prove that they hadn't, either. When would he get a break on this damn case? "Whose sample matched?" he asked, resigned.

The tech shuffled his feet again. "That's just it. I retested two times, because I thought I'd made a mistake. Then I checked your labels again, and I was wondering if you'd mismarked the samples—"

Michael ground his teeth. "I didn't screw up the samples, for Christ's sake. Just spit it out. Which one matched?"

"The cigar."

Michael froze. "Say that again."

"The cigar's a match to the hair follicle. Where'd you get it, anyway? We didn't find anything like that on the boat, or—"

Michael dropped the paperwork and sprinted for the door, taking the basement steps three at a time.

Sonofabitch! Sykes had been playing him all along. His blood iced. And Kaz was at the station. Surely Sykes wouldn't try anything in front of the other cops—he wouldn't be that brazen. But who knew how many of them were working with him?

Racing across the parking lot to his car, he used his cell phone to dial the station. Ivar answered Lucy's phone. "Where is she?" Michael shouted.

"In the interrogation room with Gary," Ivar answered. "Why?"

"No time to explain. Tell Kaz not to move. I'll be right there."

"She's not here."

Michael skidded to a stop at the car door, one hand in his pocket, reaching for his keys. Zeke barked at him from inside the car, jumping up and down. "*What?*"

"Yeah, she left about half an hour ago."

"Fuck! Where was she headed?"

"She said something to Lucy about heading to the mooring basin and then to the tavern."

"Is Sykes there?" Michael asked, terror's grip making it hard for him to form the words.

"Hold on." Ivar put the phone down for a few seconds, then came back online. "He must've gone home already; I don't see him in his office."

"Keep me posted." Michael disconnected and yanked open the car door. He started to toss the cell phone on the front seat when he saw that he had a message. Why hadn't it come through? Because he'd been in the basement at the time, that's why. He cursed again. While he started the car and pulled on his and Zeke's seatbelts, he listened to the message from Kaz. Then checked the time stamp.

He didn't have much time.

Kaz kept the *Kasmira B*'s running lights off and stayed far enough back so that Karl wouldn't see her in the approaching darkness. But with the wind picking up, and conditions becoming choppier, she found it hard to keep him in sight. Luckily, they were headed over the river bar—there wasn't really anywhere Karl could go to lose her until he was across. But if he crossed faster than she did, or if she were delayed or made any navigational mistakes, she could easily lose him on the ocean side. If she did, her only option would be to head for the location he'd given out over the radio the day before and pray that she was right.

She'd filled the *Kasmira B*'s tanks before going to the Redemption, which had given her the edge she'd needed to track Karl from the tavern to the marina without being spotted. Once out of the Redemption, she'd driven along Marine Drive, keeping his small skiff in sight as he took it upriver to the mooring basin. By the time she'd gotten there and parked, he was fueling up at the pumps and hadn't seen her sneak down the docks and onto her own boat.

The *Kasmira B* bounced harder than usual, sending alarm skittering along her nerves. The weather report coming across the marine channel wasn't good—a storm surge of up to fifteen feet was predicted just offshore, with more than thirty feet out at sea. Add to that winds up to forty knots, and it would be hell coming back across. If she could make it at all.

She couldn't think about being caught out for the

night. Whatever she learned out here she *had* to be able to communicate back to Lucy. For whatever reason, maybe simply that sense of connection she'd always had with Gary, she didn't believe that he'd survive the night. And that scared her far more than crossing the river bar under the wrong conditions.

Keeping closer to shore than Karl did, she paralleled him, staying as far back as she dared off his port stern. Only half an hour after turning south, he cut his engines to an idle and ran alongside a buoy. Just as she'd suspected, his location matched the position he'd given out on the radio yesterday. He'd employed the fishermen's habit of broadcasting false locations, but his intent all along had been to tell the drug suppliers which crab pots were the drop location. She had to admit, it was a clever idea. Someone had once said that the best place to hide something valuable was right in plain sight. This was just a fisherman's variation on that theme.

Karl's running lights provided just enough illumination so that with binoculars, she could watch him pull the crab pot out of the water, open it up, take out some kind of package, and then drop the plastic-wrapped package he'd taken from the office into the cage. Then he lowered it back into the water.

Grabbing a pen and paper, Kaz noted the longitude and latitude, as evidence for later. Karl had brought himself down by following every ship captain's habit—writing down all his movements in the ship's log. With her notes as corroboration, they had him. Now all she had to do was follow him back to port and then on to his meeting with his in-town contact.

"Gotcha," she murmured out loud. She was one giant step closer to proving Gary's innocence.

"No," a voice behind her said. "We've got *you*."

The blackness of all darkness lay around him. . . .
Then he remembered that he was Coyote,
the wisest and cunningest of all the animals.

CHAPTER TWENTY-FIVE

As Michael skidded onto the wharf, his cell phone warbled. He picked it up and flipped it open. "Talk."

"I found Lucy," Ivar said. "Knocked out cold in the men's room. Gary's escaped."

Michael started swearing. "Were you able to revive her?"

"Yeah, she says Kaz planned to observe the hand-off of the cash at the Redemption and then follow Karl Svensen from there."

"Follow him where?"

"That's not clear, but I'd bet out on the water somewhere. Makes sense."

Michael got out of the car and searched the boats on the docks below. "Both boats are gone, Svensen's and Kaz's. Goddammit! What did she think she was doing, taking this on by herself?"

"My guess is she didn't have a choice. They both were at the mercy of the tides," Ivar pointed out.

He was right, but that didn't make Michael's heart pound any slower. "Yeah, okay. Listen to me. It's Sykes."

There was momentary silence on the other end. "What?"

"Sykes is behind this, dammit. You and Lucy notify the Coast Guard, have them put a rescue boat out on the water."

"You're wrong, man. Lucy says it's Clint Jackson. And Steve called from the Redemption just now, worried about Kaz. He didn't say a thing about Sykes."

Michael told him about the DNA samples. "I don't know whether Jackson is in on it, and I don't know how much Steve is privy to in this mess, but Sykes is the murderer." He could hear Lucy shouting in the background. "I can see Bjorn from here—I'll convince him to take me out. Let's just hope to hell we're fast enough. Sykes's Lincoln Navigator is parked a block from here, locked up tight."

He dropped the phone on the car seat and locked the door, leaving Zeke whining unhappily inside with one window slightly cracked. He cleared the ramp down to Bjorn's trawler in one leap.

Kaz stared at Jim Sykes, who stood on the top step of the stairs that led to the engine room, pointing a large black handgun at her chest. His smile was cold. "You Jorgensens. You never did know when to mind your own business."

"You're in on this?" she asked. "Jim, why?"

His expression turned derisive. "You think a police chief's salary in a Podunk town like Astoria will ever get me where I want to go? Money is power, Kaz. You know that from all those consulting gigs you had."

"But, Jim. Murder?"

He shrugged, seemingly unmoved. "Ken would've blabbed, sooner or later. I had to shut him up. All my life, I've done what had to be done."

Kaz shivered. He'd committed cold-blooded murder, just for money. "It was you who shot at me out by the Elk Preserve."

Sykes chuckled, but his eyes were dead. "Couldn't have you running around proving Gary's innocence, now could I? He was a necessary part of my plan—my scapegoat."

"But why Gary?"

"It gave me great pleasure to frame one of you Jorgensens." Sykes leaned toward her, his expression becoming more coldly satisfied. "You want to know the truth? I've hated both of you ever since we were kids. The great fucking Jorgensen twins—smart, popular, and with parents that every kid like me wanted to have. That night they drowned? I goddamn cheered. The only bad part was that you survived." He nodded and leaned back, pleased with the effect his words had had on her. "Now where's the fucking money?"

Kaz was having trouble controlling the trembling that had started deep inside her. She cleared her throat, hoping her voice would be steady. "Gary used it to pay off Bobby's medical bills. It's gone—you'll never get it back."

Sykes's expression turned ugly. "Well, now. That's just too bad. I was going to spare you by knocking you out, but I guess, after hearing that bit of news, I'll just let you burn alive. In fact, killing both of you is going to be a real pleasure."

"You're going to kill Gary," she said numbly.

"Clint'll handle that little task for me, later this evening." Sykes looked amused. "Your brother was always unstable. His suicide will be just one more tragedy for your family." He stepped to the side and motioned her out onto the deck. "Let's go."

She needed to keep him talking while she came up with a plan. A quick glance around the wheelhouse told her there was nothing that could be used as a weapon. "Jim—"

He reached out, lightening quick, and backhanded her with the pistol. She cried out, stars glittering in the periphery of her vision.

"That's for damn near breaking my nose last night," he said. "Now move. And no more games."

Michael stood on the bow of Bjorn's trawler, staring intently into the gathering darkness and gusting wind. When they were riding high on a crest, he could just make out the *Kasmira B.* His gut was churning, and his hands were so slippery with sweat that he could barely grip the binoculars.

Sykes had played him, using his newcomer status to control the investigation so he could frame Gary. And the mayor was no saint in all of this, either. Forbes had to have at least suspected Sykes, or he never would've visited Michael that day on the docks. Michael had thought he was just worried about old friendships, old loyalties getting in the way of the investigation. He hadn't really given his talk with the mayor any more thought after that morning. That had been his first mistake. His second had been underestimating Sykes.

Sykes had chosen arson as his method on purpose, and he'd planned on having the power to block Michael's jurisdiction over the case. Well, he'd planned wrong. But he'd still managed to slip under Michael's radar long enough to put Kaz in grave danger.

Not again, not again. The refrain played over and over in his mind. Kaz was paying the price for his stupidity. He'd been too slow to figure it out, too slow to put the details together. All along, Sykes had run the investigation from behind the scenes. He'd had access to the boat and to Gary's truck. He also had enough SWAT team training to handle shooting at Kaz that day from the Elk Preserve. "If someone sneezes out on Youngs Bay, I know about it," he'd told Michael. He probably knew all those old logging roads like the back of his hand. Michael swallowed bile-filled rage. And Sykes had been at Kaz's house last night, executing a search warrant. All the sonofabitch would've had to do was leave, wait a couple of minutes, then come back and attack her.

Where was he? He had to be out with Svensen. And Kaz was following them, trying to gather evidence. If either one of them saw her . . .

Michael walked back to the door of the wheelhouse. "Cut your running lights. I don't want anyone seeing us."

Bjorn complied without comment, and Michael held up the binoculars. He could make out Kaz in the wheelhouse of the *Kasmira B*, along with the shadow of someone else. His heart stopped.

Fiddling with the focus, he brought the man into sharp relief. As he watched, Sykes pistol-whipped Kaz, putting the weight of his body behind the vicious blow. She hit the far wall and slid out of sight.

An icy calm settled over Michael. His heartbeat slowed to a strong, steady, focused rhythm. He set the binoculars down carefully, then turned to Bjorn. "Do you have an inflatable raft?"

"Yeah, but in these kinds of conditions—"

"Get it."

CHAPTER TWENTY-SIX

Kaz pulled herself up from the wheelhouse floor and walked past Sykes out onto the deck on shaky legs, her right hand holding her throbbing face. As the storm moved closer, the *Kasmira B* was starting to pitch in earnest. She stumbled once, then regained her balance.

Sykes motioned for her to stop just outside the door. Keeping the gun trained on her, he braced his feet and switched on the radio, then picked up the handset. "Karl."

"Yeah."

"Give me five minutes, and then come alongside."

"Make it ten—we've got storm surge."

Sykes switched off the radio and then yanked out the cord of the handset, tossing it on the floor. Then he came out and motioned Kaz toward the stern. She staggered, almost tripping over the can of gasoline that was sitting against the winch. Funny how she hadn't seen it when she'd come on board. If she had, she wouldn't be in this mess.

Keep him talking. "What did you do—stow away?"

Sykes's expression was smug. "I figured you wouldn't check the head. I was in there the whole time."

He motioned to her to sit on the stern bench, then took out a roll of duct tape, taping her hands and feet so tight that her circulation was cut off. He gave her a hard shove, and she fell onto the deck.

The shoulder she landed on protested, and she gritted her teeth. "So you were the one who broke into my house and attacked me. I knew there was something familiar about you."

He laughed. It was an ugly sound. "Yeah, I enjoyed that. It's a shame I was in such a hurry, or I could've had some real fun with you." He picked up the can of gasoline, opened it, and started pouring it on the deck. The acrid smell burned Kaz's nose as the liquid flowed across the planking toward her. She rolled as far away from it as she could.

He walked toward the bow, pouring the gasoline as he went, then put the can down and stepped inside the wheelhouse, pulling a small timer and some rags out of his pocket.

He was going to burn the boat, with her on it. If she didn't do something, and quickly, she would die. She thought of Michael. By now, he had to be frantic. Anger surged through her. As she felt the first splatter of raindrops on her face, she made her decision. She wasn't going to die. Not today.

Trying not to alert Sykes, she felt along the edge of the stern compartment, but she found nothing she could use as a weapon. She kept her bait cleaver in a slot behind the winch. Could she get to it? She would have to scrabble across the deck, through the gasoline, which would soak into her clothes. And if the fire started before she freed herself, she'd burn to death in seconds. Hey, no pain, no gain, she thought, a small, hysterical giggle escaping.

She pushed herself along the deck toward the winch, using the rubber edges of her running shoes to fight the rolling of the trawler. Spray slapped her down, soaking through her clothing. She closed her eyes, now stinging from the salt, and kept going.

When she heard a slight thump on the decking, she jolted. Was someone else on board? Or was that wishful thinking? Had it just been the wind moving the gear around? Craning her neck, she glanced at Sykes. He was busy pouring gasoline and hadn't seemed to notice the sound.

Quickly, she used her feet against the stern bench to shove herself the last several feet. The pooled gasoline was slippery and made her progress easier. She maneuvered around so that her hands and back were to the winch, feeling frantically for the cleaver. *There*. Her hands closed around the handle. She slid it under the edge of her sou'wester just as Sykes came back out of the wheelhouse.

He stared down at her in her new position, and his expression clouded with fury. He raised his gun.

"Drop it," Michael said, appearing around the corner of the wheelhouse, his feet braced, his gun trained on Sykes.

At the sight of him, relief flooded through Kaz, followed instantly by terror for his safety.

Sykes kept his gun trained on her and glanced over his shoulder. "I don't think so. You shoot me, and I shoot her."

Michael shook his head. "You don't want to die, Sykes."

Sykes tightened his finger on the trigger. "Drop your gun, Chapman, or she dies. Now."

Michael's lips tightened, and he shot a tormented look at Kaz. Then he complied, leaning down and placing his gun on the deck.

"That's better," Sykes said, turning and aiming his gun at Michael. "Kick it away."

Michael did as he was told, and the gun slid across the deck and over the edge, disappearing into the waters below.

Kaz closed her eyes, her shoulders slumping. They were going to die if she didn't do something. Sykes's finger tightened on the trigger, and he took careful aim at Michael.

"*No!*" Kaz raised her bound feet and kicked the back of Sykes's knee. The shot went wild as Sykes lost his balance and fell to the deck. Michael launched himself through the air, across the space that divided them, landing on top of Sykes.

They rolled and grappled for the gun. The gas can toppled, spraying gas in all directions, some of it hitting Kaz. She shook her head to clear the burning liquid out of her eyes, trying to focus on the two men. They rolled toward the stern, fighting viciously and silently.

Sykes landed a hard punch, then managed to roll on top of Michael and slam his head into the deck. Kaz whimpered.

Positioning the cleaver, she sawed it back and forth against the edge of the tape, her hands now so numb that she couldn't control the angle of the cleaver or what she was cutting. She felt something warm and wet flow over her fingers, but she kept sawing.

Michael scissored his legs, throwing Sykes off him, then landed on top of him. Sykes raised his gun. Michael gripped Sykes's hand with both of his, deflecting his aim, and a second shot went wild.

Kaz felt the tape on her hands give and she wrenched them apart, then sat up to work on her feet. She was almost finished when the gun went off again. Her head flew up, terror locking her throat.

Michael fell back, and Sykes shoved him out of the way so that he could get to his feet, gun in hand. "Nice try, Chapman." He was panting heavily.

Kaz got to her feet stealthily, the cleaver still in her hand. She advanced on Sykes quickly, the cleaver raised. But he turned, and seeing her, kicked her feet out from under her. On a deck covered with a mixture of sea water and gasoline, she didn't stand a chance. She went down hard, the cleaver flying out of her hands. She rolled onto her back and looked up. He was pointing the gun at her head, his finger on the trigger.

She glared at him defiantly. He laughed.

Then he jerked, his face registering surprise. He lurched awkwardly. His fingers sagged, nerveless, as he dropped the gun. Twisting around, he tried to grab the fish hook that was embedded in his back. Staring at Michael, he started to fall, his arms flailing wildly. Landing on the deck railing, his momentum carried him over the side.

Kaz got to her knees and crawled to the rail and peered over, but there was no sign of him in the churning waters. She turned back to Michael.

He lay where he'd fallen a few feet away, his eyes closed. A dark, rapidly spreading pool of blood stained the decking beneath him.

CHAPTER TWENTY-SEVEN

Sobbing, Kaz crawled over to him. "Michael!" She grabbed the front of his shirt. "Don't you dare die on me, dammit!"

"Okay," he said calmly, not opening his eyes.

"What do you mean, *okay?* You're bleeding!"

"Yeah, but I got the bastard." He opened an eye and tried to smile at her, then frowned at the blood on her hands. "Are you okay?"

"You're the one who's been shot!" She started pulling at his clothes, ripping open his shirt, feeling along his rib cage.

"My leg," he managed. "I think he got lucky and hit the bone." He tried to rise up on one elbow, but the effort was too much and he sank back, closing his eyes. "Go into the wheelhouse and disconnect the timer before this damn boat goes up."

She glanced back at the wheelhouse, then at Michael. She didn't want to leave him. Taking off her coat, she quickly pulled off her sweater, then her cotton turtleneck. Folding it into a pad, she pressed it to the bloodiest area on his leg. Then she laid her coat over him to conserve his body heat. "Hold the pad in place until I get back."

Getting to her feet, she slipped and slid into the wheelhouse, clad from the waist up only in her bra. She might be freezing, but at least she had less gasoline on her. Grabbing the timer and the pile of rags, she leaned out the door and threw them overboard. Then she started searching for something, anything she could use as a tourniquet.

The *Kasmira B* rocked to port, hard. Standing up, she looked out the window. They'd drifted north, putting them closer to the river bar. But the swells were getting huge. Restarting the engines, she turned the trawler into the oncoming waves. Leaving the engines on idle, she ran back out onto the deck.

Spying a length of line, she fetched the cleaver. Kneeling beside Michael, she drew the line around his leg, above the bleeding area, and tied it tight.

"Tighter," he said, his voice more faint than it had been a few minutes ago.

A wave crashed over the railing, its icy foam hissing and bubbling as it engulfed them. Michael sucked in a breath, and his body started shaking, hard. He was going into shock, his lips turning blue. She had to get him out of the water, or he'd die before she could get help.

She used the cleaver to rip his jeans to take a better look—there was a small entry wound about midway up his thigh, and an exit *crater* on the opposite side. She let out a sob. The leg looked funny—it was bent at an awkward angle. "Is it broken?" she whispered.

"Yeah, I think so. . . . Feels like it." He managed to

get up on one elbow and look at it. "You'll have to tie it tighter, love, or I won't make it back to port."

Ripping her turtleneck in half, she fashioned two pads out of it, then rolled him to press the second one to the back of his leg. She positioned the line over each pad and pulled it tighter. He let out a sound of pain. The bleeding slowed but didn't stop. Her makeshift bandages were already turning bright red.

"I've got a better idea," she said. The deck was pitching hard with the larger waves now, but if she could get him below before he lost consciousness, they stood a fighting chance. "Come on."

She put an arm around his shoulders and helped him sit up. His face was white, his teeth gritted, and his skin clammy with sweat. She had to move fast—he wouldn't be conscious much longer. "Okay, on the count of three, we're going to stand up, and you're going to use me as a brace to get down the stairs."

"You're insane, you know that? I've got a perfectly good deck I can lie on right here—"

"A deck that you'll slide right off of when we go over the bar. Plus, I can get your leg elevated down below, and tie you in, in case you conk out."

"Make that cruel and insane." But when she said "three" he heaved himself up, leaning heavily on her. "Here you are almost naked," he panted, "and I'm in no shape to follow through."

She shot him a look. "I am not amused, Chapman."

They almost lost balance twice on the greasy planking before she got him to the stairs. Bracing her body below his and using the stair railing as leverage, she had him lean on her as they hopped down the stairs. Once in the galley, she laid him down so that half of his body was on the dining table, then hauled his legs up until he was lying flat. Then as gently as possible, she propped his injured leg on the hanging spice island. The platter was designed to move with the boat's motion, and it would keep his leg elevated.

She raced back up on deck, fetching the roll of duct tape Sykes had left behind. Using long pieces of it, she taped Michael to the table, then taped his leg to the hanging platter. Through it all, Michael kept his eyes closed. His face had lost all color.

"Are you still with me?" she whispered.

". . . Yeah."

The elevation had slowed the bleeding, but he was still losing blood too rapidly. "I have to tighten the rope again. Hang on." She retied it as a slip knot, and tightened the rope by degrees. When he groaned, she sobbed, cringing at the excruciating pain she had to be causing him. Once she had the bleeding down to an ooze, she tied the rope in a double knot and then yanked a blanket off the berth and threw it over him.

"Hang on. I've got to get us over the river bar." She rummaged in the locker for a sweater and pulled it on.

"Lucy and Ivar called the Coast Guard . . . when I left port. They should be looking for us . . ." his voice faded.

"Yeah, but Sykes ripped out the handset, I can't get off a signal. And with the weather like this, our best bet is to cross the bar and hope to meet them on the other side." She took a precious moment to lean down and kiss him, then lay her cheek against his. "Try to stay conscious, okay?"

". . . yeah." He grimaced, then leered half-heartedly at her. "Liked you better . . . just the bra."

She laughed softly. "Another time, I promise. I'm going to get you back over that bar, you hear? So no wimping out on me."

There was no response.

"Michael?" She felt for his pulse. It was too rapid, and his breathing was too shallow.

He didn't have much time left.

"*Kasmira B,* come in. *Kasmira B,* can you read?" Bjorn's voice crackled through the radio.

Sobbing with relief, Kaz took the stairs two at a time to the wheelhouse and grabbed the radio mike. She twisted the ripped wires together, praying that the radio would work, and flipped the switch. "This is the *Kasmira B.* Bjorn, Michael Chapman is on board, badly injured." She gave him their position. "Do you copy?"

"*Kasmira B,* do you read? We have you in sight. State your condition."

Kaz stared at the mike, flipped the switch again, and retransmitted.

"*Kasmira B,* do you copy?"

She threw down the mike in frustration. She could receive, but not transmit. She went out onto the deck and searched the churning waters around her, but she could see nothing. Climbing to the flying bridge, she searched again.

Nothing.

Jumping back down to deck level, she threw open the stern seat cover and searched for a flare. Breaking it apart, she held it up as high as she could for a few moments, then tossed it into the waters off the stern. She just hoped Bjorn would see it.

She returned to the wheelhouse and waited. After an agonizingly long minute, the radio crackled to life.

"*Kasmira B,* we have the flare in sight and have transmitted your position to the Coast Guard. They are currently just east of Sand Island. Kaz, you have to cross the river bar—they can't get to you where you are. If you have navigational capabilities, set off a second flare to confirm."

After complying, she waited for the next response. "Confirmed, *Kasmira B*. We will follow you through the bar. Over and out."

Quickly, she assessed the conditions. The storm surge was still building, the winds now howling through the rigging. She pushed the throttle bar forward and heard the trawler's engines roar to life.

For a split second, she thought about that night fifteen years ago, the old fears resurfacing. Then she shoved the memories down deep and forgot about them. Failure wasn't an option. In that horrifying moment when Sykes had shot Michael, her choices had become crystal clear. If she lost Michael, her life would never be the same.

Taking a deep breath, she steeled herself, then climbed back to the flying bridge, where her visibility—what was left of it—would be best. Her feet planted wide, her body braced against the wild pitching of the fishing trawler, she peered into the wind-whipped darkness, then turned the trawler into the oncoming breakers.

The boat labored up the steep crest of a massive black wave and then slid sickeningly down, bottoming out with a bone-jarring thud in the next trough. The trawler's timbers creaked loudly, and for a moment, just one second, Kaz lost her nerve.

She couldn't do it, she didn't have the skills. Maybe she was better off turning around, heading back out to sea. Bjorn could notify the Coast Guard, maybe they could get a helicopter up in this . . .

And then suddenly, Gary's voice was there with her, inside her head. *You've got to know what you're doing to get lucky on the river bar, Sis. First thing, get your bearings. Then steer based on your instinct, on the feel of the water beneath you.*

She took several deep, calming breaths. She could do this, she could. Shaking, she managed to take a reading off the whistle buoy at the mouth of the river, then adjust her course.

Cold rain was falling, obscuring the channel markers, the faint outlines of land and blurry halos of lights on shore disappearing into the blackness.

Hold her steady, Kaz. Don't panic. Wait for the next lull in the storm to get your bearings again, then correct your position.

Number 4 Buoy bobbed past, off to starboard, its beacon so pale that she almost missed it. The *Kasmira B* shuddered as the next wave hit, her rigging clanking against the boom. As the trawler pitched hard to starboard, she gave a second's thought to Michael down below, praying that her makeshift setup was keeping him strapped in.

"*Kasmira B.* You're looking good. Adjust one degree to starboard." Bjorn's voice came to her faintly. His next words were so uncannily supportive, it was almost as if he had heard her thoughts. "Kaz, you're gonna make it. Hang in there."

Tears streamed down her face, mixing with the rain. As she neared Clatsop Spit, huge breakers slammed into the trawler, their giant, white-foamed crests almost obscuring the buoys. She wrenched the wheel to the right with all her strength, forcing the trawler to sluggishly change course again.

We lost both Mom and Pop, Sis. What would I do if I

lost you, too? She shivered when a spate of icy sleet hit her numbed face like hot needles. She couldn't fail, dammit. *Not this time.*

The roar of the surf was so loud now that she could barely hear her own thoughts. The radio crackled again, and Bjorn said something, but it was lost on the wind.

She was on her own.

She eased her way toward the Lower Desdemona Shoal, where shifting sands made passage a literal game of Russian roulette. The trawler's diesel engine coughed, and Kaz froze, terror sliding sickeningly along her nerve endings. If she lost power now, they wouldn't stand a chance.

The engine coughed again, then resumed its ponderous chugging. She slumped against the console, then steered for the next buoy.

Another wave crashed over the trawler, surprising her, slapping her down and washing her halfway over the railing of the bridge. She clung to the wheel as it spun wildly under her weight, dragging herself back to her feet. Using most of her waning strength, she willed the trawler back on course.

After several agonizing minutes, she caught a glimpse of another buoy, enough to adjust her course again, just before fog enveloped the boat and obscured everything around her. Concentrating on keeping her course and speed even, she released another trembling breath when the next buoy loomed out of the murky darkness in front of her, right where it was supposed to be.

You're almost there, Sis. Home free. Instinct caused her to glance to stern. A wave slid silently and with deadly intent under the trawler, tilting the stern up high, pointing the trawler straight down.

Kaz swallowed the scream at the back of her throat, waited three seconds for the bow to start back up, counting them off inside her head, and then she yanked the throttle full open. The *Kasmira B*'s engine growled under the strain, fighting the river current. She felt the full power of the wave catch the boat and heard the roar of the water under the hull as the boat surged forward, surfing the flood. Moments later, the waters smoothed out.

She was across the bar. Braced against the console with both hands, she stood there, her head down, letting the tears fall.

Out of the darkness in front of her, the running lights of a large ship blinded her. "*Kasmira B*, this is the United States Coast Guard. Prepare to be boarded."

CHAPTER TWENTY-EIGHT

Kaz and Lucy backed up the stairs from the engine room, ahead of the two medics carrying the stretcher with Michael on it. Lucy cursed, her feet slipping on the treads made treacherous by the rocking of the trawler and the spilled gasoline.

Kaz hadn't wanted to let go of Michael's hand, but there wasn't enough room in the galley for two EMTs, a stretcher, and her. She'd had to stand off to the side and watch, terrified, while they pushed plasma into Michael's veins in an attempt to stabilize him. They'd been able to bring his blood pressure back up and were now preparing him to be air-lifted to the hospital. The Coast Guard helicopter hovered overhead, its spotlight illuminating the deck of the trawler, the noise from its rotors deafening.

"Creative use of duct tape," Lucy shouted as they moved into the wheelhouse to let the men by. "I'll bet you didn't learn that at your fancy school down south, did you?"

Kaz tried to smile, but tears leaked out, and suddenly, she was crying again. She'd been crying off and on for the last half hour.

Lucy put both arms around her and held her tight. "He's going to be all right, you know," she said. "You saved his sorry hide by elevating his leg." Then she straightened abruptly, sniffing Kaz and then her own clothes. "Ewww. Do you have *gasoline* all over you?"

Kaz nodded, wiping the tears off her cheeks with the palms of her hands. "Sykes poured it everywhere, and I had to roll through it to get to the cleaver that I used to cut myself free."

"Dammit! I just bought this blazer—you could've warned me." Lucy's disgust was comical as she surveyed the damage to the camel hair blazer she had on under her life vest. The EMTs had given Kaz a blanket to hug around herself, and it was the only item on her that didn't reek or that wasn't soaked with gasoline and seawater.

"Sykes went overboard," Kaz said as she watched the medics navigate the wildly rocking boats to attach the hooks to the basket Michael was lying in. "I couldn't save him."

Lucy nodded. "Probably for the best. I don't think this town could've stood the stress of the trial." Then her face crumpled. "God, Kaz. I was the one who told him everything, including where to find you. This is all my fault."

Kaz shook her head. "You couldn't have known."

"I *knew* there was a dirty cop, but I thought it was Jackson. I never even considered that the chief might also be involved. I blabbed everything to him, trying to get him to hold off on arraigning Gary until we could check out Jackson."

"Jackson *was* in on it, according to Sykes." Kaz hugged herself. "Gary's okay?"

"He's fine." Lucy started pacing in the cramped space. "The jerk! I ask him to knock me out—just a small tap to my jaw is all it would've taken—but does he do it? Noooo. He uses some kind of Kung Fu crap to put me out for about fifteen minutes. I'll never live it down."

"Gary escaped?" Kaz asked, confused.

Lucy looked embarrassed, then shrugged. "I was worried about him, so I cut him loose."

Kaz stared at her, then started laughing. It felt good, even though she was still pretty shaky. "You purposely engineered a prisoner's escape."

Lucy's expression was defensive. "I was afraid they were going to—"

"You don't have to explain," Kaz said. "Really." Then she laughed some more.

"Gary radioed in a little while ago. He and Jacobsen nabbed Svensen, along with the money and drugs as evidence. They're on their way back in. And Ivar is questioning Jackson, to see what his involvement was." Lucy looked even more disgruntled. "So far, this evening is *not* helping my career. A prisoner escapes on my watch, and then my friends apprehend the bad guys."

Kaz patted her shoulder. "You'll get over it." But she noticed that Lucy's expression remained troubled.

One of the EMTs stepped into the doorway of the wheelhouse and crooked a finger at Kaz. "You're going with us. We've got to get that gasoline off you before you have a toxic reaction, and we need to check you out for hypothermia."

Kaz's heart leapt at the thought of being allowed to go in with Michael, but she stayed where she was, shaking her head. "I have to bring the *Kasmira B* in to port."

"I'll handle her—you go on," Lucy said. "What the heck—it beats filling out paperwork, which is all you guys have left for me to do."

Then Coyote turned himself into his
own form and went back to his people.
He told them he had killed Grizzly Bear.

CHAPTER TWENTY-NINE

Six hours later, Michael woke up in a hospital room.
Machines were beeping incessantly, making his head
ache. His leg felt like someone had jammed a hot
poker into it, then wrapped the poker inside some
kind of huge, immobile casing. A bag hung overhead,
dripping clear liquid into his left arm, and his other
arm wouldn't move.

He angled his head slowly, so that he could see
what was on his arm. Kaz sat in a chair beside the bed,
both her hands wrapped around his right one. Her
head laid on their joined hands, and she was sound
asleep. That explained why his right arm was numb.

His expression softened as he gazed at her. Her hair
was a mess, half pulled out of the braid she'd put it in
the afternoon before. He could smell a faint odor of
gasoline, overlaid by some kind of hospital detoxify-
ing agent. Her face was scrubbed clean, but the pur-

ple and green bruises from Sykes's beatings were a garish contrast to her pale complexion.

Someone had brought her clean clothes—Lucy, probably. She'd obviously gathered them in a hurry. The football jersey Kaz wore was wrinkled, the jeans so ratty they were almost indecent. Michael smiled. She was more beautiful than any woman he'd seen in his entire life.

He must have shifted slightly, because she woke with a start, her sleep-softened brown eyes staring into his in momentary confusion. She straightened abruptly, her expression turning anxious. "You're awake," she said, her voice raspy. "How do you feel? Are you in any pain?"

He grimaced. "I'm okay."

Her expression became more worried, and he smiled to reassure her. "Any chance you can break me out of here any time soon?"

She shook her head. Then her lips trembled. "I thought I'd lost you."

He reached up to run a hand over her hair. The movement caused pain to shoot through his leg, but it was worth it. He needed to touch her. "Same here," he said, his voice gruff. "When I saw Sykes hit you . . ."

"You saw that?" she asked, surprised.

He nodded. "From Bjorn's boat." That image was still haunting him, and would for some time to come.

"I'm fine," she reassured him, accurately reading his expression.

". . . Chuck?"

"He's still listed as critical, but improving. He lost his spleen and one kidney, but the doctors are hopeful that he'll pull through." She pressed her lips together. "He was trying to protect me."

Michael grunted. "It's a good thing that Sykes is dead . . ." His voice trailed away as she reached out and placed a hand over his mouth. He held her hand there, pressing his lips to it. Emotion clogged his throat. He cleared it, then said lightly, "Since we've—"

"So you're awake." The voice came from the doorway, interrupting them, and they both turned. Wallace Forbes stood there, looking tired. "May I come in?" the mayor asked, pointing inside the room, clearly not sure of his welcome.

Kaz stood on stiff legs and moved toward the door, giving Michael a small smile. "I'll be back in a few minutes."

He shifted, and the fire that traveled up his leg made his vision blur. He gritted his teeth and rode it out. "Where are you going?" he asked, not wanting her to slip away.

"I'm giving you two some privacy. And besides, there's someone who's anxious to see you. I'll go find him."

After she left, Michael motioned the mayor in. "You set me up," he said without preamble. "You used me to flush out Sykes."

Forbes nodded, his eyes somber. "That I did. My town was sick, Michael. I had no choice." He put the stack of magazines he'd been holding on the table next to Michael's bed. "When your resume came across my desk, I knew I'd been given my only chance to bring someone to town who could take Jim on. But I didn't think you'd have to move so quickly, or that Jim would be clever enough to use the situation the way he did."

"Kaz damn near got killed." Michael's voice was arctic cold.

Forbes sighed and reached into his pocket for his

cigarette case, then realized that he couldn't smoke in the hospital room and grimaced. "I'll have to live with that for the rest of my life. I never meant to put her in danger."

"You must have known that she'd do whatever she had to, to protect Gary."

"Yes, but I didn't know he was involved, not until the fire." Forbes shook his head and sighed. "Jim was more ruthless than I gave him credit for. I'm afraid I underestimated him."

Even though Michael had done the same, he wasn't ready to let Forbes off the hook. "Why didn't you tell me about your suspicions that morning after the fire?"

"Because that's all they were—suspicions. I had no proof, and I didn't want to influence your investigation one way or the other."

"No one influences me. You should've said something."

Forbes looked out the window into the hospital parking lot for a minute, considering. Then he turned back, nodding. "That was my mistake. But that's done. We can move on now, as a community."

Michael pinned him with a hard stare. "If you ever do anything like that again—"

"There won't be a need." Forbes frowned. "You have any ideas about who I can get to fill the new vacancy in the police department?"

"I might," Michael said after thinking about it. In fact, the idea of luring a certain friend out here from Boston had some appeal. He grinned a little, envisioning Mac's reaction to Astoria.

"Good. Have his resume on my desk by next week." Forbes walked toward the door, then turned back. "I know you think less of me because of this little affair, and I'm sorry for that. But answer me this, Michael. What's a little manipulation by an old man who wanted to save his town really worth when you stack it up against a chance for personal redemption?"

He watched the comprehension dawn on Michael's face, then nodded and turned to leave. "You think about it, son. In the end, I did you a hell of a favor."

Michael stared after him for several long moments. Unfortunately, the bastard had a point.

When Kaz entered Chuck's room, she found Gary sitting in the chair beside his bed. One of the ER nurses had obviously convinced him to let them treat him— his wounds had been cleaned and stitched, and through the open neckline of his shirt, she could see the edge of the white tape bandage around his ribs. The swelling over his left eye had gone down slightly. He turned and smiled slightly at her.

"How is he?" she asked softly, approaching the bed. Chuck lay still and silent, his face pale beneath the bruises. He looked so vulnerable lying there that it hurt to look at him. Chuck never looked vulnerable.

"He made it through the night—the nurse says that's a good sign." Gary shook his head. "I figured I'd better hang around, though, just in case he wakes up. He'll try to drag himself out of here—he can't stand hospitals since his stint in one after the war."

Kaz sympathized. "You okay?" she asked softly.

Gary shrugged. "The bastards are either dead or behind bars. I figure that makes it a good day." He straightened and stretched. "I'll be better when Chuck wakes up."

"I hear Lucy busted you loose at the station."

He grinned a little at that. "Yeah. Right about now, I

don't think she's talking to me. I was pretty sneaky when I put her out."

"You sure as hell were."

They both turned toward the doorway. Lucy stood there, looking tired but calm.

"Everything under control?" Kaz asked.

Lucy nodded. "Svensen's crew is behind bars, along with Jackson. Clint is talking a mile a minute, hoping to use the information he has as a bargaining chip for a lighter sentence." She dragged another chair from the adjoining cubicle and fell into it. "Like Gary told you, the buyer was offshore—we'll probably never be able to lay a hand on him. I've notified the DEA, but . . ." She sighed. "Sykes was the in-town contact, running everything from behind the scenes and moving the drugs upriver. Svensen was making the drops and pickups for a cut of the profits. Jackson was the muscle, when needed. He's the one who beat up Ken."

"How did Ken find out about them?" Kaz asked.

"According to Jackson, by pure dumb luck. He saw Karl remove something from a crab pot, right after he'd spent that day baiting and laying pots in a different location. That didn't make sense to Ken, so he asked Karl about it. Karl reacted badly, which made him suspicious. Ken started watching more closely, put it all together, and confronted Karl that night six months ago in the tavern. Karl exploded." Lucy glared at Gary. "Which is where you came in."

Gary shrugged again. "I didn't know what it was about—just that Karl was threatening Ken for some reason. And I wasn't about to stand by and let that happen." He shook his head. "I should've been suspicious, though, when Karl didn't press charges. It wasn't like him to just let it go. And he had no reason to be nice to me—he's never liked me. But I didn't have a clue until Ken turned up at the boat ten days ago, badly beaten. That's when I made him tell me what was going on."

Kaz pursed her lips. "So Karl broadcast a 'fake' location, which was the signal to the sellers that he was leaving the money in one of his pots with a buoy attached, at that location. He goes back out when no one is around and leaves the money, picking up the drugs. He probably figured that anyone who saw him would think he was either stealing some crabs for dinner, which happens all the time, or repairing a line." She frowned. "Why did it take six months for Ken to put it together?"

"I wondered the same thing," Lucy said. "But crab season only runs for six months—they had to have a strategy for the rest of the year. Karl said whenever he was drag-fishing off-season, they simply met in international waters when no one was around."

"So they had the advantage of using two different types of drops, which would confuse anyone who was on to them."

"Yeah."

"And," Kaz realized, "right after the fight, the season ended and they switched over to meeting in international waters, so it was a while before Ken could steal the money. Meanwhile the medical bills probably piled up . . ."

Lucy nodded. "There you go."

"What about Steve?"

"Jackson says Sykes had something on him from the time of his divorce, but he didn't know what it was, and Steve isn't talking. I'm not going to push it—other than turning a blind eye, Steve wasn't involved. And he did call the station last night, worried about you."

Kaz heaved a sigh of relief. She liked Steve; she hadn't wanted to hear he was under arrest.

Lucy stood. Her expression was tired and sad, her demeanor subdued. Not at all like her. "I'm going home to get a few hours' sleep, then I have to return to the station. Moral is real low in the squad room—two of our own involved in a drug ring, and one man dead, a good man just trying to keep his head above water but making bad decisions." She shook her head, then took a deep breath. "But we'll get over it."

They were all silent for a moment.

Lucy seemed to shake herself out of her brooding. "I left Ivar with all the paperwork, which means he's in hog heaven. I still have the murder of the drug dealer to handle—but my snitch is finally talking. It looks like Sykes took the dealer out in a fit of rage when the guy threatened to expose him after the drug supply was cut off. But there are a few more details to nail down." She headed for the door, avoiding Gary's eyes, then cocked her head at Kaz. "Six o'clock at the tavern. If I don't get a chance to cream you at pool tonight, I might just slit my wrists."

Kaz smiled. "Deal." Lucy left, and Kaz turned toward Gary, her eyebrows raised.

Gary grunted and stood. "Looks like I have some explaining to do about the way I put her out."

"I think there's more to it than that." She watched the panic come and go in his eyes.

"Maybe." He started down the hallway after Lucy, then hesitated, hanging his head. After a moment, he squared his shoulders and headed in a different direction.

Troubled, Kaz reluctantly turned away. So her brother was back in martyr mode, unwilling to take a chance. This was one battle she couldn't help him with—he was on his own. But she hurt for both of them, and she hoped they could work it out.

She sat down in the chair he'd vacated and reached for Chuck's hand. She held it for a long moment, trying to will some of her strength into him. Was it her imagination, or was his color better than it had been when she'd come in? She hoped so.

She used both hands to warm his. "Thank you," she whispered.

For a brief moment, his hand tightened on hers.

Zeke burst through the door of Michael's room with Kaz in tow, slipping and sliding on the linoleum as he ran across the floor. He launched himself at the bed. Monitors jerked and beeped, and the IV line swung wildly, almost ripping out of Michael's hand. With both paws on the bed, Zeke slathered Michael's face with dog saliva.

Michael laughed and scratched Zeke's ruff with his free hand. "Easy there, boy. I'm okay."

"Mawrooo, rooo."

Zeke then tried to climb into the hospital bed, and Kaz grabbed his collar, hauling him back. "Sit," she told him firmly, trying to avert disaster.

He grumbled, his expression accusing, but sat down beside the bed. Then he slapped one giant paw against the edge of the covers and grinned, his tongue hanging sideways out of his mouth.

It felt good to see the two of them together, Kaz realized. To see Michael's face relax as he rubbed Zeke's ears. She smiled. "Zeke hasn't slept a wink, worrying about you. I promised him I'd sneak him up here as soon as I could."

Michael grunted. "Good. Maybe the hospital staff will discover him and it'll get both of us expelled."

"Fat chance," Kaz said, but she secretly commiserated. "You're in here for a while, at least until the pin they put in your leg starts to knit with the bone."

She could see that he didn't like the sound of that, but he regrouped quickly. "So," he said, his voice casual. "Since we've now slept together—"

"I beg your pardon?" Kaz interrupted, her eyebrows arched, a slight smile on her face. "I don't remember getting a lot of sleep."

"—how about, when I get out of here, I take you out on a date?"

She made a production out of hesitating. "A real date, huh? Like dinner, and maybe a movie?"

"Yeah," he said. "I could put the moves on you after the lights go down."

"*That's* appealing." She laughed softly, but her heart turned over. "I haven't necked in a movie theater since high school."

"Then you've been missing out," he said firmly. He reached out, took one of her hands and kissed the inside of her wrist. A small jolt of desire ran through her. "You'll stick around?"

"Of course. I've got a lot of work on the *Anna Marie,* and Gary still needs help with the business. We'll have to recoup from our losses—" She shivered when he used his teeth on her palm, instantly going hot all over. The man knew how to turn her into mush, thank God.

"I meant," he growled, "will you stay around for us? Because if not, we're going to be trying out a long-distance relationship. I'm not letting go of you any-time soon."

Something deep down inside broke loose, and a feeling of contentment washed over her. *So this is what it feels like to finally be home.* She smiled, tears of joy blurring her vision. "Yes." She'd work out whatever she needed to with her business partner. She'd probably have to commute back and forth, but it would be worth it. There was no way she was going back to California on a permanent basis. This was where she belonged now.

"Yes, what?" he demanded.

"Yes, I'm sticking around." She leaned down and kissed him, placing her hand on his cheek. "For us."

HEAT LIGHTNING

COLLEEN THOMPSON

An unidentified man is terrorizing Luz Maria Montoya. Almost strangled to death outside a deserted parking lot, she has no idea who is the perpetrator of this very personal hate crime. Investigator Grant Holcomb has been assigned to find her attacker, but he makes no secret of his conflicting feelings. As Luz Maria receives threatening phone calls and grisly warnings, part of him wants to protect the sultry Latina, while the other half hopes the escalating tension between them will explode in an electrifying burst of . . . *HEAT LIGHTNING*.
